far far
away

far far away

Tom McNeal

Definitions

FAR FAR AWAY
A DEFINITIONS BOOK 978 1 909 53127 7

First published in Great Britain by Jonathan Cape, an imprint of
Random House Children's Publishers UK

Jonathan Cape edition published 2013
Definitions edition published 2014

1 3 5 7 9 10 8 6 4 2

Set in Goudy

RANDOM HOUSE CHILDREN'S PUBLISHERS UK
61–63 Uxbridge Road, London W5 5SA

www.**randomhousechildrens**.co.uk
www.**totallyrandombooks**.co.uk
www.**randomhouse**.co.uk

Addresses for companies within The Random House Group Limited
can be found at: www.**randomhouse**.co.uk/offices.htm

THE RANDOM HOUSE GROUP Limited Reg. No. 954009

A CIP catalogue record for this book is available from the British Library.

Printed and bound by CPI Group (UK) Ltd, Croydon, CR0 4YY

For Sam and Hank

What follows is the strange and fateful tale of a boy, a girl, and a ghost. The boy possessed uncommon qualities, the girl was winsome and daring, and the ancient ghost . . . well, let it only be said that his intentions were good.

If more heavily seasoned with romance, this might have made a tender tale, but there was yet another player in the cast, the Finder of Occasions, someone who moved freely about the village, someone who watched and waited, someone with tendencies so tortured and malignant that I could scarcely bring myself to see them, and even now can scarcely bring myself to reveal them to you.

I will, though. It is a promise. I will.

§

§

Let us begin on a May afternoon when the light was pure, the air scented with blossoms, and the sky a pale blue. Lovely, in other words, and brimming with promise. The village trees were in full leaf, and there, in the town square, under the shade of one such tree, a boy named Jeremy Johnson Johnson stood surrounded by three girls.

Jeremy was a shy boy, so as the girls inched nearer, their eyes bright, he lowered his gaze. One of these girls was Ginger Boultinghouse, whose coppery hair grew long and wild and whose amber eyes possessed the hue, sparkle, and—or so it seemed— effect of a strong lager. The soft sun was behind her. As she leaned closer to Jeremy, she tilted her head so that her unruly hair fell in a dazzling display.

"About that insane word problem that our insane reading teacher assigned today," she said in a low voice. "Was that what you were slaving over at lunch?"

It was indeed.

I had witnessed it all. At the end of the class, the teacher distributed a little poem called "A Boat Beneath a Sunny Sky" and then asked the students to solve a riddle: "Find hidden in the poem the person who inspired it." The class bell had rung. "It is deceptively simple!" the teacher called after the students as they filed from the room.

Well, what the teacher said was true. It took me just a moment and a half to find the answer (though it must be admitted that I spent all my mortal life as a linguist). For Jeremy, it was more difficult. He sat alone during the lunch hour and contemplated the problem, trying this and that while others joked and ate their food and wandered out of doors to enjoy the warm sunshine. *Would you like a hint?* I whispered, but he shook his head no. When finally the hour was nearly over and he sat alone

2

with his lunch untouched, he whispered, "Okay. But not the answer—just a hint."

And so I gave him a small hint. *Acrostic*, I whispered.

He needed no more than that. A few moments later, the problem was solved.

"Yeah, I was working on it," he said now to Ginger Boultinghouse, and such was the effect of the girl's eyes that he again had to look away.

The girl teased free several strands of her coppery hair, held them in front of her face, and studied them for a moment. "And you figured it out, right?"

Jeremy nodded his head.

In the old tales, kindness is the purest form of heroism. Find the character who meets the world with a big heart and an open hand and you have found your hero or heroine. Jeremy was like this—whatever was his was yours. He would give up his answer the moment Ginger asked for it. But here was a surprise: the girl did not ask for it.

She pressed the gathered strands of hair between her lips and stared at Jeremy. Her gaze was strange, and somewhat alarming. She seemed not just to look *at* Jeremy but *through* him, as if he were a window to something far away. A moment passed, and then another.

When finally she spoke, it was not of the riddle within the poem but of something completely different. "Did you see the green smoke last night?" she asked, and I noted that the girl-friends' faces retreated into mild disappointment.

"Yeah," Jeremy replied, but at once he became flustered. He touched the leather cord that looped about his neck, the cord

3

from which his house key always hung. "Well, no, I didn't *see* the green smoke. But I heard people talking about it."

"But you know what it means, right? 'Green smoke at midnight; Prince Cakes at first light.'"

Jeremy murmured yes. Everyone in town knew what the green smoke meant. But I knew that Prince Cakes meant something even more to Jeremy.

"We're headed for the bakery," Ginger said, looking off, but then she let her amber eyes settle fully on Jeremy for a long moment. "You want to come, too?"

Well! I can tell you that this was unexpected. Usually these girls took Jeremy's answers and departed, but now . . .

Jeremy's eyes slid away. "There won't be any left."

"There *will* be for us," Ginger said.

But Jeremy still shook his head no. "I'm not that hungry," he said. "And, besides, Prince Cakes are kind of expensive."

Ginger smiled and said she wouldn't worry about that.

"Why not?"

The girl's dark eyes shone. "I just wouldn't." She drew closer. "You should come with us," she said. "You like Prince Cakes, right?"

Again Jeremy dropped his eyes. "I've never had one."

As Ginger released an astonished laugh, a pleasant scent of cinnamon blossomed into the air. "You've never had a Prince Cake?"

"No," he said, but he did not give the reason.

"Not even a bite?" Her smile turned frisky. "Not even . . . a nibble?"

With each shake of Jeremy's head, Ginger's eyes grew brighter.

4

As if it were a wand, she touched a single finger to his forehead and said, "Then today is the day."

He wanted to go—I could read this in the flush of his cheeks—but he was uncertain, and as he turned away for a moment, he placed a finger lightly to the side of his head between the eye and the ear. He wanted my opinion.

I was there to protect this boy—that was my sole reason for coming to this village—but, truly, he lived so much in isolation. I myself had investigated the bakery and found it harmless. It was time that he saw this as well, and, besides, what harm could come from a visit to the bakery in the company of three pretty girls?

None.

That was what I told myself.

But in this matter, as in others, I would be proved wrong.

So I whispered no warning to Jeremy, and in the next moment Ginger and her girlfriends were leading him toward the bakery in search of his first bite of Prince Cake.

§

§

While our group strolls down Main Street, allow me to provide a word or two about Jeremy Johnson Johnson. When he was six or seven years of age, he told one of his schoolmates that he sometimes heard voices, "a strange whispering," he did not know whose, but if he pressed a finger *right here*—he pointed to his temple—he could hear the voices more clearly. "Jeremy hears voices!" the other boy sang out, and from there the news worked its way up and down the streets of the village.

Some in the town believed there was something askew in Jeremy's mind, some believed he was too suggestible, and some believed his silver tooth fillings received transmissions from distant radio stations.

But I can tell you with certainty that Jeremy Johnson Johnson did hear unworldly voices.

How do I know this?

Because he heard mine.

So! Perhaps you had already guessed. I am the ancient ghost mentioned at the outset of this tale. The one whose intentions were good.

As a mortal man, I was known as Jacob Grimm. Yes, the very one! With my younger brother, Wilhelm, I lived once in Germany, in the village of Steinau in the Kingdom of Hesse. (The house is still there—I took the guided tour some years ago. Ha!) Both of us were linguists, but our collection of household stories—fairy tales, they are now commonly called—is what you doubtless know.

I have been dead since the Saturday afternoon in September 1863 when I saw the elm tree in the garden dissolve into nothing, and also the window before which I sat, and the wicker chair, and my niece Auguste, who had just inquired what I, *lieber Onkel*, would like for tea. I lay with a dead tongue and a dead right hand. The next day, I stopped breathing.

As a dead man, I had two surprises.

6

In death, I expected to be greeted by Wilhelm, who had died before me. All of our lives, my brother and I played and studied and worked as one. He was less sturdy than I, and often unwell. I forgave him that, of course. But his was a dreamer's nature, and he was given to wistful song, longings to travel, matters of the heart. *The studies*, I would say. *The studies, the studies, the studies.* If he came reluctantly to the work, still he came. We were strapped to the same yoke. Our desks stood side to side. When Wilhelm married, I joined his household. So of course in death we would travel together—was I so foolish to believe that?—but here I was, and Wilhelm was not to be found.

That was my first surprise.

I set out to look for him. I asked the dead if they had seen my brother, but the dead who remain here are less numerous than you might imagine, two here, one there—that sort of thing. I speak English, French, High German, Low German, Serbian, Italian, Latin, Greek, Swedish, and Old Icelandic. In various languages I asked about my brother, the famous, the esteemed, the revered Wilhelm Grimm.

No, nej, nein, non.

Several of them did not answer at all but merely stared at me with their dead eyes. To the dead, who was famous means nothing.

I hastened to the national library in Paris, where I had first learned the ecstasy of comparing words to words, where Wilhelm might wait for me, but he was not there. Around the tables hovered three dead scholars, whose only interest, to my surprise, was in keeping a watchful and suspicious eye on one another. To these men I announced that in July 1805, after a day at this very

7

table, I had written a letter to my brother to say that we must never be apart, that we must do our life's work together as one.

The ghostly scholars did not speak. They kept their suspicious watch on one another.

I asked the scholar next to me if he knew my *Bruder*, Wilhelm Grimm.

Upon hearing this name, the three scholars turned their suspicious eyes on me.

Oh, the first scholar said, *the famous Brothers Grimm, who followed the footsteps of von Arnim and Brentano, then claimed the trail as their own.*

Who collected the stories of peasants, said the second scholar, *then diluted them for pedagogical nursery use.*

Who, the third scholar said, *changed first the words and then the meanings and held still to the pretense of scholarship.*

I slipped away. When I looked back, the scholars had again turned their distrustful eyes upon one another.

I went to the kingdom of Hesse, where we were born, and then to Kassel, where we went to school. I walked to the Amtshaus in Steinau, because Wilhelm and I had been happy there. I went to wait, like a child playing hide-and-go-find, in the room with the green-and-white wallpaper. But Wilhelm did not come.

In the street, I met a woman, a specter who now inhabited the kitchen space of a grand home, where she had served as a maid. She had hollow eyes and a strange smile. I inquired of her, and she asked if my brother had been satisfied with his life.

Yes, I said. *Of course.* My brother was a romantic man, and his work, his wife, and his children had met all of his romantic expectations. For all of his days, he had been at ease with his life.

Then maybe he has passed on, said the maid. Her hollow eyes stared fully at me. *Very few do not pass on.*

It was she who explained to me that only the troubled remain here in the *Zwischenraum*, those who are agitated and uneasy, still looking for what this maid and others since have called the thing undone. "Vengeance, for example," she told me and then, eyeing me slyly, "or some other unknown yet unmet desire. It is unique to every ghost, tailored to his own failures, disenchantments, or regrets." The dead maid set her hollow eyes on me. "It all depends on you."

These phrases—*the thing undone; unknown yet unmet desire*—have caused me lingering unrest, but allow me now to speak only of the second surprise: the *Zwischenraum* itself.

Examine, if you will, the vibrating space around you, what is between and around your hands and your hearths and your homes. This is where I, or another like me, might be: in the *Zwischenraum*—the space between.

Specters are not, as often imagined, agents of physical change. We cannot move table lamps or cause knockings in walls. There is about us a slight drafting of warm air—perhaps you have occasionally had one of us pass near you and, feeling a subtle current of warmth, wondered what it was. With effort, we can use this drafting to move a paper or, with greater concentration, perhaps even cause a door to swing closed. But more than that is beyond us.

Here is what we can and cannot do in the *Zwischenraum*:

We see but cannot touch.

We smell but cannot taste.

We suffer but cannot weep.

9

We hasten but cannot fly.

We rest but cannot sleep.

We speak but are not heard.

So! And what of Jeremy Johnson Johnson, who heard me?

He was one of the Exceptionals. They come rarely, and in odd variations. I once came upon a woman in Romania who could see my *Heiligenschein*—my aura—well enough to distinguish my age and gender, and I have crossed paths with a number of mortals—younger people, primarily, but sometimes older mortals grieving the loss of a spouse or a child—who can sense our presence. And there have been several who have heard me speak, though none in my experience so clearly as Jeremy Johnson Johnson.

But wait!—I will offer you an example, for as Jeremy and the girls amble toward the Green Oven Bakery, an opportunity to illustrate his strange abilities will soon present itself.

§

§

They had just crossed to the shady side of Main Street when a passing pickup truck slowed and drew alongside them.

The truck was bright red, and its driver was Conk Crinklaw, a hearty boy whose father was the village mayor. In the back of the pickup, several boys sat on bales of hay. "Hey, Ginger," one of these boys called out, "going to make the Moonbeam your summer go-to guy?"

Ginger Boultinghouse smiled pleasantly at the boys. "No, but if you mean Jeremy, he beats most of the local competition."

This drew hoots from the boys, and one of them said, "But, then, Gingerkins, you might have to *vie* for Jeremy with Frank Gaily," which generated more raucous laughter, and another boy sang out, "Catfight!"—which they then begin to chant in a husky singsong. "Cat-*fight*, cat-*fight*, cat-*fight*!"

Well, there was no Frank Gaily. He was properly called Frank *Bailey*, and because he was a large yet delicate boy, he, like Jeremy, was the object of the bully's sport.

Jeremy's skin glazed with sweat. He touched his hand to his temple to receive anything I might say to him, but it was a poor time for this. One of the boys noticed.

"What's up, Jeremy?" he called out. "Got a long-distance call coming in?" And another said, "Picking up a news flash from Jupiter?" And yet another called, "Or maybe something from Uranus?"

Well, that is how people can be. I should have restrained myself, but I could not. I gave Jeremy something to say. *Mögen Sie eine endlose Wüste auf dem Rücken eines furzenden Kamels durchqueren.*

"*Mögen Sie eine endlose Wüste auf dem Rücken eines furzenden Kamels durchqueren,*" Jeremy repeated. He had an excellent aural memory. His pronunciation was perfect.

Ah! *Exzellent!* The boys in the back of the truck stared as cows might.

But Conk Crinklaw was not so easily stupefied. With a broad grin, he leaned from his open window. "Now, what have I told you about speaking Martian, Jeremy?" he said. "No possible good

11

can come of it." The boys in the back laughed grandly at this, and Conk Crinklaw stretched his grin wider. "No girl's going to want to do the *significant deed* with a guy who talks . . . you know, *Martian*." Again he paused. "But maybe that don't matter so much to you."

The boys drove away amidst heavy, derisive laughter.

"Idiots," Ginger muttered.

One of the girlfriends was called Maddy Saxon. She had a dark allure that seemed deeply seated within her and surfaced only in the thin pink scar that ran the length of her cheek. This gave her a daunting stare, which she directed now toward the receding red truck. "Conk's tempting, though," she said in a low voice, watching the truck turn the corner, "in an odious kind of way."

But Ginger had turned her gaze to Jeremy. In the soft sunlight, her coppery hair shimmered prettily.

"So?" she said. "What did you say to shut those goons up?"

Jeremy shrugged and looked off. "I don't know for sure. It just came to me."

Ginger's eyes shone. "C'mon," she said. "Tell."

"No, really," Jeremy said, lightly rubbing his temple. "Sometimes when something like that comes out of my mouth—it's not very often, but when it does—I just have to ask myself, 'What in the world did I just say?'"

I knew that he meant this question for me. It was part of a pact we had made. If he spoke words I delivered him, I must divulge their meaning.

It was a low curse, I said to him. *One that should remain unexplained*.

But ever so discreetly he shook his head.

So I told him.

A smile spread across Jeremy's face. I will admit it. That he was pleased was pleasing to me.

"What?" Ginger said, her eyes full of mischief. "You know, don't you?"

Jeremy did not deny it—he was a poor liar—but still he said nothing.

"C'mon, tell," Ginger said, then softened her voice. "If you tell, I promise we won't ask for any more of your homework the rest of the year."

Jeremy laughed. "There's only a week of school left."

"Yeah," Ginger said, her smile demure as you please. "That's why I can do the deal."

Well, it is true. Honesty is often disarming.

Jeremy looked at Ginger and said, "Promise you won't tell Conk?"

"I do," Ginger said, then glanced at the two girlfriends. "And they do, too, or else some of their juicy little secrets will go pinballing around this little burg."

Jeremy took a deep breath. "Okay . . . what I said was, 'May you cross an endless desert on the back of a flatulent camel.'"

A merry laugh burst from Ginger. "Where do you get that stuff?" she asked. "I mean, how'd you ever learn a foreign language?"

Jeremy shrugged. "It's beyond me."

"Beyond you," Ginger repeated, and this time when she stared at him, her gaze seemed not to pass through him so much as to burrow into him, as if to find clues to a puzzle she was intent on

13

solving. "So," she said finally (and do not be mistaken, her voice was shaded with flirtation), "what's life like there in Johnson-Johnsonville?"

Jeremy shrugged at this question, and Ginger smiled, as if to say, *Okay, okay—the puzzle can wait,* and soon the group of four was again moving along the street, through the shadows, and deeper into their tale.

Since I had come to this town, the green smoke (which was, in fact, a greenish gray) had appeared every four or five months or so, infrequently enough to make it seem special. The smoke would begin rising from the circular brick chimney during the night, and the next morning the bakery's gleaming display cases would be lined with exquisite pale green marzipan cakes, each layered and filled with strawberry paste and topped by a frosted pink rosette.

These were properly called *Prinsesstårta,* or Princess Cakes. But the baker, an immigrant from Sweden, soon observed that only the women were purchasing his Princess Cakes, so he changed the name to Prince Cakes in hopes that the men might consume them, too. The strategy succeeded—you will always witness a great rush to buy the cakes by men and women alike.

There was something else that Jeremy had heard about the

Prince Cakes from his mother, and as they walked toward the bakery, he said, "Have you ever heard of a kind of enchantment that can go with the cake?"

They had not, but they were interested, Ginger especially.

"Tell," she said, and he did.

Over the years, certain villagers—his mother, for example—had grown to believe that whatever living thing was looked upon during the first bite of *Prinsesstårta* would steal one's heart. It was said that this enchantment was so steadfast, it could be reversed only by the touch of a salted tear upon the parted lips of the spellbound.

"*God*," Maddy Saxon said. "What if the first thing you saw was a donkey?"

"Or Mr. Finnifrock," the other girlfriend said.

Mr. Finnifrock was a very nice but very large man, without many teeth.

Ginger seemed to be thinking about the story. "I like that salted-tear-upon-the-parted-lips-of-the-spellbound detail." She looked at Jeremy. "So do you think it's true?"

He avoided her gaze. "Depends who you ask."

This was true as true can be. I did not believe the Legend of the First Bite, but, as in all such matters of the heart, there were wishful souls who did. And then there was the strange but true story of Jeremy's mother herself. . . . But that tale must wait, for tendrilous aromas from the bakery had reached out to the group and were pulling them forward with a quickened pace.

A handsome old delivery truck stood parked in the street, and served as a billboard for the bakery. Its paint was a deep gleaming green, and on the side, scrolling over a painting of a circular brick oven, were the words GREEN OVEN BAKERY in gilded letters.

A small overhead bell tinkled cheerily as the girls pushed open the door, and the town baker emerged from the kitchen wiping his hands on his apron.

Sten Blix was a round man with doughy-soft features, but his face had a robust reddish glow, and with his full white beard and arctic-blue eyes, he was often asked to portray *Weihnachtsmann*—Father Christmas—during the holiday season.

"Ah," he said, grinning merrily. "*Hallå! Hallå!* Is it not a great day to be alive?"

"If you say so," Ginger said genially, letting her amber eyes fall on the baker. "So," she said, "how's life in Blixville?"

"Yes, yes, all is well in Blixville," said the baker, who seemed amused not just by the question but by all things, and why not? He was beloved in the town, and his shop was a pocket of warm benignity, as Jeremy could now see for himself. The glass-and-cherrywood cases were filled with a beautiful variety of breads and cakes, two small tables were brightened by vases of flowers, and the rich scents of baked dough, sugar, coffee, and chocolate made me yearn for my mortal sense of taste.

"And," he said, turning his jovial face to Jeremy, "is this not Jeremy Johnson Johnson?"

Jeremy nodded, and color rose in his cheeks.

The baker's face brimmed with pleasure. "You used to come in frequently. Do you remember it?"

Surprise rose in Jeremy's eyes, then confusion. "Not really," he replied.

"Yes! Your dear mother used to bring you into the bakery all tucked away in your little carriage. You were a great burrower! Sometimes she had to dig through the covers to find you."

Ginger turned her eyes to Jeremy and said in a crooning voice, "I'll bet you were just the cutest little mole-creature," which only enriched the blush in Jeremy's cheeks.

But the baker came to his rescue by turning to the real business at hand: "So, my dear children, how may I help you?"

"Well, that's the problem," Ginger said as she scanned the gleaming cases. "I don't see any *Prinsesstårta*."

A laugh rumbled up from the baker's belly. "No, you don't," he said. "Because by nine o'clock this morning the *Prinsesstårta* were all sold out."

To my surprise, Ginger's expression brightened at this news. "You sold them all?"

"Yes, yes," the baker said merrily, and waited a full second before adding, "Almost all."

Ah! So this was a little game they played!

"But you kept a few slices back for your most special customers?"

"Yes, yes, my dear girl. For my most special customers"—here he dramatically peered past Jeremy and the girls toward the street—"and they may be in yet."

"You're a funny man," Ginger said.

A pan rattled in the kitchen to the rear of the bakery. Someone else was at work.

"There is just one little thing," Ginger said to the baker.

"I see, I see. There is just one little thing."

I could see that this, too, was part of their game.

"We're a little low on cash reserves."

"Oh, well now . . ." The baker shook his head solemnly and made several small tsk-tsking sounds. "This is really too bad. Too bad indeed."

"Of course, we could write you four IOUs," Ginger said, and then one of the girlfriends chimed in with, "Or one big *We-Owe-You*."

Behind the white beard, the baker's round face brightened. "I like that! One big We-Owe-You!" He winked and gestured the group toward a sunny window-side table with a vase filled with cobalt-blue irises. "Sit, please sit. My last four slices of *Prinsesstårta* will be yours. With coffee?"

The girls all nodded, and Jeremy nodded, too.

After the baker disappeared to the back of the shop, one of the girlfriends leaned back in her chair, lazily stretched her arms, and looked across the table to Jeremy. This was Marjory Falls, a pretty girl with milk-white skin and ink-black eyes. "Just so you know," she said, "I spent half my study hall trying to work out that stupid riddle and didn't even come close. 'Find hidden in the poem the person who inspired it.'" She opened her dovelike hands. "God. What's *that* all about? Hidden where, exactly?"

As we have said, Jeremy's was a generous nature—he gladly gave to others, and he was on the brink of it now. But as he opened his mouth to speak, Ginger interceded. "Hey, now," she said. "We made a deal about asking for his homework."

Marjory's hands fluttered up. "This isn't homework. This is extra-credit."

A fragile argument, and one that Ginger began to refute, but this time it was Jeremy who interrupted. "Something told me it was an *acrostic*," he said.

The two girlfriends leaned forward like hungry diners to a meal, but Ginger sat back in her chair, once again studying Jeremy.

Maddy Saxon ran a finger along her thin pink scar. "What's an acrostic?"

"It's where a particular letter in every line goes together to spell something," Jeremy said, and when the two girlfriends still seemed confused, he went on. "You're supposed to find the inspiration for the poem hidden inside the poem, right? So if you read particular letters up and down instead of left to right—"

But Ginger did not let him finish. "What did you mean when you said *something* told you it was an acrostic?"

"Well, it was like the idea suddenly came to me that it was an acrostic." Jeremy was not comfortable with this sort of half-truth—his forehead glazed with sweat.

The girlfriends had pulled out the poem and were poring over it, but Ginger's eyes were still fixed on Jeremy. "And you knew what an acrostic was?"

"Yes." He said this firmly, for that much was completely true, and Ginger fell silent when Jeremy wrinkled his nose, stifled a sneeze, and then eyed the irises on the table. From their open mouths yellow pollen lay loosely on their brushy tongues. Jeremy rubbed his nose and pushed the vase a bit farther away.

"Got it!" Marjory sang out. "It's the name of Alice Pleasance Liddell. She must have been the girl who inspired the poet to write the poem!"

Ginger was still staring at Jeremy. "So did it come to you as a vague idea or the actual word?" she asked, but at this very moment the kitchen door swung open, and a large pink-cheeked boy entered the room, carrying a tray filled with cups of coffee.

This was Frank Bailey. His plump face and arms were smudged with flour and frosting.

"Well, well," Ginger said as he neared the table. "How's life in Bailey City?"

Others in the village made sport of Frank Bailey. Ginger, to her credit, did not.

"Okay," Frank Bailey answered, setting the tray on the table, then tugging so hard at his earlobe that it stretched like rubber. "I'm working here now."

Ginger smiled at him, which prompted him to further awkwardness.

"I always liked to cook . . . and my mother thought I ought to learn a trade . . . so I'm kind of an apprentice, I guess. Mr. Blix is really nice to me." He finally released his ear. "I like it a lot."

"That's fabulous," Ginger said, and when Frank Bailey seemed to wonder whether she was serious or not, she said, "No, really, it is."

Sten Blix pushed through the kitchen door carrying another tray, this one filled with dessert plates.

Oh, the *Prinsesstårta* were an eye-filling sight! Each slice, topped with pale green marzipan and a frosted rosette, was nestled among red ripe strawberries.

"Zounds," Ginger said. "They're almost too beautiful to eat." Then, smiling at the baker, she added, "Notice I said *almost*."

Marjory said, "I noticed you said *Zounds*, which I hope to God you will never say again."

Ginger regarded her. "How do you feel about *Egads*?"

"Worse."

Ginger smiled and sprang her little trap: "Then *Zounds* it is."

The baker stood close by during this exchange but now gave a cheery laugh and departed. The three girls stared at their portions of *Prinsesstårta* as one might stare at a bow-wrapped gift. But Marjory and Maddy could not stare for long—they grabbed their forks and began to eat.

Probably they did not believe Jeremy's Legend of the First Bite, but, still, they took no chances—they chewed with their eyes tightly closed. They did not open their eyes when the bell over the door tinkled and two customers entered. They did not open them when Jeremy, reacting to the pollen from the irises in the vase before him, wrinkled a napkin and dabbed at his nose. They did not open them when Ginger said, "Oh sweet mother of God, why would Conk Crinklaw ride a bicycle buck-naked down Main Street?"

This was, of course, untrue.

The two girlfriends smiled at this ploy, continued chewing, and kept their eyes clamped closed. They did not open them until their first bites were safely swallowed.

"Mmm," purred Marjory.

Maddy, who rarely smiled, smiled.

Jeremy did not go quite so far as the girls. He merely finished his first bite with his eyes steadfastly cast down at his plate.

"Verdict?" Ginger said when he was done.

"Good," Jeremy said, nodding slowly. "Really, really good."

Ginger seemed pleased. "Told you," she said.

But here was an interesting something. Ginger, who had gone to such trouble to acquire the *Prinsesstårta*, had not begun eating hers—indeed, seemed in no hurry to begin. After a sip of coffee, she pressed several strands of coppery hair between her

21

lips and regarded the baker as he whistled a merry tune and slid fresh loaves of bread into the display cases.

"What?" Maddy asked, following Ginger's gaze to the baker.

"*Him*," Ginger whispered, nodding toward the baker as, still whistling, he pushed through the half doors into the kitchen. "Do you think the reason he's so glad to see us when we come in is that his life is as dull as ditchwater?"

"Are you kidding?" Maddy Saxon said in her low voice. "There are tons of boring people in this town, and none of them are happy to see us."

"Maybe he's just nice," Jeremy said.

"Yeah, maybe," Ginger said. She gazed again toward the kitchen. "It's just that all he does is bake all day, and then he goes home to that big old house, where he tends his flowers and lives alone without even a dog or a hamster or a horny toad."

"Who says he doesn't have a horny toad?" Marjory said, licking a bit of frosting from her fork, which led all three girls to muffled laughter, while Jeremy could do nothing but smile awkwardly and blush.

Ginger was still staring toward the kitchen when her gaze suddenly narrowed and she glanced from Maddy to Marjory. "Maybe," she said in the smallest whisper, "the boring little kingdom of Blixville needs some . . . *investigating*."

At once Marjory's hands flew up in excitement. "Night mission!" she whispered, and Maddy in a low tone added, "Stealth patrol."

I had no idea what to make of this, and neither did Jeremy. He merely continued to eat and, occasionally, stifle a sneeze. He pushed the vase of flowers even farther away from him. The girlfriends meanwhile had slowed the consumption of their last morsels of Prince Cake as if to forestall its complete disappearance. That theirs was reduced to crumbs seemed to please Ginger, who ceremonially cleared her throat and cut the first bite from her portion. Then, simultaneously closing her eyes and opening her mouth, she slipped the first forkful of cake into her mouth.

"*Mmmmmmm.*"

The girlfriends stared at her. Maddy said, "You are the queen of sadistic eating."

With eyes still closed, Ginger made a murmuring laugh and kept chewing.

Across the table, Jeremy stilled his fork. His expression contorted, relaxed, then suddenly contorted again. He jerked his head back and an enormous sneeze exploded from his mouth.

This sneeze was so wild and boisterous that the baker poked his head through the kitchen door and all of the girls turned their eyes to Jeremy in astonishment.

All of them.

Even Ginger, with the first bite of *Prinsesstårta* still on her tongue.

§

§

Laughter erupted from the two girlfriends—the notion that Ginger had just fallen under Jeremy's enchantment seemed to them unmatched for hilarity. But Ginger merely smiled. "Could've done worse," she said. "At least I didn't look at a tail-less ape."

"Thanks heaps," Jeremy said, which drew more laughter from the girls.

After a moment or two, Ginger held suddenly, theatrically, still. "Uh-oh." She stared at Jeremy. "I already feel the reversed polarity. The *powerful, irrefutable* pull of my body to yours."

At this, the girlfriends laughed happily, but oh, poor Jeremy—his face was again blazing.

Let us go now, I said to him. *Home to feed your father and return to your studies.*

He seemed ready to push back from the table, but Ginger laughed a merry laugh. "'Gads, Jeremy. You are such an idiot! That first-look, heart-stealing stuff isn't true! It's just a goofy story your mother told you." She gave him a saucy smile. "Not that I see why you're so stressed about it."

Maddy issued a snorting laugh. "*I* can see why he'd be stressed. I *pity* the fool who draws the Ginger card."

The girls chortled merrily at this, but here was an interesting something. When a silence developed, Jeremy said, "The first-bite stuff reminds me of a story called 'The Lady and the Lion,' where a man gets caught trying to steal a lark from the kingdom of a lion, and the lion gives the man the choice of giving up his life or returning home and giving over to the lion the first living thing that lays eyes on the man."

Jeremy stopped talking and resumed eating.

"And then?" Ginger said.

"Oh," Jeremy said. "The man takes the deal. He doesn't really want to, but his servant tells him the first living thing that will look upon him when he comes home will just be a pig or a sheep or a cow. But the servant is wrong. The first living thing to look upon the man turns out to be his youngest and most beautiful daughter."

Again Jeremy fell quiet, and again Ginger said, "And then?"

So Jeremy told the whole of the tale, from the girl returning to the kingdom in the forest and marrying the lion to following him all over the world, rescuing him from a dragon-turned-princess, and flying home on the back of a friendly griffin. Ginger and the girlfriends sat attentively through these several episodes until Jeremy was finished. Then, after a moment or two, they snapped back into their customary roles.

"Same old story," Ginger said, pushing her empty plate away. "Girl meets lion, girl loses lion, girl gets lion back."

There was some laughter. Then Marjory said, "Where did that story come from? I've never heard it before."

Jeremy looked away. "It's just an old story I read in one of my mother's books."

So! He did not want to say that this was a fairy tale collected by Wilhelm and Jacob Grimm?

"Like a book with damsels and dragons and all that stuff?" Maddy asked.

A second passed before Jeremy nodded yes.

Then, when the girls were again chatting, he said to me in the thinnest whisper, "*Sorry.*"

But Ginger heard him, and she pounced on his whispered word as a cat would a mouse. "What?" she asked.

Jeremy went blank for a moment but then recovered. "I burped. Then I said, 'Sorry.'"

Ginger was again studying him. "Must not have been much of a burp."

"No," Jeremy said, his eyes sliding away. "It wasn't."

And then Ginger kindly released him. "That's okay, though," she said, casting a look at her two girlfriends, "a little politeness is a nice change from what I get out of the Queens of Slobopolis."

The two girlfriends beamed as if they'd just been paid a fine compliment.

And so our little group ate and joked and enjoyed their repast. Before they departed the bakery, Ginger used a napkin to write the following promissory note:

We Owe the Baker 1 Big Favor
OR
$12,
whichever comes first.

The girls all signed their names.

Then Jeremy signed it, too.

I will report one further observation. As the group stepped from the bakery and turned down Main Street, I happened to look back, and there, within the bakery, the slightest movement drew my eye. Deep in the shadows of the bakery's wide window, Frank Bailey stood holding a tray of dirty dishes and staring fixedly at Jeremy and the girls as they disappeared from view.

§

§

When the two girlfriends peeled off to the Corner Pocket (where a friendly employee would let them play pool free of charge), Ginger and Jeremy walked on alone, and their slack pace soon caused me worry. Studies awaited. This was the last week of classes before the summer holiday, the week of critical cumulative examinations.

The studies, Jeremy, I said. *The studies, the studies, the studies.*

If he heard me, he gave no indication of it. Ginger folded a stick of chewing gum into her mouth and said, "'So how's your father?' she asks, just to be polite."

Jeremy gave a small laugh. "The same, more or less. How about your granddad?"

"Same. Goes to bed every night at eight o'clock and gets up every morning at four. Eats his Grape-Nuts, drinks his Sanka, leaves his dirty dishes on the table—*for me to wash*—then goes out to the barn, letting the screen door slam at exactly four-thirty a.m. Every day. Truly. You can set your watch by it." She looked at Jeremy and shook her head. "Now, why would a human being live like that?"

So that he might get his work done! I said, but it was clear that the girl believed there was no good answer to such a question, and indeed, Jeremy offered none.

A few moments later, she said, "Any news on the eviction front?"

Jeremy turned in surprise. "Who told you about that?"

"C'mon, Jeremy. Small towns come with big ears. Everybody knows everything."

This was not quite true. Nobody knew, for just one example, who the Finder of Occasions was. But evidently everybody did

27

know that Jeremy and his father were only months away from losing the store, which was also their home.

"So?"

"No, nothing new. It's pretty straightforward, really. We have until August to pay the money or else the bank gets it."

"Wow," Ginger said quietly. "That's awful."

"It's my own fault, really. I should never have let my father talk himself into taking out a loan with a huge payment due at the end." He glanced at Ginger. "He thought he was going to get this inheritance and it would all work out fine, but the money went to a different cousin." He shook his head.

"You do yard work, though, right?"

"Yeah, and I'll try to get more when school's out. But that won't be enough."

She seemed to be considering the situation. "Maybe I can think of something," she said, and she gave him one of her frisky looks. "I'm pretty good at hatching things up."

This drew a small laugh from Jeremy. "Yeah, I bet you are," he said, which seemed to please her.

After passing Elbow's Café, Ginger said, "So, what are you doing tonight?"

"Studying."

She pulled a leaf from one of the trees planted along the street and teased it across her lips. "Yeah, me too, I guess. But probably not as much as you." She gave him a longer look. "You really want to go off to some fancy college, don't you?"

"Not fancy," Jeremy said, but it was true that, with my encouragement, he had been studying hard so that he might be admitted to a fine university.

"I wouldn't mind going off to school someplace far, far away," she said.

It was quiet enough to hear the scuff of their shoes on the pavement. No one else was on the street, but that did not mean that there were not eyes peering from windows.

Ginger said, "My grandfather says there's no point in traveling. He says all that happens when you go far, far away is that you discover you've brought yourself along."

Well, there is truth in that. Look how far I have traveled, and yet here I am.

Jeremy said quietly, "Something like that might have happened to my mother."

Ginger turned. "Yeah? Do you ever hear from her?"

Jeremy shook his head no.

"Isn't her name something glamorous like Zondra or Zelda?"

"Zyla," Jeremy said. "Her name was Zyla."

"Was?"

"Is. I meant *is*. It's just that it's been, you know, a long time."

From his odd expression, Ginger might have glimpsed the tip of a secret, but she was not looking at Jeremy. She broke the leaf in her hand, brought it to her nose to smell, then cast it aside.

"Maybe your mom's out on some big adventure, seeking her fortune like they used to do, and before the bank note is due she'll come home and dump a huge bag of . . . *doubloons* or something on the table, and you'll be able to keep your place and everybody will live happily ever after." She glanced at Jeremy as if expecting him to chuckle at this idea, but he didn't. "Guess you don't think it's so likely, huh?"

"Nah," Jeremy said. "Not that likely."

They walked past Rawhouser's Western Wear toward the Twinkle Tub Laundry, where a hand-lettered sign, yellowed and crinkled, was taped to the lower corner of the front window:

PoSSY I Am Still Here

Behind the window, a strange figure bent over a raised ironing board. Despite the warmth of the day, she wore a hooded cloak. As Ginger and Jeremy drew near, she straightened her back and stared mutely out from within her hood.

"Hey, Mrs. Truax," Ginger called out with a small wave.

The hooded figure made no acknowledgment. She stared at them for another moment, then looked down and continued her ironing.

"Wow," Jeremy said when they were beyond her. "You say hi to Mrs. Truax? She gives me the willies." To be truthful, Mrs. Truax made everyone somewhat uneasy. Hers was a sad story, full of dark corners and odd circumstances. Long ago her son, Possy, only five years old, disappeared, as if into thin air. "Has she ever said hi back?" he asked.

"Nope," Ginger said, and she gave a careless laugh. "But I don't give up easy."

They walked on. When several men sitting in the Intrepid Bar & Grill paused in their drinking to pointedly watch Ginger pass, she faced the open glass window, stuck out her tongue, and gave her unruly hair a violent tossing, a strange performance that sent some of the drinking men into laughter and made others shake their heads in disapproval.

"Blockheads and idiots," she muttered.

I agreed, and at my prompting, Jeremy chimed in with, "*Vollidioten* and *Dummköpfe*." Ginger gave him a quizzical look, so he translated: "Blockheads and idiots."

She studied him for a few moments and said, "Everybody thinks you're funny-strange, but I'm thinking maybe you're funny-mysterious instead."

"Thanks," he said. "I think."

When they reached the corner of Main and Elm, they lingered a moment before heading off in separate directions. They watched as a black-and-white patrol car slowly passed by—Deputy McRaven's massive head could be seen in silhouette—then Ginger stared off toward the pale blue sky. "Know what language I'd like to learn? French. There's just something about it—how soft and beautiful it sounds. It's not as guttural and grating as German or whatever that was you were speaking in."

Mein Gott! Well, I might have given Jeremy something pleasant to say in my native tongue, but it would have merely prolonged the conversation and distracted him further from his studies. And perhaps this was the girl's intention! Almost without notice, she had drawn close enough to Jeremy that I could detect the tangy cinnamon scent of the flavored gum she was chewing!

"So," she said, "does any French just come to you, like the German or Martian?" Something saucy slipped into her voice. "Because if you could talk to me in French, you might really kick that whole enchantment thing into high gear."

Poor Jeremy's tongue was tied, and the color in his cheek was again rising.

Ginger laughed. "It's okay. I didn't really expect you to."

Well, what could I do? As she turned to go, I whispered a few pleasing words for Jeremy to say: "*Au revoir, mademoiselle aux jambes longues.*"

Ha! *Exzellent! Exzellent!* Now it was Ginger who was dumbstruck. A few seconds passed before she found the voice to say, "So you *do* speak French?"

Jeremy made a modest shrug of his shoulders.

She eyed him. "It sounded like you said, 'Good-bye, maiden of the . . . logjam.'"

Long-legged.

"Legs," Jeremy said uncertainly. "It might've been 'maiden of the long legs.'"

A small, satisfied smile appeared on Ginger's lips, and with that, she turned on her heel, gave a quick shake of her coppery hair, and used her long legs to stride away.

Well, I said. *At last that is over. Now let us hurry home to our studies.*

But Jeremy stood watching the girl's progress until she threw a quick, smiling glance over her shoulder to let him know she knew he was watching her.

Jeremy, with face burning bright, ducked his head and turned toward home.

§

§

Jeremy's home was unlike anyone else's in this village. He and his father lived in a small apartment attached to the Two-Book

Bookstore, of which Jeremy was the sole proprietor—and sole employee. The store was his inheritance from his grandfather, and its shelves were stocked with just two books, volumes one and two of his grandfather's autobiography.

No one wondered why Jeremy's father hadn't inherited the store. Harold Johnson had not worked a day for the past five years, nor even left their apartment. It had not always been so. As a young man, he built caskets for Jeremy's grandfather's Coffin Shop, and when that was converted to a bookstore, he began driving a truck for the delivery of heating oil to citizens throughout the countryside. Though a quiet man, Harold Johnson liked to sing as he did his solitary work. One day, a young woman came out of her farmhouse to sit on the wooden fence and listen to him sing his songs while he pumped the heating oil. She was called Zyla Johnson, and though she and Harold Johnson shared the same last name, they were in no way related. They had never before exchanged a word, but on this day Zyla's presence so distracted Jeremy's father that he forgot some of the songs he had always known by heart. When he made ready to leave, Zyla looked at his delivery truck and told him she'd always wanted to ride around the countryside in a big truck like that. After several days of riding together, Harold Johnson asked Zyla Johnson to marry him. She thought about the proposal for half of half a second and then said the answer was yes because at least she wouldn't have to change her name.

They went to live in the apartment behind the bookstore on Main Street. Within the year, Jeremy was born, and his mother gave him the middle name of "Johnson," so that he would be sent into the world as Jeremy Johnson Johnson, a redundancy Zyla thought both amusing and befitting the marriage of one Johnson to another. She also passed on to him her fondness for fairy tales, which she had collected since childhood, as had her mother and grandmother before her. She was not very interested in Jeremy during the day, but at night she would let him sit in her lap and she would read him a tale. When he reached the age of five and could climb a ladder, she built into the attic a little library full of tales. Jeremy's father helped with this construction and even converted a gabled window into a half door and tiny balcony, where on pleasant evenings Jeremy could sit in his mother's lap and stare out at passing cars on Main Street while she read him tales. For a year or so, this attic was where his mother could most often be found if she went missing from other parts of the building. But there soon came a time when his mother no longer stole away to the attic, but instead drifted farther from home, and one September night, at the annual Harvest Festival, she began to dance with men other than his father, who finally drew her aside. Their conversation started softly but grew louder. "Because I am your husband!" Jeremy's father was heard to say, a declaration that drew the attentive eyes of other citizens as well as a laugh of contempt from Zyla. "Husband?" she said. "I would call you more of a minor inconvenience."

Well, that is how it can sometimes be between unhappy men and women.

Not long thereafter, Jeremy came home from his first-grade classes and, to his surprise but perhaps no one else's, found his mother absent.

"She's gone," Jeremy's father told him.

"Gone where?" Jeremy asked, and his father's eyes slid away.

"I don't know. In search of a happy ending, I guess."

34

Jeremy did not understand. "When will she be back?"

"I'm not sure," his father said. "When she's ready, I guess."

In time, Jeremy learned the story that had kept him from entering the Green Oven Bakery until the very day on which our own tale has begun, for that was where, on her final day in the little town of Never Better, Jeremy's mother had been sitting and eating a slice of Prince Cake when a traveler from Canada walked through the door. Minutes later, she followed the man to his car and was heard asking him for a ride out of town. No one could explain this behavior—her manner was described by one villager as "mechanical" and by another as "confounded"—and Jeremy had always wondered if she had looked up from her first bite of Prince Cake when the man from Canada walked through the door, if the legend of the first bite had come true for his mother because she really believed it could.

That night, Jeremy climbed the ladder to the attic. Her books were all there.

"That was why I thought she would come back," Jeremy said when he related this sad tale to me. He looked down. "I wasn't sure she'd come back for me, but I always thought she'd come back for her books."

It was not long after his mother's disappearance that Jeremy began to hear voices, though none of them would be the voice he wanted most to hear: the voice of his mother.

Jeremy's father did not speak Zyla's name, nor did he try to find her and bring her back. He made his oil deliveries, but he no longer sang his songs. His supervision of Jeremy was absent-minded.

Then, about five years ago, Jeremy heard his mother's voice, faint and sorrowful, but, still, he was certain that it could be no one other than his mother. *I'm sorry*, the voice said. *I'm sorry, sorry, sorry.*

The voice fell silent then.

Perhaps ten days thereafter, Jeremy's father received in the mail an envelope with no return address. It contained a *Todesanzeige*—an obituary—scissored from a paper in Saskatchewan, Canada. I have seen the document myself—Jeremy brought it out one day to show me. It announced the death of Zyla Johnson Newgate, who had suffered death by drowning after her canoe capsized among rocks and boulders in fast-moving water. She was survived by her husband, Theodore Newgate, and two stepchildren, aged seven and nine. A photograph of the woman was positioned above the text. It was of Jeremy's mother.

When Jeremy arrived home from school that afternoon, he saw the obituary lying on the table. Even after reading it again and again, he was hardly able to believe its meaning. He put his head on the table and closed his eyes. Some moments went by, and then all at once he became aware of the deep and strange stillness of the house. He went to look for his father. He found him in his bed completely covered with blankets.

"I'm awful cold," he told Jeremy.

"She married and became somebody else's stepmother," Jeremy said. "I didn't even know you were divorced."

"Neither did I," his father said. His eyes were red.

That his father had been crying scared Jeremy. He had never seen his father cry before.

Jeremy looked again at the picture of his mother in the newspaper. "Guess she didn't find her happy ending."

The only sound in the room was the tick, tick, tick of the clock. Finally, his father said, "You can't tell anyone what's happened to your mother."

"Why?"

A second passed, then another. "Because I'm asking you not to."

"Okay," Jeremy said. "What do I tell people?"

"Nothing." His voice, to Jeremy, sounded not quite alive. "No one needs to know anything."

Jeremy thought it was strange that his father wanted to turn his mother's death into *Their Secret*.

"Okay?" his father asked.

"Okay," Jeremy said.

"I need to stay here," his father said. He stared up at the ceiling. "Here in this room. Okay?"

"Okay."

Jeremy counted the ticks of the clock. He had reached one hundred ten when his father said, "Here's what you tell people. Tell them that I have a rare sickness that not even the doctors can understand and I just want to be left alone. Okay?"

Jeremy nodded, and his father closed his eyes. "I'm sorry, Jeremy," he said in a whispery voice. "I'm sorry for you and I'm sorry for me and I'm sorry for Zyla."

This was the first time in five years he had spoken her name, and he would never speak it again.

Jeremy sat in a chair beside the bed until his father fell to sleep, and then he slipped back into the kitchen, for an idea had occurred to him, one that, when he again read the obituary and inspected the calendar on the wall, proved to be true: the afternoon that his mother died was the very date that he had heard his mother's voice whispering that she was *sorry, sorry, sorry*.

Jeremy climbed into the attic to be with his mother's books, and that night he dragged his bedding up the ladder. Ever since that darkening day, the attic above the bookstore had been Jeremy's private room and the apartment behind the bookstore had been his father's sanctuary, and also his prison.

§

§

After saying *au revoir* to Ginger Boultinghouse, Jeremy pulled out the key attached to the long leather cord around his neck, unlocked the bookstore door, and found a letter from the bank lying on the floor below the mail slot. "Final Notice of Trustee Sale" was written at the top of the letter, followed by a dense text containing terms like *default, unpaid balance, collection fees, late fees*, and *lender's legal department*.

"God," Jeremy said under his breath, and still carrying the letter, he pushed through the door that led from the bookstore to the apartment, where his father lay in bed watching television.

"There you are," his father said in the tone of a person both relieved to see someone and annoyed by his late arrival.

"I went by the bakery," Jeremy said, and his father's face turned rigid, for he, too, had heard the story of his wife asking the man from Canada for a ride.

"I had to go sometime," Jeremy said.

Well, it is true. Sometimes avoiding something can give it more and more meaning rather than less and less.

His father tipped his chin and poked his fingers into his gnarled beard, which seemed to irritate Jeremy and make him go even further. "I had a piece of Prince Cake, too," he said, and this was too much for his father—he clamped shut his eyes, as if not seeing his son might put him beyond hearing him as well.

"I had a piece and it tasted really good and nothing happened." He softened his voice. "Nothing happened, Dad." He waited another moment and made his voice softer still. "It wasn't the bakery's fault that Mom left."

Mr. Johnson pulled at his beard, kept his eyes clamped shut, and said, "I know what I know."

"Well, here's something else for you to know," Jeremy said a bit tensely. He held out the letter from the bank. "Open your eyes and take a gander at this."

Harold Johnson gave the letter a squinting look. "What is it?"

"It's from the bank. They're going to schedule the sale of the store."

His father said nothing and turned his eyes to the television screen, where several men in cowboy hats shot at one another from behind barrels, feedbags, and horses. One dying man splashed into a watering trough. A bleeding man dragged himself across the street while bullets sprayed up dirt all around him. Yes, yes, it was quite a spectacle.

"See that guy who just got shot and is writhing in the dust?" Jeremy said. "That's us, Dad. We're going to be put out on the street. We're going to lose the store and our home, and we're not even shooting back." His father kept gazing at the television. Jeremy raised his voice. "Are you even listening?"

His father pried his eyes from the television. "We aren't shooting back," he said, "because we don't have any bullets." He let his gaze drift back to the television.

Jeremy seemed about to say something more but thought better of it and instead pushed open the door to the kitchen. There he grilled three cheese sandwiches, one of which he ate quickly with a glass of milk made from powder. That, I knew, would be his supper. Then he served the other two sandwiches on a tray just as his father liked them—double-tiered and spread with a generous layer of a maple-flavored syrup, moderately heated.

Jeremy's father sat up in bed and ate his sandwiches almost without taking his eyes from the television screen.

Jeremy said, "I'll be studying."

His father turned his head slightly while keeping his gaze fixed on the screen. "But you'll come back for our quiz show, right?"

"I'll try."

Uncommon Knowledge was the only show that Jeremy and his father enjoyed watching together, and I confess that I, too, found it diverting. "The quiz show that celebrates the uncommon knowledge of the common man!" a rich voice always proclaimed at the beginning. Then the host would describe how the show's talent scouts had scoured the far corners of the countryside looking for ordinary men and women who possessed extraordinary knowledge about some particular thing—the history of the carrier pigeon, for example, or the terra-cotta soldiers of Emperor Qin, or the life cycle of skinks. These self-taught experts were then questioned by renowned authorities in the field. The audience rooted for the commoners, as they always have.

"You should watch it with me tonight," Jeremy's father said. "They've got a woman who knows everything about chasing tornadoes."

"What we need is somebody who knows everything about dodging foreclosures."

His father seemed not to have heard. "Tornado chasing could be real interesting." He smiled hopefully at Jeremy. "You'll watch it, won't you?"

"I'll try," Jeremy said again. "But it's finals week."

His father's eyes faded slightly, and he slowly raked his fingers through his unkempt beard. "Okay," he said. I believed I knew what troubled him. He was afraid that Jeremy would go away to a university and leave him alone. But that is the way of the world, is it not? Every day a child steps away from the parent by the littlest distance, perhaps just the width of a mouse-whisker, but every day it happens, and the days go by, one after another after another.

So Jeremy sat at the long table in the other room, removed his shoes and stockings so that he could feel the age-worn Persian carpet underfoot, and opened his books. After studying geometry, there was world history, but then he folded his book over a finger and whispered, "Jacob?"

Yes?

"What do you think of Ginger Boultinghouse?"

What I thought was that she was a saucy girl whose saucy ways could become a distraction from Jeremy's studies. But over my long life as a mortal I had learned that it is best to answer such questions as positively as the truth will allow.

She does not allow herself to be bullied by Conk Crinklaw and his friends, I said, *and she is kind to Frank Bailey. I think well of her for those things.*

Jeremy nodded. "That it?"

Well, she is very comely. I watched his face. *Would you not agree?*

He tried to manufacture a casual response. "I guess so, yeah."

And she is clever, I said, and then—I could not keep myself from it—I added, *Perhaps a bit too clever.*

Surprise registered in Jeremy's face and he seemed about to ask something more, but at this moment his father shouted loudly from the other room, "Two minutes till *Uncommon Knowledge!*"

"Okay," Jeremy called back, but he did not stand up. Nor did he question me further about Ginger Boultinghouse. He silently resumed his studies, though more than once his eyes drifted toward the window, his expression softening, as if he were thinking of something pleasant, and I would have to whisper a reminder, just as I did long ago with my younger brother, Wilhelm.

The studies now. The studies.

§

§

As the sun's last rays soften the room's light and Jeremy turns his pages and makes his notations, I will tell you a short tale about Jeremy and his beloved grandfather, who opened the Two-Book Bookstore in his old age.

Lucian Johnson had spent his entire life working as a steamfitter, dynamiter, water witcher, cardsharp, and coffin maker, and when his working days were at last behind him, he thought a written account of his life might be of interest to the public. He spent several years on the project, and it grew to two volumes in length. But when he was finally done, no one wanted to publish it, so he had the book printed at his own expense, and he converted Johnson's Custom Coffin Shop to the Two-Book Bookstore, the store's two books being *My Life & Times by Myself, Lucian A. Johnson*, volumes I and II. He lined the walls with bookshelves, rolled out a soft Persian carpet, set an old oak library table in the middle of it, and brought in a red velvet sofa and two stuffed armchairs purchased at an estate sale. Then he hung out a sign that said OPEN.

For a time, his doddering friends came to the bookstore to play dominoes at the library table, and while playing, they would pretend to be on the constant lookout for potential retail trade.

"That a customer?" one of them would say when somebody approached on the sidewalk, and then when the pedestrian had passed by, another would say, "Guess not."

This droll ritual finally drove Jeremy's grandfather into such a state that one afternoon he threw the domino players out, and the dominoes, too. During the months that followed, Jeremy was the only person whose company his grandfather could tolerate. He took seriously the voices Jeremy heard, even going so far as to have Jeremy repeat the words whenever he received them. "Ghosts," his grandfather finally surmised. "You're hearing ghosts." He squinted at Jeremy. "Do you see 'em, too?"

Jeremy said he never saw any ghosts, and a few days later his grandfather, having done his research, announced that Jeremy was not a *clairvoyant* but a *clairaudient*. "That's a person who hears voices from the spirit world." His grandfather had also come to another conclusion. "When these books sell out," he said, waving a hand vaguely toward the shelves stuffed with his autobiographies, "I'm going to add a chapter about you for the next edition." He smiled at Jeremy. "You're quite a curiosity."

Jeremy and his grandfather became friends of the best type. Each saw in the other the subtle but estimable qualities no one else saw. One day, Jeremy came into the store with his cheeks red from crying. Somehow he had lost his house key—again—and it seemed to him to signify something larger. "I'm nothing but a loser," he said, and flopped down on the old red sofa.

Jeremy's grandfather sat right down beside Jeremy and said, "You may be a loser of keys, Jeremy, but that doesn't make you any other kind of loser." The next day, he presented Jeremy with the long leather cord that he still wore, beautifully knotted, on which hung a brand-new house key. He slid it over Jeremy's head, tucked it into his shirt, and said, "There. That should do it."

It did. Thereafter Jeremy never lost a house key again.

Days, weeks, and months traveled not unpleasantly by.

Then, three years ago, on a chill wintry day while Jeremy was at school, the old man's heart failed and he fell dead. He evidently passed quickly through the *Zwischenraum*, but before departing, he found Jeremy in his school classroom.

You're a dear, good boy, he said, *and I love you more than the sun and the moon*.

Jeremy, who had been at his desk doing math sums, sat stock-still and wondered how the voice he was hearing could sound like his grandfather's.

He rubbed at his temple more and more frantically, but his grandfather's voice did not come again.

"No!" Jeremy said in a strange, strangled whisper, and then, dropping his pencil to the floor, he rose from his desk and, in spite of the teacher reproachfully calling his name, ran straight to the Two-Book Bookstore, where he found his grandfather lying dead on the old Persian rug.

§

§

For several days, the final examinations proceeded well. The first few tests came and went without difficulties.

On Thursday night, however, something happened.

The evening began in quiet study. Only two exams remained—one in geometry and one in classical vocabulary. Our contemplation of geometry had taken most of the evening, with Jeremy, at my promptings, reciting his axioms and postulates. This had aggravated his father as he lay in the next room watching television. "Not so loud!" he yelled from time to time.

And so, when geometry was finally finished, Jeremy took his vocabulary book up to the attic, where I could quiz him without annoyance to his father. I would pronounce a word and Jeremy would give its definition, followed by the Latin or Greek derivation. Unlike other subjects, vocabulary came quite easily to Jeremy. It was just a matter of taking the time to rehearse the words. He remembered that *digital* comes from the Latin *digitus*, meaning *finger*, but had forgotten the Greek root for *podiatry*. "Don't tell me," he would say, but finally I would have to tell him.

"Pous, podos," he repeated, *"pous, podos,"* and, really, he was so earnest that something in my ancient soul went out to him.

Accord, I said, and he said, *"Agreement*, from the Latin *ac* or *ad*, meaning *to* or *toward*, and *cor, cordis* meaning *heart."*

Exzellent, I said, and had begun to pronounce the next word when suddenly I heard a strange tapping sound.

Jeremy cocked his head.

And then it came again: *tap, tap, tap.*

It seemed to come from the small door between the attic and the tiny gabled balcony.

By the clock, it was 9:40 p.m., a time when few in the village ventured out.

Louder now: *tap, tap, tap, tap.*

"See what it is," Jeremy whispered to me, but he knew I could not, not unless he opened the door. (As a rule of thumb, I tell Jeremy that if a cricket can get in, so can a ghost.)

The tapping grew even sharper and more insistent: *tap, tap, tap, tap, tap!*

Jeremy crept slowly toward the half door, but as he approached, the tapping stopped as abruptly as it had started. Now silence itself seemed eerie. Jeremy leaned toward the window and was staring out when a masked face suddenly appeared in the glass!

"Eh!" Jeremy said, or perhaps, "Ek!" and lurched backward. Who could blame him?—a masked face in the window will give any mortal a turn—but now the terror in Jeremy's expression was caught by a beam of light directed in from the window.

How was this? How did a lantern get up to this high balcony?

But look! The light slowly turned on itself and a hand appeared, gripped the knitted mask, and slowly pulled it free to reveal the face of . . . a grinning Ginger Boultinghouse!

And perched precariously on the balcony behind her were her two girlfriends, also in high mirth.

Ginger motioned for Jeremy to open the small door, and the girls came spilling and laughing into the attic, each carrying a rucksack and each dressed from head to toe in black clothes.

"Very funny," Jeremy said in a peevish tone.

But Ginger was unrepentant. "You're right," she said, grinning. "It was, very." She looked around. "Zounds," she said. "Kind of stuffy up here in Johnson-Johnsonville."

Maddy walked over to the window that gave onto the back of the alleyway and began to unlatch it.

"Wouldn't do that if I were you," Jeremy said, but she already had, and a foul smell streamed in.

The girl slammed the window closed and held a hand over her nose. "Wow," she gasped. "Are you storing, like, a thousand rotten eggs out there?"

"It's the hot springs behind the building. It can be kind of bad when the wind's from the north."

"*Kind of bad?*" Maddy said. "How about cruel and unusual?"

Ginger meanwhile was looking around the attic. "This is pretty fabulous, Jeremy. Awful snug, though. You'd have more room if you had fewer books."

He glanced at the shelves. "Yeah, well. They aren't really mine. They're my mother's."

She regarded a small cane-seated rocking chair. "That for when elves visit?"

"No," Jeremy said. "It was mine. When I was . . ."

"Little?" Ginger said.

"Yeah."

Ginger plopped onto Jeremy's mattress, the other girls sprawled on the floor, and Jeremy said, "So how'd you get up here?"

"Not hard," Ginger said. "Only tricky stretch was climbing the cast-iron pipe to the roof. From there, your cute little balcony is within arm's reach."

Marjory said, "That's if you have monkey arms like Ginger. For me and Maddy, we're talking near-death experience."

It was true. I often took this route myself, but I would not have thought it easy for mortals.

Jeremy, too, seemed impressed. I could see that his peevishness was receding.

"Okay," he said, "that takes care of *how*. What I don't get is *why*."

"He's got the how," murmured Maddy Saxon, the one with the smoldering eyes and scarred cheek, "and now he wants the why."

She and Marjory Falls sat on the floor, leaning back to back with their legs in front of them. When I slipped past Maddy Saxon, she said, "Whoa! Did you just feel that weird draft of warm air?" and Marjory said, "Oh! Sorry," which, for reasons I did not understand, sent them into laughter.

"The why is very simple," Ginger said, and her smile had slyness in it. "We saw the light on and wanted to talk to you. Is that so bad?"

Studies, I said into Jeremy's ear. *Examinations*.

But Jeremy said, "Talk to me about what?"

"We're going on a night mission," Ginger said, "and we thought you might want to come along."

No, Jeremy, you do not.

"You need to get out more," Ginger said, "I mean, it's a little sad, you sitting up here in the attic"—she paused—"talking to yourself when you could be out on a night mission." She grinned at him. "Speaking metaphorically here, Jeremy, I can hardly see your life through all the dust and cobwebs."

Metaphor, I said. From meta—beyond—and pherein—to bear. To bear beyond! It is one of your vocabulary words. Words that we need to study!

"What kind of night mission?" Jeremy asked. He was ignoring me completely!

"The most fabulous kind," Ginger said. "We're going to perform a *zounds*-worthy act of *derring-do*. We've got it all planned out"—she fixed her golden eyes on him—"but we kind of need your help." She leaned forward, bringing the scent of cinnamon with her. "And you're already dressed for the occasion."

It was true that Jeremy was also wearing dark clothes, but what did that signify? Nothing whatsoever!

Your studies! I shouted. The vocabulary! The classical roots!

"I don't know," Jeremy said.

Maddy Saxon cast a meaningful look at Ginger. *"Told you."*

"Maybe Jeremy is going to read himself a fairy tale and put himself to bed," Marjory said. She pulled a book from the shelves, and when she read its title aloud—*"The Big Book of Fairy Tales"*—Jeremy's face clouded.

"Could you put that back?" he said. "It was my mother's."

Marjory did put it back, but she at once pulled out another

49

and read the title aloud: *"Told Under the Green Umbrella: Favorite Fairy Tales and Legends."* She looked up at Jeremy with dancing ink-black eyes. "Is everything up here a fairy tale?"

Jeremy's face flushed red. "Not all of them," he murmured.

The girl turned the pages to the first story. "'The Frog King,'" she said, and then in a singsongy voice began to read, "Once upon a time, when wishes still came true—" but Jeremy suddenly cut her off.

"Okay," he said.

His manner was stiff and serious. The girls all looked at him.

"Okay what?" Ginger asked.

"Okay, I'll go with you."

This time it was Ginger who cast a meaningful look at the other girls, after which she leaned forward and gave Jeremy's arm a gentle squeeze.

One after another, they crept down the ladder from the attic, not that they needed to—nothing could be heard over the din of Mr. Johnson's television. Jeremy took the key from around his neck and locked the bookstore behind him.

Do not do this, Jeremy, I said. *Please do not do this.*

But my warning was like a hand raised to stop the wind.

§

§

Away the girls went, all dressed in black, rushing ahead like rampant shadows, with Jeremy chasing behind. The girls slipped through backyards, cut across bare lots, vaulted fences, slid between buildings, loped along alleys. Upon reaching a collection of rubbish bins in the alley between the bakery and the baker's house, they stopped and waited for Jeremy to catch up. When at last he did, he bent at the waist, taking in great gulps of air.

"You should join the track team," Ginger genially chided. "It's good cross-training for night missions."

"Or," Jeremy gasped, "I could, you know, just stay home."

Ginger pulled a black stocking hat out of her rucksack and handed it to Jeremy, but while the girls tucked their hair into their hats, he just held his and looked around. The Green Oven Bakery stood on one side of the alley. Over the fence on the other side loomed the large wood-and-stone home of the baker.

"Now, tell me again," he said. "What exactly are we doing here?"

Ginger smiled, blinked, and—I could hardly believe my ancient eyes—suddenly sprang from an overturned bucket to an overturned trash bin to the top of the fence. Balanced there, she tossed her party a grin and then, grabbing on to an outreaching tree limb, swung out of sight.

At once, the girlfriends pushed a board up and over the top of the fence. Then in quick fluid motions they, too, were over the fence, leaving Jeremy alone.

We could go back to our studies, I said. *It is not too late.*

"Jeremy?" Ginger called lightly through the fence. "Ready?"

The studies, I said.

Jeremy slowly pulled the black cap over his head. He climbed onto one bucket without difficulty, but as he pushed away from it, both the bucket and the trash barrel tipped over and crashed to the pavement. Jeremy's hands clutched the top of the fence and his knees banged hard against the planks, but he dragged himself up. He teetered for a moment at the top and then, reaching for the tree limb, he lost his grip on the fence and skidded to the ground, where he landed with a *whump*. His hands and arms were badly scraped, but such was the excitement that he must not have felt it.

"This way," Ginger called in a hushed voice, and when he'd drawn close, she whispered, "Just so we're clear on the concept, we're going for stealth here."

Beyond them, the baker's house stood nearly dark. Only one rear window was illuminated, and the light there was dim.

"What are we doing here?" Jeremy whispered.

An excellent question!—but Ginger merely nodded at the wood plank laid out in front of them. "We're using this handy board to cross the mud," she said.

The plank spanned a broad swath of the backyard that collected drainage and appeared to remain perpetually muddy.

"No, I mean after that," Jeremy murmured.

"You'll see." Ginger depressed a button that illuminated her watch. "Seven minutes," she whispered. She pulled two small bags from one of the rucksacks and shoved them into her rear pockets, then turned to Jeremy. "Once we cross the mud, we split up. You follow me. Don't make a sound and everything will be all right."

Jeremy looked at the large dark ivy-covered house and then back at the fence. "What's our exit strategy here?" he asked.

"Exit strategy? We haven't even gotten in yet."

"In *where*?" Jeremy said. His voice was low but full of alarm.

"Shh."

Light appeared in one window of the house, then another. The flickering glow of a television followed, and the large passing shadow of the baker.

"Showtime," Ginger said, and she deftly stepped across the board toward the house.

Jeremy followed. The board wobbled, but he crossed without falling.

The girlfriends approached the house, too, but at a different angle. They took tightly rolled foam pads from their rucksacks and unfurled them across a gravel walkway that inadvertently composed a kind of noise moat around the house. They stood carefully on the foam pads beneath a window and gave Ginger a thumbs-up sign. Jeremy followed Ginger toward the front door, where Ginger used the same kind of pad to creep quietly to a position in the ivy behind a large electrical air cooler and directly below another window.

The muted voice of a television newsman seeped out from the house. Also another sound—what seemed to my keen ear to be a refrigerator door opening and closing.

"Okay," Ginger whispered to Jeremy, "here's the deal. We've been watching the jolly baker the last few nights and he's got a surprising little routine. Every night he reads the newspaper and then he goes somewhere we can't see and then, a little before ten, he comes back, turns on the TV news, and pours out a bowl of Trix."

"Trix? The baker eats *Trix*?"

"I know!—who would've guessed? But every night, like clockwork, he sets out his bowl and his spoon and his bottle of milk, and then he does something even weirder."

"Weirder than eating Trix every night?" Jeremy said.

"Yep. He takes out his trash, then, right over there by those far bushes, he pees."

"He pees," Jeremy repeated. He seemed surprised, but I was not. Several men in the village conducted the same nightly ritual.

Ginger nodded. "The trash and the peeing take between two and two and a half minutes. That's where we come in."

"We?"

She pulled the two bags out of her back pockets and handed them to Jeremy. "Well, actually, you."

"What?"

He peered at the two small packets she had handed him. They were marked *Pop Rocks*. On past occasions, I had seen Jeremy pour these *Kiesel* into his mouth, and I had heard the strange electrical crackling they produced there, but why he liked them I could not guess.

"As soon as the baker comes around the corner," Ginger told him, "all you have to do is sneak in and dump the Pop Rocks into his Trix. Then when he gets back and pours in the milk . . ." She let him imagine the rest.

After a moment, Jeremy said, "I'm not doing that."

Exzellent thinking, I said.

"Okay," Ginger said. "I'll do it myself. It's just that . . ."

"Just that what?"

"I don't know. It's just that"—she gestured to the girlfriends positioned in the shrubbery two windows away—"they were so totally against my bringing you. Like, you couldn't help and would slow us down. . . ." Her voice had trailed off; now it lifted just a bit. "But maybe you could keep watch for me?"

54

Nein, I said. *Let us go now, Jeremy, and leave these girls to their foolishness.*

Good advice, and had Jeremy listened to it, this would be a less dark tale.

Ginger extended her open hand to take back the Pop Rocks, but Jeremy, to my surprise and consternation, suddenly stuffed them into his pocket.

Jeremy, do not think of doing this!

"Okay," he told Ginger. "I'll go in."

"Yeah?" she said.

Jeremy's tone was resolved. "Yeah."

"Okay, then," she whispered. "Quick, take off your shoes."

Inside the baker's house, the television news ended. Seconds later, the front door opened, followed by gravelly footsteps, and then the rotund baker, whistling a little tune, passed in front of us carrying a small bin of trash toward the rear alley.

As his footsteps receded, Jeremy crouched to spring.

No, Jeremy, I said. *Nein, nein, nein.*

"Go!" Ginger whispered.

And off he went.

§

§

When I slipped through the front door with Jeremy, I stopped to take in the marvelous smells of sugar melted and sugar baked, but

Jeremy rushed to the baker's wooden table and frantically twisted the edge of the first bag of explosive candy.

Mein Gott! I said. I could not keep myself from saying it, for Jeremy's hands were red from having torn them on the fence. He, too, saw the blood for the first time, and in his alarm, he pulled even harder on the packet, ripping it nearly in two and scattering candy crystals all over the table.

Jeremy swept the *Kiesel* into one hand and dropped them into the bowl.

Dimly I could hear the sound of shoes.

Jeremy! He is coming!

Jeremy took a backward step, but there on the table lay the empty bag, the very edge of it smeared red with his blood.

The outside gravel popped louder and louder.

Jeremy stepped back to the table, grabbed the bag, and shoved it in his pocket.

To my horror, I saw another scrap from the bag lying under the table, but one of the girlfriends was tapping rapidly at the window, waving him out, and so we flew through the door and around the corner and settled into Ginger's hiding place just as the baker passed again, still whistling his little tune.

He locked the front door behind him, and then only the muted sounds of the television penetrated the walls.

"You okay?" Ginger whispered, squeezing Jeremy's arm. "I hope you're okay, because you were pretty freaking fabulous."

Jeremy, too, seemed to feel exhilarated. Well, that is how it is when mortals do something foolish and escape unharmed. Jeremy pulled on his black canvas shoes but did not tie them. "Okay," he whispered. "Let's get out of here."

"Before the grand finale?" she whispered. "I don't think so."

Jeremy rubbed the sweat near his temple. To my surprise, he actually wanted my opinion. *We should go*, I told him. *Run! Eile! Fretta! Haast!*

"Let's get out of here," he whispered again to Ginger, but she merely swatted at something crawling up her leg from the ivy, then rose just enough to peer through the window. When she motioned to Jeremy, he did the same.

Within the dining room, the portly baker could be observed as if on a lighted stage. He sensed nothing unusual. He brushed something from his full white beard and was still whistling as he pulled out his chair and sat down with his eyes on the television screen.

He leaned forward and twisted the cap from the milk carton.

"Here goes!" Ginger whispered, but just then the baker stopped to stare at the television, where there appeared a close-up picture of a missing person—a robust young man with a gap-toothed smile. A sign above his picture said MISSING? . . . and a sign below said OR MERELY AN OVERSEAS ADVENTURE? A woman moderator then came on the screen, but her words could not be heard. Behind her, there appeared a map of Europe with a red arrow pointing to Amsterdam. The baker was attentive throughout this story, and when it ended, he shook his head with an attitude that suggested concern or sadness.

For this we are playing window peeper? I said.

"Let's go!" Jeremy said in a tight whisper.

But Ginger was transfixed.

She watched the baker lift the carton of milk and pour.

The instant the liquid touched the cereal, the baker's face

froze and he wrenched his hand back. Rising quickly and stumbling away from the table, he dropped into a crouch, stricken, as if something dangerous had leapt up from the bowl. I felt pity for him, but at the windows, the girlfriends had to cover their mouths to smother their laughter.

After a moment, the baker began to stand up straighter. He regarded the cereal bowl, milk dripping from the table to the floor, spreading to the top of the candy package Jeremy had left behind. The baker's eyes went to the front door and then to the kitchen and a doorway beyond. He disappeared down that corridor, evidently checking other rooms, for light appeared in a succession of windows.

Jeremy tugged at Ginger's arm, but still she waited and watched.

Soon the baker returned to the dining room. He bent close to stare at the floor, at what I knew to be the scrap from the package. But he didn't pick it up.

And then the moment arrived that must always arrive in such situations.

The baker's gaze lifted. It moved from window to window until, at last, it was directed at us.

Ginger and Jeremy ducked out of the way. I did not. I watched the baker walk heavily across the room and put his hand to a switch on the wall.

Mein Gott!—suddenly the whole yard was flooded with light!

"Code red!" Ginger shouted. "Go! Go! Go!"

Maddy and Marjory were already bouncing over the mud on the wooden plank and racing toward the high fence, with Ginger close behind. The plank shifted abruptly under Jeremy's weight, and in the next instant his foot was sucked into the deep gummy mud. He stumbled forward, trying to pull himself free.

Up! I urged. *Up! Up!*—but the mud oozed around him and pulled at his feet and hands. Suddenly, Ginger was there, leaning forward from solid ground, extending her hand, and his foot wrenched free of both shoe and mud, and Ginger and Jeremy ran for the fence as if chased by demons.

The baker stood at the leafy window peering out at the yard. But what could he see? In their black clothes, Jeremy and the girls were but shadows.

Maddy took a running jump at the fence, caught hold of the top, and scrabbled over, but Marjory needed help. Jeremy and Ginger boosted her up and over, then, as Jeremy stirruped his hands for Ginger, she fell back, grabbed at his collar—he would remember later a quick tug at his neck—and she fell almost to the ground before he could get hold of her. At once she was upright again, and this time she stepped back, launched herself toward the fence, and pulled herself up and over.

The baker opened the window. "*Hallå!*" he called. "Who is out there?"

Jeremy pulled off his remaining shoe and tossed it over the fence.

"*Hallå!*" the baker shouted. "Stop there! Stop there right now!"

Jeremy flew for the fence and, springing almost out of himself, caught hold of the fence top and spilled over it, bouncing off clattering trash cans and rolling to the ground on the other side.

Where, to my utter surprise, he sat up, looked at Ginger, who was standing there with his shoe in her hand, and began to laugh.

"*Code red?*" he said. "I don't remember anybody talking about *code red.*"

"Yeah, well," Ginger said, and now she was laughing, too. "I didn't think it was going to come up." She extended his muddy shoe. "Here you go, Cinderella!"

"Hope it fits," he joked, stuffing his muddy foot into the muddy shoe and half limping, half loping after her as they all scampered down the alleyway.

I, however, paused at the fence to look back.

Framed by the large window, the baker stood talking into the telephone while gazing out toward the yard, the fence, and the unseen me.

Ein Anruf bei der Polizei.

I was sure of it.

The baker was contacting the sheriff.

§

§

Maddy and Marjory had gone in one direction, Ginger and Jeremy in another. I caught up with them just as they rushed around a corner and—*mein Gott!*—knocked someone down!

Mrs. Jenny Applegarth.

In fact, Ginger had also gone sprawling, and Jeremy hardly knew whom to help first.

Jenny Applegarth, he decided.

"Sorry," he said, extending his hand to pull her back up. "Are you okay?"

They had fallen within a circle of light thrown by one of Main Street's three streetlamps. When Jenny Applegarth looked up at him, a smile came to her lips. "Is that you, Jeremy—all dressed in black?"

"Hi, Mrs. Applegarth," Jeremy said. "I guess we weren't paying attention."

Jeremy did yard work for Jenny Applegarth and had always liked her. Now she was brushing herself off and regarding Ginger, also dressed in black.

"It's me," Ginger said, peeling up the front edge of her black watch cap. For once the girl seemed not to know what next to say.

Mrs. Applegarth gazed down the empty street for a moment. "I thought I heard someone else, too."

The girlfriends, probably.

"Maybe," Ginger said, and offered nothing more.

Jeremy said, "Well, I guess we'd better go now."

Jenny Applegarth nodded and then added a small smile. "I'll let you know if I run into your missing shoe."

Jeremy glanced down at his muddy feet and started to offer an explanation, but Mrs. Applegarth held up an open hand to stop him. "The less I know, the better I like it." Again she smiled. "Night, kiddos."

She began to walk away.

"Mrs. Applegarth?" Ginger called softly, and Jenny Applegarth looked back.

"If anybody asks—probably they won't, but, I mean, let's say they did—could you just forget you saw us tonight?"

Jenny Applegarth regarded her for a moment. "It depends," she said, "but maybe." Her expression softened. "My memory always *has* been kind of dicey."

She turned the corner, disappearing from sight, and Ginger said they'd better keep moving.

I glided smoothly ahead and soon confirmed my worst fear: I saw Sheriff Pittswort's black-and-white patrol car wheeling from the police station and turning toward Main. I slipped back to Jeremy and advised him to hide at once.

"What?" he said.

"I didn't say anything," Ginger said.

Sheriff Pittswort. He's coming this way. Hide.

"Quick," Jeremy said, grabbing Ginger's arm. "In here."

He pulled her behind a short wall of blue plastic bins stacked in the alcove of Crinklaw's Superette.

"What are you doing?" Ginger said.

"Hiding."

"Because?" she asked. But at this moment the arcing beams of headlights swept onto the street. "It's Pittswort!" she said, ducking back. She looked at Jeremy in amazement. "The baker called the freaking *sheriff*? Over freaking *Pop Rocks*?"

Ginger and Jeremy crouched behind the bins as the sheriff's car prowled down the street. Mounted to the car was a strong lamp that the sheriff used to probe into dark nooks and crannies, including those around the superette, but Jeremy and Ginger were well hidden, and the patrol car slowly passed by.

"Okay," Ginger whispered, "that was an unnecessary thrill." She stood and looked around. "Let's get out of here."

Wait, I said, for I had seen something else as well.

62

"Just a second," Jeremy said.

"Why?" Ginger said. "Let's just—"

At that moment a second set of headlights turned onto Main. It was Deputy McRaven in a second patrol car. It, too, passed slowly by.

All right, then, I said, and was about to tell Jeremy to hurry home when to my dismay I heard something else! *Wait!* I said. *Wait. And hush.*

Jeremy took hold of Ginger's arm to keep her quietly in place.

Footsteps, I said, and in the next moment they could hear them, too—slow, shuffling footsteps coming this way. Behind the grocery crates, Ginger and Jeremy shrank into their smallest selves and held their breath.

Closer and closer came the shuffling footsteps of a dark hooded figure.

It was Mrs. Truax.

And then, a few feet away, on the opposite side of the grocery crates, she stopped. She peered that way and this.

"Possy?" she said at last in a dry, hollow voice. "Possy?"

The stillness seemed to stretch beyond the earthly world. And then, at last, this strange hooded woman turned and shuffled slowly on, and Jeremy and Ginger fled toward home, where yet another unhappy surprise awaited.

At the bookstore door, Jeremy pulled the leather thong from inside his shirt and . . . found it broken.

"What?" Ginger said.

Jeremy stood holding one end of the broken leather thong. "My key. It's gone." He looked back down the street. "I'd better go look for it."

63

"With Pittswort and McRaven and crazy Mrs. Truax crawling the streets?" Ginger said. "Are you doing any kind of thinking here at all?"

Jeremy admitted that he probably was not.

They circled to the side of the building, where Jeremy pried open a window that he knew was never latched. As he got set to climb through, Ginger grabbed hold of his arm. "So," she said, grinning at him through the darkness. "How'd you like your first night outside the Jeremopolis city limits?"

He gave a small laugh. "I'm not sure. It was all right, I guess."

"Not sure? My God, Jeremy. You were amazing! I said you had potential, and I was totally right." She reached for his one remaining shoe. "I'm going to jettison this."

"Why?"

"What good's one shoe going to do you? Besides, from this minute on, you never owned a pair of black Converse." She folded a stick of cinnamon gum into her mouth. "I'd also advise throwing all your muddy clothes in the washer."

"Yeah, okay." He paused. "I think I'm not really suited to a life of crime."

"You might be surprised. Besides, it can have unexpected rewards."

She took off her wool cap, shook out her long red hair, and leaned forward as if to kiss Jeremy, but she did not. She let her hair graze his cheek, and when she whispered, "I think you'd make a great sidekick," the sweet smell of cinnamon bloomed into the air.

She touched a finger to the tip of his nose and stood smiling at him. "*Au revoir,* Jeremy Jeremy Johnson Johnson," she said, and disappeared into the night, leaving her spicy scent behind.

"Whew," Jeremy said, though whether to himself or to me was uncertain. Then he climbed through the window and fell safely inside, or so he believed.

§

§

Jeremy laid the broken thong on his bedside table and stared for some moments at its fancy knots tied tight by his grandfather. Thereafter he began to ready himself for bed.

Doubtless there are specters who do not respect the privacy of mortals, but I am not one of them. At day's end, I kept Jeremy company only until he said, "Good night, Jacob," and then I took my leave. Sometimes, when he was feeling solitary, he would delay saying good night and we would talk before he fell to sleep. When his spirits were low, I would remind him of one of the day's pleasant occurrences—a kind word from a teacher or the sight of a gliding nighthawk silhouetted by the moon. Such thoughts sometimes helped him slip into the sweet arms of sleep.

This night, however, Jeremy was ready for slumber. Still—I could not help myself—I reminded him that we had not finished our vocabulary study.

"Wake me early," he said. "We'll study then."

Of course, I said.

"Good night, Jacob."

Good night, Jeremy.

After retiring from Jeremy's attic, I made my way to the belfry of the white church built by the town Lutherans. Here I passed my solitary evenings no matter the season, for while I might behold the beauty of snow, I was not chilled by it, and though I might hear the buzz of the summer's mosquito, I was beyond its bite.

I stretched my vaporous legs and gazed out at the vast prairie and sky and thought my disquieting thoughts. Distractions occurred—a star might shoot by, a browsing mouse might rustle a dry leaf, an owl might swoop from a nearby tree—but my apprehensions always returned.

The thing undone.

The unknown yet unmet desire.

This riddle is my prison; I am trapped within it. The answer— *the thing undone*—is the door that might release me from the *Zwischenraum*, but if I could not find the door, how could I open it?

What could it be—this thing undone? The *Deutsche Wörterbuch*, the monumental dictionary that Wilhelm and I undertook to compile, was of course undone. This was my first thought. When Wilhelm died, we were on words beginning with *D*. At my death, the work was in its seventh volume, and yet I had gotten only to *F*. But this could not be the thing undone, for it was a thing I could not do. From the *Zwischenraum* I could not continue our work on the great dictionary, or even encourage others to take it up. So it was not that.

Had Wilhelm and I been alive, we would have discussed the

thing undone, approached it with reason, determined its nature, devised a method of correction. But I was alone in the *Zwischenraum*. I had no advice and no answers and no methods. I had only a tender, terrible yearning for my absent brother.

I wondered if the *Zwischenraum* was not a riddle to be solved and escaped from but, in fact, *Hölle*—hell itself—or *die Hölle auf Erden*—a living hell. And with that came the nagging fear that the maid in Steinau had been right, that Wilhelm was not here because he had passed beyond to a better place, a place I had no way of reaching.

The thing undone.

The unknown yet unmet desire.

Finally, I remembered how, one night in a meeting hall, an aged traveler regaled Wilhelm and me with tales of faraway places, the Russian steppes, the Ganges and Nile rivers, the Great Wall of China, the Canadian Yukon, the American Badlands, on and on, each place more fascinating than the last.

That night, as we had walked home under a cold moon, Wilhelm said, "All those marvelous places." It was a soft, damp evening. The village butcher, passing by with his terrier, touched his hat to us. We had just turned up our lane when Wilhelm said, "We must go to these many places, Jacob, before we rest."

But we had our tales to transcribe and then the great dictionary to compile. One works and works, and then one morning the elm tree outside one's study shatters into the smallest of pieces, and the room in which one sits shatters, and the niece with whom one sits shatters, too, and—*blitzschnell!*—in the quickest instant the life that one has taken as one's daily due has been converted to this . . . what? . . . this place between smelling and tasting, between speaking and being heard, between living and finding peace.

But Wilhelm's words—*We must go before we rest*—had given me an excuse for movement. In one of the tales, a princess searching for her twelve brothers says that to find them she would travel as far as the sky is blue. It is a beautiful phrase, one that Wilhelm himself added, and it seemed now to command my own quest. I would travel as far as the sky was blue to find him. I needed no shelter, no food, no fire, no rest. However forlorn a ghost might be, he moves quickly and smoothly, without pause or break, and that was what I did.

China, Mongolia, the Yukon, on and on, all of those places Wilhelm had wanted to go, everywhere looking for Wilhelm's genial face, but I did not find him, and as months passed and then years, my hopes grew fainter. He was not here. He had not waited for me. He had passed on, and I had not.

Decades slipped past. Wars, famines, inventions. A century, finally, and half of another.

Then one day I found myself drifting with the wind across the grassy American plains, and I spied at a distance a specter working his way into the wind. He moved slowly—with the wind behind me, I covered four lengths to his one—and soon we approached each other.

I nodded at him and saw in his dull, desperate eyes my own dull desperation.

Wait, I said. To my own surprise, I said this.

I did not expect him to turn, but he turned and hovered, leaning into the wind, waiting for me to speak again.

I am looking for my Bruder Wilhelm Grimm.

The dead man stared at me for a few moments and then—
how surprised I was!—his lips curled into the slightest smile,
which I beheld as a man in the desert might behold water.

I know who you were, he said, *and who your brother was, though
I have not seen him. As a boy, I read your tales.*

This news had a soothing effect on me.

For a long time, he said, *I thought the Brothers Grimm wrote
those fairy tales. Not until I was a grown man did I learn you had
collected them from others.*

From this I knew he had not been dead as long as I, for when
I was alive, few would have made this mistake. *Yes*, I said, *most of
the tales came from citizens of Hesse, where we lived for a long time,
so, for my brother and me, the associations were tender.*

We talked for some time, though the man's smile had now
dried up and he kept peering north, into the wind, as if he had
some appointment there to keep. I asked him if we might travel
together in search of my brother, but he said he could not. He
must travel on, against the wind.

For how long?

He looked at me with hollow eyes. *Until I no longer must.*

Why? I asked. *Why into the wind? What for you is the thing
undone?*

He bent his head and said, *On the answer to that question I will
float away from this wretched place.*

So he, too, was enduring his own form of living *Hölle*.

We parted company, that desperate soul and I, but a short
time later I detected his voice carrying downwind to me: *Hallo,
hallo*.

I turned and saw him at a great distance motioning me his

way. He could not come with the wind, so I must go into it. It took some effort, but in time I had overtaken him.

Yes?

I have remembered something that may be of interest to you. In a town some distance from here, there is a boy who can hear us. The slight smile again formed on the specter's face. *A boy who sleeps in an attic full of fairy tales.*

I felt something hopeful stirring within me.

It is more even than that, the stranger said. *I was told by another specter—a small, nervous woman from Moldova—that there was also in this town a Finder of Occasions who would bring harm to the boy.*

A Finder of Occasions? I asked, and the stranger replied, *Someone who lies in wait until the opportunity is afforded to do harm or wreak havoc*—here he cast his ancient, unhappy eyes at me—*without leaving a trace behind.*

How will I know this boy? I asked. *What is his name? Where will I look for him?*

He lives in a bookstore. The village itself can be seen only from the corner of the eye.

What?

It is difficult to find but, once found, you will never lose it. The stranger closed his eyes and searched his memory. *There were red buttes nearby. Red-stone buildings in the town. The smell of sulfur. A bakery with wondrous scents.* He sighed and squinted into the wind. *I cannot tarry. I must go.*

How do I locate this Finder of Occasions? I asked, but already the stranger had turned and begun to work his way into the wind.

Off I hastened, full of expectation, but this boy and his store filled with books and his attic full of tales were not easily found. From village to village I went, from house to house and shop to shop until finally—I cannot tell you how many days had gone by—I stopped one evening and stood perfectly still. I closed my eyes and let the night wind move past me as the water moves past a rock in the river. How much time slipped by in this manner I cannot say, but when I again opened my eyes, the stars had scattered and the moon had moved and off to the side, almost behind me in fact, in the thinnest sliver of vision, I could just detect a strange and faint illumination.

I hastened toward this light with uncertainty, and there, taking shape in silhouette, was an array of looming buttes, and a sign that said WELCOME TO NEVER BETTER, and along Main Street there was a bakery producing wondrous aromas, and there, in the last of the business district's red-block buildings, was a bookstore where a boy sat alone, reading in an armchair under lamplight.

The window was open.

When I drew close and whispered, *Listen, if you will*, Jeremy Johnson Johnson looked up from his book, cocked his head, and said hopefully, "Mom?"

Honestly, I was sorry to disappoint him. *No*, I said.

Instinctively, he touched a finger to his temple. "Grandpa?"

Again there was hope in his voice. Again I was sorry to say no.

"Who are you, then?"

I cannot explain the phrase I chose. A *beggar*, I said, echoing words from one of our tales, *an ancient beggar with a broken heart. May I stay here awhile?*

Well, what have I told you about this boy's kindness?—he did

71

not hesitate an instant. "Sure, if you want," he said, and asked me my name.

Jacob. I pronounced it as it is pronounced: *Yaw-kub*.

But this was strange to the boy, so he had to repeat it. "Yawkub?"

Yes.

"Your accent is different. Where are you from?"

And do you know what I said? *I come from long ago and far away*.

"You do?" he said, and I could hear pleasure in his voice, and truly, for the first moment in all my time in the *Zwischenraum*, I felt something like lightness myself.

Well, that was how it was. As rapidly as that, I stepped into Jeremy's tale. I will not deceive you. I hoped that by protecting him from the Finder of Occasions, I might somehow achieve the thing undone, and be released at last from the *Zwischenraum*. I contrived a plan. Jeremy was young and clever, and I believed that the best way to protect him was to move him from this town, and I saw no better way to do this than by his going away to university. So I became not only his protector but also his teacher. And all had gone well, until . . .

On this fateful night I stared out at the thinning darkness and heard the first cock crow, with more soon joining in from one farm and another.

And what was this? Human voices? At this early hour?

Yes. *Mein Gott!*—down on Main Street—Sheriff Pittswort and Deputy McRaven were walking door to door, trying a particular key again and again, looking for the particular lock that it would open . . . as if in some fairy tale.

I hastened down from my belfry to investigate.

§

§

A very few minutes later, my anguished fears bore unhappy fruit: When the sheriff tried the key at the Two-Book Bookstore, it slid easily into the lock. It was followed by a smooth *click*, and with a twist of the knob the door swung open.

"Bingo," Sheriff Pittswort said, and poked his head into the bookstore. "Morning, folks!" he called. "Time to rise and shine! Sheriff's here for a visit!"

No one answered, though I heard the faintest stirring in the attic.

"Sleepyheads," the sheriff declared, casting a sly smile toward his deputy.

They were a peculiar pair. Sheriff Pittswort was so large that, in the old tales, he might have been called a giant. His deputy had a squashed aspect and resembled, if it is possible, a large dwarf, with short legs, broad shoulders, and an outsized head. His breath—I knew this even though I hovered some distance away—smelled sourly of coffee.

They stepped into the room. When the sheriff found large pieces of hardened mud near the window, and then a track of smaller pieces leading to the door at the rear of the shop, he said, "I think what we got here, Deputy, is a Person of Interest."

Deputy McRaven's laugh sent another wave of stale coffee-scented breath into the air.

"Hey, folks!" the sheriff yelled, louder this time. "Up and at 'em!"

No one answered.

Possibly Mr. Johnson could sleep through such clamor, but I had no doubt Jeremy was awake in the attic, lying still, wondering what to do next.

"Official business!" the sheriff yelled in a voice that boomed.

Jeremy poked his head over the top of the ladder, his hair stiff and uncombed. "You'll wake up my dad," he said quietly. "He has a hard time sleeping."

A derisive smile cut across the sheriff's face. "What I've noticed is that your dad has a hard time getting himself out of bed."

Deputy McRaven laughed hard at this. I turned to avoid his breath.

Jeremy pulled on his clothes and descended the ladder.

"Guess you know why we're here," the sheriff said when Jeremy faced him.

Jeremy put a hand to his temple. He wanted me to advise him. I knew I should recommend only that he tell the truth, but I did not trust this Sheriff Pittswort and I did not want Jeremy at his mercy. So I advised him as I advised myself when Bonaparte's brother assumed authority in Westphalia: *Tell no lies, but volunteer no truths.*

"I guess I don't really know what you mean," Jeremy said to the sheriff.

Sheriff Pittswort's smile was mocking. He whispered something to his dwarfish deputy, who at once stumped out the door and disappeared. The sheriff drew a small notebook from his rear pocket and uncapped his pen. "Okay," he said, "just for starters, where were you last night between nine and eleven p.m.?"

Jeremy stared down at his bare feet, then looked up, and was about to speak when a voice from the rear of the shop said, "He was here."

Mr. Johnson stood in the doorway, his long hair and beard both a greasy tangle.

"Well, well," Sheriff Pittswort said. "He has risen and it ain't even Easter."

Mr. Johnson raked his fingers through his beard with some difficulty.

The sheriff said, "So where were you last night, Harold?"

"Here," Mr. Johnson said. "Right here."

"Here in this room, Harold?"

"No. In the other room. Right there." Mr. Johnson gestured toward the room behind him. "My room."

"And your boy was in the room with you?"

Mr. Johnson's gaze slid away. "Some of the time." He touched his beard. "I was watching TV. He and I don't always like the same shows."

"So where exactly was your boy, Harold, when you were watching the shows he don't like?"

"In here. In the bookstore. Or up in the attic. He likes to read there."

"I was studying geometry," Jeremy said. "I was trying to memorize—"

But the sheriff cut him off by saying to Mr. Johnson, "So the fact is, Harold, you wouldn't have known if your boy'd gone out for an hour or two, would you? If, say, he'd had a sudden notion to break into somebody's house?"

"Jeremy wouldn't do that!" Mr. Johnson said with surprising vehemence. "Jeremy doesn't do those kinds of things!"

"Maybe he don't." Sheriff Pittswort smiled. "Then again, maybe he do."

Deputy McRaven came back into the room carrying a paper bag. The sheriff glanced into it, then turned to Jeremy. "Why don't you go put your shoes and socks on, son."

Jeremy looked at his father, who nodded begrudgingly, and after Jeremy had passed from the room, Mr. Johnson said, "Remember, Victor, I knew you before you were sheriff. Back then, you were just the town bully."

Sheriff Pittswort laughed. "And you were the town pissing post, so I guess we both just kind of *parlayed* our natural-born talents into what we are today."

Well, this is how men can speak when they are circling one another.

Jeremy appeared wearing an old pair of canvas-and-rubber shoes, which both the sheriff and deputy regarded closely.

"Them's what you wore last night?" the sheriff said, nodding at the shoes and then up at Jeremy. "When you went out?"

"Did I say I went out?" Jeremy said.

The sheriff smiled. "Okay, let me put it to you, then: Did you go out last night?"

In an even voice Jeremy said, "Either last night or the night before I took a walk up Main and back again. I do that sometimes before I go to bed."

The sheriff stared at him with a cold fixed eye. "See anybody on the street?"

"Not that I remember. But I was kind of lost in my own thoughts."

"You didn't see Jenny Applegarth?"

"Maybe. I do see her sometimes when I go out walking at night."

The sheriff reached into the brown bag and pulled out the muddy black shoe abandoned the night before. "This yours?"

"Doesn't look like mine," Jeremy said.

"You never owned a shoe like this?"

"I used to, yeah. But I don't now."

"When did you used to?"

"A while ago."

"A while ago," Sheriff Pittswort repeated. "As in, last night?"

"He said a while ago!" Mr. Johnson said. "What more do you want from him?"

Sheriff Pittswort smiled. He was clearly enjoying himself. "Well, one more thing I want from him is to try this shoe on." He grinned. "It'll be just like Cinderella."

"Don't do it!" Jeremy's father said.

"It's kind of a dainty shoe," the sheriff said, laying it next to Jeremy's foot. "But then you have kind of a dainty foot."

Jeremy's face was burning red as everyone noted the similar size of the shoes.

The sheriff took the muddy shoe over to the window and compared the hardened mud on the shoe to the hardened mud on the floor. He looked up at his deputy and nodded toward the floor. "Let's get a sample of that mud there, deputy."

The sheriff turned to Jeremy. "You mind holding out your hands?"

"What for?" Mr. Johnson said before Jeremy could answer.

"Settle down, Harold," the sheriff said mildly. "I just want to have a look at them."

Jeremy held his hands out, palms down.

"Other side?" the sheriff said.

Jeremy complied. The inner surface of his hands had been heavily abraded and were now softly scabbed.

The sheriff nodded as if this was exactly what he expected. "I'm afraid you're going to have to come up to the station, son."

"Why? Because he scraped his hands doing yard work or something?" Mr. Johnson said. "It's not even six in the morning and you come barging in here?" He was actually sputtering. "This isn't right! This is still America, isn't it? He needs a lawyer!"

The sheriff said, "Christmas Hunt is the only lawyer in town, and I know from personal experience that he don't rise early."

"Then *I'll* represent Jeremy!" Mr. Johnson said. "I'll be his legal representative."

Sheriff Pittswort looked past Mr. Johnson to Jeremy. "Let's go, son."

"Not without me!" Mr. Johnson said.

The sheriff stared down at Jeremy's father. "Don't bother coming if you ain't dressed decent, Harold. We got a no-shirt, no-shoes, no-service rule."

Again Mr. Johnson tugged his fingers through his beard. I doubted that he had proper clothes. In all my time there, I had never seen him in anything but a nightshirt.

"It's okay, Dad," Jeremy said. He was frightened, I could see it in his eyes, but he was trying to pretend he was not. "I'll be all right."

§

§

When Jeremy and the sheriff walked into the station, the baker was already there waiting. He stood in the vestibule staring at the posters of missing children. He had been called from work—he wore the white flour-dusted clothes he normally wore in the bakery and he carried the pleasant aroma of baked goods. As he spied Jeremy passing through the door, a look of surprise registered in his kindly blue eyes. While the deputy led Jeremy into the next room, the sheriff lingered behind.

"Morning, Sten," he said, bending a little as he looked down at the baker.

"*Hallå*, Sheriff," the baker said quietly.

The self-possession lost the night before had been restored—his white beard was once again combed, his cheeks again ruddy, his blue eyes again bright.

"Think you'll be happy with our work on this one, Sten," the sheriff said. "We got one of the kids nailed and mounted. After that, the rest will tumble."

The baker did not seem especially relieved. His eyes returned to the posters on the wall, in particular to a poster of Possy Truax that showed a photograph of him as a five-year-old boy alongside a sketch of him as he was imagined to look now.

The baker glanced up at the sheriff. "You really think he might still be alive?"

"Probably not," the sheriff said. "But who knows for sure except Possy himself . . . and maybe the person who took him." His eyes lingered for a moment on the poster. "I'll tell you what, though. I will never understand how anybody could've done that little boy a bit of harm." He shook his head wearily, and I will say it: In that moment, he did not look like a bullying sheriff—he looked like a pitiable human being.

I had heard that Possy, who had no father, trusted the sheriff more than he trusted anyone, and used to ride around in the sheriff's patrol car and sit with him at the café and wear a badge made especially for him while eating chocolate chip pancakes that the sheriff paid for and called *Possy cakes* because they weren't on the official menu. I had also heard it said that no one searched longer or harder for Possy than the sheriff.

The baker's gaze drifted over the other posters of missing youths. "So many children disappearing," he said.

The sheriff sighed. "Kids run away from home, Sten. Always have and always will. What we're seeing now is the same old deal, only more so."

The deputy poked his massive head through the door to say he had everything ready, including a chair for Jeremy's father, just in case he showed up.

In the inner room, the sheriff eased his bulk into his giant padded armchair and loomed over his desk. "Don't need introductions, do we? You know Jeremy Johnson Johnson, don't you, Sten?"

"Yes," the baker said, letting his gaze fall on Jeremy. "I do."

I thought I detected disappointment in the baker's voice. Sadness, even.

"So, Jeremy," the sheriff began conversationally, as if he were about to pose the most prosaic question, "why would you want to break into the baker's house last night?"

"I didn't say I did," Jeremy said, but he looked at the floor.

"Well, let's see," said the sheriff. "We found *your* key on *Sten's* property. And we found *your* shoe on *Sten's* property. And the mud in *your* house matches with the mud on *your* shoe, which is the mud of *Sten's* property. We found blood on his fence and blood on his table, and we found blood on your hands. So that kind of points to *you* being on Sten's property. And breaking into Sten's house. And then running like a banshee when Sten's yard lights come on." He smiled. "How's that for a *scenario?*"

The room filled with tight silence—everyone stared at Jeremy.

But the sheriff then did something unexpected. He softened his voice. "You know," he said, "what we have here ain't real *real* serious. It's a little bit bad, all right, but it ain't *murder* or anything. More of a prank than anything else. And the truth is, Jeremy, we'd just like to get it all sorted out. We know you was there, and we know there was other fellas, too, and if you was to fill in the blanks, that'd help your own situation a little. More than a little, even." The sheriff's smile seemed the smile of a friendly uncle. "So, Jeremy," he said, "who were your *compadres?*"

Jeremy did not say Ginger's or Maddy's or Marjory's name, and I knew he never would. Nor did he touch his temple. There was no point. What could I do? The misery in Jeremy's face gathered around his mouth—he was fighting away tears.

Across the room, the baker's eyes were fixed on Jeremy, and as he studied him, I detected uncertainty in his face, or even confusion. But about what? The case that the sheriff had presented left no doubt.

The sheriff must have noticed this, too, for he said, "Something the matter, Sten?"

The baker kept staring at Jeremy, and as he did, I saw a sudden sureness come into his eyes, as if something had come clear to him. "It wasn't him," he said in a quiet voice.

The sheriff leaned forward in surprise. *"What?"*

"It wasn't him," Sten Blix repeated. He nodded toward Jeremy. "He's much taller than any of the figures I saw."

The sheriff's face stiffened. "You just said *boys* when you described them to us, Sten. You didn't say *little* boys or *short* boys."

"That may be true," the baker said. "But now when I think of the voices and their size, I think they must have been small boys." The baker cast a kindly glance at Jeremy. "Immature boys, but probably good boys at heart. Boys who didn't know the prank they were playing might be seen as something more serious than a prank."

The sheriff smirked. "And the size-eight shoe, Sten? And the key that fits? And *your* real estate on the floor of *his* house?"

The baker shrugged. "I only know what I know, Sheriff. And I know that this isn't the boy who was in my yard last night."

The sheriff's face was as stone. "That your final word on the subject?"

The baker nodded yes.

The sheriff exhaled heavily, pushed back from his desk, and raised his great form. "Then I guess we're done here," he said, and he lumbered out of the office.

The deputy, however, did not move. He continued to stare at Jeremy. "The baker knows what the baker knows," he said in a low, seething voice. "But I know what I know."

Jeremy nodded but seemed barely to hear the words. A brief minute earlier he had been fighting tears, and now, to his utter surprise, he was free. As he passed by the baker, he whispered, "Thanks, Mr. Blix."

The baker nodded and returned a gentle smile, a smile the deputy saw. The moment Jeremy was gone, Deputy McRaven said, "Backing out on your story don't make our job any easier, Sten."

"I understand," the baker said, "but this episode started to seem a small thing beside . . ." His voice trailed off and he pointed to a photograph on the sheriff's desk. In it, Possy Truax sat beside the sheriff at the counter of Elbow's Café. Possy was smiling and the sheriff was smiling and no one could imagine a future in which Possy would disappear without a trace.

Deputy McRaven was not impressed. "Sure, that was worse, but you don't turn a blind eye to housebreaking just because there's bigger crimes in the world."

"Yes, yes, I take your point," the baker replied, smiling and nodding slowly. But he did not change his story.

§

§

When I caught up to Jeremy as he headed home, he seemed anxious to talk.

"What just happened?" he asked. "Why did the baker let me off?"

I do not know. He was studying you when something seemed suddenly to come clear to him. That is when he said that it was not you. And just now he told the deputy that the crime seemed small compared to the loss of that boy Possy and the others who are missing.

Jeremy kept walking. The waking village had begun to stretch and scratch. A man retrieved his newspaper, waved genially at Jeremy, and went back into his house. "And that's it?" Jeremy whispered to me. "The baker just thought it was too small a crime to worry about? You think that's the whole reason?"

Perhaps also that you seemed repentant.

Jeremy considered this. "Maybe it was a test. Like in one of your stories. It was a test of the baker's kindness, and he passed."

Perhaps, I said. But in truth I did not know. The mystery was still unfolding before me, and I had little sense of how dark its nature would become.

§

§

We found Jeremy's father in his room sitting on the side of his bed. He had tried to comb his gnarled hair and he had tried to put on long pants and a shirt, but they were so tight, they could not be fastened. His eyes were puffy. I smelled salt. He had been crying.

"You okay, Dad?" Jeremy said.

Mr. Johnson did not look at Jeremy. "I wanted to come help."

"You didn't have to. They let me go. It was all some kind of mistake."

Mr. Johnson seemed relieved but not consoled. "I wanted to come help, but I couldn't get into any of my clothes." He clamped his eyes to keep back tears, but one escaped. "I've gotten . . . I don't know what's happened to me."

"It's okay, Dad," Jeremy said. His voice was gentle. "Everything's okay."

But Mr. Johnson lay down on the bed and pulled the covers over his face.

When Jeremy looked in on him a few minutes later, his head was still under the covers. "I'm going to school now," Jeremy said, for he had remembered what I had nearly forgotten: he had to go to school today, and take examinations—examinations for which he had not properly studied. "Dad?"

His father poked his head out. In the distance, the first school bell could be heard. "You're going to be late," Mr. Johnson said, but then, as Jeremy swung his book bag onto his back, he said, "Jeremy?"

Jeremy looked at him.

"I'm sorry," his father said.

"For what?"

His father's eyes slid away. "For everything. For just about everything."

Yes, I thought. *You should be sorry. Your example is beschämend. Shameful.* That is what I would have said. But Jeremy's way was kinder. "I'm not sorry," he said. "I'm just glad to have a father at all." He looked at his father. "Okay?"

Mr. Johnson did not seem to believe Jeremy's words, but still he said, "Okay."

§

§

Jeremy burst into the classroom just as Mrs. Kilgarten was distributing the examinations.

"Eyes forward!" she barked, and Ginger, who had turned to give Jeremy a questioning look, swiveled back around. "You all know the importance of this exam. While taking it, there will be no talking and no straying eyes." The teacher sternly scanned the room. "Very well, then. You may . . . begin!"

Such a rustling of papers! Such a concentration of faculties! Generally, I enjoy a scene like this, but this morning my pleasure was only momentary, for Jeremy, who had slept little and studied less, was passing over half as many questions as he answered!

He would never ask for help, nor would I customarily offer it. Still, it was the sheriff's visit that morning that had preempted Jeremy's last chance to study, so it did not seem quite fair to let him fail.

I tried something new.

At the next difficult question, I produced the answer in just the way he would have memorized it—*ossify from os, ossis, Latin for bone*—but I spoke in so thin a whisper he might think he was reaching into the dark corners of his own memory.

And, look here!—he entered the correct answer on his paper.

A few questions later, I whispered, *Phobia from phobos, Greek for fear or flight*.

Really, I must admit it, it was all quite satisfying. I almost looked forward to the difficult questions so that I could whisper the answer so softly that he was not even aware he was hearing it.

Gastric from gastro, gastreros, Greek for stomach.

Oration from orare, Latin for plead, speak, or pray.

I was clever. In order to avoid arousing his suspicion, I withheld answers to two questions altogether, no matter how long he stared at them. Finally, he expelled a deep breath, laid down his pencil, and turned his paper over.

"Time!" Mrs. Kilgarten called out in a piercing voice. "Pencils down, papers forward, no talking. *Henry Hollis and Samuel Thompson! Did I not just say No talking?*"

Henry Hollis and Samuel Thompson exchanged rascally smiles. Like every other student in the room, they knew that when the bell rang in precisely two minutes, they would be beyond the reach of Mrs. Kilgarten until autumn.

Ginger caught up to Jeremy as soon as he had left the classroom. "So?" she said.

"What?"

"Your little visit to the sheriff's station this morning?"

"Wow," Jeremy said. "News travels fast."

"Like I said, Jeremy—small towns, big ears. So what happened?"

He shrugged. "Not a thing."

She looked at him in disbelief. "Seriously?"

"Seriously."

Even after he had given her all the details, she shook her

head. "So Sten Blix knew you'd done it . . . and he sprang you, anyway." She slid several strands of coppery hair through her lips. "I guess we really kind of owe him one."

"I do, maybe," Jeremy said, "but you don't. Your name never came up."

She turned to him and her eyes shone. "I knew you'd never give Pittsworт any names. I just knew that about you."

The corridor had grown quiet. The few remaining students moved off toward their next classes.

"So how'd you do on that *demonic* test we just took?" she said.

"Okay, I guess. At first, I was tanking, and then all of a sudden it was like I slipped into the Vocabulary Zone or something."

I shimmered with pleasure. Well, it is true. Even a ghost has his vanities.

"I think I was in the Not Enough Sleep Zone," Ginger said. "That police-pursuit deal last night was like a quadruple espresso. I thought I was never going to fall asleep."

The warning bell rang and Ginger sailed away. "Bye-ya," she said over her shoulder. Farther down the hall, Conk Crinklaw slammed his locker shut, then turned and bumped into Ginger in a way that did not seem accidental. After untangling himself, he doffed his cap and made an elaborate show of apology, which drew a gaze of disbelief from Ginger and then—I was quite sure of it—a look of mild amusement.

Jeremy observed this, too. I followed him toward his geometry classroom for his last examination of the year, but as he drew close to the door, he stopped and looked around to make sure no one was nearby. "Okay, Jacob," he whispered, "no help with the answers this time."

Mein Gott! I felt like one of those toys that looks like a ball made of metal leaves, but when its spring is pumped and made to spin, the leaves open to reveal a standing figure. Well, that is how being caught at something can make you feel.

"I'm not mad or anything," he said, "but . . . you understand, don't you?"

Ja, ja, I said quietly, and kept myself still, craving the covering of the metal leaves.

§

§

I slipped away from the school but had no time to contemplate my misdeed because, once beyond the school campus, I saw that something graver was amiss.

Whispers carried in the warm spring air, moving from house to house and street to street, a strange, dark animus wrapped in everyday phrases. On the sidewalk of Main Street, in the aisles of the market, across fences and hedgerows, the whispers met and bred more whispers.

"The baker's house. Broken into. That's right, the Swede's."

"The Johnson boy. Harold Johnson's boy."

"The strange one. The one who hears voices."

"Last night. Around ten p.m. Broke right into Sten's house."

"They say the Johnson boy had been stalking him for months."

"Botched the job, though, and left behind his shoe!"

"Not just his shoe. His key, too, and his blood."

"They had him dead to rights."

"They say his father was behind it."

"What kind of father would send his boy out to steal?"

And so it went, the fantastic, malevolent whisperings stretching and reconfiguring until at last their shape was one on which the villagers could agree: Jeremy Johnson Johnson had broken into the baker's house to steal something but had been disrupted by the return of the baker himself. Then the boy had been thoroughly found out by Sheriff Pittswort, but because of the baker's misplaced kindness, Jeremy had escaped the punishment he deserved—and the citizens were ready to do something about it.

Well, that is how it is. No matter the time, no matter the place, a village will often take a false story into its clenched fist.

I repaired to my belfry and gazed out across the flat plains in the direction from which I had hastened that fateful day after coming upon the traveler who walked endlessly into the wind, the man who told me about a boy who read fairy tales and heard voices and needed protection from . . .

Suddenly, I had this thought: Perhaps the rumors moving through the town, evil as they were, were a strange gift to me! Only two people might have played out the leading thread of the twisted information: the sheriff and his deputy. So perhaps I was a step closer to identifying the Finder of Occasions.

From the steeple I scanned the town—how small the cars seemed! how harmless the humans!—until I spied a black-and-white patrol car sliding under the railway trestle toward the business district, and I descended to investigate.

It was Deputy McRaven, prowling along Main Street. I followed behind, an easy thing given his lax pace, and when he turned onto a leafy residential street and pulled up in front of the garage over which he lived, I drew closer still.

The neglected building stood in the shade of a large, overhanging tree. The deputy huffed his way up the outside stairs, unlocked two locks, and pushed open the door. But he did not enter. I was distracted by the short-legged bed, the short-legged desk, and the short-legged chair. The deputy stood studying things, as if to see if everything was exactly as he had left it. He was especially intent on the papers spread across the short-legged desk in the far corner of the room, so I slipped in and, by passing rapidly above the papers, caused them to stir.

One paper fell from the desk.

At this, the deputy stumped hurriedly across the room, picked up the paper (it was nothing, merely an advertising notice), and then did something interesting: he looked around the room one more time and pulled open the lower right-hand drawer. He then lifted aside a false bottom that lay within it and regarded a large envelope hidden below.

That this envelope was safely in place seemed to quell whatever fear had come over him—the apprehension drained at once from his face.

He locked the front door, took a bottle of ale from a small refrigerator, and went back to the desk. He took two long draughts from his bottle, then laid open the large envelope.

Inside lay a packet of photographs that the deputy began shuffling through. One was of a man alone in a car reading a letter. One was of a man and woman embracing behind a building. Another was of a man handing cash to another man in the shadows of the municipal park. The deputy studied each photograph— often they were blurred, as if shot from some distance—before going on to the next. There were perhaps a dozen, each one evidence, it seemed, of behavior that the pictured villagers would not want known. There was also something that sent a tremor through my ancient soul: an exact copy of the obituary of Zyla Johnson Newgate, the very one that had been posted anonymously to Jeremy's father.

When the deputy got to the last pictures in the packet, he took out a magnifying glass and held it over the blurry images. There was one of a boy and a girl walking along Main Street, one of a boy and a girl laughing on Main Street, one of a boy and a girl standing on the corner of Main Street and Elm.

Yes, you have doubtless guessed it.

The girl in these photographs was Ginger, and the boy was Jeremy.

The deputy returned the envelope to the bottom of the drawer, twice-locked the door behind him, and clumped back down the steps to his patrol car.

So, who was this Deputy McRaven?

A man who accumulated bits of information about villagers and hid them away, as a miser might money.

A man who was particularly interested in Jeremy and his father.

A man, in other words, who might be the Finder of Occasions.

§

§

I waited for Jeremy at the school. When at last the final bell rang, the front doors flew open and the students streamed out amidst a raucous din, Jeremy among them.

Listen, if you will! I shouted to Jeremy, but the boisterous noise could not be penetrated. This was the last day of school—children waved and shouted and threw papers into the air.

Finally, when he separated from the other students, I drew close and fairly shouted. *Jeremy! It is I, Jacob. Listen, if you will.*

But he had begun to whistle! He was happy, and something in me went out to him. He knew only that his examinations were over and that the summer holiday lay ahead, time he could use to earn money toward saving his bookstore and home.

Jeremy! Listen, if you will!

Still he did not hear me.

No, what finally stopped his whistling were the cold stares from citizens on the street, and the way, when met by Jeremy's genial nod and smile, these villagers stiffly tipped their chins and turned away.

Jeremy slipped into an alley and rubbed his temple. "What's going on?"

I have been trying to tell you, Jeremy. Someone has spread word of the clues that led to your door.

"But Mr. Blix told them it wasn't me."

Yes. And so now you have been tried in the court of community opinion.

After a few seconds, Jeremy said, "Tried and found guilty, from the looks of it."

I said nothing. I could not disagree. We turned onto Main Street.

"And my punishment?"

One of the oldest.

He cocked his head quizzically.

Public shunning.

Barely had I spoken these words than I saw the town banker turning curtly at Jeremy's approach; two other villagers did the same.

Poor Jeremy lowered his head and bolted for the bookstore. Once inside, he locked the door, scrambled up to his attic, and flopped onto the bed.

His father called from the other room. Jeremy did not answer.

Someone rapped on the front door. Jeremy did not stir.

The telephone rang several times. Jeremy stared at the ceiling and listened to the voices leaving messages.

The first voice said, "Jeremy, this is Norman Harang. I no longer need your gardening services."

A few minutes later, Eva Tanner said, "Don't come to do my yard tomorrow or ever after. I think you know why."

Then Melvin Blood said, "I am calling to inform you that I have found someone else to do my yard work."

And then as it grew dark, a softer, warmer voice flowed from the answering machine: "Jeremy? Are you in there? It's me, Ginger. I'm sorry about everything. It's all so horrible and it's all my fault." A pause, then: "Could you please pick up?"

But Jeremy simply turned on his bed and stared at the wall.

Jeremy?

"What?" His voice was snappish.

Perhaps there is a silver lining.

"And what would that be?"

I think this chapter of your tale has revealed the Finder of Occasions.

Though I had told Jeremy of the Finder of Occasions—and more than once!—he neither believed it nor feared it as I knew to do. So he said nothing.

I think it is the deputy. He collects information about the villagers that is embarrassing or incriminating so that he might hold it against them. He is the one who sent your mother's obituary to your father. He has taken photographs of you and Ginger.

In a sullen voice Jeremy said, "This is not a chapter in a tale, Jacob. It's my *life*. And even if there is such a thing, what difference does it make if McRaven *is* the big bad Finder of Occasions?" He looked in my direction. "He found his occasion and he used it. Game over."

I started to disagree, to defend my ideas, to defend myself, to tell him that worse might be coming, and might yet be avoided, but he was in no mood for it.

"Good night, Jacob," he said.

Well, what could I do?

I said, *Good night, Jeremy*, and departed.

§

§

The next day was the first of the summer holiday, the day Jeremy had meant to look for more work.

Instead, he left the CLOSED sign hanging in the window of the Two-Book Bookstore and did not venture out of doors. He sat watching television with his father. They did not just watch *Uncommon Knowledge*; they watched anything that appeared on the screen. They ate popcorn. They drank a sickeningly sweet-smelling fruit beverage made by stirring sugar and water with powder poured from a small packet. When the telephone rang, they did not answer it.

Finally, I could bear no more.

You cannot do this, Jeremy. You cannot do what your father has done—lie down and stay inside and stop living.

He made no sign of hearing me.

You must listen, Jeremy! I said. *You need to face the town. Let them know that, yes, you did something wrong but not a large thing and that you intend to make amends and perhaps even learn something from the episode.*

Jeremy sat staring at the television. "What I learned is that you do almost everything right for most of your life and then you screw up one time—*one stinking time!*—and everybody thinks you drip with slime."

A silence followed this pronouncement, and then Jeremy's father said, "Who're you talking to?"

Jeremy's face flushed. "Oh . . . myself. I was just thinking how unfair this all is. Well, not unfair, exactly, but not completely fair, either."

"Yeah," his father said, "learning that things aren't always fair is a bad lesson." His gaze drifted to the window. "Sometimes I think it's the worst lesson of all."

Surely he was thinking of Zyla Johnson. I think Jeremy

sensed this, too, for he said, "How about I pop another batch of popcorn?"

While they munched their popped corn, Jeremy said, "What are we going to do, Dad?" His father did not speak, so Jeremy continued. "What are we going to do about losing the store and the place where we live?"

His father kept staring at the television, but I could tell he was not really watching it. "I don't know," he said finally. "If this was one of those fairy tales you and your mother used to read, I'd send you out to seek your fortune, and you'd do some impossible thing and a king would give you a kingdom." He smiled miserably and turned to Jeremy. "But this isn't some fairy tale we're in the middle of, is it?"

"No," Jeremy said, "it isn't." He stared dully at the television. "Maybe we should leave," he said. "Maybe we should just let them have the store and we could just go somewhere else."

"Go where?" his father asked. "And do what?"

It was true. If they had no money here, they would have no money anywhere else. It was as Ginger's grandfather had said. It did not matter how far you go, you always take yourself with you.

§

§

That night, Jeremy climbed the ladder to the attic, drew down an edition of the *Household Tales*, and began reading "Iron

Heinrich." It was a conciliatory gesture—he knew this to be one of my favorites. He read to himself, as did I, but my ability to read is akin to my ability to hasten about—I read with unnatural rapidity.

Often, waiting for Jeremy to catch up, I was left to reconsider a line or a paragraph. It was true that during my mortal life I did not want to tamper with the tales for scholarly reasons, but it was also true that I had no talent for such tampering. It was Wilhelm who had the deft stylistic hand. His smoothing and shaping drew the characters up from the paper and set them free—the princesses and princes, giants and dwarves, talking foxes and frogs, huntsmen and shepherds, fishermen and their wives.

I will give an example. In the story before us, "Iron Heinrich," the king's youngest daughter was described as being "so lovely that even the sun, which had seen so many things, was filled with wonder when it shone upon her face." Beautiful words, yes?—but they will not be found in the first version of the story. Again and again, Wilhelm's flourishes would enrich a tale. Enrich, and change, too, and I resisted these changes. For my brother, the transformation of the tales rose from his deepest being. "Its source is simple," he told me once when I questioned him. "It comes from belief."

I remembered how he looked at me as he spoke these words—his eyes full of kindness but sorrow, too. Yes, it was true. He felt sorrow for me. I loved the search for our people's history in the tales. But Wilhelm loved the tales themselves, and the princes and princesses who lived within them.

"Want to read more?" Jeremy said when he had finished "Iron Heinrich."

Would you?

"I'm kind of tired, but I could just turn the pages for you if you want."

He knew that I liked that very much, to swim through the familiar words as rapidly as I liked. *A bit faster*, I said as he flipped the pages. *A bit faster yet*.

We were midway through "The Cunning Little Tailor" when we heard a sudden tap-tap-tapping and spied Ginger Boultinghouse smiling through the window of the small balcony door.

Jeremy unlatched the window and let it swing open. He looked past her for the girlfriends, but Ginger was alone. He said, "You could just come to the front door like a normal human being."

"Tried the front door," she said. "Found the 'closed' sign discouraging."

"And then there's the telephone," Jeremy said.

"Tried that, too"—she smiled at him—"nobody seems to answer."

Jeremy's gaze fell away. "Maybe that's because nobody here wants to talk to anybody."

Ginger sighed. "The village idiots have gotten you down, I guess." She paused. "The village idiots aren't worth it, you know."

"Yeah, well, it's still a little weird, walking down the street and having people stare at you like you're a . . . *child molester* or something."

Ginger slid several strands of hair through her mouth.

From some distance, I detected the dull rhythm of a freight train. So did Ginger. "Hear that?" she said. "When the coal train goes up Clearlake Grade, it makes my grandpa's house tremble."

She listened for another moment or two. "That's how I would leave if I had to—jump on a freight train. I've taken a couple of short rides but nothing long. I was talking to Conk today, and he said one weekend he rode to Omaha and back in empty freight cars. He knows a railroad guy who tells him where they're all going. He said it was cold, but he still really liked it." She shrugged. "'Course he's an idiot." She turned to Jeremy. "What do you think? Want to do that sometime with me?"

Careful, Jeremy, I whispered, but it will be no surprise to you that he did not listen.

"Maybe," he said. "Sure."

"You could teach me French while we ride the rails." She smiled. "Could be *très romantique, oui?*"

She stretched, yawned, and picked up the book whose pages Jeremy had been turning for me. "You were reading a fairy tale?"

Jeremy's whole body tensed. "Not really. I was just looking through it for a particular story."

"Yeah? What story?"

"'Bearskin,'" Jeremy blurted, and, once started, went stumbling on. "It's about a man who can't wash or comb his hair for seven years. It's kind of a love story."

"Kind of a gamey love story, I'd say."

"Yeah, well, that's the part I was trying to remember. Two of the princesses won't have anything to do with him, but the youngest one agrees to marry him because of a kindness the man did for her father."

"So it has a happy ending."

"Yeah. Except for the two sisters who refused him. They—"

But Ginger cut him off. "Don't tell me," she said, and handed him the book. "Just start at the beginning."

Jeremy appeared confused. "You want me to . . ."

"Read me the story. Exactly. But wait just a second." She slipped off her shoes, lay down on the bed, and closed her eyes. "Okay," she said. "From the beginning. From 'Once upon a time.'"

Jeremy began to read, and by the time he turned the third page—*mein Gott!*—the girl was asleep! Jeremy closed the book and regarded her for a moment.

Then an even more disturbing turn—he leaned over and switched off the light!

Jeremy?

"Mmm?"

Do not allow her to sleep here.

He turned the light back on and quickly set the alarm clock.

"There," he said. "It'll wake us at midnight. Then she can go."

But—

"Good *night*, Jacob," he said, so what else could I do? I took my leave.

But before dawn the next morning, when the cocks began to crow, I stole down from my belfry and hastened to the attic, where I found an alarming sight: Jeremy lay asleep, and there, beside him, with her head nestled into his outstretched arm, was Ginger Boultinghouse, also fast asleep.

§

§

Jeremy! Jeremy! Wake up! Wake up!

Jeremy's eyes flew open and fell at once upon the clock and then upon the girl.

"Ginger!" he whispered, and when she awakened and saw the hints of daylight through the window, she became a flurry of motion, scrambling out and over the balcony and scaling down the outside pipe just as the night sky gave way to the yellowish gray of morning.

She dropped from the pipe, slipped around to the alley, and on her long legs flew past the hot springs and red-stone buildings. She had just started to cross Main Street when she heard whistling and ducked back. It was Frank Bailey, dressed in white, heading down the street toward the bakery, where dark gray smoke was already pouring from the tall chimney. The boy's whistled tune was somber. His eye seemed to flick in Ginger's direction; in the next instant, he was placidly looking straight ahead, still whistling his soft tune.

Once he had passed, Ginger peered up and down the street, saw no one, darted across, turned the corner, and broke into a graceful loping run down the dirt road into the country. *Why did I follow? Perhaps I wanted to see her safely home. Or perhaps I wanted to see the home where she chose to spend so little time.* In any event, she kept a steady pace, but she was also wary. Whenever dust rose from an approaching car, she ducked into a field until the car had passed by. She ran a great distance before finally cutting across a plot of green alfalfa and approaching a tall, dilapidated farmhouse from the rear.

She crouched behind a hedge of blooming lilacs to take the measure of the place. Roosters crowed, sheep bleated. Ginger's gaze alighted on the old farmhouse, which stood decrepit, unpainted, and quiet, and then shifted to a dull red barn, where the motor of an unseen tractor suddenly chugged to life. A moment later, it emerged from the barn, purple-gray smoke puffing into the sky and a stiff upright elderly man at the wheel.

Once the tractor had turned away, toward the fields, Ginger darted to the house, but she did not go through the front door. She quickly climbed a rickety trellis onto the back-porch roof and from there slipped through an open window.

The room was doubtless hers—clothing of all sorts had been slung everywhere. She studied the bed—at first it seemed she had a sister who lay sleeping there—but when Ginger sat on the mattress, she pulled out the pillows she had shaped into a human form, an old trick but serviceable still. Then she walked to her closed bedroom door and inspected something—a length of tape stretched from the edge of the door to the doorframe. From this she knew that her grandfather had not looked in on her during her absence—if he had, the tape would be broken or unaffixed. Another tried-and-true tactic.

Ginger went back to the bed and sat on its edge.

Then this reckless girl with the wild hair did a surprising thing.

She placed both hands over her eyes and began to speak very softly.

"Please don't let Grandpa find out I was gone last night, because I didn't do anything and he will think I did." She was quiet a second or two. "God bless Jeremy," she whispered, "and help me figure out a way to help him. And God bless Grandpa, but please don't put off calling him to you on my account."

This last sentiment caused me to chuckle—not that she could hear me.

She quickly concluded. "Please give shelter to those without shelter, food to those without food, and hope to those without hope, amen."

A kind prayer, I thought, drawn from a well of pure belief. I had once had such a well from which to draw and felt a fresh pang that I no longer did. Still, as I drifted back to the village, my assessment of Ginger Boultinghouse began to soften. Perhaps she would yet prove a hypothesis that Wilhelm believed to be found again and again in the *Household Tales:* that beauty is goodness, and goodness beauty.

§

§

The next morning, Jeremy pedaled his bicycle through the alley behind the red-stone buildings of Main Street and the smoldering hot springs that lay behind them, a route I knew he had chosen to avoid being seen. It was a sultry Saturday, the sun sealed off by a thick cushion of clouds bearing the prospect of rain. Behind his bicycle he pulled the little trailer his grandfather had built him for carrying his equipment.

A woman out walking with her dog began to smile at Jeremy, but upon realizing that it was he, she turned her face to stone and looked pointedly away.

Jeremy stood on his pedals to power his bicycle along more quickly and did not stop riding hard until he reached a neat yellow bungalow trimmed in green and surrounded by a small, tidy yard.

This was the home of Jenny Applegarth, the very woman Ginger and Jeremy had run into the night of their misadventure. She was presently unmarried, after four previous attempts at such unions. Over the years, the smoothness of her beauty had eroded somewhat, but she still possessed the kind of physical advantages that men noticed and women regarded warily.

She worked two daily shifts at Elbow's Café, one in the early morning and one at the noon hour, which allowed her to come home for an hour or so in between. This morning, while Jeremy was pulling weeds in the flowerbed, she turned up the walkway, wearing denim pants and a pink sleeveless blouse.

"Is that Mr. Johnson Johnson among the irises?" she called out in a friendly voice.

"Hi, Mrs. Applegarth. How's it going?"

"Oh, it's going," she said, and then went inside and returned a few minutes later, nudging open the screen door with a tray laden with sandwiches and beverages. "Hungry?" she asked.

They sat on the steps of the green porch, the sandwiches smelling of butter and cucumber, Jeremy smelling of mown grass and turned earth, and Jenny Applegarth smelling of lavender soap. Well, that is how it is in the *Zwischenraum*. You taste nothing, but your sense of smell grows keen.

"Sticky weather," she said, pushing her loose hair from her neck and looking off toward the red buttes, silhouetted now against the purple clouds, a pretty sight in itself, but Jeremy seemed distracted by Jenny Applegarth's caramel-brown shoulders and streaky blond hair. "I bet it rains," she said almost to herself.

When she let her hair drop back down over her neck and turned to Jeremy, he quickly averted his eyes and took another bite of his cucumber sandwich.

She regarded him with a kindly expression. "Guess you know you've been the main subject of conversation the last couple of days in the café."

Jeremy kept chewing.

"So how're you doing?"

He shrugged. "Just okay."

After a moment or two, Jenny Applegarth said, "And your father?"

Jeremy opened his mouth to speak but suddenly stopped.

"What?" she asked

"I don't know. I was going to say, 'About the same,' which is what I usually say. But when Sheriff Pittswort took me down to the station, my dad wanted to go, too, to help defend me or something crazy like that." Jeremy lowered his eyes. "But it's been so long since he's gotten dressed to go out, he couldn't get into any of his clothes."

"Oh, dear," she said. "The poor man." She sipped her tea. "Doesn't he have friends?" she asked. "He used to have friends."

Jeremy appeared surprised. "When was that? That he had friends, I mean."

"When he was in school. He was shy, but he was nice to people and, really, he had the nicest smile. He had a good voice, too. For a while, he sang in the madrigals."

"My father sang in a choir? Who told you that?"

"Nobody told me, Jeremy. I was in it with him. We were in school together."

"But isn't he lots older than you?"

She laughed mildly. "Your father and I graduated the same year." She swirled the ice cubes in her glass. "He didn't stay in the madrigals, though. He was the only boy, so he ran for it." She looked off. "You know, all my husbands were different, but they could all sing. Every one of them, even though a couple of them didn't like to." She smiled at Jeremy. "So your dad's pretty down, huh?"

"Yeah. All he does is watch TV, but, really, he hardly even pays attention. The only show he's interested in is that goofy one called *Uncommon Knowledge*, where—"

"I know that show!" Jenny Applegarth exclaimed. "And it's not goofy! I watch it all the time! I loved the one with the woman who studied prairie dogs."

Jeremy smiled. "Yeah, I watched that one with my dad. He liked it, too. He liked the clip of the male prairie dogs fighting over a mate."

Jenny Applegarth gave a small laugh. "There's the difference between men and women. I liked the part about how they kiss when they go visiting."

It was quiet for a moment or two. Then she said idly, "They're coming through the Plains this summer, you know."

"The prairie dogs?"

Another chuckle. "The scouts for *Uncommon Knowledge*. They're looking for contestants." She sighed. "I'd love to go on that show, but all I'm an expert on is how not to pick husbands."

"I could go on for being good at getting a whole town to hate you," Jeremy said.

Jenny Applegarth yawned, arched her back, and stretched, which distracted Jeremy from his gloomy thoughts, as I suspect she intended. Then she said, "You know, if you and your dad want to feel better about things, you need to make a plan." She smiled at him. "Everybody needs a plan."

"Do you have one?"

She laughed. "I've had dozens."

As she began to tidy up the tray, she said, "Just for the record, I didn't tell the sheriff I saw you the night of the . . . *incident*, I guess you'd call it. He asked if I'd seen anybody on the street and I said, 'Not that I could remember.'"

Jeremy turned. "Did he believe you?"

Jenny Applegarth's laugh was so cheerful, it seemed musical. "Not for a second, but I said, 'That's my story and I'm sticking to it.'"

"Well, thanks," Jeremy said.

It again grew quiet.

A question had formed in my ancient mind, and when Jeremy moved away and Jenny Applegarth stood and stretched and stared out across the lawn, I drew close and whispered, *Listen, if you will.*

Well, here was something! She caught her breath and cocked her head!

I said it again: *Listen, if you will.*

She turned intently toward the trees, as if *they* were speaking, but the next time I said *Listen, if you will*, she gave up. She shook her head and heard nothing.

"That was odd," she said.

Jeremy turned from his gardening equipment. "What was?"

"This faint . . . *oboe-like* sound—I heard it for a second, and then it was gone." She looked at Jeremy and smiled. "Maybe I'm losing my marbles."

It was me, I told him. *She almost heard me, but not quite.*

It seemed a shame because, in my experience, it never went any further than that.

As Jeremy wheeled his bicycle and cart toward the gate, Jenny said, "Jeremy?"

He stopped and turned.

"You know, you might tell your friend Ginger that male chauvinism can have its happy byproducts."

"How's that?"

"When the sheriff was grilling me, he asked if I'd seen you or any other *boys*." She grinned. "The sheriff seems to think girls wouldn't be able to climb fences and run as fast as, to use his term, the *perpetrators* did."

"Yeah, okay," Jeremy said. "I'll tell her."

Jenny let her eyes settle on him. "When would that be, Jeremy? The next time she spends the night in your attic?"

So! Somebody *had* seen her!

Jeremy's pale skin burned red.

Jenny Applegarth slipped a napkin under a plate and said quietly, "Morley McRaven saw her shinnying down the drainpipe from your attic."

So, I thought. *Once again, our Deputy McRaven.*

"It's not what you think, Mrs. Applegarth," Jeremy said. "I was reading her a story and she just fell asleep and I didn't have the heart to wake her up and then I messed up setting the alarm clock. It was all my fault." His expression was miserable. "I set the alarm for twelve *p.m.* instead of twelve *a.m.*" He raised his eyes to Mrs. Applegarth. "But all we did was sleep. Nothing happened."

"I believe you, Jeremy, I truly do. Problem is, in a town like this, the appearance of doing something wrong can be as bad as actually doing it."

Jeremy's jaw tightened. "What else can they do to me?" he blurted. "They've already crowned me the scummiest kid in town! What else can they possibly do?"

Jenny Applegarth shook her head and picked up the platter. "More," she said quietly. "They can always do more."

§

§

She was correct, of course.

Normally, Jeremy did nine jobs every Saturday. Five had canceled by telephone, but, not counting Jenny Applegarth's job, that still left three.

When he arrived at the first house, a sign hung from the gatepost that said JEREMY — DO NOT COME INTO OUR YARD YOUR SERVICES NO LONGER NEEDED.

At the second house, the note was shorter: JEREMY, NO MORE WORK FOR YOU!

When he got to the third house, he did not need to look for a note. Another boy was already at work in the yard, running his mowing machine back and forth.

On past Saturdays, Jeremy had a little ritual. After finishing his last yard work of the day, he would ride to Crinklaw's Superette, purchase groceries, select a bottle of root beer from the refrigerated case, and then sit on the wooden bench in front of the market to drink it. It was always a pleasantly reassuring scene—a tired boy drinking a cold refreshment in front of his bicycle and gardening equipment—and passersby would nod and smile and tip their hats.

But this was before the public shunning and the loss of nearly all of his jobs.

Today he purchased the barest necessities at the market and was about to pedal away when Dolores Broom pulled up in her postal truck and stepped out, holding a letter.

"Been looking for you, Jeremy," she said, waving an envelope and a pen. "Certified mail. You've got to sign for it."

Dolores Broom seemed to hope Jeremy would open the letter then and there, but he merely stared at it.

"Looks official, doesn't it?" she said.

It was true. It did. The return address was *High Plains National Bank*.

"Guess it's important," Jeremy said, and the mail carrier replied, "'*Course* it's important. You don't pay for certified unless it's important."

She waited, but Jeremy merely folded the envelope in half and stuffed it into his rear pocket.

"Okay, then," Dolores Broom said, plainly disappointed. She glanced up at the darkening sky. "I better get to it before things turn damp."

She climbed back into her truck and drove away.

§
§

Jeremy pedaled to a remote corner of the municipal park and seated himself on a picnic table. A grumble of thunder issued from the north.

Jeremy touched his finger to his temple. "You here?" he whispered.

I am.

"Kind of a bad day," he said.

Yes. But things will turn for the better. Often in the tales it is when circumstances seem most hopeless that good fortune intercedes.

"I thought you didn't really believe in the tales."

That does not mean I would not like to.

He took a deep breath. "Okay, let's just see." He pulled the envelope from his pocket and tore it open.

Notice of Foreclosure Auction was the first line, followed by particulars: Barring payment of all monies due, Jeremy's property would be auctioned on the steps of the county courthouse in sixty days.

"Sixty days," he whispered. "We'll never get the money by then."

His eyes fell again on the letter.

But listen!—a soft footfall, and there was Ginger Boultinghouse slowly stealing up on Jeremy from behind.

Do not look now, I said, *but the girl is sneaking up behind you.*

She is going to try to scare you. I will tell you the moment before she is going to pounce.

This was in fact what I did, at which point Jeremy leapt up, spun around, and let loose a hair-raising scream!

Ginger shrieked, recoiled, and tripped backward onto the grassy lawn.

Jeremy found this extremely entertaining. I was myself somewhat amused.

"Very funny," she said, dusting herself off. She was wearing a white shirt and white shorts. She looked around. "How'd you know I was there, anyway? That was my stellarest stealth mode. Plus you seemed so . . . lost in thought."

"Guess stellarest wasn't stellar enough," Jeremy said, sitting again on the table.

Ginger sat nearby and let her long, freckled legs stretch to full length.

"What's that?" she said, nodding at the letter beside him.

He handed her the auction notice, and she read it through.

"Okay," she said. "We've really got to think of something here."

"Yeah, well, if you happen to have twenty-two thousand one hundred and six dollars in your piggy bank, we would have something to think about."

"I could probably scrape together the six-dollar part," she joked, "provided you give me a little time." A low roll of thunder carried from the distance, but she ignored it. "There's got to be some way to come up with the money."

He folded the letter and put it back into his pocket. Ginger was rubbing her index finger over a softening scab on her freckled knee when Jeremy said, "So did you know Morley McRaven saw you this morning?"

She turned with a stricken look. "Saw me where?"

"Coming out of the attic. Jenny Applegarth told me people at the café were saying you'd stayed the night."

"Oh, God." She paused. "I *wondered* why some of the fossils were looking at me funny." Another pause. "Well, let them think what they think." Then: "But it means I'll get it from my grand-dad." Her voice dropped. "Get it and then some."

Another rumble of thunder, deeper, angrier, and it seemed to stir the air.

"Where are Maddy and Marjory?" Jeremy asked, because, it was true, they were usually like shadows to her.

Ginger shrugged. "Their parents threatened them with total lockdown if they get caught, as they put it, 'associating with that housebreaker kid,' so when we were at the bakery and I said I was going to go find you, they stayed put."

"It's okay," Jeremy said. "I don't blame them."

"Yeah, well, I kind of do. I prefer my friends to come with a backbone."

She held up a maple leaf and watched it bend in the wind. "So last night, when I fell asleep, did you kiss me good night?— you know, like on the forehead or ear or lips or something?"

Jeremy shook his head. "Why? Should I have?"

She shrugged, then tossed the maple key into the wind and watched it whirl sideways. A few moments passed and she said, "So what happened to the selfish sisters at the end of that Bear-skin story? Something bad, I'm hoping."

"Pretty bad. When Bearskin returns as a fine gentleman and

marries the nice sister, one mean sister drowns and the other mean one hangs herself. Then the devil shows up to say he got two souls instead of one."

"Zounds. That's kind of severe."

"Yeah, well, those Grimm Brothers." He grinned. "They love a bloody ending."

Ja, ja. He was having his sport with me! But, truly, those were the cautionary elements and the rules were observed. Evil would not be punished with mere finger wagging!

Another boom of thunder, sharper, almost crackling.

Ginger looked up at the sky. "Maybe my granddad will get hit by lightning."

"Seems unlikely."

She shrugged and grinned. "A girl can hope."

The gray sky deepened toward black. Ginger slid several strands of hair through her lips and regarded Jeremy for a second or two.

"Just for the record," she said. "I'm sorry about everything."

"It's okay. It's not your fault."

"That's just it. It is. If I hadn't—"

Jeremy cut her off. "And if I hadn't agreed to go into the baker's house and if I hadn't dropped my key and if McRaven hadn't gotten the town all riled up and if and if and if."

"Yeah, but my *if* is the *if* that started it all."

A moment passed and then Jeremy said quietly, "Yeah, but if that *if* hadn't happened, we wouldn't be sitting here right now. Which I kind of like."

They fell silent, and with a casual ease she set her hand to his bare arm. This time, unlike others when she had touched him, he did not flinch. She ran a finger experimentally along his bare inner arm and he, to my surprise and perhaps his, turned and leaned subtly toward her.

And, at this exact expectant point of time, a sharp crack of thunder shook the trees and the first fat drops of rain spattered on their picnic table.

Ginger and Jeremy sat as if paralyzed for a moment before he quickly stuffed the auction notice into his pocket. Lightning and thunder crackled together, and the scattered fat raindrops soon turned into a watery throb.

It must have been a warm rain. Ginger grinned at Jeremy, spread her arms, and turned an open mouth to the sky.

Jeremy, however, stood abruptly up.

"Hey, now," Ginger said. "Where're you going?" She looked about. "We could go over there to the bandstand and ride it out."

Jeremy glanced at the covered band shell, but shook his head. "Naw. I'd better get back. My father will be waiting on his lunch by now."

Ginger studied him, her face glistening with rain. "Okay," she said.

"Okay," he said, but he did not move.

They stood letting the rain run over them, looking at each other.

A small smile formed on her lips. "Know what?"

"What?"

"When a girl falls asleep on your bed, you really should kiss her good night." She pulled her wet hair back and grinned. "For future reference."

And she was off, loping across the wet green grass as frisky as a deer in the meadow.

Jeremy found his father napping when he returned home and slipped through the room without waking him. He changed into dry clothes, took a bowl of cereal to the front of the bookstore, and saw that the light on the answering machine was blinking. He pushed the button and listened to a new message from Ginger.

"Okay, Jeremy, weird but good. I was walking by the bakery soaking wet and Maddy and Marjory were gone, but Sten Blix waved me in, gave me a coffee, and asked if you and I would like to work for him at his house tomorrow! See? Weird but good, like I said! I know it's Sunday, but I told him we could." A pause. "Which I hope is okay. He said nine a.m." Another pause. "I'll come by beforehand and we can go together."

The smallest smile appeared on Jeremy's face.

Jeremy spent the rainy afternoon reading, but that evening, when the rain had ceased, he put on his shoes. "Going for a walk," he called out to his father.

"*Uncommon Knowledge* is on tonight!" his father shouted back.

"Okay," Jeremy called, which, his father knew, was not the same as saying he would return in time for it.

"So you'll be back?"

"I'll try," Jeremy yelled, and set the door closed behind him.

It was the pleasantest sort of evening, with streets gleaming from the rain and billowing clouds floating past a nearly full moon.

Where are we going? I asked.

"Nowhere. Anywhere. Out of the house."

Yes, of course, and yet I observed that our circuitous route took us by the Corner Pocket, where Ginger and the girlfriends could sometimes be found, and then past Maddy's house, and then Marjory's.

Jeremy saw no one in any of these places, but on the way back to the bookstore, he passed in front of the Intrepid Bar & Grill and, glancing in, suddenly froze. There, in a booth near the front window, Ginger Boultinghouse, Conk Crinklaw, and the two girlfriends all sat watching a television screen mounted on the wall. Conk sat closest to Ginger, at the end of the row of girls.

They were watching *Uncommon Knowledge*, and when Conk said something—evidently about the contestant's answer—the girls all laughed and Ginger bumped him softly with her shoulder. Jeremy stared at this tableau as if mesmerized and was prompted again into motion only when the beams of headlights swept past. It was a patrol car, and it slowed to a stop next to Jeremy.

Deputy McRaven leaned from the window. "She gets around, don't she?"

"Who?"

The deputy snickered. "Your little girlfriend. Or is she Conk's little girlfriend?"

Jeremy said nothing and resumed walking.

The patrol car moved forward, too. "Where you headed?" the deputy asked.

"Nowhere. I'm just out walking."

"I see that. But out walking where? And doing what, exactly?"

"I'm not *doing* anything," Jeremy said, his voice rising.

Jeremy's irritation seemed to please the deputy. "Casing things, maybe?"

"What does that mean?"

"Oh, I think you know what *casing* means, Mr. Johnson. It means looking over a place to see how it shapes up for robbing it."

A malicious grin spanned Deputy McRaven's broad face, but before Jeremy could say something in anger, I gave him something more obscure to say.

"Nur wenn die Sonne niedrig steht, kann ein Zwerg einen langen Schatten werfen."

For a moment, the deputy was nonplussed, but for only a moment. "And right back at you," he said calmly, and let the patrol car ease away.

"What did I just say?" Jeremy whispered.

Only when the sun sets low can a dwarf throw a long shadow.

Jeremy issued a small laugh.

It was perhaps unkind, I said. *Our deputy is not a true dwarf.*

Jeremy said, "Close enough that he gives dwarfs a bad name."

He continued past the darkened businesses, then veered toward the municipal park and the table where he and Ginger had visited earlier in the day.

The park was dark and quiet now, the light of the moon shone in small puddles of water, and the trees threw slow-moving shadows. The flutish call of an owl carried on a gentle breeze. Jeremy had been sitting at the table for perhaps a minute when his hand brushed across something on the table, something odd and startling. He leaned away so the moon could illuminate whatever it was.

Wedged between the planks was a tightly folded piece of paper.

Jeremy stared at the paper for several seconds before pulling it free and unfolding it in the moonlight.

Within it lay a single strand of long reddish hair.

Written on the paper was this:

I was here thinking of somebody, possibly you.

A smile eased across Jeremy's face. But then, abruptly, his face clouded and he stared off toward town. He folded the strand of hair into the paper and wedged it back between the planks of the picnic table so that it would seem unfound.

From the west, a coal train approached with a loudening throb. Through the trees, it could be seen slowly passing in the moonlight, black car after black car, loaded with coal, the wheels clicking rhythmically over the rails. When finally it had passed, Jeremy said, "Jacob?"

Yes?

"Did this ever happen to you?"

I'm not sure what you mean.

"Where when you think of someone, it's like your whole body is lighter than air and you feel like you're floating off to another world or something."

I said nothing.

"Jacob? Did that ever happen to you?"

No.

It was quiet, a mild breeze stirred the leaves, and I could see her face.

120

Well, I said. *Perhaps once.*

He looked toward my voice. "Really? When?"

I could see her face, and I would tell him. But I would start at the beginning.

While immersed in my studies, I resisted the temptation of the Mädchen—the girls—but I always supposed that some faraway day I would become a husband and a father. But it was not until I joined the household of Wilhelm and Dortchen that I saw what actual sustenance such company might provide.

The breeze bore the last faint whistle of the freight train.

I found myself looking forward to Dortchen's casual questions and friendly banter. I became comfortable with her company. Yes—perhaps you have guessed it—I fell slightly in love with her.

There they were: words I had never spoken. I will tell you, it was a relief to pass them to another.

"What happened?"

Nothing. If she heard my thoughts, she pretended not to. I loved my brother, as she did, so I would not speak and she would not hear.

Such a long time ago. Such a long, long time ago. But there was more.

One day while Wilhelm and I were at our desks, Dortchen came in with a tray of boiled eggs and black bread and butter, a pleasant surprise for both of us. After she departed, Wilhelm looked up and quizzed me about my bachelorhood. Would I never have a wife of my own? I constructed a careful answer. Had I met someone like Dortchen, I said, I might easily have found my way to wedlock. He nodded and did not speak, but later, while I was out of the room, he wrote something on a small piece of fine paper and slipped it into the book I was reading.

I fell quiet and Jeremy said, "Do you remember what it said?"

Oh, yes, I remembered the words. I could see them as if that slip of paper were still in my hands. *One does not know love until it arrives, and its arrival will always surprise.*

My thoughts drifted away, then returned. *It was characteristic of Wilhelm to take my subtle confession and convert it to a hopeful prospect. I did not discard the slip of paper. I used it to mark my place in books for several years, until* . . .

But suddenly I was faced with images of my nephew on the dark night that he looked at me with pleading eyes as he searched for another breath.

"Until what?" Jeremy asked.

Until something happened to my nephew and I turned to the work in earnest.

"What happened to your nephew?"

It cannot be discussed.

"But why not?"

I did not answer.

Finally, Jeremy said, "So the surprise that Wilhelm talked about never happened?"

No, Jeremy. I barred the door against surprises. I kept to the work. It was for the best.

But as I spoke these words, I heard them with new ears, and wondered at the wisdom of the barred door and the endless hours of work, of the great dictionary, which, at my death, I had taken only to the letter F. The last word to fall under my scrutiny was *Frucht.*

Fruit.

From the Latin *fructus: to enjoy.*

I hovered there in the darkness, debating my course, but finally I spoke.

Jeremy?

"Mmm?"

Perhaps you should take out the note in the table and jot a word or two in response. So she will know that you appreciated . . . her little gesture.

"Really?" he asked, and why would he not be surprised at such a suggestion passing my lips? The very one who had held the bridle and fixed the blinkers was now the one removing them.

Yes. Really.

And so he unfolded the paper and under the words *I was here thinking of somebody, possibly you*, he wrote *Me too*, then folded the paper and wedged it into its place between the table's planks.

§

§

Later that night, as Jeremy settled himself for sleep, he said, "Jacob?"

Yes?

"I'm glad you told me about Dortchen." He was quiet and then he said, "It makes you seem realer."

Realer?

"More real."

Ah.

"Will you ever tell me about your nephew?"

Before I could think, I said, *I cannot. I cannot.*

A few moments passed. "Okay," he said. "Good night, Jacob."

123

Good night, Jeremy, and sweet repose.

Well, I must tell you one other thing. Later, after I had taken my leave from Jeremy and repaired to my belfry, I spied Ginger Boultinghouse turning from Main Street and walking alone in the moonlight, toward the table in the park.

§

§

When the baker built his home, he had his workmen coat it with a paint containing pigment from a mine in the town of Falun, Sweden. This, I had once heard him explain, was the traditional Swedish red.

Sunday morning, standing at the gate and gazing at the house, Jeremy said, "There's something about the color and the way the sun makes it sparkle that makes me think of gingerbread."

"It makes me think of weirdness," Ginger said. "I mean, where on the entire planet would this house fit in?"

"Sweden, maybe," Jeremy said, and Ginger said, "Or maybe the Twilight Zone," a term I did not understand but which made Jeremy chuckle.

At this moment, the baker stepped from the front door, smiling and waving them forward. "*Hallå,*" he called out. "Is it not a great day to be alive?"

"If you say so," Ginger said, smiling herself. "How's life in Blixville?"

"Sunny as ever," the baker said, and stepped aside to let them enter, but they hesitated. "Come, come," he said, and his blue eyes twinkled. "No one will eat you."

As they stepped inside, they were at once greeted with the pleasantest smell of baked goods. And on the very table where Jeremy had poured explosive candy into a bowl of cereal, a platter was stacked with fruit-filled pastries.

"Sit, sit," the baker said, and began pouring coffee for both of them.

"Zounds," Ginger said, tasting a pastry. "I'd get fat fast living in Blixville."

The baker laughed and said he doubted that very much.

Though Jeremy had accepted a pastry, he had not taken a bite.

"It is a raspberry cut," the baker said in a coaxing tone. "People generally find them agreeable."

"No," Jeremy said. "It's not that. It's because . . ."

Everyone waited. The baker, at the point of pouring himself coffee, held the pot still in his hand.

"It's just that before anything else"—Jeremy took a deep breath—"I wanted to say I was sorry for what I did that night."

The baker's expression moved from surprise to kindliness.

"Me too," Ginger blurted. She lowered her eyes. "I was the one who kind of planned it."

The baker's blue eyes swung to her. "Ah. The brains behind the operation." A small chuckle escaped him, and he shook his head. "It did have a *gingery* flavor to it all."

He set the coffeepot down and composed his thoughts. "It was a misunderstanding. You meant it only as mischief. At first, I

125

took it as something else, but now . . ." He waved a hand dismissively, as if to send the whole matter away.

"Really," Jeremy said, "we didn't mean anything by it."

"I know, I know," the baker said in the most kindly voice. "And I trust that you now know that all is forgiven."

They ate for a time, and the baker again passed the tray of pastries. "Try the lemon," he said. "You won't be disappointed."

And they were not.

As they ate, Jeremy posed the very question that had been on his mind since the morning in the sheriff's office: "So why did you decide to say it wasn't me?"

The baker's gaze turned almost melancholy. "I felt sympathy," he said. "I saw how glad the sheriff and deputy were to have caught you and I thought, No, this cannot be. The sheriff will look like a hero, but really, he has done nothing." He turned from the window, and his voice stiffened. "We have young people vanishing without a trace, but instead of focusing on these matters, the sheriff finds it a great thing to catch a boy who has made a small bit of mischief." He sipped his coffee, and his voice softened. "I suppose you heard that a boy disappeared last week in the next county, a boy not yet fourteen—*poof!* gone!—and the sheriff there even more clumsy than our own Mr. Pittswort."

"I heard about it," Ginger said. "But I didn't know who he was."

"He was an idler, according to the newspaper, a truant from school. The sheriff there said what all the sheriffs say. 'He ran off. He'll turn up.' But they never turn up, do they?"

"I guess not," Ginger said, and Jeremy added rather weakly, "It seems like some of them do, though."

The baker dipped his head in a gracious nod. "You're right, of course. Some do." He sighed. "But enough of that. Let us discuss the work at hand."

He opened three large, velvet-lined cases containing a massive collection of exquisite silver forks, spoons, and knives.

Jeremy and Ginger stared into the cases as if at jewels.

"It is the Franska Liljan pattern," the baker said. "I'm not sure what it means, but it has been a favorite in Sweden since the 1700s."

"French lily," Jeremy said, after I'd whispered the translation to him. "Or possibly Fleur de Lys. That's what it means, I think."

A surprised laugh issued from the baker. "You speak Swedish and French?"

Jeremy flushed slightly and shrugged. "Not really. It's just that sometimes this stuff kind of comes to me."

The baker seemed amused by Jeremy's strange talent, but Ginger's response was even keener. While the baker went to fetch polish and rags, she kept staring at Jeremy. Her eyes shone, and her smile stretched from one ear to the other.

"What's the matter?" Jeremy said.

"I've got it," she said in a tone of absolute sureness. "I've totally got it."

"Totally got what?"

"The answer to our prayers."

"What prayers?"

"What do you think?—the ones for finding a way for you to keep your store."

"I think you lost me," Jeremy said, and he would stay lost, because at that moment the baker bustled into the room carrying metal polish and soft flannel rags.

§

That morning, the baker gave Jeremy and Ginger a thorough education in the polishing of silver, and as the hours wore on, the stacks of gleaming silver grew. The baker hovered amiably nearby, helping here and there, bringing a platter and teapot for cleaning, taking the others away.

When the silverware was finally finished, other tasks were assigned—the feather dusting of his collections of nutcrackers and novelty salt and pepper cellars, for example—until at last the noon hour came and the baker set out plates of sandwiches, plump with preserves and cream cheese, their crusts neatly trimmed, and served with a thick fruit nectar that the baker poured from a porcelain pitcher.

Well, I will say it. How delectable it all looked! And how envious I felt!

Ginger sipped from the nectar, then gulped. So did Jeremy.

"Zounds!" Ginger said. "In fact, I'll go zounds squared." She grinned appreciatively at the baker. "That's totally fabulous. What's in it?"

The baker shrugged. "Whatever I thought might blend well. Banana, strawberries, a kiwi"—his blue eyes twinkled—"the left foreleg of one small frog."

"Yeah," Ginger said. "I *thought* I caught just a hint of frog-gishness."

And so it was the pleasantest of little picnics, and when it was done and nothing was left, the baker handed them each an envelope.

"No," Jeremy said, glancing at the money inside. "That's too much."

"Speak for yourself," Ginger said with a laugh, then looked at the baker. "But we still do owe you for the Prince Cakes that day. Our big We-Owe-You. How about we pay up for that?"

"All taken into account," the baker said. He was nodding benignly. "You make a very good team. I'll find another job for you soon"—a merry smile—"something to better utilize your skill and industry."

Once they were down the lane, Ginger knuckled Jeremy softly on the shoulder. "Ha! Was that gig freakishly fabuloso or what? Less than four hours' work and we get a great breakfast, a great lunch, and some serious loot in our boot."

"Loot in our boot?"

"I know," she said. "Weird phrase. My folks used to use it." She extended her share of the money to Jeremy. "Here. For the Bookstore-Retention Fund."

Jeremy shook his head, and when Ginger persisted, he said it more emphatically: "No."

Ginger raised her hands in mock surrender. "Okay, okay." Then, without quite looking him in the eye, she said, "Look, I've got some stuff to do. Maybe I'll catch up with you later on."

Jeremy nodded. "Yeah, sure . . . I've got some stuff to do, too."

But as she began to stride away, he said, "Ginger?"

She turned around. "Yeah?"

"So what exactly *is* the answer to all our prayers?"

"Oh, that." She teased a strand of hair through her lips. "Can't say."

"When can you say?"

"Can't say."

"That's helpful."

"Let me put it this way. When you need to know, you'll know." Then she coated her voice in honey. "Bye-ya, Jeremy Jeremy," she said, and her words lingered in the air like a sweet scent after she was gone.

§

§

The next week brought a series of thunderstorms and several more notices from the bank, which Jeremy put away without opening. Under my direction, he had commenced a summer's reading list of classic literature, beginning with *Beowulf*.

When Ginger stopped by to visit, she picked up the book, flipped through a few pages, put it back down, and said, "You know, you don't have to read weird books like this. You're already the honorary mayor of Nerdsville."

She stared at the shelves filled with his grandfather's autobiography. "That's a lot of copies of the same book." She glanced at him. "Is it any good?"

"Not really sure," Jeremy said. "I was ten and did a lot of skimming."

On the stiles of the old bookcases, Jeremy's grandfather had mounted a number of his ancient tools—adzes, mallets, baling hooks, those sorts of things. As Ginger bent close to look at a brass level, she said, "I was in the bakery today. Mr. Blix said McRaven had been in to talk to him about employing us."

"You're kidding! For one day? What did McRaven say?"

"He said that the good people of Never Better would feel obliged to boycott the baker if they found out he was giving us work."

"*Us?* They don't want *you* to earn anything, either?"

"Ever since I got spotted leaving your attic . . ." Ginger shrugged. "Anyway, Mr. Blix was great about it. He just laughed and told me that we'd have to be a little less conspicuous next time." She glanced out the window. "The baker's one of the good ones," she said, "and believe me, there aren't that many."

She sat down at the old desk and began going through its drawers.

"You're kind of snoopy, aren't you?" Jeremy said, a question Ginger did not bother answering. By then, she was waving the recent letters from the bank. "What *are* these?"

"Letters not addressed to you."

"Yeah, yeah, yeah. But what *are* they?"

Jeremy flopped down sideways in the big chair. "Take a wild guess."

"Don't you think you should open them?"

Jeremy said nothing.

"Can I open them?"

"Sure. But what's the point?"

After going through them, Ginger said nothing, but her expression hardened. She put the notices back into the drawer and slid it closed. For a few seconds, she pressed several strands of hair between her lips, and then suddenly, decisively, she said, "Okay. That's it. We're doing it."

Well. These words alarmed me. They seemed to worry Jeremy as well.

"Doing what?"

She barely looked at him. She was striding for the front door. Over her shoulder, she said, "You'll see."

§

§

A day passed, and another. Ginger did not visit, Jeremy read *Beowulf*, and I was content.

After Beowulf, I said, *comes El Cid.*

"After *Beowulf*," Jeremy said, "comes my investigation into the most painless method of suicide."

When Jenny Applegarth telephoned that afternoon to ask Jeremy if he could help her with a painting project, he threw *Beowulf* down and leapt for the door.

A half hour later, he was sitting on her front porch helping her paint a set of brown chairs green. Jeremy's mood, for once, was tranquil, and why not? The sky was blue, Jenny Applegarth sang prettily under her breath as she worked, and through the trees, dappled sunlight fell on her brown arms and legs.

Once she interrupted her singing to ask if Jeremy's father was doing any better.

"Not really. I keep telling him what you said—you know, that we need a plan?—and he keeps saying he's waiting for inspiration." Jeremy issued a small, mirthless laugh. "I think the only inspiration we're going to get is an eviction notice."

Two elderly women—the Downs sisters—were passing on the sidewalk. They paused to stare pointedly at Jeremy and Jenny at their work. After the women had moved on, Jeremy said, "They're going to try to get you not to hire me anymore."

Jenny Applegarth smiled. "Already have. You'd be amazed how my tips have gone down in the last week or so."

At this, Jeremy stilled his paintbrush. "That's what McRaven told Mr. Blix after he hired Ginger and me—that if he did it again, the town would boycott his bakery." He stood up abruptly. "Really, I should go."

"Oh, don't be foolish," Jenny said. "Sit down and keep painting." She pushed up her streaky blond hair with the back of her hand. "You can't let buffoons run your life." She glanced down the street at the Downs sisters, who were almost to the corner. "Especially cranky old buffoons."

For several minutes, she brushed long, smooth ribbons of green across the chair, but then she looked suddenly up. "Know what? I have the feeling that things are going to get better soon."

Jeremy's smile was dubious. "Yeah? Based on what?"

"Who knows? Gut feeling . . . Cockeyed optimism." She smiled. "Applegarth intuition."

Jeremy laughed and said, "What about 'none of the above'?"

Jenny Applegarth shrugged and smiled. "You'll see I'm right," she said.

And for a time, it seemed as if she was.

§

§

"Guess what?" Ginger said.

Three days had quietly passed without a word from the girl, but now she stood at the door of Jeremy's small garage, beaming.

"What?" he said. To his right, the circular grindstone he had been using to sharpen the blade of his mowing machine still spun.

"Well," she said, "I want to tell you, but I can't when you're wearing those extremely weird safety goggles."

He took them off. "Okay. What?"

"I'm taking you someplace tomorrow and we're going to do something you've never done before and it's going to be really fun." She snapped her cinnamon-scented gum. "It's a surprise."

"I don't really like surprises," Jeremy said. "In fact, I hate surprises."

That is correct, Jeremy. We hate surprises. What is more, you need to know exactly where it is she wants to go, and what it is she wants you to do once you get there.

Jeremy said, "So what would we be doing?"

Ginger held the back of her hand to her nose. "Those hot springs are *evil*. If there's ever a Totally Gross Smell Contest, I'm putting all my money on the hot springs."

Jeremy closed the garage door and turned on the fan. "Okay. I repeat: What kind of surprise?"

"We leave early," she said. "Be ready by six a.m. Eat a good breakfast and wear clean, comfortable clothes." She unfolded a paper from her hip pocket and glanced down at it. "A solid blue shirt will be good or a solid pastel color, but don't wear white or black. And no patterns or stripes."

"I don't get it. What are we doing?"

She was still looking at the paper. So, in fact, was I, but the writing was messy enough that I could not decipher it. "And be wrinkle-free," she said.

Jeremy! I said. *Agree to nothing,* and for once he seemed to listen.

"It's a simple question really," he said. *"What are we doing?"*

She smiled demurely. "Can't tell." She put the paper back into her pocket. "Except it's nothing illegal. That much I can tell you. And it's a happy surprise."

"Yeah," Jeremy said, "but I really need to know what the surprise is."

She laughed. "Wish I could help. Really, really do."

She smiled, touched the tip of her finger to the tip of his nose, and left.

§

§

That night, against my warnings, Jeremy ironed a blue shirt, laid out his other clothes, and set his alarm clock for 5:30. Then, in the midst of a final plea that he go nowhere at all with this girl, he interrupted to say, quite firmly, "Good night, Jacob."

Well, then, what could I do? *Good night, Jeremy,* I said, *and sweet repose.*

The evening was pleasant and the town was quiet, except for occasional laughter spinning into the night from the Intrepid Bar & Grill. All of the other businesses were dark. I drifted through the streets of the village, and when I heard a distant wistful melody, I recognized the voice as Jenny Applegarth's and found her sitting alone in a chair on her patio, softly singing an old folk tune.

> *The keeper did a-hunting go;*
> *And under his cloak he carried a bow;*
> *All for to shoot a merry little doe;*
> *Among the leaves so green, O.*

She sang so prettily that I lingered until she finally rose and went indoors. Even then I carried her melody with me as I drifted toward the church belfry.

I could never sing. And on this night, gazing from the belfry, I remembered a time when my failure to sing caused discomfort not just to me but to those I loved.

It was my little nephew's fourth birthday, and he came up to my study to entreat me to join the celebration. Perhaps Wilhelm sent him, or Dortchen, for they knew there was little I could deny the boy. I went down and smiled as best I could, but when the singing began, I remained mute. Wilhelm spied me standing silent. Between choruses, he called out to me. "Come, Jacob, join us in the singing," he said, and when I demurred, he prompted my nephew. "Please, Uncle Jacob," the boy said in his sweet voice, "won't you sing?" Something brittle within me snapped, and I shook my head so furiously that the boy in confusion and dismay dropped his eyes and his lips began to tremble. He was saved from crying only by the commencement of the next merry tune. Through all of the song, he did not glance at me and I stood in a state of suppressed chaotic rage at this conspiracy to have me do what I would not, and—oh, my senses worked at high pitch!—nothing brought greater offense than that my brother, my own brother, would use this small, kind boy as a weapon in the onslaught! When the song was over, they all laughed as one and I began to take my leave. "Jacob?" Wilhelm called to me as I reached the doorway. "Where do you go?" "To our study," I told him, "to work with doubled effort to compensate for your absence!" They all pretended to take this as a joke and laughed heartily. And so with burning ears I strode off to my solitary desk to do my work. Then, as now, in the dark night of the *Zwischenraum*, I felt the full weight of my solitude.

The night stretched long and hollow, and then—the clock had just struck twelve times—I saw something that I knew would make the villagers happy: greenish-gray smoke rising from the bakery's tall brick chimney.

§

§

The following morning, a few minutes before six, Ginger rapped on the door of the bookstore. This was expected. What was not expected was Conk Crinklaw's red pickup truck parked in the street behind her, with Conk himself sitting sullenly behind the steering wheel.

"Zounds," Ginger said, eyeing Jeremy's shirt when he opened the bookstore. "That's a blue you don't see every day. Would you call it fluorescent?"

"How about calling it the only blue I had," he said, then nodded toward the truck. "What's Conk doing here?"

She glanced back. "Oh, him." Her tone was merry and her breath smelled sweetly of cinnamon. "He's our driver for the day."

Conk cast a wooden look at them both. "No eating in the cab," he said, then fixed his eyes on Jeremy. "And no talking to Martians, either."

As they climbed into the truck (and I with them), Ginger said, "Martians couldn't be any weirder than you, Conk. In fact, I'm not a hundred percent sure you aren't one."

He stared at her. "Well, I'm a hundred percent sure I'm about to lose a day that I'll never get back."

"Which is a real shame," Ginger said, "because I know that a day in Conkopolis is a day chock-full of noble deeds and profound thinking."

Conk shook his head and guided the truck away from the curb, but they were barely under way when Ginger pointed excitedly toward the chimney of the Green Oven Bakery. "Hey, take a look! Green smoke! We've got to stop! Prince Cake for the road!" She turned to Conk. "Got any money, Conky-poo?"

Conk did not say yes and did not say no. He simply kept driving. Ginger turned to stare as the truck passed the bakery. The kitchen lights were on, but the store in front was dark and the sign on the front door said CLOSED.

"Maybe he'll save some for us," Ginger said.

Conk stared forward, down Main Street. "Why would he do that?"

"Maybe because he thinks I'm a ray of sunshine on a cloudy day."

Conk gave her a quick sidelong look. "He said that?"

"Yep. Direct quote."

Conk shook his head in disbelief and said in a low tone, "There's something fundamentally wrong with that guy."

A laugh burst from Ginger, and the sweet smell of cinnamon filled the cab. "Like what, Conky? Like what is fundamentally wrong with Mr. Blix?"

"Well, just for starters, he's not from around here."

"C'mon, Conky-poo. *Nobody* is from around here, except the Lakota."

Conk shrugged and reached forward to turn on the radio.

As the truck approached the Twinkle Tub Laundry, Mrs. Truax could already be seen at her ironing board behind the front window. Ginger leaned past Jeremy and shouted, "Bye, Mrs. Truax!"

Mrs. Truax stared darkly in return.

In a bland voice, Conk said, "That's one scary human being."

Ginger grinned at him. "Scarier than the town baker?"

Conk considered it and said, "Too close to call."

Ginger rode between the two boys and seemed not at all uneasy with the arrangement. Just the opposite, in fact. Once the truck was out on the highway, she extended an arm over the shoulder of each boy and said, "There. That's more comfy." Then, to Jeremy, "That shirt may be a freakish shade of blue, but it's nice material. What is it?" She turned, pressed into him, and folded back the collar to read a small tag stitched there. "One hundred percent cotton," she said, finally leaning back. She smoothed her hand over the sleeve of Jeremy's shirt and grinned at Conk, whose expression was as stone. "That's why it's so soft and nice to the touch, Conky," she said. "It's one hundred percent cotton."

Conk drew a long, steady breath, then bent forward to look past Ginger toward Jeremy. "So I hear you talk German and about three other languages."

"Sort of," Jeremy said.

"Well," Conk said, "maybe you could give us the German word for *she-wolf*."

There seemed no real need to translate, for Ginger said, "While you're at it, Jeremy, maybe you could give us the German for *warthog*."

I did, and Jeremy repeated it: "*Warzenschwein*."

Jeremy and Ginger shared a small laugh over this; then she repeated the word, "*Warzenschwein*," which set her off on another round of mirthful laughter.

Conk exhaled heavily and turned up the volume of the radio.

Many miles and minutes and fields and farms passed with the three young people talking very little while a great deal of loud, nerve-jangling music streamed from the radio. Ginger often knew the lyrics, and sang along happily, but the boys did not sing at all. As the sun rose in the sky, Conk pushed a button to lower the windows and air rushed into the truck. He was driving quite fast, and the gush of warm, summery, farm-scented air was so exhilarating that I was somewhat disappointed when we came upon a town and slowed down in order to search for a particular address on Bank Street.

"What's there?" Jeremy asked.

Conk was incredulous. "What's there? The TV studio is what's there."

"Why are we going to a TV studio?" Jeremy said.

Conk's look of surprise moved from Jeremy to Ginger. "He doesn't know why he's here?"

"Why *who's* where?" Jeremy said.

Ginger shifted slightly in her seat. For the first time all day, she seemed uneasy. "Look, Jeremy, I didn't want you worrying about this."

"Worrying about what?" Jeremy said.

"At this studio"—she pointed toward a building we were now approaching—"they're doing an audition today for *Uncommon Knowledge*. That TV show where—"

"I *know* what it is," Jeremy snapped. "But what am I doing here?"

"I told them about you—how you're only fifteen and know a bunch of languages."

"But I don't!" Jeremy said, panic rising in his voice. "I just know a few words here and there."

It took a moment to grasp the situation unfolding, but once I did, a prideful pleasure began to suffuse me. *But I speak thirteen languages, Jeremy*, I said. *I can help*.

"That would be cheating!" Jeremy blurted, and Ginger said, "What would be cheating?" and Jeremy, realizing he had just spoken out loud to me, was irrationally angry at Ginger! "I don't want to do this!" he yelled. Then, less loudly but no less peevishly, he added, "I *told* you I don't like surprises."

Now it was Ginger's turn for petulance. "You need money, Jeremy, and you can earn money on this show. Lots of money."

Jeremy fell quiet as Conk guided the truck into a paved area filled with many other cars. An attendant in a small booth asked for two dollars, which Conk paid, but as he pulled ahead, he said, "I'd rather be shot right between the eyes than live in a town where you have to pay to park your truck."

Ginger seemed relieved by the change of subject. "You've already been shot right between the eyes, metaphorically speaking," she said.

Conk turned. "You know what? I don't speak metafornically, or whatever it is, and the truth is, I don't much care for those who do."

This only enlivened Ginger's spirits. "Uh-oh. Turbulence in Conkville! Conky, sweetie, how can I give the driver a nice big tip when he goes negative like that?"

Conk stared at her with the cold eyes of an unhappy god.

The building we were approaching was square and beige. Inside, we were directed to a large room filled with people sitting in metal chairs. The sour smell in the room, it soon became clear, was from nervous perspiration. All the people seated here appeared both anxious and miserable. Even though Ginger, Conk, and Jeremy were much younger than anyone else in the room, no one paid them any attention, and they found three chairs in the most distant corner.

There were only two doors in the room, the one through which we had entered and another one at the front of the room, painted blue, and standing closed.

After taking his seat, Conk looked around. "Man, this is worse than church. At least a church has got windows so you can at least look outside and imagine being there."

"You said 'at least' twice," Ginger said.

Conk looked at her evenly and said, "And I just might say it again."

The three of them settled into the room's uneasy silence. From time to time, the blue door at the front of the room opened, a large bald man came out and called a name, and the man or woman of that name walked somberly through the blue door, which quickly closed behind them.

"Cows going to slaughter," Conk said. He turned to Jeremy. "Next time we see you, you'll probably be shrink-wrapped and labeled extra-lean."

Jeremy smiled a little nervously, and Ginger said, "Whereas, Conk, you'd probably go out to the meat counter as oaf loaf."

"That's a good one," Conk said in a flat voice. "Oaf loaf."

Another long silence stretched out. After a time, the woman sitting next to Conk turned to him and said, "What do you know about?"

"Not much." He gestured toward Jeremy. "He's the one with the weird abilities."

The woman glanced at Jeremy but did not seem particularly interested in him. "I can name every bone in the body," the woman said. "Also all the nerves and muscles. I can go head to toe or toe to head, either way, it don't matter."

Conk stared straight ahead and said, "Well, I'm sure your knowing that makes the world a better place."

"I can also do them in alphabetical order," the woman continued, and she began to recite them alphabetically in a tight, low voice, more to herself than to anyone else.

* * *

An hour passed, then another, and another. One by one, men and women went through the blue door; they did not come back. Finally, only a few people remained in the room. Still, after all this tedium, it was a bit of a jolt when the large bald man opened the blue door and said, "Jeremy Johnson Johnson?"

Jeremy rose and began to walk toward the blue door. Ginger and Conk followed, but at the door, the bald man said, "Which one's Johnson?"

"I am," Jeremy said, and the bald man looked at Conk and Ginger and said, "Sorry, prospective contestants only."

A sensible rule, of course, but not one that applied to me.

Jeremy looked uncertainly at Ginger, who said, "It's okay, Jeremy. We'll wait out front." She produced a smile. "Knock 'em dead, Jeremy Jeremy."

This was an idiomatic expression I did not understand, but Jeremy seemed to take it as encouragement. He smiled wanly and allowed himself to be led away, the blue door closing behind us.

§

§

The room to which we were escorted was small. Two women sat at a long table, each positioned behind separate electronic devices with illuminated screens.

"Have a seat," the bald man said, nodding toward a single

wooden chair situated opposite the women in the very center of the room.

Jeremy sat and looked around. "Where's Milo Castle?" he asked. Milo Castle was the *höfliche*—you would say *debonaire*—master of the show who visited briefly with the contestants and then asked them the specialized questions composed by a panel of experts.

Neither of the women looked up, but the large bald man said, "Mr. Castle doesn't come to the screenings."

The bald man left the room. Overhead, several intensely bright lights snapped on and shone down on Jeremy, who blinked and brought up a hand to shield his eyes.

"Take a moment to adjust," one of the women said, and the other woman leaned close to a recording device and said in a flat monotone, "Jeremy Johnson Johnson, Caucasian male, aged fifteen, claiming special knowledge in various languages."

"Are you talking to me?" Jeremy said, squinting through the lights, and the first woman said, "We'll start with something easy. Please say good morning in at least six languages other than English."

This was no problem and I begin going through them one by one, with Jeremy reciting them afterward: "*Guten Morgen.*" "*Bonjour.*" "*Buenos días.*"

"Hold it," the first woman said. "Why are you pausing before each answer?"

Jeremy stared at her blankly. "I guess I just have to think it through."

"For *good morning?*" the second woman said.

Well, it degenerated from there. The women asked two or

three more questions, but when Jeremy had to wait for me to translate before he could speak, the women became visibly impatient. One of them said, "Look, Jeremy, this whole time-delay thing isn't working for us. It would be fine to deliberate if we were asking questions you needed to search your memory for, but you're supposed to *know* these languages. The answers should come flying right back to us, *bam-bam-bam*."

I felt chastened. So did Jeremy. "Okay," he said. "I'm sorry. Thank you."

He stood up. He seemed so young and lost that evidently even these brusque women felt the need to soften the blow. "You seem bright and nice and photogenic," the first one said, and the other one added, "It would've been great having a contestant your age."

"It's okay," Jeremy said. "It's not your fault." He looked around for the door.

Tell them that you are an expert on the Brothers Grimm.

"What?" Jeremy said.

"Pardon me?" the first woman said.

Tell them that you are an expert on Jacob and Wilhelm Grimm and all their tales.

Jeremy said, "I know a lot about the Brothers Grimm."

The women looked dubious.

"You mean fairy tales?" one of them said.

At my further urging, Jeremy told the women that he could tell them almost anything about the lives of the Grimm Brothers, about their methods of collecting the tales, and about the tales themselves.

The women looked at each other, and one of them shrugged.

They motioned him to sit back down. They each made clicking sounds on the keyboards in front of them and then stared at their illuminated screens.

"Okay," the first woman said, "give me the first and middle names of the two Grimm brothers?"

I told Jeremy, who said, "Jacob Ludwig and Wilhelm Karl."

"Which brother was married, to whom, and what tale did this woman relate to the brothers?"

Slowly, Jeremy said, "Wilhelm. To Dorothea Wild. 'Little Red Riding Hood.'"

The two women turned to each other in surprise, then looked again at their monitors. The first woman said, "What was Dorothea Wild's father's chosen profession?"

"*Apotheker*," Jeremy said, and when the women looked confused, I guided Jeremy to revise his answer: "What we would today call a pharmacist."

"That is correct," the second woman said, and it was clear that the mood in the room had brightened. These women were now rooting for us.

This was fun, I had to admit, and Jeremy and I answered several more questions without difficulty. Finally, after the women had conferred for some time in front of one of the television sets, the first woman said, "Explain what might be meant by the term the *Göttingen Seven*."

So! These women thought they had us, but it was we who had them! Slowly, deliberately, Jeremy gave our answer: "When Wilhelm and Jacob were teaching at the University of Göttingen, King Augustus abolished the constitution. The Grimm Brothers publicly protested, along with five other professors, and they became known as the Göttingen Seven. They all were dismissed from the university, and several of them, including Jacob, were deported."

For a moment, it was very quiet in the room. Then the women rose as one from behind their table. Their faces were radiant. "That's right!" one of them said. "That's absolutely right!"

They nearly lifted Jeremy from his chair as they escorted him into an adjoining room. "Get everything on this young man," the second woman said to a man sitting at a desk. "Get his Social, complete bio, release forms, everything." She grinned at Jeremy. "We might well need it."

A half hour later, when Jeremy finally made his way out to the foyer, Ginger looked up expectantly. Conk, too, looked up from the sporting page in his hands.

"Well?" Ginger said.

"I don't know. It wasn't too bad."

"Are you going to go on the show?"

Jeremy shrugged.

"But how did you do?"

"Okay, I think," he said, but from behind him a woman's voice said, "*Okay?* I think you did a little better than *okay*." It was one of the two questioners hurrying up, smiling. "So, Jeremy, are these your people? Agents and handlers and so forth?"

She was joking in some manner, but only Ginger realized it. She grinned and said, "Actually, Conk here is Jeremy's driver, and I'm his agent."

The woman laughed, and hands were shaken and names exchanged. At the exit, the woman said, "You made my day, Jeremy Johnson Johnson, you really did. No promises, but chances are, you'll be hearing from us." She turned to Ginger and Conk. "Jeremy is a regular demon on the Brothers Grimm and all their fairy tales."

Everyone was grinning, and it must be admitted that I, too, felt a bit giddy. Conk's grin, however, seemed oddly lopsided, as if there was some source of humor here that the others did not yet see.

"When will Jeremy find out?" Ginger asked the woman. "I mean, how soon will he hear if he's going to be on the show?"

The woman seemed amused by Ginger. "Maybe you *should* be his agent," she said. "But if he's accepted, he'll hear soon, because we're doing the show in this region in just a few weeks."

"How will he hear?"

"Bad news by mail, good news by phone—that's the general rule. And if Milo Castle himself calls, you're golden. Milo likes to be the bearer of good news."

Before they parted, the woman said, "Oh, and, Jeremy, one little thing. If you are on the show, you might think about a different shirt. Something a little less . . . *distracting*."

Jeremy smiled and said he'd see what he could do.

§

§

Good spirits prevailed among the young people as they walked through the late-afternoon light to the truck and when they stopped at a small restaurant for sandwiches. But on the long drive home, an odd discord arose. When Ginger said, "I still can't believe it—I think you're going to be on the show!" several seconds passed, and then Conk said, "You're not actually going to do it, are you?"

"What do you mean?" Ginger said. "Why wouldn't he?"

"C'mon, Ginger. *Fairy tales?* He hears voices, he's the only kid in town who can't throw a football, and now he's going to go on TV as an expert on *fairy tales?*"

Jeremy stiffened and swung his head away.

Ginger, seeing this, said, "You are such a complete idiot, Conk."

"Truth hurts," Conk said, and kept driving down the highway for a few minutes before he broke the silence by saying, "Well, why are you doing it, anyway?"

Jeremy, staring stiffly off, did not answer. I was not even sure he had heard.

"Because he needs the money, Conky," Ginger said. "And do you know why he needs the money?"

"No, I don't. So why don't you tell me?"

"Because the bank is going to take back his store. Which is where he lives."

Conk seemed actually surprised. "Okay. I didn't know that." Then he said, "Couldn't the bank cut you some slack or something?"

Ginger stared at him. "What do you think?"

They all fell silent. As the radio played softly and the passing wheat fields turned golden in the dusky light, Ginger grew sleepy and dozed for a while against Jeremy's arm, and then, half waking, she shifted and nestled her head onto Conk's shoulder.

It was dusk by the time they reached Never Better. As Conk wheeled the truck onto Main Street, Jeremy leaned forward and said, "Could you just let me out here?"

"Hey, c'mon," Ginger said, awake now and restored. "I thought we could go see if the baker saved us any Prince Cake."

"Naw," Jeremy said. "I'm kind of tired."

"You sure?"

"Yeah, I'm sure."

Conk pulled up to the curb, and Jeremy slid from the cab. "Thanks," he said, looking past Ginger to Conk. "That was pretty nice of you to drive me all that way."

Conk shrugged. "No problem." He looked forward. "And you know that bank-loan thing? I'll talk to my dad about it. Maybe he can do something."

This was doubtless a surprise to Jeremy, and it seemed to impress Ginger, too. Her eyes lingered on Conk for a moment before she turned back to Jeremy. "Sure you don't want to come along? A piece of Prince Cake could perk you right up."

"No, but thanks, anyhow," Jeremy said, and stepped away from the truck. He stood watching until it disappeared from view, and then he turned for home.

I could not help but remember a night from long, long ago. Wilhelm and Dortchen had made plans to attend the opera. I was opposed—Wilhelm and I had work to do. He and I had been upstairs at our desks working late and ignoring Dortchen's entreaties that Wilhelm cease work and dress for the evening. *"Ich tue es auf der Stelle,"* Wilhelm kept saying—*I'll do it this minute,* but under my severe gaze he did not leave. Finally, Dortchen came into the room holding Wilhelm's evening clothes. She was already dressed in a black gown, looking—I remember it perfectly—absolutely enchanting. "If you don't put these clothes on this very instant," she said, "I am going to stuff them with hay and go to the opera with Herr Strawman." Wilhelm laughed with delight and, ignoring my gaze, was soon himself within the clothes. I walked out to the lane as they were stepping into their carriage. It was a cold, starry night, and they snuggled close together under their lap robes. They waved back at me and called out merrily. As the clatter of the horse and carriage fell away, I felt as cold and dark as the night's sky, and then, of course, I returned alone to my study, just as Jeremy, now, returned alone to his bookstore.

But the day's surprises were not over. As Jeremy stepped into the bookstore, he was met with another.

Floating through the store from the direction of his father's room was a delectable aroma and something else, something even more unexpected.

The sound of singing.

A man's and a woman's.

§

§

Jeremy crept across the room, put his ear to the closed door to his father's room, and listened to a woman's voice singing alone now, high and light:

> The keeper did a-hunting go;
> And under his cloak he carried a bow;
> All for to shoot a merry little doe,
> Among the leaves so green, O.

I knew this lilting voice to be Jenny Applegarth's. But then there were two voices, weaving one with the other in a dance of questions.

Jacky boy? Jenny Applegarth sang, and a surprisingly resonant tenor answered:

> Master.
> Sing you well?
> Very well.
> Hey, down.
> Ho, down.
> Derry, derry down.

On the last line—*Among the leaves so green, O*—they joined their voices, and then continued on with this cheerful melody shadowed by dark lyrics:

> The sixth doe she ran over the plain;
> But he with his hounds did turn her again,
> And it's there he did hunt in a merry, merry vein,
> Among the leaves so green, O.

After they were finished, Jenny Applegarth laughed and said, "Well, listen to us! Aren't we something!"

Jeremy pushed the door open and found his father sitting up in bed grinning. Jenny Applegarth sat in a chair pulled close by. Their faces were radiant.

Jeremy's surprise at the scene caused his skin to burn, and all he could think to say was, "How'd you get in?"

"Well, that's a fine way to say hello," Jenny Applegarth said with a laugh. "Through the front door is how. What did you think, down the chimney?"

Jeremy, flustered, shook his head. It *was* quite a surprise, this sight before him: Jenny Applegarth in her summery yellow dress, with her apricot-brown arms, and his father's eyes bright in spite of his tangled hair and beard. The tantalizing aroma of baked goods was even keener here—it emanated from the kitchen.

"What's cooking?" Jeremy asked.

"Chicken pot pie," Jenny Applegarth said. "In fact, could you just peek at it and see if the top's brown?"

No sooner had Jeremy opened the oven door and peered in than Jenny Applegarth slipped into the kitchen behind him. "You can't just stand back and look at it," she said. "You need to lean in a little bit."

Jeremy instead used a heavy cloth to pull the rack toward him.

Jenny Applegarth glanced at the pie and said, "Let's give it three more minutes."

She closed the oven door and gazed out the kitchen window for some little while before she turned her eyes to Jeremy. "Guess you're kind of surprised to find me here."

"No," Jeremy said, his face blazing again. "I mean, yes, I was, but I'm not now. I mean, it's fine. It's really good, in fact."

Jenny Applegarth smiled. "It was kind of spur-of-the-moment. And I knew if I tried to arrange it all, he'd just say he didn't want company."

"No," Jeremy said, trying to recover himself. "I'm glad you came. It's the first time I've seen him smiling in I don't know how long. How'd you do it, anyway?"

Jenny Applegarth shrugged, but there was a shine to her eyes I had not seen before. "Okay," she said, again. "Let's see what we've got."

The chicken pot pie she pulled from the oven was wondrous to behold.

"Yum," Jenny said, and she served portions onto three plates, laid forks across each edge, and then, with the ease of a practiced waitress, carried all three into the next room.

"Think you're going to like this, Harold," she said, and Mr. Johnson (who, I noticed, had now run a wide-toothed comb through his hair) said, "Yes, indeed."

While they ate, his father said, "So what did you do with your day?"

Jeremy did not look up from his plate. "Nothing much."

His father snorted. "Well, for nothing much, you sure got up early and came home late."

"I went to Bank's Bluff with Ginger and Conk."

"With Ginger and Conk?" His father was looking up now. "What for?"

"No good reason. We just got something to eat and came back."

This answer did not satisfy his father. Jenny Applegarth, too, was looking at him with curiosity. His father said, "Well, you must've had a reason. You don't just drive a hundred something miles to get a hamburger and come back."

Jeremy kept eating.

His father took another bite, and said carefully, "I've been to Bank's Bluff. It's not a place people drive to for the fun of it. So there must've been—"

Jeremy suddenly jumped up. "Look," he said, "I didn't do anything wrong. But I don't want to talk about it. Is that okay with you?"

And before either of the adults could answer, he had bolted from the room, through the Two-Book Bookstore, and out into the street.

§

§

Jeremy turned toward the park. Even in the pale evening's light I could see that his face carried a dark gloom.

Are you well, Jeremy? Are you feeling well?

If he heard me, he did not respond.

What is the matter?

Still he did not speak.

I waited until he had seated himself on his favored picnic table. He looked for another note from Ginger squeezed into the table planks, but there was none.

And then I again said, *Are you well, Jeremy?*

He turned toward my voice. "Am I well?" His mocking tone was unmistakable. "Am I well? Why can't you just talk like everyone else? Why can't you just say, 'How you doin'? You doin' good?'"

Very well, then, I said. I look forward to the day when every schoolchild will read Shakespeare's great comedic play All's Good That Ends Good.

We both fell silent for a long while, listening to the chorus of crickets and frogs. From a distant corner of the park a child shouted, "Olly olly oxen free!"

Finally, I said, *Jeremy, what is the matter?*

"Everything's the matter!" he blurted. "Every single freaking thing!"

Ah. And may we consider them particularly, one by one?

"Okay, sure. For starters, there's the foreclosure problem. And there's the Ginger problem, and then there's the Ginger plus Conk problem. Then there's the everybody and his brother thinking I'm a slimeball problem. And then you have the Conk and possibly everyone else wondering why I know so much about fairy tales problem. Oh. But wait! I forgot maybe the most important problem of all—which would be you!"

Me?

"You. *Definitely* you. Maybe mostly you. You're the one, for just one example, who got me into this whole fairy-tale mess with the TV show."

I was trying to help, if you will recall.

"But look where it's gotten me! If I go on that show as a fairy-tale expert, not only will I look like some dweebish weirdo, but I'm going to feel like a fraud."

I did not understand this. *A fraud? Why a fraud?*

"Because it's not *my* uncommon knowledge! It's yours! And that makes *me* a fraud!"

I collected my thoughts and said, *Jeremy, it may be true that it is not your knowledge, but it is your talent. Your talent to hear me.*

"Yeah, well, in case you missed it, this isn't a talent show. It's not called *Uncommon Talents*."

There is little difference, Jeremy. Some have a talent for memorization; you have a talent for listening.

He breathed deeply in and out. "Yeah, that sounds good, but then, throwing a few Pop Rocks into the baker's cereal sounded good at the time, too."

And here I made the mistake of pointing out to Jeremy that going into the baker's house had never sounded good to me, and I had said so at the time.

"Okay, that's it!" Jeremy said. "Just leave me alone. Leave me absolutely alone."

I was quiet. I knew that I must be. Time passed. Somewhere in the park a child shouted, "Hello, hello, hello," and waited for the dim respondent echo: *oh, oh, oh.* The town clock struck nine, and parents began calling their children home. Jeremy stretched out on the table and stared up at the starry sky. A coal train strained its way up the grade and out of town. Finally, Jeremy sat up and said in a low voice, "You still there?"

Yes.

"I'm sorry if I was rude."

Do not worry, Jeremy. I know you are caught in a gloom.

He was quiet for a few seconds. Then he said, "I don't know. It's just that after my mother left and then after my grandfather died, it was pretty bad. But you came, and I got used to just doing my studies and my odd jobs and taking care of my father and having you nearby and everybody else just leaving me be. It wasn't great, but it was okay. Now all of a sudden, it's like I'm under everybody's microscope."

Yes, I said. *I understand. But we must work together, I am here to help you—*

But I did not finish.

We heard footsteps behind us, then a girl's voice softly calling, "Jeremy?"

§

§

Ginger stepped from the darkness, holding a small paper bag from the Green Oven Bakery. "So where've you been?" she asked.

"Since when?"

"Since fleeing Conk's truck like it was on fire."

"Home. Then here."

"For, like, four hours?"

"I guess. I kind of lost track."

She sat on the table beside him and pulled from the paper bag a single slice of Prince Cake, which she handed to him.

"The bakery was closed," she said, crumpling the bag into a ball, "but it turns out that Conk's dad has a standing order for the first Prince Cake anytime Sten bakes them." She paused. "Guess being the mayor has its fringe benefits."

Jeremy broke the cake in two and handed her the bigger

piece. As they were eating, Ginger said, "Conk talked to his dad about the bank loan, and his father thought maybe he could do something. Maybe not a lot, but something."

"Yeah?" Jeremy said quietly. "That seems good."

It was silent except for the frogs and crickets, and then Ginger said, "Conk is such a moron. He wants to go to Brazil and start a cattle ranch."

"Conk Crinklaw?" Jeremy said in a surprised tone. "In Brazil?"

Ginger chuckled. "Yeah, I know. A concept and a half. But he's been listening to Spanish tapes and everything."

I told Jeremy something that he passed on to Ginger: "I think they actually speak Portuguese in Brazil."

Ginger laughed a quick snorting laugh. "There it is—Conk in a nutshell—studying Spanish to go live in a country where they don't speak Spanish."

The words were disparaging, and yet she seemed amused. "Know how all the Crinklaws have those weird names, like Intrepid and Dauntless? Well, I found out that Conk has one, too. His real name is *Stalwart*. But as a baby, he kept crawling headfirst into things all the time, so they started calling him Conk."

Jeremy laughed softly. "Conk's not a bad name, I guess. Better than Stalwart, anyway." Then, staring off into the darkness, he asked, "So if you actually jumped a freight train, who would you go with? Conk or me?"

His seriousness appeared to surprise her. "Why would you ask that?"

"I don't know. Because I was thinking it, I guess."

Ginger seemed to be considering the matter. "And it has to be either-or, right?—I can't ride the rails with both of you?"

Jeremy gave her a decisive shake of his head.

160

"Okay, then. I guess if I was having to deal with thugs and stuff—like I was in a hobo jungle or something—I'd choose Conk, because, well, he's Conk. But if I were just riding along in a freight car, I'd want to be with you." She looked at him. "That help?"

"I guess," he said, but I could detect the disappointment in his voice. "Also, just so you know, I don't think they have hobo jungles anymore."

"Well, there you go, then. If there are no hobo jungles, I don't need Conk at all."

She stretched out on the table, put her head in his lap, and stared up at the sky. "Why don't you tell me a story—one of those fairy tales, one with a happy ending."

"Which one?" he said.

"I don't care. You pick."

Perhaps "The Fisherman and His Wife," I said, because, truthfully, I thought the shameful influence of the greedy wife might cloud the romantic climate that I felt was developing, but Jeremy would not listen.

"Okay, I've got one," he said, and a strange ease came into his voice as he began: "Long ago and far, far away, there was an old king who, as he lay dying, called for his faithful servant . . ."

It was the tale of Faithful John, a wide-ranging story of enchanted love and of amorous abduction and, most of all, of the servant who gave his life to save his master's. When the king's son enters the one room he has been forbidden to enter, his eyes fall upon a portrait of the Princess of the Golden Dwelling, and he is, as Jeremy recited, "possessed by a love so great that if all the leaves on all the trees were tongues, they could not declare it."

161

An appreciative murmur escaped Ginger. "Zounds . . . ," she said softly. "That's a whole lot of love."

Jeremy gave a small laugh and continued. At Faithful John's direction, he said, the prince's artisans were soon crafting beautiful objects of gold, to be used to lure the Princess of the Golden Dwelling. "And so," Jeremy related, "the ship laden with golden objects set sail for the land of the Golden Dwelling when—"

His voice broke abruptly off.

A dazzling light had split the darkness and now held Ginger and Jeremy in a tableau of startled surprise. Ginger shielded her eyes and pushed herself upright.

"Curfew," said a hard, gruff voice. It was Deputy McRaven.

Ginger squinted into the searing brightness. "Curfew?"

"That's right. I should write you up."

"For what? Sitting in the park telling stories?"

The deputy kept his bright light shining into their eyes. "For breaking curfew, littering, and loitering. And I'd probably have to mention that the subject female was lying prone on the picnic table."

At this, Ginger abruptly jumped down from the table. "C'mon, Jeremy," she said, and strode past Deputy McRaven. Jeremy followed behind. "We're leaving," she said, "but if you still need to write us up on your cute little curfew charge, you should also note that the subject female referred to the subject deputy as a giant horse's ass."

The bright beam of light followed them as they retreated through the trees. Behind the light, the deputy's large face looked both resentful and strangely miserable.

"Your time will come!" he called after them. These were his exact words, and he soon repeated them. "Don't be fooling yourselves! Your time will come!"

Three days quietly passed, and Jeremy neither saw nor heard from Deputy McRaven. Nor did he hear a word from the game show. Two more letters came from the bank, letters that Jeremy signed for but did not open.

There was another development: On the morning of the fourth day, Jenny Applegarth stopped by to pick up Jeremy's father, to what end no one would say, but his father had showered and combed out his unruly hair for the occasion. In his old loose-fitting athletic apparel, he looked like a prisoner being led out into the light, which, by a certain line of reasoning, was exactly what he was. He blinked and gaped and allowed Jenny Applegarth's hand to guide him along the street. And so, for the first time since I had come to the village, Mr. Harold Johnson crossed the threshold into public life.

I was hovering there, watching him and Jenny walking side by side down Main Street, when Ginger turned the corner and bore down on the bookstore. She strode past me, pushed open the door, and didn't waste time saying hello.

"So?" she demanded. "Did he call?"

By *he*, she of course meant Mr. Milo Castle, from *Uncommon Knowledge*.

"Nope," Jeremy said. He held a broom in his hand. When I had requested that he resume his reading of *El Cid*, he said that he needed to sweep the floor. That will tell you how much he liked *El Cid*.

Ginger checked the telephone to be sure it was working, then set it back down. "What's up with those people, anyhow? I mean, they all but said you'd be on the show."

Jeremy shrugged and kept sweeping. I had observed that he was not nearly as anxious for Mr. Milo Castle's call as she was.

Ginger flopped down in the stuffed armchair. "So am I losing my mind or was that your dad and Jenny Applegarth I just saw walking down the street?"

Jeremy nodded. "It was them, all right."

"That's big news, right? I mean, when was the last time he left his room?"

"I can't even remember." He stilled his broom. "It's good but also a little weird. I guess I'd started to think he wouldn't come out of that room until he'd—you know—cashed it all in."

Ginger pressed several strands of hair between her lips. "Really, when you think of it, it's so once-upon-a-time."

Jeremy's face twisted into a dubious look.

"Sure," she went on. "As in 'Once upon a time, there was a lonely old king who would never leave his castle, but one day a beautiful woman warrior presented herself at the gates.'" Ginger produced one of her saucy grins. "Not bad, huh?"

Jeremy said, "Let me get this straight. Mrs. Applegarth is a woman warrior and this"—he gestured around the room—"is a castle, and my father's a king?"

164

"Yep." She beamed. "Which means . . . you're now a prince!"

"Yeah?" He looked about the room. "Where's all my treasure and stuff?"

"We're working on that." She stretched and yawned. "So where were they going? Your dad wasn't exactly wearing the royal duds."

Jeremy issued a small laugh. "Yeah, I don't know where he got that old sweat suit, but at least he could get into it. As for where they're going, they wouldn't say."

Ginger pulled a newspaper clipping from her pocket and extended it toward Jeremy. "Not to change the subject," she said, "but read this."

The article concerned the boy in the adjoining county who had disappeared, the one whom Sten Blix had mentioned a few days before. It was just as the baker predicted. The authorities had given up the search. "We think he'll show up in San Francisco or Miami, someplace like that," the sheriff was quoted as saying.

"Maybe they're right," Jeremy said. "Maybe he *will* show up there."

"Maybe." Ginger slipped the clipping back into her pocket. "But it's kind of weird how kids keep going missing."

A small smile appeared on Jeremy's face. "Hey, maybe their mothers sent them out to seek their fortunes. Or maybe they've been called away to slay a dragon somewhere. Like when Beowulf goes after Grendel."

I was, of course, pleased by this allusion to his summer reading, but Ginger gave him a deadpan look and said, "I was wrong. You're no mere mayor of Nerdsville. You are the emperor of Greater Nerdistan."

Jeremy grinned and drew down a board game from a nearby

bookshelf. "And now the emperor of Greater Nerdistan will an-nihilate the cheeky delegate from rural Never Better in a friendly game of Monopoly."

Ginger seemed aroused by the challenge. "You'd better hold on to your valuables, your highness, and no, I don't mean those valuables."

This made Jeremy laugh out loud, and truly, happiness had been in such short supply that it was a relief to see it. And so the two of them passed the time playing their game, with dice rattled and thrown, followed by cajoling comments and the passing of mock money either to the bank for the purchase of properties or to the other player for rent on those already purchased. Really, it was quite intricate, and a shameless waste of an afternoon, but it also offered a quiet retreat from larger complications.

But as the afternoon lengthened, Ginger pressed strands of hair in her lips and, instead of studying the playing board, seemed more and more to be studying Jeremy.

She was plotting something, I was sure of it.

Jeremy, I said calmly, matter-of-factly, trying to mask my growing alarm. *We need to read and to study. Please suspend your game and ask her to return another day.*

But I was too late.

"To be continued," Ginger said, and pushed away from the library table.

"Just when it's getting good?" Jeremy said, but his voice trailed off. He was watching her as she stretched lazily and began to wander about the bookstore.

"That your grandfather's pipe wrench?" she asked, drawing close to a large open-jawed tool hanging from a bookcase stile.

166

"Yeah," Jeremy said, drifting over. "It was the first one he bought when he became a pipe fitter. Even after he retired, he still took it down and used it sometimes. He said the nice thing about a pipe wrench is that it doesn't lose much in its dotage."

Ginger made a murmuring laugh, and they stood quietly, side to side.

Jeremy, I said. *Our reading.*

In a soft voice, she said, "You know what I was thinking about?"

"What?"

"That goofy legend about falling for whoever you look at when you have a first bite of Prince Cake."

"Yeah?"

"Yeah. Because . . . I don't know . . . sometimes it doesn't feel so goofy. I mean, sometimes I feel like something I don't understand keeps—you know—pulling at me."

Jeremy went looking for the literal meaning in this. "You mean like something *magnetic* or *invisible* or—"

But Ginger touched a finger to his lips to keep him from speaking further. She leaned nearer. Very softly she whispered, "Close your eyes."

"What?"

With a finger, she gently touched one of his eyelids. "Close your eyes."

He did. He closed his eyes, and as she stood regarding him in the empty store, the only sound to be heard was the *tickentock* of the clock and—did I not hear it? was this not what I had feared?—the beating of two hearts.

Ginger now closed her own eyes, but just as she drew her lips feather-close to his, there came a robust *thump! thump! thump!* from the front door.

Jeremy's and Ginger's eyes flew open and there, peering through the glass of the door, was the square-jawed face of the town mayor.

§

§

As he stepped into the bookstore, the mayor removed his cowboy hat and flashed a broad smile at Ginger. "Hope I didn't come at an inopportune time," he said, and turned at once to Jeremy. "It's just that I've been doing my *due diligence*, and, well, let's just say that time is of the essence."

Dauntless Crinklaw was like a stretched-long version of his son—where Conk was blocky, his father was tall and lean—but they both shared the same white teeth, square jaw, and dark eyes, which he now directed again at Ginger. "The thing is," he said, "I need to talk a little business with Mr. Johnson here."

"No problem," Ginger said, ignoring the mayor's hint and draping herself comfortably across the arm of the stuffed chair.

"*Personal* business," the mayor said.

Ginger turned to Jeremy, who shrugged.

"Okay," she said, heading for the door. "I don't stay where I'm not wanted."

The mayor's laughter was so sharp it seemed to crackle.

"Well, that's good sense," he said. "I wouldn't make it my personal motto or anything, but, still, it's good sense." Then, after watching her slip through the door, he turned back to Jeremy. "Fine girl. Smart as a whip. Conk's nuts about her, but I don't encourage it. He'd bore that girl in a year, if not sooner." He shrugged. "Probably anybody would." A grin spread across his broad jaw. "What do you think?"

"I don't really know," Jeremy said.

"No, a'course you don't!" the mayor said in his booming voice. "Nobody does! It's all by guess and by golly, though we hate like heck to admit it. Right?"

Jeremy said he guessed so, sure.

The mayor looked around the store for a few seconds, as if frankly assessing things. Then his eyes fixed on Jeremy. "You know why I'm here, right?"

"Not really."

"Well, okay, then, I'll tell you. I'm here to save your bacon."

Jeremy stared at him.

"That's right," the mayor said. "I'm your white knight."

"I don't think I understand."

"Well, let's see. As I understand it, come Friday at one p.m., you and your father are out on the street, right?"

"What?"

"Sure. Conk mentioned it, so I looked into it. The bank sent you final notice. Certified mail. You got that, right?"

Jeremy's eyes dropped. "Maybe. I don't open them all."

"Don't open them? Holy Harry, boy! I heard you was smart!"

Jeremy said nothing.

"Well, okay, look here. What that last letter says is that if you don't pay off your note in full by one p.m. Friday, they're going to ask you to vacate. And if you don't go quiet, the sheriff will forcibly remove you and your possessions and lock you right out." He gave a sympathetic murmur. "As scenarios go, son, it isn't pretty."

Jeremy went to the desk, found the most recent envelope, tore it open, and read the letter, as did I, over his shoulder. Everything the mayor had said was true. "Oh my gosh," Jeremy said in a small voice. "Friday. That's . . . the day after tomorrow."

"Well, yeah, but listen here. This is where your white knight rides in." He grinned. "I'm going to loan you that money."

"You will?" Jeremy said. And then: "Why?"

The mayor scaled back his wide smile. "Okay. I'm not going to lie to you, son. I wouldn't mind owning this building myself, and I'd just as soon not go through the bank to get it. I know those jaspers. They're difficult." He turned the rim of his hat in his hands. "Now, Conk tells me you might go on some quiz-show deal and answer questions about fairies and such, and that's just fine. And if you make a pot of money, you can pay me back without a single penny's interest and keep your store and live happily ever after."

"And if I can't pay you back?" Jeremy asked.

"Well, then, you don't owe me a dime, but I get the building."

Jeremy still seemed puzzled. "But why do you want it?"

The mayor laughed. "Hellfire, son, that's just what I *do*. I *acquire* things." He nodded at the game Jeremy and Ginger had been playing. "It's just like Monopoly. You try to buy stuff up. So right now I own all the other buildings on the block, and if I was to buy this one, I'd have me a nice little monopoly. *¿Comprendo?*"

Jeremy thought about this. "And if you get it, will you keep it a bookstore?"

Dauntless Crinklaw sighed. "I'll tell you what, son. Thirty years ago you might have kept it as a bookstore and made a few dollars, but not today. And just because that don't make you or me happy don't mean it's not true."

Again the only sound in the bookstore was the *tickentock* of the old clock.

"What will you do with it, then?"

Dauntless Crinklaw released one of his crackly laughs. "Maybe nothing. But maybe something. My granddaddy had this crazy idea of taking all the buildings together and using those old hot springs out back to run a fancy spa to cater to high muckety-mucks, or at least their aging brides." He was again grinning. "I said crazy, but sometimes it don't seem so crazy, if you know what I mean." He paused. "But what I do with it isn't the issue at hand. The issue at hand is my lending you the money so you can keep the place long enough to give yourself a shot at paying it off."

The mayor unfolded a document and laid a pen on the library table. At the top it said PROMISSORY NOTE. "This is absolutely no-interest, you understand. You buy some time, but you don't pay a penny."

Jeremy was staring at the document. "How much time?"

"Six weeks," the mayor said.

Jeremy touched a finger to his temple.

It is not good, I said, *but the alternative is worse. This gives you a small reprieve. If you go on the show, we can win the money.*

"We can win the money," Jeremy repeated in a small voice.

"We?" the mayor said. "Who's *we?*"

Jeremy did not answer. He stared out the window for a long time. Then he turned, picked up the pen, and signed his name to the promissory note.

There was another line for his father's signature. "My dad's gone right now," Jeremy said. "I'll have him sign when he gets back."

"And that won't be a problem?" the mayor asked.

"No," Jeremy said. He was looking down at the floor. "It won't be a problem."

"I hope you're satisfied," Jeremy said the moment the mayor stepped from the shop.

Wie bitte? I said, and repeated it in English: *Pardon me?*

"Now I have to hope the game show calls me. And if they do, I have to go on."

But think of it, Jeremy. This is a chance to be free of debt. To restore quietude to your life. To return to our summer classics and prepare for university.

For a long while, Jeremy stared out onto Main Street, and then finally he sighed and said, "I think I need to be alone for a while, Jacob."

Well! At least the Boultinghouse girl and I agreed on this much: we would not stay where we were not wanted. And so I ventured out, enshrouded in my own dour mood, a wanderer without intentions. For a time, I caught a breeze from the south, and then I allowed a gliding trio of starlings to draw me along. Presently, I heard waves of clamorous cheering, and I followed it to the knolltop home of Mayor Crinklaw.

In his wide, shaded yard, a crowd of agitated young villagers had gathered in a tight circle, watching something. Conk Crinklaw was among the onlookers, and so were Ginger's two girlfriends, but I did not see Ginger herself.

As I slipped close, I discovered why. Ginger lay on her back on the ground opposite a boy I recognized as one of Conk's churlish friends. They lay with their heads at reverse ends, and their hips evenly aligned. Both wore expressions of confidence.

Some kind of event was about to ensue, for the boy sat forward and, staring at Ginger, made a strange pronouncement: "My name is Burpo Bowen. You, Ginger Boultinghouse, have insulted the universe. Prepare to die."

The girlfriends hooted at this. "How did she insult the universe, Burpo?"

"By beating *him*," Burpo Bowen said, tipping his gaze toward another of Conk's friends, a tall boy with stiff, strawlike hair, who looked deeply abashed. Burpo Bowen said, "Thoust girly-girl shall not beat a maley-male in a manly-man sporting event." He blinked slowly. "And so it is written."

"Well, it just got erased!" Maddy said, and the boy on the ground said, "And I am about to rewrite it in idyllics."

"*Italics*, you idiot," Ginger said. "And oh, by the way . . . no, you're not."

Another of Conk's friends stepped in. "Ladies and gentlemen," he announced, "for the global championship of Never Better County, we have Ginger Boultinghouse, the temporary

173

champeen, and Burpo Bowen, her worthy challenger." He glanced at Ginger and the boy, both now lying flat on the ground, their nearest arms interlinked. "All right, contestants," he said, rhythmically chopping his hand through the air, "one . . . two . . ."

As he counted, the two rivals each raised a leg up into the air like an inverted pendulum. Twice they swung past each other. On the third such swing, their legs suddenly interlocked, and each contestant began straining to pull the other forward.

The boy grunted and heaved.

Ginger, to my very great surprise, began to smile.

The boys in the crowd shouted, "Do it, Burpo!" and "Nail her, dude!" and more of that sort of inane encouragement.

Ginger yawned, then flipped the boy ferociously forward, where he lay sprawled on the lawn.

Ginger's girlfriends exploded with shrieks of laughter. The boys stared in stony silence. Ginger rose and, with a pitying look, extended the boy on the ground a hand. "My condolences, Burpatoid."

Burpo Bowen was not a gracious loser. He batted away her hand, pushed himself up, and slipped sulkily to the back of the gathering.

"Well," Ginger said, dusting off her shorts and looking around, "I guess that concludes the festivities."

After a still moment, somebody said, "Not quite."

The crowd parted as Conk Crinklaw strode forward.

A mischievous grin spread across Ginger's face. "Really?"

Conk gave his broad shoulders a modest shrug. "I've done a little of this Indian leg-wrestling thing." He gave his friends a wink of the eye. "And I don't ever recall getting beat."

"Not until now," Ginger said pleasantly.

"Well, let's just us see," Conk said, and lowering himself onto the ground, he began methodically to stretch this way and that.

His confidence seemed warranted. The boy was the quintessential specimen of brutal power—all muscle and gristle and grit. I found myself fearing that Ginger might actually get hurt.

And so, when the legs again began to swing and the count again reached three, I was not surprised when in that first flashing instant, Conk pulled Ginger quickly forward. But it was only for a moment. In the next instant, Ginger had regained her position, and their upright legs were locked in a state of fiercely resistant equilibrium.

Three times Conk gathered himself and with a great throaty grunt launched a surging offensive.

Three times these attempts had no effect whatsoever on Ginger.

In truth, while Conk strained and grunted and his friends coaxed and cajoled, Ginger seemed to be studying the clouds overhead. After a time, she held out an open hand and said, "Beverage, please."

One of the girlfriends gave her a bottle of water, from which she sipped while Conk again groaned and heaved and strained to overcome her.

But Ginger, holding Conk's leg steadily in place, merely passed back the water and said, "Napkin, please," and, with Conk still straining and red-faced, she daintily daubed her lips.

Mein Gott! She was trifling with the boy! Even Conk's friends grew quiet.

"Had enough, Conklodite?" Ginger teased after a time.

"Just . . . going . . . to . . . ," the boy huffed, "ask . . . you . . . the . . . same . . . question."

His face had moved beyond red to purple, and truly, it seemed his bulging eyes might pop from their sockets.

"You could call Ouchies," Ginger teased. "I could mercy you if you called Ouchies."

This was too much for Conk, who, straining harder, said, "Why . . . don't . . . you . . . just . . . go . . . ."

Well! Whatever indecorous remark was about to spill from his lips Ginger preempted with a pull of her leg that was as startling for its suddenness as for its ferocity.

It was a thing to see! Conk Crinklaw flew forward, as if flung from a catapult, and landed flat on his back with a severe *whump!*

The girlfriends filled the air with loud whoops, and it took several moments for the shock on Conk's face to drain away. He sat up and looked around questioningly, as if wondering how he, Conk Crinklaw, could possibly have come to this. But Conk Crinklaw was no Burpo Bowen. He rose, grinned, and with as much graciousness as he could muster, shook Ginger's hand.

"That was flat-out impressive," he said. His square-jawed grin widened slightly. "And you know what you won, don't you?"

"What's that?"

"A big ol' smoochy kiss from the likes of me."

Once the ensuing raucous laughter began to wane, Ginger said, "Sounds more like the booby prize."

Conk grinned and said he'd always been partial to the booby prize himself, which drew more hooting laughter from his friends.

This raucous interplay went on a while and might have gone

on a good deal longer had Deputy McRaven's patrol car not wheeled around the corner. The deputy slowed the vehicle and stared pointedly at the young people until one of Conk's friends called out, "Loverly day, ain't it, Deputy?"

Deputy McRaven stared at them another long moment before moving slowly on. Once his patrol car had turned the corner, Ginger said, "That guy is *everywhere*. It's like there are three of him or something."

No one responded to this, but Burpo Bowen said, "Know why McRaven has never gone to Disneyland?" and before anyone could speak, he answered his own question: "Because he's not tall enough to get on any of the rides!"

This struck everyone as richly comical, though I myself had no knowledge of what this Disneyland might be, nor of the rides for which the deputy might be judged too short. In any case, it was poor timing that Frank Bailey should pass by at this boisterous moment. He carried a Green Oven Bakery bag and walked head down, as if lost in thought. If he saw the gathering in the mayor's yard, he gave no indication of it.

"Hey, Frank, how're you doing?" Burpo Bowen called out in a false, bright tone, and when Frank Bailey looked up, Burpo said with exaggerated politeness, "You'll be glad to know you're looking more like a cream puff every day."

It took a moment for these words and the laughter that followed them to deliver their sting. Then Frank Bailey again ducked his head and trudged forward, as if cruelty, like rain or wind, was just another element he had learned to move through.

"Don't rush off!" Burpo called. "It's not that often we get to see a real, live Frankopotamus!"

Harsh laughter followed, but once it was quiet, Ginger fixed her eyes on Burpo Bowen and said, "You'd be more interesting, Burpo, if you had a brain."

"Ouch," somebody said, but before the banter could be taken further, Ginger broke away from the group and headed through the yard gate.

"Hey, where're you going?" Marjory called after her.

Ginger stopped and turned. Her face was stone. "To Jeremy's," she said, her gaze moving from one girlfriend to the other. "Want to come?"

The girlfriends lowered their eyes.

"Okay, then," Ginger said in a tone that seemed to mix disappointment with acceptance. "See ya."

In a few long, purposeful strides, she rounded the corner out of view.

"Weirder by the day," said Marjory, and Maddy replied, "I'd say by the minute."

Conk Crinklaw stared at the corner Ginger had just turned, then finally broke his gaze, manufactured his trademark grin, and said to those who remained, "Okay, what'll it be? Pitch horseshoes, shoot pool, or swim at Klimmer's Bridge?"

Maddy said, "We don't have our suits," and Conk Crinklaw, slipping mischief into his voice, grinned at her and said, "That settles it then. We swim at Klimmer's Bridge."

§

§

178

When I found Ginger, she had caught up to the baker's apprentice from behind. "Hey, Frank," she said.

"Leave me alone," he said over his shoulder.

"Burpo's an idiot, Frank." She stepped in front of him to cut him off. "It makes a difference whether the person insulting you is an idiot or not."

Frank Bailey peered at her from his white doughy face. "It's okay. I'm kind of used to it. And it's not them. It's this place, which is why . . ." But then his expression stiffened and his voice trailed off.

"Which is why what?" Ginger asked.

Frank Bailey was looking at her with the abashed yet yearning look I'd seen on his face when he watched from within the shadows of the bakery that day as Jeremy, Ginger, and her two girlfriends left the bakery. "You'd never understand," he said.

"I might."

Again he seemed on the verge of saying something, but he did not. He just ducked his head, stepped around her, and continued walking toward his home.

Ginger watched him for a moment, then turned back toward Main Street.

I looked from one to the other, and followed Frank Bailey. I could not help myself. I was intrigued by the secret he would not speak.

Listen, if you will, I said when I drew alongside him.

Nothing. No response whatever.

I tried it more loudly: *Listen, if you will.*

Still nothing. He walked on, pulling at one ear and occasionally expelling a deep breath. He crossed over to a dirt lane and turned up a buckling stone walkway to a small house in terrible need of paint.

"Is that you, then?" his mother called out when he entered.

Frank Bailey gave a murmuring assent, and his mother appeared from another room, her fading hair pulled tight to her skull, her skin aged by cold and wind and worry. I knew a little of her story. She had come from Scotland in her late girlhood and, prettier then, and livelier, she quickly found a husband whose work for the railroad initially kept him away a few days at a time, and then a few weeks and a few months. And then, at about the time that Frank, their only child, gained *Pubertät*, the railroad man was gone for good. There were citizens who said it was because he could not face the kind of dainty boy his son had become. Not just one or two said this but many.

"Pastries, then?" she said, peering into the paper bag Frank Bailey had just presented her. "From Mr. Blix?"

"Mmm," the boy said as if he was speaking here and thinking somewhere else. He pulled at his earlobe, stretched its flesh.

"He's a nice man, Mr. Blix," she said, and the boy nodded distractedly.

Mrs. Bailey put a kettle on the stove, and they did not speak again until she poured boiling water into a teapot.

"So?" she said as she rearranged her empty cup.

"Pardon?" he said, brought back from his thoughts.

"You're tugging at your ear, then, aren't you? So I guess you have something to say."

"Oh." The boy broke off a section of a small cake dusted with powdery sugar. "Mr. Blix gave me a funny choice today."

Mrs. Bailey looked up from her steeping tea. "A funny choice, you say?"

"Mmm. He said I could stay here and work with him, which he said he would like. And I would, too." He swallowed. "But he also said that there's a really good cooking school in California. He said if you graduate from this school, you can get a good position anywhere in the world."

Mrs. Bailey seemed to be studying her son.

"He meant it, Mother. He's been watching me in the kitchen." He looked down. "He thinks I have a talent."

"This school," she said. "How in the world would we pay for it?"

The boy regarded the bit of cake in his hands. "Mr. Blix said he would pay for it," he said, and then looked directly at his mother. "I know how you are about charity, but he said once I have a position, I can pay it back bit by bit."

Mrs. Bailey watched him. "Why would he do that?"

"Because he's nice, and because he really does believe I can be—I don't know—a *master baker* or something." The boy took a breath. "And also because he said he knows"—and now something crumpled in the boy's face, and the look that it left there was heart-wrenching—"he said he knows what it's like to be . . . misfitting." A moment passed. "That's why he left Sweden."

Mrs. Bailey looked off.

In a small voice, the boy said, "Maybe he'd come back—you know, the old man—if I was gone."

Her face hardened. She shook her head.

"He might, though," the boy said.

"No. It wasn't you at all. He just wasn't the right kind of a man for being a father or a husband, either one."

"No, Mom. It was me. He couldn't stand the sight of me. He just couldn't."

This time, she did not argue. "California," she said.

"Mmm."

Her face broke down, too. It seemed she might cry. "You wouldna' come back, then?"

"Yes, I would," he said. "Even if I didn't live here, I would always come back, you know"—there was a slight crack in his voice—"to wherever you are."

Oh, the tender misery here! I could not bear it, and took my leave.

§

§

When I returned to the bookstore, Ginger was rapping frantically at the locked door. She cupped her hands to each side of her face and peered through the window and then knocked again, harder. She had balled her hand into a fist to pound even louder when the door swung open and Jeremy stood before her.

He seemed both glad to see her and amused at her agitation. "A little chill factor might be good here," he said. "Just a suggestion."

Ginger's expression relaxed. "I know. I kind of overreacted." She breathed in and out. "It's just that I was with Conk and all of them, and all of a sudden I wished I was with you and then creepy McRaven was parked right over there"— she glanced across the street—"and so I waited for-freaking-ever for him to leave and then you didn't come to the door right away and . . ."

Jeremy brought her a tall glass of water. Once she had sipped from it and settled into the overstuffed armchair, she relaxed and told him about her gratifying leg-wrestling competition (though she deleted mention of Conk's assertion that she had won a "big ol' smoochy kiss"). Jeremy told her about the mayor's visit, including the promissory note he had signed (though he omitted Mayor Crinklaw's observation that Conk was nuts for Ginger).

"So, how'd you beat Conk and those guys? Conk's pretty strong."

Ginger pretended indignation. "I'm pretty strong, too, just for the record, or at least my legs are. Plus I'm super flexible. I mean, have you seen me do the splits?" She illustrated by lowering herself to the floor with one leg extending forward from the torso and the other leg behind. "And straddle split," she said to herself, extending her legs to left and right.

Why she did not yelp in pain I could not say.

She held her position but glanced toward the telephone. "I guess the show didn't call."

Jeremy shook his head.

"They'll call," she said. "They will. I just know it."

And, truly, something in my ancient soul went out to the girl, so badly did she want to believe her own words.

Jeremy idly rattled the dice in their little cup, Ginger drifted over, and soon they went back to their game of Monopoly. Ginger had just moved her marker—a small silver terrier—seven squares to one of her own properties when she said, "Oh! I do have a little bit of good news."

Jeremy dropped the dice into the cup. "Yeah?"

She nodded. "The baker wants us to work for him tomorrow morning."

"But I thought he wasn't supposed to—"

"I know, but he has a plan so nobody'll know. He didn't tell me what plan—he just said he had a plan. We're supposed to go to the bakery a little after seven-thirty and act like we're customers."

"I don't get it. How do we work for him without—"

But Jeremy's question hung in the air, because the storefront door swung open and in walked Jenny Applegarth, followed by a man who was barely recognizable as Jeremy's father.

§

§

"Wow," Jeremy murmured, and Ginger said, "Yeah, me too. Zounds, even."

Jenny Applegarth glowed with well-being; Mr. Johnson appeared happy but dazed. His face was shaved clean, his hair was trimmed, and he was wearing nice clothes, smart and neatly pressed. He looked ten years younger, and almost handsome.

"Where'd you get the clothes?" Jeremy asked his father, but it was Jenny Applegarth who answered.

"Oh, those," she said. "I had them in a closet at home." She gave a small, frisky laugh. "Seems a couple of my exes were the

184

same size as Harold here." She turned to Jeremy's father. "That scare you, Harold? That you're just the right size for me?"

Mr. Johnson's face sent contradictory signals: he beamed with pride while shaking his head as if to say, *Why would a woman speak like that in public?*

"I'm not real scared, no," he said.

Jenny Applegarth regarded him approvingly. "It's a whole new Harold," she said, and then, turning back to Jeremy, went on, "Oh, and by the way—he's also gainfully employed."

Jeremy's father nodded. "Yep. Elbow needed a busboy at the café. Except what he got is more of a bus*man*, I guess."

Jeremy stared in astonishment at his transformed father. "And how do you feel about that—about being a bus . . . man?"

"Good," Mr. Johnson said. First he smiled happily at Jenny Applegarth. Then he smiled at Ginger. When he turned to Jeremy, his smile turned earnest. "Real good, in fact."

§

§

The following morning, Jeremy and Ginger arrived at the Green Oven Bakery promptly at 7:30. There were several customers already there, all older women, and their collective bearing grew stiff when Jeremy and Ginger walked in. The rotund baker, however, greeted them as always.

"*Hallå! Hallå!*" he called out. "Is it not a great day to be alive?"

"If you say so," Ginger said pleasantly, as she always did, but one of the older women shook her head and another said in a stage whisper, "*Impudence!*"

The baker pretended not to notice the women's irritation, and soon Jeremy and Ginger were enjoying coffee so rich, cream so heavy, and pastries so golden-glazed that I myself was treated to a large serving of envy. The baker stood nearby enjoying the pleasure they took in his wares.

"Good?" he said, beaming.

Ginger laughed. "Let's leapfrog *good* and go straight to *fabulous*."

The baker's round face glowed.

The older women paid their bill and exited in arch silence.

"Oh, my," the baker said, watching them go. "The women were chilly this morning." He turned to Jeremy and Ginger. "But they can also be friendly and generous. I'm sure you'll see their better side again someday."

"Right now," Ginger muttered, "their better side is their big-behind side as they're walking away."

A laugh rumbled up from the baker's ample belly. "Charity, charity," he sang out, and then, casting a quick look toward the door to be sure they were alone, he said, "And where did you leave your bicycles?"

"At the park," Ginger said, and Jeremy said that he had walked.

"Good! Then it is time to put you to work!"

"Here?" Ginger said. "Won't everyone know?"

The baker merely chuckled. "This way," he said, and led Jeremy and Ginger through the counter and into the kitchen, where Frank Bailey was brushing butter over a large pan of hot rolls. He turned and smiled, at home here among the ovens and rolling pins, happy as I had never seen him happy before.

"Pardon us, Frankie," the baker said. "We're just heading to the storerooms." Though before moving on, the baker took a moment to examine the pink frosting Frank Bailey was about to apply to the raspberry cuts.

Well, while the baker is occupied, let me describe his kitchen. It smelled divine, of course, and shiny racks, counters, and ovens lined the room, but what drew the eye, amidst all this gleaming steel, was the cylindrical green-brick oven that rose from the center of the room. The craftsmanship of its slightly concave surfaces was obvious, and the oven itself was enormous—its door large enough to admit a full-grown man. So remarkable, in truth, was this oven that Jeremy and Ginger stared at it as if spellbound.

"Perfection, Frankie!" the baker was saying about the pink frosting. "You really do have the gift!" Frank Bailey beamed at the compliment, and then the baker, gesturing to Jeremy and Ginger, said, "This way, please," and led them through an accordion metal door into an elevator.

"You're in charge, Frankie!" the baker sang back to his helper and then, with a push of a button, the caged compartment began slowly to descend.

"Zounds," Ginger said. "This is pretty fabuloso." And Jeremy asked, "Where're we going?"

"Down to the storerooms," the baker said, and again his cheeks were glowing. It was endearing, this pride that he took in his bakery and its complex inner works.

In another moment, the elevator opened onto a stone-lined tunnel.

"After you," the baker said.

The passage was so dry and well lit it seemed more a corridor than a tunnel.

"Where *are* we?" Jeremy said. "Are we going north under the alleyway?"

The baker held a finger to his lips. "Our little secret," he said, and just then the passage opened into a great, softly illuminated chamber. A series of three metal doors ran along one of its concrete-lined walls, and four simple wooden chairs hung from pegs on another wall. At the far side of the room a long, spiraling, metal-lined chute descended from an unseen point overhead.

"Wow," Jeremy said quietly. "Is this a basement?"

"Yes, yes," the baker said with twinkling eyes. "It is how it is done in Sweden. With thick walls, the temperature is almost constant, so it is an excellent place to store goods year-round."

He unlocked two of the three metal doors. Each revealed a large storage room paved with white ceramic tiles and lined with sturdy metal shelves.

"These are two of my storerooms," he said. "I need you to scrub the floor and walls and shelves to make them suitable for the storage of baking supplies."

"Are you kidding?" Ginger said. "They already look freakishly clean."

The baker was carrying a bucket filled with cleaning supplies. He set the bucket down and removed three of the chairs that hung from pegs in the wall. "Sit," he said genially, "and I will tell you a story."

And once they were seated, he said, "This is the story of the mouse who slew the baker," and he rubbed at his white beard while he assembled his thoughts. "All right, then . . . Once upon a time, there was a baker's apprentice who was so splendid at his baking that his master feared to lose him. He kept him locked inside the kitchen day and night. The boy had no friends except a brown mouse who lived in his coat pocket. 'What am I to do?' the boy would ask his mouse each night before falling to sleep. 'I do all the baking and I am locked in the kitchen and the master goes home to his beautiful wife.' And this was true. The apprentice's baked goods were so marvelous that each day they were delivered to the king himself, and because of this, the boy's master had grown rich and had married the village beauty. And so each night the boy would hold the brown mouse in his hand and ask, 'What am I to do?' and the mouse would say nothing.

"But one night, the brown mouse said, 'I have the answer.' The mouse asked the boy to pluck just one whisker from its nose. 'No, I will not,' the boy said, 'because it will cause you pain,' and the mouse said, 'But you must, and though it will cause me a moment of pain, it will bring you a lifetime of joy.' So the boy closed his eyes and plucked a single whisker from the mouse's nose and put a small poultice to the spot where the whisker was gone. It was a fine black whisker, and the next morning, as instructed by the mouse, the boy mixed it into the batter for the baker's famous walnut-and-raisin breakfast rolls, the very rolls the king ate to begin his every day. 'Ho! And what is this?' the king declared angrily as he drew the mouse whisker from his roll.

"And that, my dear young friends, was the end of the baker. The king bought no more of his goods, and soon no one else did, either. Before the next winter was over, the baker's beautiful wife had deserted him and the baker had grown old and died of grief."

Sten Blix smiled and let his twinkling blue eyes fall on Jeremy, then Ginger.

"So do you see how it is? One mouse whisker and I live unhappily ever after. That is why my storerooms must sparkle."

After a moment, Jeremy asked, "What happened to the apprentice?"

At this, the baker's blue eyes began to twinkle again. "Oh! What a sorry storyteller I am! I forgot the happy ending! So let me remember. . . . Ah, yes. . . . After his master died, the boy opened his own bakery in a nearby town, and one day the king's daughter, dressed as a peasant, stole away from the castle and walked all the way through the countryside to the nearby town, where she peered into his shop. The boy, seeing how pretty she was and knowing how penniless she must be, offered her a pastry. She took one bite, then another, and then she knew she was eating the very roll she had often been served at her father's table. 'I have no money,' she said, 'but I would like to take a whole plate of these rolls to my father.' 'Who is your father?' the boy asked, and the girl was careful in her reply: 'A broken man who once tasted such rolls and has not tasted one since.' Even dressed as a peasant, the princess was too beautiful to refuse. The boy gave her every roll he had. So she took the rolls to her father the king, and soon the apprentice was supplying the king and his court with baked goods." Sten Blix broke into a broad smile. "And before long, to the delight of all the king's subjects, the baker and the princess were wed and lived happily ever after."

They were all quiet a moment, then Jeremy said, "That's a good story. I've never heard it."

I had not heard the story, either, but it would be untrue to say I did not enjoy it. It was of the very kind that Wilhelm and I loved to collect.

Sten Blix gave a jolly laugh and seemed to drink in the appreciation on the faces of both Jeremy and Ginger. "Who knows?" he said. "It may be popular only among Swedish bakers."

He stood then and showed Ginger and Jeremy how to scrub the tiles until they shone. Once he had them started, he made to leave. "And now I will see how Frank Bailey is managing our bakery!"

But before he could go, Jeremy pointed to the third door, the one that the baker had not opened, and said, "What's in there?"

"Oh," the baker said, his eyes falling on the door. "Nothing, nothing. Please do not open it."

Again the baker made to leave, and again Jeremy stopped his progress. "Mr. Blix?"

"Yes?"

"You can't do that."

The baker seemed confused. "Can't do what?"

"You can't leave and tell us not to open the door, because that happens all the time in fairy tales and movies, and everyone knows that sooner or later whoever isn't supposed to open the door is going to open the door, and . . ."

"Yes?" the baker said.

"And that's when things start happening."

A laugh rumbled up from the baker's belly. Then he walked over to the third door and lifted the latch. He pushed the door gently open and stepped aside so that Jeremy and Ginger could peer in.

Well! This room was just like the other two, except that the gleaming shelves were already stacked with sacks of flour and sugar, baking soda and salt.

"Frank Bailey and I cleaned this one last week and loaded the shelves, which"—he winked—"you will know something about before your workday is over." He smiled at Jeremy. "I didn't mean to be mysterious. I just didn't want anything disturbed or any dust to get in. You understand?"

"Sure," Jeremy said. "Sorry."

The baker seemed unperturbed. "Not at all," he said, pulling the door closed again. "Perhaps it's been too long since I read a story or went to a movie."

He departed, and then, in this place of perfect coolness and quietude, Jeremy and Ginger set to work. The minutes passed slowly, but little by little the storerooms began to shine, and when the baker returned several hours later, he appeared delighted. "Well done," he said, beaming his blue eyes here and there. "*Very* well done."

He'd brought them fruit nectar, along with pastries, and again he seemed to enjoy nothing more than watching them eat. Then he said, "I suppose I should be sorry for you, the way the townspeople are treating you, but I think I am more sorry for our town, that they cannot see your better natures"—he smiled—"as I do. It is a shame that they spend their time shunning two young people of whom they should, in fact, be proud."

It had grown quiet as the baker made this little speech, and he had to laugh at himself. "There!" he said. "I am too serious sometimes."

And not a moment later, with a sudden *shush*, a large bag of flour came sliding down the spiraling metal chute in the middle of the room, and soon after it, several more—*shush, shush, shush*.

"Aha!" the baker said merrily, and you might have thought it was Christmas. "Our goods are delivered!" And then, calling up toward the top of the gleaming chute, "Keep them coming slow but sure, Frankie!"

So they again set to work. From the garage of the baker's house (I slipped up the spiraling chute to observe this myself), Frank Bailey pulled the bags of flour from the Green Oven Bakery van and gave them a gentle nudge that sent them sliding easily down the chute to the great room below, where the baker waited. He smiled and made happy *oof*ing sounds as he hoisted the bags onto a cart, which Ginger pushed to the storeroom. There Jeremy heaved the bags up onto the shelves. For the higher shelves, he used a ladder, and Ginger, who strained no more (and very possibly less) than Jeremy, held the bags over her head for him to take. By the time they were done, their faces glowed with perspiration.

"Well done!" the baker said, smiling first at Jeremy and then at Ginger. "We are an excellent team!"

Well, there can be no denying the pleasure of hard work properly done, and after Ginger and Jeremy slipped away from the bakery carrying bags of lemon and raspberry cuts, Ginger said, "That was almost fun."

"Yeah, it was."

"Also remunerative," she said, leaning into him gently, for this was one of their classical vocabulary words. And it was true. The baker had again paid them a generous sum.

"He's nice," she said. "I feel pretty bad I ever dreamt up the Pop Rocks thing."

"Yeah," Jeremy said. "Me too."

Several villagers stood in a cluster on the sidewalk before

them, casting stony glances their way, so Jeremy and Ginger crossed to the other side of the street, but then, seeing a patrol car on Main Street, they ducked into the alley.

It is Deputy McRaven, I told Jeremy. *When he saw you, he turned around.*

"What?" Jeremy said.

"What what?" Ginger said, and I said, *He turned around and is coming this way. It is all right, though. You are doing nothing wrong.*

But Jeremy made an impetuous split-second decision. "Quick," he said, lifting a lid from a trash container. "Get in! McRaven's coming."

"What?" Ginger said. "How do you—"

"Quick!" Jeremy said, and already he was climbing into another container and pulling the lid over his head.

Ginger did the same but peered out until the patrol car nosed into the alley, and then she eased the lid down, too. All of this made me uneasy. It created the appearance of guilt, for why would two people hide if they had done nothing wrong?

Deputy McRaven must have thought they had run, for he sped down the alley, and I thought all would be well, but then, upon reaching the street, he stopped and—*Mein Gott!*—started the car rolling slowly backward through the alley!

He is returning! I shouted to Jeremy, who relayed the news to Ginger. "Be quiet!" he said. "He's coming back!"

As the car drove through the alley in reverse, the deputy gazed into the rear doors of businesses and peered into every crevice and cranny. He slowed further as he passed the trash containers, and then . . . he stopped the car completely!

From his seat, he stared at the cluster of containers. He

turned off the engine to listen for sounds. After a moment, he said quietly, "I know you're in there, Mr. Johnson. And the thing is, I'm going to start shooting some rats right now, and I'd hate for anyone hiding in a trash can to get hurt." He waited. "Okay," he said. "Gun out. I begin firing at the count of three."

He does not have his gun out! I shouted to Jeremy, and wondered if he could hear me from inside the container, and wondered, too, what good it would do because Ginger could not hear anything at all.

"Okay," the deputy said quietly. "One. Two. *Three!*"

Deputy McRaven stared at the trash containers.

Neither Ginger nor Jeremy moved.

The deputy waited another few moments, then started the engine and continued his reversed course through the alley.

Finally, when the car was out of sight, I shouted the news to Jeremy.

"Quick!" he said to Ginger. "He's gone!"

They tumbled out of the trash cans and began to run.

§

§

Why did you hide, Jeremy?

We were back in the bookstore, the children's laughter over their escapade having finally been spent.

Jeremy, composed now, did not quite answer my question. He

merely rephrased it. "You know what's funny?" he said. "I'm not even sure why we hid."

"I do," Ginger said. "When a predator hunts you, you either run or hide. It's called instinct."

"But the truth is, we weren't doing anything wrong."

Ginger set her backpack on the floor. "With McRaven, you're always doing something wrong. If he'd found us, he would've cited some ordinance about going through people's trash." Then she held her head still and wrinkled her nose. "What's that smell?" She sniffed at her bare arm. "Oh, my gosh! It's me! I smell like spoiled armadillo!"

"What does spoiled armadillo smell like?"

She brought her arm close to his face. "Like this. And oh, by the way"—she pinched her nose for effect—"you smell like a month-old coyote carcass." She took an exaggerated step back. "I'm putting you on a maggot watch."

Jeremy stared at her and said that she was just hilarious.

Still, it had to be admitted that his scent was robust.

Ginger looked down at her soiled, sweaty shirt and then up at Jeremy. "Maybe you could offer a girl a change of clothes and a hot shower."

I did not like the sound of this. *No, Jeremy,* I said. *That would be unwise.*

"I guess so," he said.

Jeremy! Your father is not here. You should say no to her idea. It is not appro—

Well! Jeremy had begun to whistle.

And so Jeremy brought Ginger a clean shirt and pair of shorts, and gave her a clean towel in order that she might bathe while he sat in the bookstore pretending to read *El Cid*. Before long, she presented herself in her slightly oversized clothes, looking just scrubbed and smiling and running a comb through her long, wet hair.

"Okay," she said. "That felt pretty terrific. You'll feel like a whole new you."

Jeremy set down his book and headed off for the shower.

And then, while Ginger was standing at the front window, combing her hair, the telephone rang.

For a moment, the sound froze her into statue-like stillness.

Then she set down her comb, flattened her hands to her eyes, whispered, "Please, God, please," and hastened across the room. She took one final deep breath, lifted the receiver, and sounding quite official, said, "Two-Book Bookstore."

It took only a second for her rosy freckled face to lose color. "Yes," she said in an oddly formal voice. "He's right here. Well, not right here. He's in the shower. But I'll get him."

She hurried to the bathroom, pounded on the door, and shouted for Jeremy, who appeared with soap in his hair and a towel wrapped around his waist.

"They called!" she said. "They're on the phone now! It's Milo Castle's assistant! He said he has Milo Castle on the line for Mr. Jeremy Johnson Johnson!"

Jeremy tightened the towel around his waist and went out front and put the phone to his ear. "Hello?" he said.

I could not hear what was being said to Jeremy, and little could be taken from his face. He offered only a series of stiff responses. "Yes, that's me . . . No, I'm standing up." He sat down and said, "Okay, now I'm sitting down . . . Really? . . . No, I'm just kind of surprised . . . No, I think I'm happy, I really do . . . No, no, I am. I just don't show it very well over the phone and I was in the shower so I'm kind of wet . . . Okay . . . Okay . . . Okay . . . I look forward to it, too . . . Okay . . . Bye."

After hanging up, Jeremy sat staring at the telephone. Then he turned to Ginger with a look of uncertain wonderment. "They want me on the show," he said.

Really. I must confess it: at these words, I shimmered with satisfaction.

"When?" Ginger said. Actually, she screamed. She was quite excited.

"A week from tomorrow." He paused. "Mr. Castle said they'll be sending a big black car."

"A big black car?" Ginger whooped and laughed and paced the bookstore grinning and shaking her head. "You nailed it! You completely nailed it! And now somebody from Never Better's going on a national quiz show, which is a definite first." She threw her arms around Jeremy, tapped his nose with her finger, and then stood back. "And you know what else is a first?"

"What?"

"That's the first time I ever hugged a boy wearing only a towel."

Jeremy, who seemed to have forgotten his manner of dress, began to blush, which only increased Ginger's pleasure in the circumstance—she laughed a merry laugh. But then, at this jovial moment, a shadow passed the window.

It was Jeremy's father, home from his work at the café.

"Don't tell him about the show!" Jeremy said in a tight whisper as he made for the back door.

"Why not?" Ginger said, but by this time Jeremy was gone

and his father had swung open the bookstore's front door. He looked weary, but upon seeing Ginger, he straightened himself and smiled.

"Hello there," he said, and then looked around. "Where's Jeremy?"

Ginger, normally unflappable, appeared almost panic-stricken. "He's taking a shower," she said, then added, "We had work today and got pretty sweaty." She seemed to want to stop talking, but could not. "So I took a shower," she said. "And now he is."

Jeremy's father seemed confused. His gaze, drifting about the store, found the water on the floor near the telephone. "How come it's all wet?"

"Oh, that," Ginger said, glancing at the glistening floor. "That's not anything. He just had to come out and take a phone call."

Mr. Johnson's face clouded further, and Ginger said, "It was okay, though. He was wearing a towel." When that only added to Mr. Johnson's confusion, she blurted, "He's going on that show! That *Uncommon Knowledge* show!"

Well! It was true that Mr. Johnson was completely distracted from his earlier questions and concerns, but solving one problem only presented another, and when he pressed the girl for details about Jeremy's appearance on *Uncommon Knowledge*, she had no choice but to give them. She must have been sorry for this, for when she was done, she said, "You have to keep it a secret, though, because he asked me not to tell you."

But Mr. Johnson was feeling so proud of his son and so heartened by their brightened prospects, he seemed barely to hear her words.

"Sure," he said. "Sure."

§

§

The following week passed slowly, in a state of uneasy anticipation. Jeremy told no one about his upcoming participation in the show. He and I studied the tales. Ginger often dropped by to encourage him, but she never stayed so long that he (and I) could not continue our preparation.

One thing should be mentioned. On the third or fourth day of our studying period, I witnessed a bittersweet scene involving young Frank Bailey.

It was well before dawn, and I was drawn down from my belfry by the headlights of the Green Oven delivery truck pulling up in front of Mrs. Bailey's tumbledown cottage.

It was a warm, moonless night, and as Mrs. Bailey, Frank Bailey, and the baker met on the sidewalk, they talked in hushed voices.

"*Hallå*, Mrs. Bailey," the baker said, "is it not a great day to be alive?" and then, stowing the boy's suitcase in the van, "So, Frankie, are you ready for your grand adventure?"

The boy nodded. The plan, I learned, was for the baker to drive Frank Bailey to the airport, two hundred miles away. From there, the boy would fly west to San Francisco, where his enrollment in the fine cooking school had already been arranged, thanks to the baker's largesse. In the boy's attitude I could see two distinct and opposing elements at work: the immediate sadness in taking leave of his mother, and the larger unfolding excitement of setting out on a course of his own.

"You'll write, then," Mrs. Bailey said, "and remember always who you are?"

"Yes, mother," the boy said.

"And you willna' forget your mother?"

He shook his head. He could see she was waiting for a hug, but the boy instead leaned close to give his mother's forehead a quick but slightly misguided kiss—in his awkwardness, it was more of a glancing bump.

They stood back. It was time to go, and yet Mrs. Bailey seemed so apprehensive that the baker was prompted to speak. "I'd ask you to ride along, but there are only the two seats." Then he had a thought: "But it would only take me a minute to run back to the house and put the rear seat in, and then we could all three go and there would still be room for supplies." He seemed to warm to the idea. "We'll make a day of it, Mrs. Bailey! We'll see the big city and I'll show you where I shop for provisions."

The baker was nodding now, as if liking the plan more and more, but Mrs. Bailey said, "No, no. A good-bye two hours before dawn or two hours after—it's all a good-bye."

Frank Bailey's face was illuminated for a moment when he got into the passenger's seat of the cargo van, then, when the door shut, his face fell into shadow. He waved from the window, and Mrs. Bailey waved, too, and did not stop waving until the beautiful old van turned from view. Even then she did not move. She stood and stood with her head slightly cocked until finally the last strains of the delivery truck's engine had been swallowed by the night. Only then did she turn and go back inside her little cottage.

The day before he was to appear on the show, Jeremy sat in the bookstore with the edition of the *Household Tales* that we had been poring over all week long.

"Knock, knock," Ginger called, poking her head in the front door. She entered with a box under her arm. "So," she said, "ready to nail your big oral exam?"

"I guess so."

"You *guess* so? C'mon, let's be thinking positive here!"

Jeremy made a wan smile. "The truth is, I have a really bad feeling about it."

Ginger laughed and shook her head. "The medical term for what you have is Early Onset Little-Old-Ladyism. But it's all going to work out *fabulously*."

Jeremy stared at her for a second, blinked, and went back to his studying.

After a while, Ginger said, "Everything I know about the Brothers Grimm I got from Disney movies—*Snow White* and *Sleeping Beauty* and *Cinderella*."

"I never saw those," Jeremy said. "And by the way, *Sleeping Beauty* isn't a Grimm Brothers."

Ginger ignored this correction. "Really and truly? You never saw the Disney movies? How'd you live to fifteen and manage that?"

He did not answer, and after a few seconds of silence, she said, "Hey, I've got one for you!" She set down her cardboard box and pretended to read from a card. "Question: How many frogs do you have to kiss before you find a prince?" She turned the imaginary card over. "Answer: Way too freaking many."

She laughed at her own joke, then held out the cardboard box for display. "Okay, I know you have me pigeonholed as a brainy athletic teenage love goddess, but today I stand before you in my new role as your . . . very . . . own . . . personal . . . *shopper!*"

Jeremy stared at her. "What does that mean?"

"It means I've been out shopping on your behalf." She opened the box and spread three new shirts across the library table, all in shades of blue.

"Pick one," she said, "and I'll take the other two back."

"How'd you pay for them?" Jeremy asked.

"With my grandfather's credit card." She grinned. "This will teach him to go to sleep and leave his wallet hidden in a secret compartment under the false bottom of his sock drawer." She shook her head in mock chagrin. "I call that just plain careless."

"A hard lesson," Jeremy said, playing along, "but one that has to be taught."

He had taken one of the shirts into his hands. They all looked expensive and up-to-the-minute. "Where'd you get them?"

Ginger named a shop in a town an hour's drive away. "Conk took me," she said.

Jeremy's grip on the shirt loosened slightly. "Did he help pick them out?"

203

"Are you kidding? I didn't even let him come into the store with me. His fashion sense is worse than yours, and that's going some." She looked from the shirts to Jeremy. "C'mon, aren't you going to try them on?"

"Can I do it later?"

She gave her head a slow shake. "You think I'm going to trust you to decide which one looks best? You're the guy recently seen in toucan blue."

"I thought you called it phosphorescent blue," he said, and she said, "Whatever."

Whatever? What, as a reply, can this possibly mean?

Jeremy slipped on the first shirt, which was a restrained shade of blue.

"Okay, that's a ten," Ginger declared, and eventually this was the shirt they chose, though she insisted he try on the other two, followed by a reprise of the first.

"Yep, that's the one," Ginger said. "That's the shirt that's going to turn you into a teenage heartthrob." She snapped her cinnamon gun and grinned. "What time's that big black car coming?"

"Seven a.m."

"Okay, then," Ginger said. "Don't let it leave the station without me."

§

§

"Just relax."

This was what the peppy female employee of the television company had just told Jeremy. "You have three or four minutes before you go on, so just relax."

Jeremy closed his eyes. He took deep breaths. He did not look relaxed.

I, on the other hand, was less apprehensive than excited. I am embarrassed to admit it, but I was looking very much forward to answering questions about myself.

To this point, everything had gone as planned. The television company's long black car was waiting for Jeremy at the bookstore well before seven. With very little crowding, Jeremy, his father, Jenny Applegarth, and Ginger were able to sit comfortably in the facing seats in the back. Jeremy was wearing his new blue shirt, and I must say, he looked quite handsome. When Conk Crinklaw happened by the bookstore in his red truck, Jeremy was clearly surprised.

"Just wanted to see you off," he said to Jeremy, and then, even more surprising, he said, "Hope you do good." Well, the grammar was poor, but the sentiment was kind. He offered his hand and Jeremy shook it. Then Conk had stood back, looked Jeremy over, and said, "At least they didn't dress you up as a fairy prince or some damned thing."

Suddenly, the peppy employee popped her head into the room. "Okay," she said. "It's showtime."

Jeremy was led to a dimly lighted stage with the curtains drawn closed. In the middle of the stage was a small room made of glass panels, though the front panel had been temporarily lowered. This was "the climate-controlled, soundproof booth." Inside the booth was a podium composed of clear glass. The woman positioned Jeremy behind the glass podium and instructed him to fold his hands on top of it so "you'll look calm"—a smile—"even if you aren't."

Jeremy did as he was told, and the woman gave him a nice smile. "You're going to do great, Jeremy," she said, "and have I mentioned that that shirt is to die for?"

An odd, nervous laugh escaped from Jeremy.

A moment later, overhead lights came bursting down with great intensity, and the curtains were pulled away. We saw nothing but could sense people breathing and murmuring in the darkness until, as if on cue, they fell completely silent.

"Thirty seconds," a voice within the booth said. "Stage lights."

The lights on the stage clicked abruptly off.

Jeremy, rigid in the darkness, touched his hand to his temple. *Everything is satisfactory*, I said. *We are perfectly fine.*

"We are totally screwed," he whispered.

At once, the voice within the booth shushed Jeremy and said, "Mike on, Jeremy! Mike on!" Then the voice said, "Five, four, three, two, one," and suddenly our booth blazed with light and a different voice, full and mellifluent, said, "Greetings, America! Today on *Uncommon Knowledge from the Common Man* we present the youngest contestant ever to appear on this stage, a boy just fifteen years of age with uncommon knowledge of the lives and tales of the Brothers Grimm. But first"—and now the whole stage was lighted and the voice climbed in register—"here is your host, Mis-ter Mi-lo Cast-le!"

Milo Castle strode into the light as applause burst from the audience, which was also now illuminated. Hundreds of beaming faces smiled up at us from the packed auditorium, and—what was this?—in the foremost row of chairs, Conk Crinklaw and his friends sat whistling and raucously carrying on! This was a pleasant surprise, for, otherwise, there were few representatives of the town. Ginger, Mr. Johnson, and Jenny Applegarth were there, of course, beaming with pride, and a few rows behind them sat Elbow Adkins, Sten Blix, and Mayor Crinklaw. There was one other pleasant surprise. Seated together toward the rear of the audience were Maddy and Marjory, whose presence, once discovered, would bring them certain punishment from their parents, yet here they were, smiling and clapping for Jeremy.

"Well, Jeremy Johnson Johnson," Milo Castle said, waving an arm toward the audience, "looks like you have quite a fan base."

Jeremy gave a stiff nod of the head. "It's kind of a surprise," he said softly.

"Speak right up, Jeremy," Milo Castle said. "We're all friends here."

"It was supposed to be a secret," Jeremy said, a little more forcefully.

"Tell your father that!" Mayor Crinklaw called from the audience, and clamorous laughter followed. But, if you will, a sad observation: If it was not a secret—and clearly it was not—then it was remarkable how much of the town had chosen to stay away, not that Milo Castle would want to say so.

He had some rectangular cards in his hands, and after looking at one, he said, "So, Jeremy, I understand you own a business called the Two-Book Bookstore. Does that mean you only sell two books?"

Jeremy nodded. "Actually, it's kind of only one book, but it comes in two volumes. It's my grandfather's autobiography."

"And what other businesses do you have there in that little

town of yours? Do you have the Two-Tire Tire Shop and the Two-Flower Flower Stand?"

These remarks were greeted with mild laughter from the audience, and Jeremy said, "No, sir."

"Well, how's business at the Two-Book Bookstore, Jeremy?"

"Not that great. That's the reason I wanted to be on your show, so I could pay off a loan that's due."

Milo Castle nodded. "And it says here that you live in the back of the bookstore with your father. Does he help you with the store, too?"

"No, he works in a restaurant."

Jeremy said this with such evident pride that Milo Castle asked a question without looking at his card. "Does your father run the restaurant?"

"Oh. No. He just does whatever Elbow Adkins asks him to do, like busing tables and stuff."

This would have been an even more awkward moment, but Elbow himself yelled from the audience, "And he only does that so he can flirt with a particular waitress!"—which, while not an especially witty remark, distracted everyone from the pathos of Jeremy's answer.

"Okay, Jeremy," Milo Castle said. "Enough visiting. Let's get down to business. You know how the game is played. In our studio in Boston, we have collected three internationally renowned experts on the Grimm Brothers and their tales"—here a vast screen to one side of the stage revealed two women and a man sitting in a book-lined study—"and they will be the final judges as to the correctness of your answers. Their green light means you've answered correctly and may go on; their red light means your answer is incorrect and the game is over. With each new question, the amount of your earnings doubles, and the questions get more difficult as we go. After the fourth question, you will have the choice to retire with your winnings or risk your earnings and go on. Answer seven straight questions correctly, and you will take home over *one hundred thousand dollars*! So, Jeremy, are you ready to play?"

Jeremy nodded. I will be truthful: he seemed frightened almost beyond speech.

I said, *Listen, if you will. Can you hear me, Jeremy?*

Again he nodded.

Milo Castle said rather theatrically, "Then we'll seal off your climate-controlled, soundproof booth and . . . start the game!"

A window in front of us slid up and sealed the booth closed.

"Can you hear me now, Jeremy?" Milo Castle asked.

In a voice that seemed barely to get out, Jeremy said, "Yes."

"Just speak up, then, Jeremy, and here we go." With a flourish, he said, "Your first question, for one thousand dollars: In several of the tales collected by Wilhelm and Jacob Grimm, a kiss casts off an enchantment. But in what tale is a frog thrown against a wall, finding himself immediately thereafter restored to a prince?"

I was answering the question even before it was completed, so that Jeremy, almost without a second's thought, could answer, "'The Frog King,' or 'Iron Heinrich.'"

The panel of experts nodded, a large green light illuminated brightly, and Milo Castle said, "That is correct! Now, question two, for two thousand dollars: What was the original title of Grimm's fairy tales, and for what audience was it intended?"

"Kinder und Hausmärchen," Jeremy said. "And it was meant for other scholars rather than children."

"Kinder and what?" Milo Castle said, looking toward the screen where the panel of experts could be viewed. I was not surprised when they nodded and the green light again brightened. One of the experts said, *"Kinder und Hausmärchen* is the German for *Children's and Household Tales*. So that is correct."

"Well done!" Milo Castle said, which, I will admit it, I found pleasing, indeed.

And so the questions continued until, after our fourth correct answer, Jeremy was asked whether he would like to retire with his eight thousand dollars or continue.

People were shouting from the audience. Though we could not hear them, we knew from having watched the show that they were shouting for us to go on. Well, that is how it is. The audience always does this—I cannot tell you why.

Still, I had to agree. Jeremy had not yet earned enough money to pay Mayor Crinklaw and retire the loan.

Let us answer one more, I said.

"One more question," Jeremy said.

Milo Castle nodded and smiled. "Okay, Jeremy . . . for sixteen thousand dollars, tell us what important change in Rapunzel's circumstances occurred in the first edition of the tales but was deleted in subsequent editions?"

Ach! I could have laughed! It was too easy!

Jeremy touched his fingers to his temples, I answered the question, and he said, "The fact that Rapunzel had become pregnant."

The experts smiled and nodded, the green light shone, and

Milo Castle said, "I guess those visits by the prince to the tower weren't exactly G-rated!" This was some sort of joke, and though we could not hear the audience, we could see that they were laughing. After this, in a low, serious voice, Milo Castle said, "So, Jeremy, retire and keep your sixteen thousand dollars or risk your winnings and go on?"

Jeremy hesitated, but I reminded him that we did not yet have the sum needed to satisfy his debt. *One more*, I said. *It will not be difficult.*

"Go on," Jeremy said, and we could see people in the audience, including Jeremy's father, clapping and nodding.

"Okay, I ask you, fifteen-year-old Jeremy Johnson Johnson of the little town of Never Better, for thirty-two thousand dollars . . . which of the Grimm Brothers illustrated a number of the stories for the later editions of the *Household Tales?*"

Simple—laughably simple. And I was happy to have a light beamed upon my younger brother.

"Ludwig Emil Grimm," Jeremy said.

The green light, the satisfying refrain of "That is correct," the exuberant if unheard applause from the audience, and then Milo Castle said, "While Jacob and Wilhelm Grimm were far more famous, their younger brother, Ludwig, was a noted artist in his own right."

Milo Castle rather dramatically took a long, deep breath. He looked at the audience and then at our glass booth. "Well, Jeremy, you have gone where no other fifteen-year-old contestant has ever gone before. Now, do you rest on your laurels or do you go on? Remember that the questions grow increasingly difficult."

Yes, it was true that the amount of money already earned was enough to take care of Jeremy's immediate needs, but an additional sum would no doubt prove useful as well. Also, it must be said, this was all quite stimulating.

Let us answer one more, I said. I really was enjoying myself.

Jeremy hesitated, so I said, *This will go toward your education, Jeremy.*

"We'll go on," Jeremy said, a decision animatedly received by the audience.

"Okay, Jeremy, for *sixty-four thousand dollars* . . . a friend and collaborator of the Grimm Brothers wrote, 'I've already heard one mother complaining that a story about a child who slaughters another child is in your collection.' Your three-part question is: One, who was this correspondent? Two, about which story does he refer? And three, in what way did the Grimm Brothers respond?"

The first two answers were not difficult—I supplied them at once.

"Achim von Arnim was the letter writer," Jeremy said, "and he was referring to a very short tale called 'How Children Played Butcher with Each Other.'"

"And how did the Brothers Grimm respond?" Milo Castle said, and while Jeremy rubbed his temples, I told him.

"Wilhelm Grimm wrote back to say the tale was useful because he had himself heard it as a child from his own mother and it made him careful about child's play."

I was waiting for the panel to lean forward to illuminate the green light, but they did not. Instead, they looked warily at one another. Finally, one of them said, "The contestant's first two answers are correct. The third answer is not incorrect, but it is

212

not complete. We are looking for the brothers' actual *editorial* response."

Milo Castle said, "Jeremy?"

Jeremy rubbed his temple. I was suddenly quite nervous. I said, *Sie haben die Geschichte von den Folgenden Ausgaben beseitigt.*

Jeremy said, "*Sie haben die Geschichte von den Folgenden Ausgaben beseitigt.*"

Milo Castle cocked his head. "Excuse me?"

But I recovered, and quickly provided Jeremy the translation, which he recited: "They eliminated the tale from all subsequent editions."

Milo Castle and everyone else turned toward the screen, where the experts were all smiling and nodding, and then, wondrous to behold, the green light shone!

In the audience, the celebration appeared exuberant.

Finally, when it had evidently quieted, Milo Castle said, "Well, Jeremy, here we are. You have earned an incredible sixty-four thousand dollars. Retire now, and you take it all home—or at least what Uncle Sam leaves for you. If you go on, and answer one more question, you will earn one hundred and twenty-eight thousand dollars, which will be yours to keep and will additionally qualify you for this year's *Uncommon Knowledge* Tournament of Champions. So what will it be, Jeremy Johnson Johnson? Keep your winnings and retire . . . or risk your winnings and go on?"

It was clear that Jeremy wanted to stop, but he gazed out at the audience and found his father. He was nodding yes. So were Ginger and Jenny Applegarth. While Jeremy was looking at them, I said, *Let us go ahead, Jeremy. We can make your small town*

213

proud of you. But it was more than that. I was shimmering with excitement. Never had the *Zwischenraum* been so exhilarating, and I knew it never would be again.

"Well, Jeremy," Milo Castle said, "stay or go?"

Say yes for me, Jeremy, if you kindly will.

"Okay," Jeremy said in a faltering voice.

"Okay?" Milo Castle said. "Okay what?"

"I'll go ahead."

Again we could see the audience applauding, although it quickly gave way to apprehension, I could see it in their faces, but this fact only doubled the sum of my pleasure. If we could not answer questions regarding my own life and the tales my brother and I collected, then who could? Besides, there was no turning back—Milo Castle was now wearing the solemn look that preceded his more difficult questions.

"Okay, Jeremy Johnson Johnson," he said in a hushed tone, "in the tale of Snow White as related by the Brothers Grimm, the jealous queen sends the royal huntsman out into the forest with Snow White for the purpose of killing her. For one hundred and twenty-eight thousand dollars, your two-part question is this: In the Grimms' version of the tale, the queen asks the huntsman to bring back what evidence to prove he has killed Snow White? And, secondly, what change in the nature of this evidence was made when Walt Disney produced his animated version of the tale?"

What? What kind of foolery was this? I was appalled by the question. Who was this Mr. Walt Disney and why were they asking questions about *his* version of *our* tale?

Jeremy was rubbing his temple, and I told him what I knew.

"In the version collected by the Grimm Brothers," Jeremy

said, "the huntsman is asked to bring back Snow White's lungs and liver so the queen might eat them."

The panel of experts all nodded in agreement.

"And in the Disney version?" Milo Castle said.

Jeremy rubbed his temples again, but what could I do? I could not have felt worse. I was of no help to him.

I do not know, I said.

"Ten seconds, Jeremy," Milo Castle said.

Jeremy stared out at the audience. All of the people were very still. They looked at Jeremy as if at somebody perched at the very lip of a high cliff.

Milo Castle said, "A small hint. In the Disney version, the queen wanted to put this into her golden jewelry box."

So this Mr. Walt Disney wanted something less ghoulish than lungs and liver! *A necklace?* I said. *A buckle from her shoe?*

Jeremy shook his head. He was rubbing his temple very hard.

Then, from somewhere within the glass booth, a man's voice, so soft that it was hardly audible, said, "Her heart."

Jeremy stiffened for a moment, then his expression turned to confusion. His skin seemed stretched in different directions. He rubbed his temples hard.

That voice was not mine, I said. *It was a mortal's voice. I do not know whose.*

"Jeremy?" Milo Castle said. "I'm afraid I have to ask for your answer."

Jeremy had heard the words. He knew the answer. But he would not speak it.

"I don't know," Jeremy said. "I'm sorry." His face was contorted—he was on the edge of tears. "I never saw the Walt Disney movie. I'm sorry."

215

"We will allow you one guess," Milo Castle said.

"Her heart," the soft voice within the booth said again.

Jeremy's expression was wretched. He cast his eyes down and mumbled, "A lock of Snow White's hair."

As if shot, Milo Castle's chin dropped dramatically to his chest. All eyes turned to the experts, who looked gravely at one another and shook their heads.

The dread red light suddenly brightened.

The members of the audience collapsed in their seats, stared at Jeremy in disbelief, clapped their hands to their head. Open mouths, I was sure, were releasing groans.

In a somber tone, Milo Castle said, "Our panel tells us that the first half of your answer is correct, but both answers are required, so, Jeremy, I'm afraid your quest sadly ends here." The moderator's voice then turned expansive. "But we and inquisitive minds across America and around the world thank you, Jeremy Johnson Johnson, for sharing with us your . . . *uncommon knowledge!*"

Everything else was anticlimactic. The door to the glass booth swung open, and Milo Castle, accompanied by applause, walked across the stage to shake Jeremy's hand. "Sorry, young man. We were really rooting for you," he said, and he did seem genuinely regretful. Then the lights dimmed, Milo Castle hurried off into the side darkness, and out in the auditorium there was a general shuffling as people moved toward the exits.

A short time later, Jeremy was escorted to some double metal doors that led into the glaring sunlight of a back alley, where Jeremy's father, Jenny Applegarth, and Ginger stood waiting.

"Sorry," Jeremy mumbled when he saw them all looking at

him. Then, without any warning at all, his face gave way and he began to cry. His father was the first to reach him. He put his arms around him and said, "You did great, Jeremy. I couldn't be prouder."

"You were fabulous, Jeremy," Ginger said. "I mean it. I couldn't believe how you answered all the hard stuff." She shook her head. "Them bringing the Disney version into it was totally bogus."

Jeremy dabbed at his eyes with his new blue shirt, then took a few deep breaths. "Well, we got a lot further than I expected," he said. "I just wish . . ." But he could not say more.

Jenny Applegarth said, "I had no idea anybody could know so much about the Brothers Grimm. Question after question. I don't know how to say it, but it was really something."

"Not really," Jeremy said. He took a deep breath. "Just so you know, it's not like I really learned it or anything. It's more like this stuff just channels through me."

Everyone in the group was staring at him. Finally, Ginger said, "So you're not an actual whiz kid—you're an actual mystic. In what way is that less impressive?"

Jeremy seemed glad to receive Ginger's kind words, but still he said, "I wasn't calling myself a mystic." Then, looking around, he said, "So where's the big black car?"

"Over there." Ginger was nodding toward a boxy orange vehicle parked down the alley. A man with a sleepy expression sat behind the wheel.

"The orange van?" Jeremy said.

Ginger offered a wan smile. "I guess the deal is that if you don't win, they send you home in a pumpkin."

§

Over the next few days, Jeremy grew very quiet. He did not rub his temples to invite commiseration from me. In fact, he seemed relieved that I kept my silence. Whether he was annoyed with me, or angry, or disappointed, I did not know. I only sensed that some strange barrier now stood between us.

As disagreeable as these days were for me, they were worse for Jeremy. He owed money he could not pay, and when he went out, the villagers seemed more scornful than ever. Mayor Crinklaw said, "Holy Harry, boy, you were so close to that pot of gold, I could smell it!" and Elbow Adkins said wistfully, "Almost, Jeremy. Almost." But it was evident that most villagers were on familiar terms with Mr. Walt Disney's version of the story of Snow White and knew the answer that Jeremy could not give (her heart, just as the mortal's voice had told us), and so in addition to the town's judgment of him as an unpunished housebreaker, many citizens seemed to feel a further measure of disdain for his inability to answer what, to them, was the easiest question of all.

Conk Crinklaw, for example, stopped by the bookstore to offer his condolences, then shook his head and said, "But c'mon, Jeremy, I knew the answer to that question when I was, like, *two*. What was in that little glass room—some kind of brain-numbing gas?"

To which Ginger, sitting on the edge of the reading table,

replied, "Nobody I know produces brain-numbing gas but you, Conky."

Conk nodded as if complimented and asked Ginger if she wanted to come over and get shellacked in a game of horseshoes. "We'll see who shellacs who," she said, sliding from the table. She turned to Jeremy. "Wanna come?" she asked, but of course he declined.

And so she went off to play horseshoes, but in less than an hour she had returned to the bookstore and sat down without a word.

"Who won?" Jeremy asked.

"Nobody," Ginger said. "He was ahead and then I was ahead and then I just didn't feel like playing anymore." She looked at him. "I just kept wondering how you were doing."

He shrugged. "I'm doing fine."

But, truly, he did not seem fine, and Ginger stayed on, like a nurse waiting for a patient's fever to break. Days passed. She stayed close and ate with him and sat with him. Sometimes an hour or two would go by and Ginger would say nothing more than "There goes McRaven again," because, it was true, the deputy continued his vigilant surveillance of Jeremy and the bookstore. But what could a Finder of Occasions do if Jeremy stayed indoors? Nothing. That was what I believed.

The mayor stopped by one day to say he was sorry about it all, and—who knew?—maybe an inheritance would come through for Jeremy, he was sure hoping so, but if it didn't, well, then, Jeremy and his father could take anything at all they wanted from the building when they went, "except"—the mayor gave Jeremy and Ginger his square-jawed smile—"the walls, floor, and roof, a'course."

That night, after Ginger had gone home, Jeremy was eating dinner with his father and Jenny Applegarth when his father said, "You know, if anybody's to blame for you missing that Walt Disney question, it's me. I remember when *Snow White* was playing over in the next town. You were six or seven, and you wanted to go, but, I don't know, that was after your mother left and I didn't like going out. And then I never would spend the money on one of those recording machines, which I thought were a passing fad . . . So it was my fault if it was anybody's."

Jeremy said, "It's not anybody's fault, Dad. It's really not."

Jenny Applegarth left a delicious-looking bite of red potato poised before her. "That's right," she said. "Besides, what matters isn't so much what you did yesterday as what you do tomorrow. What you do next is who you become."

Ah. She meant well. But a well-meaning bromide is still a bromide.

A while later, when Jeremy was alone in the kitchen with his father, he said, "I knew the answer to that Disney question. Well, I didn't really know it. I heard it. When I was in the glass booth."

His father, washing dishes at the sink, stopped. "What do you mean, you heard it? Like one of those voices in your head you said you heard?"

"No. It was a real voice. A man's voice. Soft but real. Somebody was trying to help me. It wasn't Milo Castle, but it must've been somebody from the show."

Mr. Johnson stood still for a moment thinking. "And pay you all that money? Why would they want to do that?"

"I don't know. I've wondered, too. Maybe they thought having a kid win would help the ratings or bring in a younger group of viewers—I don't know."

They were quiet for a second or two. Then Mr. Johnson said, "Why didn't you give the answer?"

"I don't know that, either. I just couldn't. I just knew it was . . ."

"Wrong?" Jeremy's father said quietly.

"I guess so, yeah." He paused a second. "And what I was trying to tell you guys that day is true. I got all those other questions because of a voice in my head, so it shouldn't have bothered me if a voice came to me outside my head. But it did. I knew it was wrong. And once I knew that was wrong, I knew using the voice in my head was wrong, too."

So. This was what had built the wall between Jeremy and me. He felt as if we had deceived, that I had coaxed him into deceiving. Well, I did coax him, yes, but I did not think of it as deceiving. Still, that he did . . . this caused me deep shame. It is true that we in the *Zwischenraum* do not feel heat or cold. Shame is another matter.

Jeremy's father put down his dishrag. "Look, Jeremy, I don't know about the answers coming from the voice in your head, because I just believe that if you hear a voice in there, it's part of you, which isn't cheating." He took a deep breath. "But I think you were right about the outside voice. I think you were right not to use that voice." He was already serious; now he grew even more so. "I'm real proud you didn't use it." His face stiffened. "More proud than if you'd won all that money."

His face twisted, and I believe Mr. Johnson might have shed a tear, but he broke the tension by roughly rubbing Jeremy's head

221

with his knuckled hand. "I swear," he said. "When they made you, they broke the mold."

Jeremy produced a bittersweet smile. "'Course if I'd won the money, we wouldn't be losing the bookstore in a few weeks."

After they finished the dishes, Jeremy's father asked if he wanted to walk down to the Superette with him and Jenny. "We're going to split an ice cream sandwich." He grinned. "She always gives me the big half."

"Naw, it's okay." Jeremy gaze drifted. "Running into people . . ."

He did not need to finish the sentence.

§

§

Jeremy wandered out to the alley and sat on a box downwind from the sulfurous vapors wafting from the hot springs. He rubbed his temple and said, "You there?"

I am.

He stared off toward the springs. "Well, after we move, that's one thing I won't miss—the rotten-egg smell."

But, truly, this seemed just another way of indicating everything he would miss.

Jeremy, I said, *I made a mistake prodding you to go on. I got carried away.*

"It's okay. I think if we actually had won, I would've felt so slimy about it that it would've been even worse."

222

But your father was right about this, Jeremy. You are hearing my voice at this very moment because of your peculiar ability to listen. Those answers came to you through your own natural, uncommon talents.

Jeremy did not speak.

You do not believe me, then?

"I don't know. If you look at it like that, then, sure, I believe you. But if you look at it from the point of view of another contestant who goes into that booth without a ghost-buddy who gives him all the answers, well, then, it might be a little different."

Not quite all the answers.

He allowed a small laugh. "Yeah. We were skunked by the Walt Disney version." Several quiet seconds passed. "It's okay. The truth is, in the back of my mind, I had the idea that if I did really well, the town would maybe feel different about me, but I'm not even sure that's true." He stared off. "The only thing that really bothers me is losing the bookstore. I think my grandfather would be disappointed that I . . ."

He could not go on.

I will tell you this: his silence made the singing of crickets seem mournful.

After a time, I heard the sound of moving feet and saw the small, dark profile of someone approaching along the alleyway. I moved forward, in fear that it was Deputy McRaven, but it was not.

"Jeremy? Is that you?"

"Oh, hi, Mrs. Bailey," Jeremy said. I believe he, too, was relieved that it was only this kind small woman.

Mrs. Bailey looked around. An empty canvas bag hung over

223

her arm. "Is there someone else here then, dearie? I thought I heard you talking to someone."

"Nope, it's just me. Sometimes I talk to myself, is all."

"Me too," Mrs. Bailey said, and laughed softly. "All the time, in fact." After a moment or two, she went on. "I was there for the show."

"You were?"

"Mmm. Way in the back. I wasna' planning to go, but when I heard the women in town saying it was all agreed that no one would go, well, I thought I hadna' agreed on anything at all and I went right home to consult my bus schedule." She gave another soft laugh and shook her head. "But, my, weren't you something? Some of those questions were so difficult, and then when you answered them all just as easy as you please, I could've collapsed in astonishment."

Jeremy nodded and smiled. "Yeah, well . . ."

"When will they play the show, then?"

"I don't know for sure. They're supposed to let me know, but the truth is, once you lose, you sort of stop existing for them."

She nodded, and it again fell quiet except for the melancholy chorus of crickets.

Jeremy said, "So have you heard from Frank?"

"Oh, yes. He writes a postcard every little bit." They again fell quiet, and Mrs. Bailey said, "Well, all righty, then. I'm just out for my evening stroll."

"Night, Mrs. Bailey. Thanks for going to the show."

"Wouldna' missed it." She shook her head. "Really, this town. Sometimes I just don't . . ."

She turned to go. Jeremy conspicuously stood and again

said good night before going indoors. I knew why he did this. He did not want her to think he was watching when she stopped at the back door of the café to see if Elbow Adkins had any leftover portions of food he might send home with her, as he often did.

The moon had risen. Jeremy climbed up to the attic but did not turn on the light. He just lay on his bed, staring up at the ceiling. Presently, he said, "You still here?"

Yes.

"Can I ask you about something?"

Of course.

"I want you to tell me about your nephew."

Oh. How quickly these words threw open the door to that dark time. At once, I saw again the *Bübchen* gasping for air. I did not speak.

After a few moments, Jeremy said, "I know you don't want to, but it's kind of like one of the tales where there's a box you're not supposed to open, but you know you have to, because until you do, you won't have the complete picture."

But that was just it. I wanted the memories of my dear nephew locked in the heaviest chest and dropped to the darkest depths of the remotest ocean, because bringing them out for observation would only make the pain fresh again.

I said nothing.

"It's okay," Jeremy said quietly, because, truly, he was nothing if not kind.

But I recalled how he had told me his darkest chapters—his abandonment by his mother, the death of his grandfather, the arrival of the obituary from Canada—and now he had asked the same of me.

A minute of silence passed, and then another.

At last, I closed my ancient eyes and gathered myself. *I had a nephew*, I began. *Wilhelm's son. Given the name Jacob by Wilhelm and Dortchen to honor me. But it was not just that he carried my name that endeared him to me. He was only four years old but like a little man. He would come into our study and take my hand. "Ich möchte dir etwas zeigen, Onkel," he would say. I have something to show you, Uncle. If I was working, no one, nothing could take me away from my studies, but when this boy took my hand, I pushed back from my desk and followed him down the stairs and out of the house to the fresh berries he had found, or the nest filled with speckled eggs, or the smooth stone shaped like a heart. He could have brought these treasures inside, presented them at my desk, but that was not his way. He led me out of doors and would watch me looking at whatever he had found, as if it could not be a treasure until I had called it one. "Yes," I would say. "Today you have certainly shown me something." Oh, he would beam.*

And then . . . a sickness. The color draining little by little from his cheeks, his limbs thinning to matchsticks. The Mediziner coming, one after another, and departing, one after another. But this boy, this little man, he would try to smile even as his eyes bulged from his face. He never complained. In his sleep, he would sometimes cry out for his mother or father or for his uncle Jacob, but he never complained.

The final two days I did not leave his side. I sat through the night. Are you there, Uncle? he would say, and I would squeeze his hand and say, Yes, my little man, I am here.

I stopped. I could not go further.

After a long silence, Jeremy said in a quiet voice, "What did you do when your nephew died?"

I died a kind of death. My heart shrank and blackened and I died. Though I did not quite know it at the time. But of course I could not tell Jeremy this. *I went on*, I said. *My life had changed and I had changed, but I went on.*

Another silence. Through the attic window, the crickets could still be heard.

Jeremy said, "How long do you think you'll stay here, Jacob?"

Here with you, or here in the Zwischenraum?

"I don't know. Both, I guess."

Of course I wished to be free of the *Zwischenraum*, but my role here was to keep Jeremy safe, to see him off to university. Jeremy knew this—it did not need repeating. So I merely said, *I think I will stay on for some little while, Jeremy.*

"But until when, exactly?"

"Until you are safe" was the thought that flew to my mind. But I tried a small joke instead. *Until I am sure you will live happily ever after.*

He snickered. "If that's what it'll take, you could be here forever."

Outside, the calm call of an owl—*hoo-hoo, hoo-hoo*.

"Jacob?"

Yes?

"I know sometimes I take you for granted, or get tired of you riding me about studying, but . . ." His voice trailed away. "I like knowing you're around and that you . . . I don't know . . . watch out for me and more or less take me, you know, *as is*."

I did not speak, but I was moved.

After a few moments, he said, "We never had a dog because my father is allergic to them, but I always wanted one because dogs are there when you leave and there when you come home and they're always happy to see you no matter how bad you might've screwed up during the day."

This strange comparison lightened the mood. *Mein Gott!* I said laughing. *I might be replaced by a dog?*

Jeremy chuckled, too, and this had a gladdening effect on me. "Well," he said, "it's true a dog can't talk. But then again a dog can't say, 'Your stutties, Jeremy. Your stutties, your stutties, your stutties.'"

His replication of my accent was quite good. I stifled my laugh and kept very still.

"Jacob?" he said. "You here?"

I am licking my wounds. Much as a dog might do.

Jeremy gave this a small laugh and pulled the quilt to his chin.

"Good night, Jacob," he said, and I said, *Good night, Jeremy, and sweet repose.*

§

§

From my belfry perch I watched the deep night settle over the village and wrap it in sleep. Deputy McRaven's patrol car prowled the streets; a mockingbird in search of a mate sent out his strange, varied calls; and a masked raccoon turned over a trash can, receded, and when it was quiet again, returned to root for food. And then, after midnight, the mockingbird settled into a gentler song and, soon, no song at all.

When my nephew passed beyond, Wilhelm comforted himself that a child in his innocence would be delivered speedily to heaven, and there be given an honored place. "In his small, simple throne," Wilhelm said, and I said, "With secret compartments for his bird's nests and smooth stones." Wilhelm believed this. He had to believe this. I, too, repeated this conception to myself again and again, trying harder and harder to believe it. But a Creator who takes a child so small, so kind, so tender? What can be made of that? The tales we collected are not merciful. Villains are boiled in snake-filled oil, wicked *Stiefmütter*—stepmothers—are made to dance into death in molten-hot shoes, and on and on. The tales are full of terrible punishments, yes, but they follow just cause. Goodness is rewarded; evil is not. The generous simpleton finds more happiness and coin than the greedy king. So why not mercy and justice to a sweet youth from an omnipotent and benevolent Creator? There are only three answers. He is not omnipotent, or he is not benevolent, or—the dreariest possibility of all—he is inattentive. What if that was what happened to my nephew? That God's gaze had merely strayed elsewhere?

Well, that is how it is. The night that I closed the lids of my nephew's eyes, the course of my life altered. During my nephew's earlier days, watching him in his sweet discovery and play, I had nursed thoughts of marriage and fatherhood and family, but these ideas fell away with his last breath. I turned. My vital principle flowed only to the studies, the papers, the essays, the dictionary. Projects without searching eyes and gasping mouths.

But enough of my morbid thoughts. The cocks were crowing, the town was stirring, and I fell again to my duties of watching over Jeremy during his sad, dark time.

Sad and dark, and soon to be sadder and darker still.

§
§

It seems strange to say that it began with good news.

"Guess what?" Ginger said. "The baker wants us to work for him again! Some kind of construction thing at his cabin up in the timber."

Several more long, dull days had passed when Ginger brought this news.

"Mr. Blix has a cabin in the timber?"

"I *know*. News to me, too. But he said we'll mix work with pleasure. We'll build a wood crib—that's the work part—but he's going to pack a picnic, and there's a swimming hole, so we should bring our swimming suits."

I will confess the truth. Nothing about these details alarmed me. Every day, all over the world, people build things and swim in ponds without particular risk.

Ginger threw her arm loosely over Jeremy's shoulder and left it there. "Know what's good here? This will get you out of the house and you won't even have to deal with any of Never Better's idiot-citizens."

They were quiet for a while, and it had to be admitted that these two youths at ease with themselves and each other made a pleasant picture, and I suddenly understood that, for Jeremy, the surprise of love would not arrive, as it does in the tales, with a strange enchantment or with a single smiting glance or with a lilting voice riding the wind through the woodland. No, for

Jeremy, the surprise of love would be carried on the lazy currents of friendship.

§

§

When the sun peered over the earth's rim that Sunday morning, it found Jeremy bicycling along the highway leading from town. A mile or two out, close by a railroad siding, he turned into a small clearing, where he stopped, stood by his bicycle, and looked around.

"You're early," a voice said, and Jeremy turned to see Ginger smiling and stepping out from a stand of trees. She was wearing a faded pink shirt that said AS IS across the front in gold, glimmery letters.

"Early," he said, "but not as early as you."

"Yeah, well, I think I told you that my grandfather gets up at an ungodly hour, and I needed to be gone before he got up." She watched him lean his bicycle against a tree next to hers. "Did anybody see you leave town?"

"You mean McRaven?"

"Yeah, I guess I do."

"Nope. No sign."

This was true. I had myself gazed through the window of his quarters above the garage. The deputy seemed to be sleeping soundly in his small bed.

"Okay, all we do now is wait for Mr. Blix," Ginger said. She poured coffee from an insulated container and offered a cup to Jeremy. "It's lukewarm," she said. "I made it last night after my granddad went to bed."

Jeremy took a sip and smiled. "Just the way I like it."

I could see in his face how relieved he was to be out of town at the beginning of this fresh new day, relieved to be away from his troubles and the villagers' stares, relieved to be alone with this girl, and truly, relief can sometimes come within an inch of happiness itself.

On the siding, freight cars stood empty in the low, sloping sun. Birds began to sing, insects to buzz. And then, beyond all that, the faint thrum of an engine could be heard, and presently the gleaming Green Oven delivery van came into view. The baker's smile beamed out from his full white beard as he turned off the highway.

"*Hallå!*" he said, after lowering his window. "Is it not a great day to be alive?"

"A little too early to say, if you want to know the truth," Ginger said, but it truly was a beautiful day, and they all seemed to feel it.

Stacked and bound in the rear of the van was a selection of wooden posts and planks to be used for construction of the wood crib, so as they rolled along the highway, Jeremy sat in the front seat with Ginger in his lap.

"An adventure!" the baker said, beaming. "That's what this feels like. A most pleasant adventure!"

"Yeah," Ginger said, smiling, too, "it does, kind of."

The highway split fields of corn and wheat, and symphonic music played within the van, quite beautiful to my ancient ear, though when the baker asked Jeremy and Ginger if they liked it, Jeremy said, "It's okay, I guess," and Ginger said, "It's kind of an audio sleeping pill."

A laugh rumbled up from the baker's belly, and he guided the van onto a dirt road leading north. The van bounced over ruts, and pebbles tinked against its underside.

"Okay," Jeremy said, "I think it's time for me to give up my seat."

"Really?" Ginger said. "'Cause I'm comfy as can be."

The van jounced again and Jeremy said, "That's because you're the sitter and I'm the seat."

He folded a red blanket into a cushion and took a position on the bundled lengths of wood.

Ginger turned to the baker. "So how far is this cabin, anyhow?"

"A ways yet. It's a beautiful spot, close to a small lake, deep in the woods."

The baker's voice was as kindly as ever, but at the mention of deep woods, a dim note of alarm sounded within me. *Wald, Forst,* and most especially, *im tiefen Wald*—in deep forests—were the words that wrapped black tendrils around a story and foretold ghastly creatures lying in wait or children losing their way. But those were the forests of fairy tales, I told myself, not the ordinary pines of everyday life.

The music played, the baker guided his delivery van along the dirt roads, and Ginger and Jeremy stared complacently out. The farms here were large, unirrigated, and widely spaced, and soon the land was given to the grazing of animals rather than the growing of grains. When the van approached a crossroads, the baker turned toward a range of dense, up-reaching conifers, and soon we were among them, the pines so thick that they eclipsed the sun. The road grew darker, narrower, rockier, more intricate in its twistings. There were no other mortals here, no fences, no gates, no visible boundaries.

"Wow," Jeremy said staring out from his seat in the back. "I didn't know there was anything like this around here. Where are we?"

"A world all its own," the baker said, his round face beaming. He turned onto a lane so narrow and overgrown it seemed the forest's own secret.

Ginger laughed with delight. "What was that? Did the directions just say, 'Take a hard left straight into the forest'?"

The passage was almost a tunnel, and when the baker approached the end of it, he slowed the van. "And now the ceremonial clearing away of the bears!" he said, and honked the car horn three long times.

"You have bears?" Ginger asked, looking slightly alarmed, and the baker, laughing, said, "Not anymore."

In another moment, he was gesturing toward a clearing before us. "There," he said, his round cheeks radiant with pride. "There is the cabin."

A *Hütte*, Wilhelm and I would have called it in a tale— a simple, single-story structure made of logs, its roof composed of earth from which grass grew.

"Zounds," Ginger said as she and Jeremy walked around the encampment, "it must be twenty degrees cooler up here." The wind through the tree limbs made a low, hollow whistle. She grinned at Jeremy. "Pretty fabulous, no?"

"Yeah," Jeremy said, "it really is," and, behind them, the baker smiled with pleasure.

234

I will be truthful. I, too, partook of the preternatural beauty. But it went beyond even that. I felt myself pleasantly transported back to the woods of Germany, and of my childhood. And so I was carried away . . . when I should have stood fast and remained vigilant.

§

§

Jeremy and Ginger hauled the wooden posts and planks from the car while the baker busied himself at the hut, folding back window shutters and setting out chairs.

"I haven't been here for a few weeks," he said. "Not since Frank Bailey left."

Ginger seemed surprised. "Frank Bailey came up here?"

"Oh, yes. He's a good boy. He helped me put down the new wood floor."

Ginger and Jeremy carried the last loads of lumber, then looked around. "Everything here in Blixville looks so just-raked and tidy," Ginger said to the baker. "How do you do it?"

"A caretaker," the baker said. "Once a week, a gentleman hikes over from his cabin a mile or so from here and takes care of this and that." The baker's blue eyes twinkled. "Then when he comes into town, I pay him in pastries."

After all the wood planks had been laid out, the baker directed Ginger and Jeremy to a large stack of pine logs, handed each of them a sharpened ax, and showed them how to split the round lengths into smaller sections. It was a funny sight, this plump, cherubic man swinging an ax and issuing a little *Oof!* each time he brought the force of it to the wood, but he was surprisingly adept at his work.

As Ginger stepped up to try her hand, she asked, "Is the grunting absolutely required?"

"Absolutely," the baker said with a Santa-like wink.

The baker left them alone with their sharpened axes. Jeremy and Ginger enjoyed the work and began racing to see whose pile of split wood grew largest.

The wood chips spewed here and there, and the minutes flew past. Jeremy and Ginger swung the axes with gusto, drawing closer to each other as the pile of logs diminished and the piles of split wood grew. They hurried and cajoled and huffed and puffed until the arcs of each ax fell perilously close to that of the other and I began to shout into Jeremy's ear . . . but he was too caught up in his race to hear.

"Careful!" a voice rang out. "Careful now!"

It was, to my relief, the baker, hurrying toward them, wiping his hands in a towel. "*Hallå! Hallå!*" he sang out. "Oh, my dear young friends, you scare me with your wild axes!" He took several deep drafts of air to regain his breath, then looked with satisfaction at their work. "But what woodpiles you have made!"

Jeremy and Ginger—shirts damp, faces slippery with perspiration—stood catching their breath. I did, too, in my own manner, for I felt the danger had passed. The baker's twinkling eyes moved from the split wood to Ginger and Jeremy. "You two put me to shame. It would take me a day to do what you've done here."

It was a pleasant moment, a compliment hanging in the air

236

along with the scent of split wood, the soft murmur of the breeze through the trees, and, somewhere farther off, the dim, watery sounds of an unseen creek.

"Yes, yes," the baker said, smiling and eyeing the woodpiles. "*Very* impressive."

"Actually," Ginger said, "if you look closely, you'll see that my pile's slightly more impressive than his."

"You had the sharper ax," Jeremy said, laughing, and Ginger said, "You had the softer wood."

The baker laughed heartily. "All we need now is a wood crib, which we will soon build. But, first, did you build up an appetite? Yes? Then you are in luck."

He led them into the hut, which was clean and welcoming, with plain, hand-hewn furnishings—a table, two chairs, a bed—and a simple kitchen arranged around a circular stone fireplace.

"Zoundsapoppin'," Ginger said, a new term for her and, I was sure, for linguists everywhere. Her eyes flew around the room. "A guy could live here." She grinned. "Also a girl."

"Yes, yes," the baker said. "I've often thought that I would retire here someday, when the bakery is finally behind me." He followed Jeremy's gaze to the enormous oven at the center of the room. "It burns wood," he said, "which some people find difficult, but not a Swedish baker." He gave a modest shrug. "The ovens and I have always understood each other."

The rear door of the hut gave on to a shaded clearing with a beamed table on which the baker had spread rolls, fruits, meats, and cheeses. One tin pitcher was filled with stalks of lavender, another was filled with thick nectar.

As the baker's eyes moved from the sumptuous table to

Jeremy and then to Ginger, one could almost see a prideful pleasure coursing through him. "Does it please you?" he asked.

"And then some," Ginger said at once, and Jeremy was smiling, too.

The baker nodded. "You know, our days too often pass one like the other. I hoped to make this a day that you would not forget." He gave a broad, beaming smile, and seemed in that moment like a real-life Saint Nicholas, one whose presents came in the form of food in all of its aspects—the baking, the staging, and finally the tasting. It looked so tantalizing that I had to avert my eyes as Jeremy and Ginger sampled one delicacy after another.

The baker, too, partook of the offerings.

"What's that?" Ginger said, suddenly stilling herself and cocking her head.

I had heard it, too: the distant cracking of a limb.

The baker stared off alertly in the direction of the sound but soon relaxed. "Probably just a falling branch," he said. "The dead limbs grow brittle and when the wind blows . . ." He broke off a bit of roll and applied a liberal coating of butter, then mentioned idly that he had seen bears here several times and, once, a mountain lion.

"They aren't supposed to be here," he said, "but they are. The foresters call them 'long-distance dispersals.'" He gave a slow-rolling laugh. "Of course, I am a bit of a long-distance dispersal myself."

"So why *did* you come here?" Jeremy asked. He was layering the most delicious-looking meat and cheese onto a butter-browned roll.

The baker considered the question. "It is a strange thing, but as a boy in Malmö I always dreamed of owning my own bakery and living in America."

Ginger dipped a strawberry into heavy cream and asked where Malmö was.

"In Sweden," the baker said. "Toward the very south. It was such a bustling town! We built ships, we caught herring, we had our own railway station—a wonderful place. But then I grew up, and had a . . . romantic disappointment." He smiled. "It is probably hard for you to imagine, but I was younger then." He sipped from his cup of nectar. "So I decided the time had come for my departure."

"Do you miss it?" Ginger said. "Sweden, I mean."

"Sometimes, my dear girl. But less and less." He glanced toward the cabin and the forest. "It is good here." And then, rather suddenly, his expression stiffened. "But I will tell you, there are times when the customs here disappoint me. The lost young people that the police cannot find and explain always as runaways. In Sweden, the authorities will not rest in cases like these, but here . . ." He waved his arm in a gesture of weary dismissal, then drank from his nectar. "And then there is the way the people in town have treated you." He smiled suddenly and winked. "And how they would treat me if they knew I was hiring you."

"No problem on that account," Jeremy offered. "No one saw me this morning, and all I told my dad was that I was doing something with Ginger, but I wasn't sure what. Which was true."

Ginger rolled a small slice of meat over a piece of cheese. "That's more than I told my granddad—or anyone else, for that matter."

"Thank you." The baker shook his head. "It's a shame we

have to take these precautions, but that is how things are in the village in which we live."

"Yeah, well," Ginger said, "someday I'm going to live somewhere else." She smiled and passed a quick glance toward Jeremy. "Someplace far, far away."

It was quiet again, except for the birdsong and the hollow wind through the trees.

After a last bite of food, Jeremy sat back and said, "That was delicious."

"And we're not done yet!" the baker announced. He went into the cabin and returned with a pot of coffee, tin cups, and raspberry and lemon cuts, which they enjoyed in a leisurely way that put me pleasantly in mind of life with Wilhelm and Dortchen before the death of my nephew. I understood the happiness in Jeremy's and Ginger's eyes. I, too, was as happy as a ghost might be.

Ginger, sipping her coffee, noticed several sheets of paper, a pencil, and a pen lying on the food tray. "What's up with that?" she asked. "You writing a letter?"

The baker smiled. "When you talked about wanting to go far, far away, I thought of something I did as a child that made me feel better," and he went on to explain that when he was young and he was angry at his parents or his school friends and wished he were far away in America, he would sometimes sit down and write a letter to his parents as if he were already gone. "Sometimes I would write as if I were stowed away on a ship crossing the Atlantic, sometimes I would write as if I were already in America selling newspapers in New York City. I would sign the letter, fold it carefully, and address the envelope, and then, when it lay there sealed and ready to go, I always felt better. It was as if writing of my leave-taking foretold it, and made it my destiny."

Jeremy asked what he did with the letters.

"Oh, put them aside, into drawers, under books. My mother found one—it made her very sad." He winked. "After that, I hid them better."

Ginger eyed the writing paper. "Could I try one?"

The baker shrugged agreeably. "Of course, if you like. But there's no need. It's just a little trick I found useful, and I thought . . ."

Ginger and Jeremy each selected a piece of paper and an envelope, hers a square one that she addressed to her grandfather, Jeremy's long and rectangular, which he addressed to his father. While the baker cleared the table, Ginger and Jeremy composed their notes. Ginger was quickly done. Jeremy was more hesitant and, when finished, folded his note into its envelope.

"Well, then," the baker said. "Did that help? What did we write?"

Ginger held up her sheet of paper and read: "Hi, Grandpa. We took a train out of town. I'm not sure where we are exactly, but it's far away and I'm happier now than I've ever been." Her amber eyes shone as she read this, and when she was finished, she looked genially from Jeremy to Sten Blix. "You're right. It really does make you feel like you've already got one foot out the door."

She turned to Jeremy. "So what did you write?"

He shrugged. "Not much."

"C'mon, Jeremy Jeremy! No fair! Cough it up."

He looked down as if abashed. "I just wrote my dad that I

241

didn't miss a lot of people in town but I missed some of them and I missed him most of all."

"Ahh, you're such a sweetheart, Jeremy," she said. "Did you say where you were?"

"Arizona."

Ginger issued an abrupt laugh. "Arizona! Why Arizona?"

Jeremy shrugged. "I've always wanted to see the Grand Canyon."

At this pleasant moment, we heard another cracking sound some distance away, and again everyone stared into the shadowy woods and waited. But we heard nothing more.

"As long as it's not a bear," Ginger said.

The baker's laugh was jovial. "Even the bears leave humans alone unless you come between a mother and her cub."

Ginger grinned. "That's a hard-and-fast rule of mine: Never come between a bear and her cub."

Jeremy said, "My rule is: Never come between a Ginger and her cheeseburger." He laughed and turned to the baker. "You should see her eat a cheeseburger. It's not what you'd call routinely carnivorous."

Well, I will tell you, it was a charming sight: a girl, a boy, and a Saint Nicholas–like baker, all in radiant good humor.

After dining, they set to work on the wood crib, a job that moved smoothly because the baker had already cut and drilled the boards according to a prescribed plan. "I like this," Jeremy said. "It's like assembling a kit."

"Seventy percent of success is planning," the baker said. "Twenty-five is execution. And"—he chuckled—"the last five percent is alignment of the stars."

By midafternoon they had finished the wood crib, and soon they had it filled with the wood Jeremy and Ginger had split earlier. Jeremy leaned against it and took in a deep breath of the piney air.

"Thanks," he said to the baker. "That was fun."

Ginger, standing nearby with skin damp from sweat, said, "Yeah, it was, kind of, considering that it was actually work." She turned to the baker. "What's next?"

"No more work. Now it is time to rest and enjoy yourselves." He pointed off. "Do you see the lightning-split pine at the crest of the hill? Beyond it is a pond that is perfect for swimming. You go ahead, and I'll follow along." He gave an apologetic shrug. "I don't swim myself."

"Don't like to or can't?" Ginger asked.

"Can't. But you both can swim, yes?"

"Oh, yeah," Ginger said. "We can swim like the fishes."

§

§

The pond, when they came to it, was as placid and picturesque as everything else in the baker's domain. An enormous boulder reached toward the sky and overhung the water, and Jeremy and Ginger changed into their bathing costumes on either side of it. Ginger ducked into the pond first, bobbed quickly up, and said, "Okay, then. Not that warm."

But soon they were splashing and kicking and reporting where they could and could not touch bottom. The breeze filtered through the trees and my mind wandered. A short time later, I noticed Jeremy regarding Ginger, who was staring up intently at the massive boulder that leaned out over the deepest portion of the pond.

"Don't even think about it," Jeremy said.

"Oh, I'm thinking about it, all right." She grinned. "What'll you give me if I dive from up there?"

"I don't know—how about the Unrivaled Stupidity Award?"

Ginger laughed. "That happens to be an award I've been dying to get."

"Excellent. Of course, you might die getting it."

Ginger emerged dripping from the water, and my ancient heart tightened as she picked her way up a series of ledges and momentarily disappeared behind the rock. When she next appeared, she was walking crablike along the rock's domed top. She stood carefully, as if on slick ice, and peered down.

"Okay," she said. "Here's the thing. It looks way different from up here."

"Don't do it," Jeremy said. "Just because something's pointless and dangerous doesn't mean you have to do it."

This advice echoed my own sentiments, but she did not reply. In fact, as she stared down, a concentration of purpose seemed gradually to be building within her.

Jeremy! I cried. *You must tell her to stop!*

"Ginger, seriously. Don't even think about this."

Her smile was frozen, but her words were full of bravado. "Oh, I'm thinking about it, all right."

Real fear took hold of me. *Jeremy! Stop her! You must stop her!*

Jeremy sought middle ground. "Look, Ginger, if you do it, don't dive. You can just jump. You'll still get the Stupidity Award if you just jump."

Ginger edged forward, looking down. She took a deep breath, bent slightly forward, but still did not dive. She stood frozen midway between fear and resolve.

Help her, Jeremy. Help her to step back.

"Ginger, listen to me. Just climb back down. I'll give you the Stupidity Award for just thinking about it. And if you dive and hit a rock, you might wind up a vegetable, which is worse than dying."

But this, if anything, had an effect opposite of what he desired. Ginger inched so close to the ledge that a gusting touch of wind might send her over. She stared straight forward, staring, staring, not moving, standing perfectly still, staring, staring . . . and then she bowed her head, raised her hands, and—*mein Gott!*—plummeted headfirst into the water, which swallowed her in one quick gulp.

For a moment, the world's heart stopped beating.

Then, suddenly, Ginger's head burst through the surface and her tightly closed face opened into an exultant laugh. "Ha!" she called, splashing water toward Jeremy. "That Stupidity Award is mine, all mine!"

Jeremy's laugh was fueled by relief. "And I can think of no recipient more deserving."

Well, there it is: youth, and the pleasures of unpunished recklessness.

They swam and paddled about for a while, and then Ginger

began walking the length of a slippery log that cantilevered over the far end of the pond. At its end, she stood on one leg posing, it seemed, as a stork.

A mourning dove made a soft *hoo-hoo*ing sound.

Only at this moment of pleasant quietude did I realize Jeremy was not here.

"Geronimo!" he shouted from above, and as Ginger broke her pose and looked up, he leapt from the top of the rock, pulled his knees to his chest, and rotating slightly forward, exploded into the water with a ferocious *whump!* Ginger turned her head from the massive splash.

Jeremy surfaced looking happy yet dazed.

"Had to hurt," Ginger said.

"Affirmative," Jeremy said. "It totally did."

He held his hands to his smarting face, but he was clearly exhilarated to be, in his own fashion, a member of this little club.

Ginger, sitting on the log now, said, "That was some serious Jeremocity."

Normally, a compliment like this would have caused Jeremy to blush, but this was no normal day, and he did not blush. He just smiled happily.

Ginger slid off the log and glided through the water, drawing closer to him, her coppery hair floating out behind. When she stood, their faces were very near. "So," she said in a soft voice, "how are things in Jeremopolis?"

"Good. Really, really good."

Her amber eyes bore into him. "I told you that you had potential," she whispered, and before he could reply, they kissed.

Yes. Just like that, before I could issue a warning or create a distraction, they kissed.

246

And, to my own surprise, I was happy for Jeremy, and happy even for Ginger, and what did this mean? Did I, the ancient and venerable Jacob Grimm, whose life had been governed by fact and reason, believe in the power of a youthful kiss, or in the nonsense of a sealed enchantment? No. That was what I told myself. *Nein, nee, nö.* It was something even simpler—I was happy that they were happy.

Ginger's laugh was so merry that it seemed musical. "There," she said. "We got that out of the way." Then, a few seconds later: "I don't know about you, but I'm freezing and have to get out of here."

They placed their towels on a flat, sunny rock and sat side by side.

"You know, Jeremy Jeremy, not only are you the first boy I ever spent the night with and the first boy I ever hugged wearing just a towel, but now you're also the first boy I ever kissed in a pond." She leaned into him. "You're knocking off some key categories in my personal history book."

"And don't forget I'm the first one to confer upon you the highly coveted Unrivaled Stupidity Award."

She laughed softly.

The wind through the trees made a low hushing sound.

There was the whisk and chatter of a squirrel.

"I really love it here," Ginger said.

"Me too."

"It's like somehow, without even knowing how we did it, we suddenly found the secret passage to the Far Far Away."

How much time passed by in this state of pure and guileless pleasure, I cannot accurately say, but it is the nature of such happiness that its intensity is often matched only by its brevity.

A sudden cracking sound broke into their reverie, and Ginger and Jeremy, turning as one, were relieved to see that it was only the baker huffing and puffing his way up the hill, carrying a woven-wood picnic hamper.

"Hallå!" he said as he drew near, and he paused to take a few deep breaths. "Whew." He issued a wheezy chuckle. "That hill has gotten steeper over the years."

But he was soon smiling again. He set down his basket, removed his shoes, rolled up his pant legs, and dipped his pink feet into the water. "Ha!" he said, and his blue eyes twinkled. "It could be Swedish water, it's so cold."

He dried his feet with a towel, then pulled from his basket a deck of playing cards and several cloth-covered bowls of nuts and crackers and small salted fishes. "Here," he said, "eat a little bit and I will teach you a card game played in Sweden."

And so, over the next long, congenial hour, the three of them played card games, and laughed, and ate the savory snacks. The baker's happiness was a match for his helpers'—it was a rare minute that passed without hearing his rumbly, gladsome laugh. Ginger and Jeremy liked the fish he had brought but favored the pretzels, and who could blame them? They had been tied and baked that very morning, with coarse salt clinging to the golden glaze.

No one seemed happier than the baker, who was gratified when he won a card game, and more grateful still when someone else did.

"Oh my, oh my," he would say when he lost. "It's a good thing we are not playing for money. I would have lost yesterday's fortune and tomorrow's, too!"

Between games, while Ginger shuffled the cards and Jeremy lay back staring at the clouds, the baker went to his hamper and drew out the insulated container he had used before, so they knew what was in store.

"Nectar?" Ginger asked, and when the baker nodded, she grinned. "Fabulous! I was getting so thirsty, I was about to drink pond water."

The baker began unscrewing the cap but then paused. "I will tell you something strange. You know who I was thinking about this morning?—Rumpelstiltskin. It's an odd story, isn't it? Because he is the villain even though he simply made an arrangement and kept his end of the bargain. He taught the girl how to weave gold from straw in exchange for her first-born but then, when she becomes queen and the baby is born, she will not give it up."

Ginger was still staring at the flask of nectar. "Well, of course not," she said distractedly. "What mother would?"

"Yes, yes, you are right, dear girl." The baker unscrewed the cap another turn before stopping again. I could almost feel Ginger's disappointment. "But of course the queen could bear another child," he said. "Poor Rumpelstiltskin could not. He was small and strange. Everyone despised him. Perhaps his only chance at companionship was to raise a kindly child who might befriend him." He had been staring off toward the trees but now turned his blue eyes to Jeremy and then Ginger. "What do you think?"

Well, his idea was, in its odd way, astute. But "Rumpelstiltskin" is a story full of greed, and no one is more greedy than the little gnome himself, so of course we are satisfied when he stamps and shrieks and tears himself in two. Here, though, is what I did not properly notice: the sudden seriousness in the baker's eyes. Nor did Jeremy and Ginger.

"I'll tell you what I think," she said, still eyeing the flask in the baker's hand. "I think I am going to scream if you don't pour us some of that nectar."

A laugh burst forth from the baker. "Yes, yes, of course. I forget my duties as host." He nodded formally at one then the other. "Allow me to serve you."

He filled two tin cups with the pale pink nectar and extended them to Ginger and Jeremy. Ginger at once sipped from hers. "Wow," she said, and took several more quick swigs. "What's in this besides strawberry?"

The baker shrugged modestly and poured a portion into his own cup. "Several fruits and soy milk."

"You should market this stuff," Jeremy said to the baker between gulps.

"But what could I call it?" the baker said, smiling and watching them drink. "I never make it the same way twice."

"Blix-Elixir!" Ginger said, and Jeremy laughed, but there was an odd thickness to his laugh, and when he said "That a good name," the words were odd and elongated, which made Ginger laugh her own odd laugh. And when she said "You soun funny," her words were so thick and muddy, she could hardly be understood.

A sudden cold fear coursed through me. Sudden, and too late.

I turned to the baker, whose smile was that of a kind father's. "Now, now, dear children," he crooned. "Just go ahead and sleep. Just relax and let go and sleep and sleep and sleep."

Jeremy sat back on his towel. He curled onto the ground. He closed his eyes.

I rushed close. *Listen, if you will, Jeremy*, I cried. *Listen, if you will!*

Jeremy's eyelids fluttered open, then closed. They did not open again.

At his side, Ginger stared at Jeremy, then clamped her hands to her ears, as if trying to ward off sounds she did not want to hear. "Whad . . . ," she said, turning to the baker, and her voice trailed off. She moved her flattened hands to cover her eyes as if to pray, but after only a moment her hands slid away.

She, too, slumped onto the ground. Her eyes, too, fell closed.

Methodically, the baker now began putting things right. He poured onto the ground the nectar from his own cup. He set the dishes and cups and cards neatly back into the picnic hamper. He gathered the towels. Then he stared again at the two unmoving youths before gazing out at the pond.

In a soft voice, he said, "*Sa börjar det igen.*"

I translated at once: *So another moment has come.*

These words, and the calmness with which he had spoken them, filled me with terror. *Nein!* I cried out. *Nein! Nein! Nein!* But of course no one heard.

And so I could disbelieve it no longer.

It was the baker.

The kind, jolly, Saint Nicholas–like baker.

The villain without villainous qualities.

The Finder of Occasions.

A few moments later, I heard the heavy crackling of a branch, and I turned to see a man materialize from the dark woods, trudging slowly, a heavy-spirited man of unknown age with a blank face and long hair pulled back and tied behind his head. The baker did not acknowledge him, nor did this man acknowledge the baker. Theirs was a prescribed pattern of behavior, as if what I was watching was an established ritual. Without any expression on his face whatsoever, the man presented a cigarette to the baker, then struck a match to light it for him. The baker drew the smoke deep into his lungs and then, after several long moments, allowed the smoke to stream through his bearded lips. Imagine Saint Nicholas with a cigarette, and you will see what I saw in that dreadful moment.

§

§

In the tales, horrific evils are routinely perpetrated against innocents—maidens are butchered before our eyes, children are devoured—yet in the end, justice is meted out, and bodies are reassembled and restored to life. Innocence is rewarded; cruelty is punished. And there is something else, too—a small but critical distance between the words on the pages and the world as we know it. Now, however, watching the man with the blank face load Jeremy's and Ginger's bodies into the Green Oven Bakery van, watching him secure them with ropes and cover them with blankets, I knew that there had been a terrible alteration.

The small but critical distance had been bridged.

The horror had escaped into the everyday world.

Beneath the blankets, they breathed—Ginger and Jeremy breathed—but between each breath stretched a terrifying stillness.

The baker finished his cigarette, then he and the man with the blank face went about the cabin putting things away, making fast the windows, and finally locking the doors. The baker took one last look around.

There was not a sign or a hint that Jeremy and Ginger had ever been there.

The man with the blank face stood and waited.

The baker went to the van and peeled back the blankets to examine once again Ginger's and Jeremy's faces. "Oh, you poor children," he whispered. "What an ordeal. But do not worry. It will all soon be over."

Then he again draped the blankets loosely over their heads.

The baker turned to the blank-faced man and gave him a nod. Silently, the man turned and dissolved into the dark woods whence he had come.

Not one word had passed the stranger's lips. Nor had the baker spoken one word to him. No, their dreadful business had been conducted entirely in silence.

I slipped into the delivery van with the baker. As he drove away from the forest, he listened to his Swedish composer, and when finally he turned onto the hard highway, he hummed along with the bucolic melody.

Can a ghost go mad? For as I hovered in the back of this delivery van, I felt myself spreading out in all directions and yet unable to do anything at all except wait in terror for the next sustaining breath from Jeremy and Ginger, and then, when it came, indulge the barest moment of relief before the fear began to build again. It made dark and ancient memories fresh, for it was in just this way that I watched my dear nephew breathe, and breathe again, until, finally, he did not.

At the edge of town, the baker stopped to service his delivery truck, adding gasoline and washing the dust and spattered wings from the front window.

"*Hallå!*" he said to Lemmy Whittle, the town grocer, who pulled up nearby. "Is it not a great day to be alive?"

I hovered close to the grocer's ear. *Call someone!* I shouted. *This man has two children drugged and bound and possibly dying in the back of his vehicle! Call someone at once!*

"Sure," the grocer said to the baker, "but they're saying heat to beat all tomorrow." He cupped his hands to his eyes and made a show of peering into the baker's van. "Not hiding any Prince Cake back there, are you, Sten?"

The baker laughed. "No, no, not today, Lemmy. But wait a few weeks, and I am sure you will see the green smoke."

The grocer smiled and nodded. "All righty, then. I'll keep an eye out."

And then the baker and the grocer went about their business just as they might have done at any ordinary moment of any ordinary day. Is this how the horrors move hidden among us—carried in the pockets and cuffs of the commonplace and the routine?

From the service station, the baker wheeled his delivery truck onto Main Street. It was early Sunday evening; the street was quiet. The van passed by the darkened bakery and—what was this?—pulled into a space near the café. The baker glanced at the covered bodies in the back—they still intermittently breathed; otherwise they were motionless—then without locking the doors or raising the windows behind him, he walked into Elbow's Café.

Upon entering, the baker genially received the welcoming nods and greetings of his fellow citizens. He found the Sunday newspaper on a seat near the front counter and, passing a friendly glance here and there, made his way to a table in the middle of the room, where he snapped open the newspaper and began to read.

Jenny Applegarth set a glass of iced water on the table. "Well," she said in her good-natured way, "to what do we owe this little surprise?"

The baker's blue eyes twinkled. "A beautiful Sunday and a strange hankering for one of Elbow's beef pies."

As Jenny Applegarth walked toward the kitchen, I said, *Listen, if you will. This man—he is the Finder of Occasions. Jenny Applegarth, listen. You must listen!*

"Beef pie," she said to Elbow Adkins through the window to the kitchen.

Fräulein Applegarth! I said in a rising voice. I was shouting, actually. *Listen! You must listen!*

She scooped a glass full of ice and poured iced tea.

Jeremy's father emerged through the swinging kitchen doors carrying an empty tray. He began clearing dishes from a vacated table.

Jeremy is in trouble! I screamed into his ear. *He and Ginger—in terrible trouble!*

He wiped the table clean, and as he passed by the baker's table, he tipped his head and said, "How are you, Sten?"

"*Hallå*, Mr. Johnson," the baker replied. "It's good to see you out and about."

Over his lowered newspaper, his cheerful face might have seemed as comforting as the rising sun.

"Good to be out," Jeremy's father said, and he cast a glance across the room to Jenny Applegarth, who gave him a quick smile in return.

"And how's that boy of yours?" the baker asked. "Getting into trouble or staying out of it?"

"Oh, mostly staying out of it, I guess. Wish he'd get out more, though."

The baker nodded. "It's the game-show disappointment, I suppose."

"That's part of it, sure," Jeremy's father said. "But it's also what went on . . . there at your house."

The baker waved his hand dismissively. "That was nothing. Some mischief by"—he winked—"whoever it was."

"Yeah, well, I wish everyone was as forgiving as you are," Mr. Johnson said.

As Jenny Applegarth set a steaming beef pie in front of the baker, he smiled and said, "You have an unusual boy there, Mr. Johnson. Very bright, very bright, indeed." He cut into his pie. "I just hope this town doesn't drive him away."

Jeremy's father, clearing the next table, stopped abruptly. "How's that?"

"Oh, it's just that I've seen it before." The baker blew softly on his forkful of steaming food. "And there have been so many runaways lately."

Jeremy's father stiffened. "Jeremy's no runner. That's just not his way."

"I'm sure you're right, Mr. Johnson. Though, of course"— he cast a twinkling eye toward Jenny Applegarth—"you can't underestimate the power of female persuasion."

Mr. Johnson, blushing slightly, brought his curled fingers to his cheek as if to rake them through his beard but then realized the beard was gone. He took up his cleaning with renewed industry, and the baker continued his leisurely meal.

I hastened back to the van and drew close to the covered bodies.

Jeremy, can you hear me? Are you there? Listen, if you will! My voice rose. *Wake up, Jeremy! You must wake up and scream and shout!*

He did not stir. There was only the occasional rise and fall of the coverlet. The time between each breath stretched almost beyond my endurance.

Back and forth I shuttled between the café and the van, between assuring myself that Jeremy and Ginger were still alive and seeking to effect their rescue. Twice more I tried to gain the attention of Jenny Applegarth and Mr. Johnson and even, with every decibel I might muster, Elbow Adkins himself.

Nothing.

No one heard me.

Once Jenny Applegarth stopped at the baker's table and stood smiling down at him. "So, Sten, maybe you'll tell me the secret of the Prince Cakes."

The baker seemed startled. "What do you mean, the secret?"

Jenny Applegarth chuckled. "How you get them perfectly, identically scrumptious time after time."

The baker's cheerful manner recomposed itself. "Ah, well. I'm afraid even a woman of your beauty cannot coax that from me. Otherwise, you would soon be making my own Prince Cakes as well as I make them!"

"Or maybe better!" Jenny Applegarth said with a laugh, and

moved on to another table. Finally, the baker paid his bill—
along with a generous tip—and then, with a wave to Jenny and
a nod to Jeremy's father, he strolled out to the van. When he
pulled himself into his seat, he did not so much as glance at the
rear cargo area but instead stared into the café with a strange,
satisfied smile.

Then, almost without moving his lips, he whispered in Swedish, "With Prince Cakes, my dear Jenny Applegarth, as with all
baking, the secret is the proper recipe, the proper ingredients,
and the proper oven."

The next moment, we were moving again, along Main
Street, then around two corners to the baker's house. Once inside the garage, he pulled down the door behind him, turned on
the lights, and set about his business. Though he grunted and
sweated, he worked with surprising efficiency, talking to Jeremy
and Ginger as if they could hear him.

"There, now," he whispered as he eased Jeremy onto a cart
and wheeled him through a door to a shadowy landing. "One
step closer to your destination."

The baker stood above the same spiral chute that they had
used a few weeks before, but now, instead of sacks of flour, the
baker dragged Jeremy to its lip, talking all the while. "Sorry, my
dear boy," he said. "Sorry. Just a few inches more now." And
then, with a small grunt: "Off you go."

Down Jeremy spiraled to the dark chamber below.

The baker followed by way of the stairs and, at the bottom,
switched on a light. Jeremy lay half off and half on a cushioned
cart set at the bottom of the twirling slide. "Almost there,"
the baker murmured. He pulled Jeremy's body all the way onto

the cart and then wheeled the cart across the great chamber. The squeak of the wheels was loud in the cavernous room—almost a shriek or a squeal—and, well, I cannot tell you how wretched and fearful I felt.

"Not far now, dear boy," the baker crooned. "Not far at all."

But the baker did not go to either of the two doors leading to the storerooms that Jeremy and Ginger had cleaned and stocked.

He went to the third door, the one that Jeremy had asked to look behind.

The baker pushed the door open and rolled the cart inside. The room was just as it was before—the shelves neatly stacked with baking supplies.

What I next witnessed I could scarcely believe.

By touching a hidden control, the baker caused the entire rear wall to moan and swing away. Yes, the whole wall was a secret door, through which the baker now rolled the cart. When the wall closed behind us, we stood in darkest darkness.

The baker pushed the cart forward into the blackness. I saw nothing and heard only the squealing wheels, but I sensed something else: the presence of someone or some*thing*, alive, shrouded in darkness, poised in waiting silence.

The wheels stopped squealing. I heard a metallic clank and the creak of hinges. The baker grunted, and it sounded as if Jeremy's body was being placed on a bed, for I heard the squeaking of springs.

"There, dear boy," the baker whispered. "Sleep, just sleep."

The hinge again creaked and the wheels again squealed— once more the baker was moving off through the pitch-black darkness.

I stayed with Jeremy. He still breathed.

Somewhere in the quiet of the room, it seemed that something else breathed. Breathed and waited. I stayed close to Jeremy, to be present if he awoke, or to be present if he were to stop . . .

Who knows how many minutes passed before I again heard the groaning wall, followed by the cart's shrieking wheels. I could not see the baker, but I smelled him. His scent, which had always favored sugar and baked goods, was now smoky and sour.

"Almost there," he whispered, and then I again heard the clank of metal, creak of hinges, screech of springs. "There you are, my dear girl," he said gently. "Isn't that soft and snug?"

In the darkness, I sensed a kind of fence separating Jeremy from Ginger, but it was easy enough for me to slip through, and as I bent close and waited, she at last took a breath of air. So she, too, was alive. Barely alive, perhaps, but still alive.

The baker stood quietly in the darkness for a few moments—thinking what, I could not guess—and then he began to move away. My choice was to stay with Jeremy and Ginger or to follow the baker out of this place in search of help.

I thought that I should not stay but found that I could not leave.

I hovered close to Jeremy and Ginger in the pitch-darkness, taking in the acrid, metallic smell of their bodies, listening for the faint movement of air from their lips—and, also, from some other being in the darkness. For there *was* some other creature hidden there in the darkness, I was sure of it.

Finally, with terrible trepidation, I eased through the impenetrable blackness toward the breathing that was neither Jeremy's nor Ginger's. I moved slowly, seeing nothing, listening, pulling odors toward me. The scent, I was almost certain, was human.

A person of unknown identity.

Who sat breathing and listening.

Listen, if you will, I said, and said again, but there was no response.

I darted close, to stir the air around the creature.

Then, softly, uncertainly, a male whisper touched itself to the silence.

"Hello?"

The silence and darkness was total.

"Hello," the voice said again, a little louder, and when it was met with silence, it became a whimper: "Oh no, oh no," the voice said, and there followed a soft, prolonged weeping so miserable that it would squeeze pity from stones. Eventually, the crying subsided and the breathing of this wretched creature, whoever it was, fell into the slow measures of sleep.

§

§

Time in that darkness passed with unbearable slowness. I endured not from one minute to the next but from one breath to the next—a breath from Jeremy, a breath from Ginger. As a ghost, I had grown used to the elastic nature of time and had learned to abide it with patience, but here, in this darkest darkness, I felt the minutes pressing in and thought I might be getting my first glimpse of what might prove a lasting madness, until, finally—oh, the relief of it!—I heard the only sound that could deliver me: the stirring of a human body.

It was Jeremy. He moved, and then he groaned.

He was in pain, but he was alive.

And, listen!—a murmur from Ginger!

A few long seconds passed.

Then: "That you?"

"Yeah."

Their voices sounded molten and thick.

"Oh my gosh," Ginger said. "Headache from hell."

"Yeah, me too. And it's so dark—I can't even see my own hand. Where are we, do you think? Is there anybody else here?"

Suddenly, another voice came from somewhere else in the darkness.

"I am."

Ginger and Jeremy drew themselves into utter stillness.

Several silent moments passed.

Then the voice said, "It's me. Frank Bailey."

§

§

"Where are we?" Jeremy asked through the darkness. "And what are *you* doing here? I thought you were going off to some fancy cooking school."

"Yeah, so did I. All I remember is driving down the highway with Mr. Blix, heading for the airport, eating these amazing homemade sweet-potato chips of his, and then I got thirsty and drank this strawberry stuff he'd brought along. That's the last I remember. When I woke up, I was here."

"Where's here, though?" Ginger asked. "Is this an old bomb shelter or something?"

"More like an underground motel room with bars," Frank Bailey said. "You'll see when the light comes up."

"When's that?"

"Whenever it does. You lose track of time."

All of them were silent for a moment or two. Then Jeremy said, "He did the same thing with us—salty pretzels and stuff, then strawberry nectar."

"Laced with something brain-numbing," Ginger said.

"It's not all bad here," Frank Bailey said. "The food's good. And there's a bathroom that has hot water and soap and stuff. Mine does, anyhow. Sten makes the food and brings it in. He's the only person you ever see."

"So he drugs us and puts us in his underground motel room—what does he get out of it?"

"Not sure," Frank Bailey said. He paused, and then, as if embarrassed, he said, "It's like he wants you to be his friend or something."

Ginger's voice filled with alarm. "What do you mean? What kind of friend?"

"I don't know. Maybe *friend* isn't the right word. It's more that he just wants you to hang out with him."

"Sounds kind of creepy," Ginger said.

Frank Bailey's voice was low: "I wouldn't say creepy, exactly.

It changes. Sometimes he's in a good mood, sometimes he's not. Sometimes it's like you've disappointed him, but you don't know why. At least that's how it is with me."

"What exactly happens when he comes in?" Jeremy asked.

"He brings food and sometimes clean clothes. In the morning, he leaves right away, but after supper he'll usually stay and talk. There's a space between your rooms and mine and there's a rocking chair he sits in."

"Our *rooms*?"

"Yeah," Frank Bailey said. "There are two rooms over there. I mean, they're cells, actually. They're separated by bars and they're a little smaller than mine. They've always been empty before."

"What is he going to do with us?"

"No idea." He paused. "I don't think anything really bad, though."

"Why not?" Ginger asked.

"I don't know. It's just that I don't believe Mr. Blix would ever do anything really bad to us."

Another short silence, and then Jeremy said, "You said he tells stories—what kind of stories?"

"Anything. Sweden comes up a lot, and his childhood, but it can be anything. He just likes it if you're polite and listen." They fell quiet for a time, and then Frank Bailey said, "It's so weird here. When the light's on, it's not so bad, but when the place gets dark . . ."

I detected the shuffle of feet. In the darkness Ginger could be heard exploring her cell. "There are iron bars," she said. "Concrete wall . . . and another room."

"Bathroom," Frank Bailey said.

"Small wooden table," Ginger said. She seemed to be feeling her way. "Plastic vase or something . . . one wooden chair . . . concrete floor." Then: "Okay, end of tour. Back on my bed." She paused. "This headache is like total annihilation."

"I had one, too," Frank Bailey said. "Must be from the knockout potion."

After a while, Jeremy said, "What if he's the one responsible for all these missing kids and stuff?"

Nobody said anything.

He said, "Most of those kids never show up again, do they?"

Silence. Silence and darkest darkness.

Jeremy said, "Are we out in the woods near his cabin someplace?"

I wondered suddenly if he was talking to me. I said, *You are in the basement of his house behind the bakery.*

"So you're here," Jeremy said. He sounded relieved. "And you won't leave?"

Yes, I am here, and no, I will not leave.

"So *who's* here?" Ginger asked. "And *who* won't leave?"

"Oh," Jeremy said. "You. So you're here. But I knew you were, didn't I, so I don't know why I said it. I guess I'm still not thinking right." He let a moment pass. "But I would just love someone to tell us how Sten got us here."

He gave you the potion. Then he wrapped you up and brought you to town. While you lay in the back of his van, he ate heartily in the café and chatted with your father and Jenny Applegarth as if nothing was wrong. And then he brought you to the garage of his house and slid you down the spiraling chute and carted you through a swinging wall in the third storeroom and put you in this darkness that is beyond

265

even my penetration. He is the Finder of Occasions, Jeremy. The villain whom it was my duty to see but did not see.

Again it was quiet.

"It's okay," Jeremy said in a small voice. Then slightly louder, "Everything will be okay."

The darkness and silence again settled over them. "When?" Ginger said.

"When what?"

"When will everything be okay?"

§

§

At longest last, after what seemed an unending night, the blackness began to lighten. It was not the rising of the sun, but it suggested it. From the darkness, forms materialized. In their separate chambers, Jeremy and Ginger could finally see each other lying on narrow cots along opposite walls and separated by an iron-barred partition. They wore the stiff, disheveled looks of hospital patients.

Their bed coverings were a deep blue, the bars of their cells had been painted Swedish red, and the stone floors were painted pastel yellow. A vase stood on a small antique table in the middle of each room. For a prison, the effect was strangely cheerful. Cut within each cell door was a very much smaller door with a fixed shelf just below it on each side. This, I supposed, was where food might be left.

Frank Bailey sat staring through the bars from within his own cell on the opposite side of the chamber. At first glance, he seemed little altered. Though his fingernails and hair had grown long, his clothes were clean, and his face was round. Fearfulness, however, had made a home in his eyes. His cell was similar to Jeremy's and Ginger's, though somewhat larger, and the vase on his table was filled with a bouquet of blue irises.

"Wow, Frank," Ginger said. "You get flowers?"

"Yeah. Mr. Blix brings them every couple of days. I think they're from his garden." He shrugged. "It's weird, but you kind of begin to look forward to it."

Between Frank Bailey's large cell and the smaller ones of Jeremy and Ginger, an open area had been made homey by a rocking chair and a braided oval rug in reds and yellows. Behind the rocking chair hung a comforting painting of a family staring into a fire while, out of doors, snow gathered on the windowpanes.

"So that rocking chair is where he sits and tells stories?" Ginger asked.

Frank Bailey nodded. He was about to say something more, but he suddenly cocked his head.

I had heard it, too: the locking mechanism, and now the groaning wall.

"Shh," Frank Bailey said. "It's him. And don't forget to play nice."

§

§

267

The baker entered, pushing a cloth-covered cart before him and looking as he had always looked—portly, cheery, hearty, and harmless.

"*Hallå!*" he said. "Is it not a great day to be alive?"

Ginger and Jeremy said nothing, but Frank Bailey smiled and said, "Yes, Mr. Blix, it is."

"Yes, yes, a great day, indeed," the baker said with a cheerful laugh. "And, for my dear young newcomers, be assured that the service here is excellent!"

"Where is *here?*" Ginger said, but the baker acted as if he had not heard. Behind him, Frank Bailey frantically gestured to Ginger to be quiet, but she paid him no mind.

"What are we doing here?" she demanded in a cold voice.

The baker, humming to himself, did not answer. Instead, with a flourish, he pulled the white cloth from the cart to reveal an array of food—breakfast pastries, grains, cream, coffee, lemon and raspberry cuts. On the lower shelf lay three bouquets of irises in three different colors—the yellow of ripe lemons, the blue of delft china, and the red of port wine. "There," he said with a hearty smile. "Did I not tell you the room service is superb?"

He began to set the food onto the ledge outside each cell, along with the flowers. "You new visitors are probably a little done in by your strange travels, but after a bite of food, you'll feel much better."

Still, the small metal door kept any of them from touching the dishes.

"Where are we?" Ginger asked again, her tone more insistent.

The baker took several deep breaths and then sat down in the blue rocking chair. He patted his white beard with his short, plump fingers. "Remember when you told me you'd like to go to the Far Far Away?" His eyes twinkled. "Well, your wish has come true! You are in the Far Far Away!"

It was quiet for a moment, and then he chuckled and pushed himself up. "Yes, yes," he said. "A great day to be alive." He crossed the room and depressed a button on the wall that immediately released the locks on the small doors beside the food.

Frank Bailey quickly reached through to grab a croissant, but neither Ginger nor Jeremy moved.

At Frank Bailey's cell, the baker accepted the old flowers that the boy nudged through, as well as a sack full of clothes, which he raised for the others to view.

"You see? Your lodgings even come with laundry service," he said. Then, noting that Jeremy and Ginger had not yet touched their food, his voice turned fatherly. "Oh, now, my dear children. You have to eat." His round cheeks plumpened as he smiled. "You need to eat and to thrive."

He piled the clothes and flowers onto the cart and began to wheel it away.

"I don't think I'm going to be doing any *thriving* here," Ginger said.

The baker, pretending not to hear, kept pushing the cart forward.

In his cell across the room, Frank Bailey was again gesturing for Ginger to quiet herself, but she would not.

"Where are you going?" she shouted at the baker.

He stopped then and turned to look at her. His expression was benign. "I'll be back. I can't tell you how much I'm looking forward to spending time with all of you. But I have duties, too.

The bakery." He smiled. "Appearances." He winked and began again to leave.

Ginger's voice rose even higher. "If anything happens to us here—"

Now the baker, as if weary, turned slowly around. "Please, dear child, you must understand. I hope very much that nothing will happen to you here. But if it does"—again his face bulged with his fulsome smile—"*no one will ever know.*"

This time, when he pushed his cart away, Ginger said nothing.

I followed the baker to the end of the corridor, where he tapped several numbers on a keypad to swing the wall open. He nudged the cart through, let his fingers dance on another key-pad, and as the wall swung shut, he stared directly through me.

Oh, to be mortal! I thought. To carry a cudgel and to own the arm to swing it!

But I am only a ghost. My sole weapon had been vigilance, and then, on a fateful Sunday in the woods, when I had most needed it, I mislaid it.

The wall groaned closed and, with a solid *clack*, locked shut.

§

§

Perhaps an hour had passed. In her cell, Ginger was stretching her arms. They had all eaten their food and drunk their water, and then Jeremy and Ginger had disappeared into their showers and come out in fresh clothes. "Okay," she said quietly. "Headache fifty percent contained."

"Yeah," Jeremy said. "I feel a little more normal, too. Or at least as normal as you can feel when you're locked up in somebody's dungeon."

Ginger was looking down at her clothes—a yellow shirt and blue shorts, both of the type she might typically wear. Jeremy's clothes—old denim pants, white T-shirt—might also have come from his own closet.

"Guess he's been planning for our visit," Ginger said.

Across the room, Frank Bailey was poking fresh irises into his vase. "Mr. Blix plans everything," he said quietly.

Jeremy and Ginger looked at him.

"I'll give you an example," he said. "On the way to the airport, before he gave me the knockout tonic, he had me write some postcards. He said he was afraid I'd get so caught up in school that I'd forget to write." He tucked the last stalk into the vase and sat on the edge of his cot. "He had me write really general stuff. 'Working hard, doing fine, weather iffy, sunny one day, cloudy the next'—that sort of thing. I remember one he dictated. 'Puff-pastry assignment really tough, but my baked Alaska was best in class.' He laughed at that one and told me to put an exclamation mark at the end of it. Then he had me sign and address them. When I was done, he said, 'There. Put those in your suitcase and just pull one out every few days and send it.'"

Through the bars Frank Bailey gave Jeremy and Ginger a mournful look. "I think he's been sending those cards to my mother so she'll think everything's okay."

"She *does* think that," Jeremy said. "I talked to her the other day. She thinks you're out in California at that cooking school."

Frank was immediately attentive. "You talked to her? Is she okay?"

Jeremy nodded. "She's fine. She misses you, I could tell, but she's fine."

"He did the same thing to us," Ginger said. "About the postcards, I mean. Only he had us write letters like we'd run away from home. I wrote my granddad that I'd jumped a train and was happier than I'd ever been." She issued a dry laugh. "When my granddad gets that letter, he'll probably be happier than he's ever been, too."

"I wrote that I was in Arizona," Jeremy said. "And my father might believe it, because he knows I've always wanted to see the Grand Canyon."

Based on yesterday's date and on the date Frank Bailey departed for the airport with the baker, they computed how long he had been down here: twenty-three days.

"Oh my God," Ginger said. "That's a long, long time."

"Seems longer," Frank Bailey said. "I would've guessed two months or something." He exhaled deeply. "The morning I left, I was so anxious to go that I hardly said good-bye to my mom." He looked down. "I knew she wanted me to hug her, but, you know, with Mr. Blix standing right there . . ."

After a moment, Ginger said, "But she knew, Frank. People who love you always know."

He looked across the room at her. "You think?"

"Yeah, I do. I really do."

And so they kept talking, mostly about what might be going

on in town, who might already be missing them, and how they might soon find them, but the questions they returned to again and again were two: Why was the baker doing this? And what did he mean to do with them?

"Maybe he just wants to have us to talk to," Frank Bailey said. "I mean, if he was going to do something to me, wouldn't he have done it in twenty-three days?"

"He abducted us, and we know it," Ginger said. "That's the big problem for a kidnapper. Once the abductee knows who the abductor is, there's no going back."

"Yeah, but he's got all these potions and stuff," Frank Bailey said. "He could just keep us here for a while, then erase our memories and have us wake up stupefied in the woods."

Ginger stared at him. "This isn't science fiction, Frank."

"No," Frank Bailey said. "There's a drug that can actually do that. They use it in cancer treatments so people don't remember the pain and will do it again."

Ginger turned to Jeremy, lying on his cot. "How come you're so quiet?"

He stared at the pale blue ceiling. "Just thinking."

"About what?"

"About how to get out of here."

She gave him a small, unhappy laugh. "Yeah? What have you got so far?"

"Not much: Keep breathing until we find a way out."

Again she gave a sour laugh.

Frank Bailey spoke up. "I have an idea about the staying-alive part."

Ginger turned. "And what's that, Frank?"

He turned his soft eyes to Ginger. "Be nicer to Mr. Blix."

This time Ginger's laugh was even more bitter. "Be *nicer* to him? My God, Frank! Where is Baileyville, anyhow—on one of the moons of Jupiter? In case you missed it, Sten Blix is a psychopathic sleazeball who's been passing himself off as the jolly baker. Not exactly the type of guy I want to be nice to."

Frank Bailey shrugged. "Okay, but just so you know, one time I got mad and was rude to him, and he left and it stayed dark for so long that I began hearing sounds and started to think I was starving to death *and* going crazy."

Ginger did not respond to this. She lay down on her cot and stared at the ceiling. After casually rubbing her eyes with both hands, she left them there for a few seconds so they covered her eyes. Perhaps the others could not guess what she was doing, but I could: she was saying one of her little prayers.

When she was done, she sat up abruptly and looked at the other two captives. "Okay, listen up. We can't just lie here stewing and worrying. We each have to figure out a way to help us pass the time."

Frank Bailey suggested a game called Twenty Questions, which they played for a time before they grew bored.

Ginger suggested exercises, which they did for a time before they grew tired.

Then Frank Bailey and Ginger turned to Jeremy, who looked like someone who had just been asked to sing for his supper.

"I don't really know any games or anything," he said.

Ginger had pressed several strands of hair between her lips. "Maybe you could tell some of those old stories of yours."

He started to decline, but I jumped in. *Yes*, I said. *It is a good*

idea. It is in the old manner of passing the time. And if you forget
something, I will prompt you.

"Okay," Jeremy said. "I can try, anyhow." He glanced at Ginger. "I mean, if you both want to listen."

"Sure," Frank Bailey said. "We could use a good story," and Ginger said, "As long as it's got a happy ending."

So Jeremy lay back on his cot with his arms folded behind his head. "This is the story of the Three Feathers," he said, and every now and then, when he was uncertain about what happened next, I would provide details. Never had the tale seemed so endearing, for it kept the prisoners distracted from their circumstances, and when the story was over, Frank Bailey and Ginger asked for another, and then another.

And so in this way the time was passed until, almost to my surprise, the groan of the swinging wall could be heard, followed by footsteps and the squeaking wheels of the baker's cart.

§

§

"*Hallå! Hallå!*" the baker called out. "Dinner is served!"

With his signature flourish, he swept the white cloth from the cart to reveal a stewpot, a plate of fruit tarts, and a full loaf of freshly baked bread, from which he began to cut slices with a long serrated knife.

I will admit, it all smelled heavenly.

"Sourdough bread," the baker said. "Frankie's favorite. And beef stew, also Frankie's favorite."

He glanced at Frank Bailey, who shrugged, as if embarrassed. "Yeah, it's really good. But I like your turkey pot pie, too."

The baker gave an appreciative laugh. "It is settled, then! Pot pie tomorrow!"

After he'd given each prisoner a portion, the baker sat in his rocking chair between the cells and watched them eat. When they were nearly finished, he questioned each of them, beginning with Frank Bailey.

"Good, yes?" he asked, and Frank Bailey said yes, it was scrumptious.

The baker turned then to Jeremy. "Good, yes?"

Jeremy stirred his wooden spoon through the peas he had left at the bottom of his bowl. Without looking up, he said, "Yeah, the food was good."

This seemed to satisfy the baker, who now regarded Ginger. "Good, yes?"

Ginger stared back at him with a contempt that could not be disguised.

"Oh," the baker said with a fallen voice. "But you see, my dear girl, if you are not an agreeable guest, I cannot be an agreeable host." He paused. "Do you see?"

Silence filled the dungeon.

"Do you see?" the baker asked again in his most patient voice.

"Yes," Frank Bailey blurted, "she sees! She definitely sees what you mean!"

The baker did not break his gaze from Ginger. "Yes? She sees?"

Ginger's face remained as stone. "The prison food's fine," she said.

For several long moments, the baker stared at her with a fixed, frozen smile, but then his expression softened and he said mildly, "Good. That is a start."

From his cart, he took out a long-stemmed clay pipe and smoked it quietly until the prisoners had finished their pastries. Then he rose and regarded the painting on the wall that I have mentioned before: the happy family seated before a cozy fire, while through the window, one can see the gently wafting snow.

"Swedish," the baker said of the painting in a reflective tone. "Swedish through and through. The painter is Swedish, the scene is Swedish, the love of warmth and family is Swedish." He turned around, a wistful smile almost hidden within his white beard. "But not everyone can find warmth in Sweden."

Well, here is a small something to report: while the baker had been staring at the painting, Jeremy removed all of the peas from his bowl and slipped them under his pillow.

The baker settled again into his rocker and repacked his pipe. "I will tell you all a story," he said. Smoke slid through his lips, and he directed his gaze at Jeremy.

"I know that you like the old tales, full of fantastic events and intrigue, but the story I am about to tell you is as strange as any fairy tale." Again he pulled on his pipe and let white smoke float through his lips.

"It will at first seem ordinary," he said, "the simple story of a boy whose father fished in the sea. The boy had troubles in school. He was clever, but none of his schoolmates saw his cleverness. They saw only his plumpness and shyness, and the more he craved their friendship, the more the other children withheld it. When the boy was seven years of age, the fisherman took him from his schooling and put him to work mending nets and cleaning fish, so that now the boy was not only plump but also foul-smelling. Wherever he went, people stepped away, so strong was the smell of herring that clung to his skin and to his clothes."

The baker paused to draw smoke. "The boy ran away," he continued. "Who could blame him? He was a clever boy, and in a faraway village he found work at a bakery, where"—the baker's eyes twinkled—"plumpness was no liability." He nodded. "Yes," he said, "things were finally going well for the boy, but this is where the tale takes a mysterious turn."

He smoked as he composed his thoughts.

"So . . . This bakery was run by a big-hearted man and his handsome, hard-eyed wife. They taught the boy everything about the trade, even its most particular intricacies, for he was a boy who listened and forgot nothing. The baker taught him the secrets of *Prinsesstårta*, which he prepared as a sweet commemoration whenever a villager died, and he taught him his method of announcing the arrival of this delicacy with green smoke. The boy forgot nothing. He heard whispers of the woman's receipt of a large inheritance, and he forgot nothing. He heard them whisper how wonderful a baker the boy had become and how much money he was making for them, and he forgot nothing.

"Several years passed, and the boy grew into manhood. He was made to work even harder, beginning long before the sun rose, while the baker and his wife slept. Still, he loved the bakery, and when he was friendly and smelled like baked goods, people no longer stepped away from him. In fact"—and here the baker chuckled—"when the proprietor was not in the room, the proprietress leaned very close."

The baker paused, as if savoring this part of the story.

"One wintry day, the woman's husband fell gravely ill and

278

did not recover. The *Prinsesstårta* were prepared, and the green smoke rose. The baker's wife grieved less than might have been expected, and before long, she had drawn the boy into the business as a full partner and sole heir. But in only a year, the woman grew into a terrible and jealous hag, and before long, she, too, fell ill. She tried to speak before she died, but her throat had tightened. She could only grunt and groan and point wildly at the boy, who shed big tears as he tenderly held her hand. 'She is trying to say that I am to carry on with the bakery if she should die,' the boy explained to the attending nurse. 'I think she is afraid it might fall into the wrong hands.'

"The old hag took a long time in dying. The boy stayed by her side, watching each small step in her slow progress until at last she was dead. The boy baked the *Prinsesstårta* and fed into the fire the crystals that turned the smoke green. He ran the bakery to its former standards, and even higher, which won him the admiration of the villagers. And then one day, he sold the business, and a week later he was gone with the widow's fortune, never to be seen in that country again."

The baker regarded his pipe, which he had allowed to go out. "The end," he said. "A wonderfully strange story, don't you think?"

He looked expectantly from one cell to the other.

"Yes," Frank Bailey said.

"Yeah," Jeremy said in a low voice.

"I guess," Ginger murmured.

The baker was smiling and nodding, for he had done as he had hoped to do—he had pulled his prisoners into his story and carried them along its dark path. He stood and began collecting dishes. When he began rolling the cart away, Ginger said, "What did the baker and his wife die of?"

The baker, as if he had not heard, continued his unhurried exit.

§

§

When the groaning wall had swung shut and the dungeon fallen quiet, Jeremy gathered the peas from beneath his pillow, washed them in the basin, and held them in his open hand for Ginger to see.

"Hope you're not trying to pass those off as magic beans."

He shook his head. "It's our calendar. We don't have a way to mark days down here, so every day I'll give you a pea and we'll know how many days have passed. Up to twenty-seven, anyhow. Because that's how many peas we have."

Ginger's eyes filled with alarm. "You think we're going to be down here twenty-seven days? You don't think we're going to be rescued?"

"I do," Jeremy said. "But—"

"Keep your peas," she said. "If we're still down here after twenty-seven days, I don't want to know it."

Soon thereafter, the lights dimmed slowly, as to suggest dusk and nightfall, and one by one, the prisoners fell into the heavy breathing of sleep. Sometime later—how much time had passed, I could not have said—Ginger began to make fearful, murmuring noises that awakened Jeremy.

"Hey!" he said in an urgent whisper. "Ginger! Are you okay?"

Her murmuring stopped, and she said, "Oh. Yeah. Bad dream. Sorry."

"And you're okay now?"

"Yeah, I'm fine. Except, you know, that we're *here*." A few moments passed. "That story he told. Didn't it sound like he poisoned the baker and his wife?"

"Yeah, it did," Jeremy said quietly. "And took the money and came here."

"What I was thinking about was how he made the green smoke when the baker and his wife died. It's like that's what he does after he's—you know . . ." She let her voice trail off. "He's worse than the villains in those stories of yours."

Jeremy gave a small laugh. "It depends. In one story, the step-mother chops up her stepson and puts him in a stew that she feeds to the boy's father."

"Okay, that's worse," she said, yawning. "Not that it's much consolation."

After a time, Jeremy whispered, "The thing is, in fairy tales, when the heroes are chopped up or eaten by the wolf, they still come back to life at the end and live happily ever after. But this isn't like that. If we die, we stay dead."

But Ginger could not reply, for she had given in to sleep.

§

§

Slowly the days passed. Often I imagined slipping out with the baker in order to try somehow to find help in the village, but I could not break my pledge to Jeremy to stay. Ginger did accept the pea that Jeremy gave her every morning—she now had seven of them. The prisoners listened to the baker's dark stories, and they ate the baker's food (all of which, it must be admitted, looked delectable). They exchanged their soiled clothes for clean, their spent flowers for fresh. They wondered who might be looking for them, and they discussed ways of escape. Nothing offered much hope. Jeremy and I continued telling the tales, one after another, always with happy endings. Often I would embellish, or even add episodes, that they might divert the others a little longer. When I did this, Jeremy would hesitate and cock his head but then go on with the amendments I provided. He and I could not talk during the day, but at night, when the others were asleep, he would whisper, "You there?" and I would say, *Yes, Jeremy, I am here.*

And there was someone else, too, making pleas in secret. Whenever she found that the others were momentarily paying her no attention, Ginger would cover her eyes with her hands and her lips would softly move. And once, when the others were in their baths and she was completely alone, she placed her hands to her eyes and whispered softly, "Please watch over Jeremy and Frank and me, too, and please help someone see the baker for what he is and discover that we're here, wherever we are, and, most of all, don't let us all die here without ever getting to—"

But she did not finish the thought. The sound of Jeremy's shower had suddenly ceased, so she whispered, "Amen," and fell silent.

Without ever getting to . . . what? I wondered. What might she be regretting not having the chance to do? And a darker question yet: If in this dungeon she were to slip free of her mortal self, would she, too, be destined to drift through eternity searching for the thing undone? It did not seem impossible. Nothing, it seemed, was too cruel to be true.

One night, when the day had seemed endless and the prisoners' stomachs were rumbling with hunger, the baker rolled in his cart and announced that he had news from the outside world. "Yes, yes," he said cheerfully, "and so much of it hitting so close to home!"

The prisoners watched him as he set the cart and uncovered a stewpot and a beautifully browned loaf of freshly baked bread.

"I will begin with my visit with our dear Sheriff Pittswort, who came in for crème-filled pastries. As we chatted, I could not keep myself from asking about our missing young people. 'Oh, them,' he said. 'They're just out adventurin'. They jumped a train. The girl wrote her grandpa telling him so.'" The baker's eyes glistened with pleasure. "The sheriff told me he did a little investigating and, lo and behold, they found Jeremy's and Ginger's bicycles near the siding, an ideal place, according to the sheriff, to catch a train." A laugh rumbled up from the baker's ample belly. "*Lo and behold!* Our Sheriff Pittswort has solved the case!"

The baker lifted the lid from the pot, stirred his stew with a wooden spoon, and sampled it appraisingly. "Yes, I think this will meet with your approval." He took out his carving knife and began drawing a flat file back and forth across its long blade.

"What other news?" he said. "Oh, yes, Dauntless Crinklaw. Our good mayor. Once he heard about Jeremy's train adventure, he said he had no choice but to start legal proceedings against Jeremy *in absentia* for his nonpayment of debt." The baker held up the knife—its blade gleamed when turned to the light. "*Lo and behold! In absentia!* What phrasemakers our villagers can be!"

He began slicing the bread—its splendid aroma spread through the chamber.

"Oh! But I forgot the most interesting news of all! There is one person in town who believes something is wrong with our narrative. Our dear Deputy McRaven believes that Miss Boultinghouse has met with foul play, and he says so to one and all. But no one pays him any attention, and do you know why?" The baker's face swelled with happy expectation. "*Because no one listens to a dwarf!*"

The baker laughed so hard that his great stomach shook.

"No," he said, catching his breath, "the deputy will never uncover our secret, but he has revealed his own!" The baker nodded to himself. "Just think of it. Our deputy isn't worried about Jeremy or Frankie, and he has never worried about all the other missing children over the years. But now he is worried sick about Miss Boultinghouse. Yes, worried sick! So what has he inadvertently announced to the town? That our poor, sad, solitary dwarf has been enchanted by a fifteen-year-old schoolgirl!"

Again the baker's stomach shook with laughter.

Could it be true? Could Deputy McRaven have been following Ginger because he was lovesick?

Yes. I saw it at once. It not only could be true but most certainly was.

"A laughingstock," the baker said. "That is what our deputy has become."

He began to ladle thick beef stew into bowls. "Oh," he said. "One last thing! Jeremy's show was on the air last night, but I'm afraid the ending did not change. A pity, really, because just think of it—if he had answered that last question and won all that money, he would not have needed to sneak away to work on a wood crib in the forest and then"—he gave his broadest smile—"we would not all be together now."

He set the food on the ledge of each cell and was about to open the little doors when Ginger said, "They're going to find us, you know."

The baker stilled his hand.

Frank Bailey said hurriedly, "But you've been nice to us, Mr. Blix, so even if they did find us, we wouldn't tell them anything."

The baker kept his eyes on Ginger. "And how will they find you, dear girl? You do not even know where you are."

"We're in your dungeon," Ginger said.

The baker laughed. "Oh, ho! Is that where you think we are? In a dungeon?"

"Yeah," Ginger said, "that's what we think."

"But you might be anywhere, dear child. You might be in a converted silage bin on a deserted farm. Or in a concrete chamber out in the woods. Or in a secret vault under the old quarry."

At these suggestions, all darkly possible, Ginger fell quiet.

The baker's voice softened. "But do you know?—it doesn't matter where you are, because no one is ever going to find you."

He smiled. "Now, my dear child, if you will just apologize for your outburst, you may all have your dinner."

If eyes could kill, Ginger's stony glare would have struck the baker dead.

The dungeon filled with silence.

Then, in a low voice, Jeremy said, "We're beneath your house."

The baker's eyes danced merrily toward Jeremy. "Oh! Do you think so?"

"Yes," Jeremy said. "I do. You drugged us, and you drove us back to town and left us in the back of the van while you went into Elbow's Café and ate and even talked with my father. Then you drove into your garage and slid us down the chute and carted us through the third room and swung open the back wall and brought us here."

It took Jeremy perhaps a quarter of a minute to say these words, and in that time the color had drained completely from the baker's face. He stared in disbelief, and when he spoke, it was almost to himself. "You were awake? But if you were awake, why didn't you call out?" Wildly, his eyes flew everywhere, and then alighted again on Jeremy. "But you were not awake. You were cataleptic. How could you see?" His voice climbed in register. "How did you see?"

Tell him nothing, I said.

The baker's eyes turned to ice, and so did his voice. "How did you see?"

"I don't know how I saw," Jeremy said. "I just saw what I saw."

The baker held his gaze on Jeremy, and then a smile slowly returned to his lips. "Your eyes were open," he said. "You were cataleptic, but your eyes were open. That is how you saw."

Then he collected the prisoners' untouched dinners and departed.

§

§

The moment the baker was gone, Ginger turned to Jeremy. "So?"

"So what?"

"How did you know all that stuff that Sten was doing while we were conked out?"

"I didn't. I mean, I think he might be right—that my eyes were open and it sort of registered in some dark corner of my mind and then, when he began to talk about it, it kind of worked itself free."

She stared at him. "Seriously?"

He shrugged. "I guess so. How else would I have seen it?"

She kept her eyes fixed on him. "Yeah, well, that was what I was asking."

From across the chamber, Frank Bailey said, "Know what I noticed?"

The other two turned toward him.

"That we're going without our dinner," he said. "I mean, everything was just fine, and then you guys had to start talking about dungeons and seeing things and getting Mr. Blix all worked up." He shook his head. "Because I can tell you that when Mr. Blix is all worked up—"

He did not finish speaking because the lights had begun to dim.

A moment later, the prisoners sat in darkest darkness.

"Oh, God," Frank Bailey said, and Jeremy asked him what he meant, but by that time he did not have to.

The sounds had begun.

"What's *that*?" Ginger said.

The sounds were soft and strange and unsettling, a kind of whisking, as if from the movements of small living creatures. Nothing could be seen. The darkness was impenetrable—we all might have been blind.

Frank Bailey said, "Sounds like mice."

"Or rats," Ginger said.

"Do you see anything?" Jeremy asked.

"Not a thing," she said, and I added, *Nor do I. I do not smell anything, either.*

Something metallic suddenly scraped across the stone floor. "That's me," Ginger said. "I'm pulling my cot closer to yours. Can you pull yours over, too?"

Jeremy did. Then, into the darkness, he whispered, "You okay?"

"Yeah. It's just that one time, when I was little, I saw some rats eating a not-quite-dead barn kitten . . . and it kind of affected the way I feel about them."

"Yeah," Jeremy said. "I guess it would."

*   *   *

The night was so long that it might have been three nights, or four, or five. The sounds of whisking rodents never ceased. From Ginger, Jeremy, and Frank Bailey, I occasionally heard the rhythmic breathing of sleep, but more often I heard heavy sighing and anxious whispering.

"You awake?"

"Yeah."

"Do you think the light will ever come on again?"

"Sure," Jeremy said.

"Yeah, you're right," Ginger said. "I mean, what would be the point of keeping prisoners in total darkness until they go stark raving bonkersville?"

Who can say how many hours passed, but at last, when the darkness finally began to thin and the dim light rose, Ginger and Jeremy lay asleep in their cots on either side of the iron-barred wall. And there was something else, too. Ginger had slipped her hand through the bars and it lay wrapped in Jeremy's hand.

§

§

Upon wakening, Ginger quickly pulled back her hand. Jeremy, too, began to stir. "Okay," Ginger said, "whoever doesn't believe in hell should spend a night in this hotel."

Jeremy stood and began inspecting the floor, looking into corners.

"No droppings," he said. "If there were mice or rats, you'd see droppings." He glanced across the dungeon at Frank Bailey. "You think it was just sound effects? To toy with us and give us the willies?"

Frank Bailey tugged at his ear. "I don't know. Maybe Mr. Blix was just trying to get our attention, or something."

"He did that, and then some," Ginger said. "I need a shower just to wash off a little bit of the bad way I'm feeling." But a moment later, she stepped back out of the tiny bathroom with an expression of shock. "No water."

"That's a new one," Frank Bailey said. He blinked. "I wonder what it means."

"I think it means he's playing mind games with us," Jeremy said.

"Yeah," Frank Bailey replied in a quiet voice. "And they're kind of working."

"No!" Ginger said, her voice stiff and rigid. "We can't let him win. And we can't let him think he's winning."

She is right, Jeremy, I said. *Perseverance is all. You must resist and adapt and never give up.*

"You're right," Jeremy said to me, but Ginger, thinking he was talking to her, said, "Of course I'm right. Who said I wasn't?"

"A motto just came to me," Jeremy said. "Resist, adapt, never give up."

"Sure," Ginger said. "We can make it an acronym. *Rangu.*"

Ginger and Jeremy then heard something they had not heard since the beginning of their incarceration: a laugh from Frank Bailey.

"Rangu," he said, and another, smaller laugh spilled out.

290

"Sounds like a spaghetti sauce." His grin seemed to leap across the chamber. "I like it."

Jeremy nodded. "And the other thing we have to remember is that there are people besides McRaven who are going to miss us. And pretty soon they're going to begin looking in the right places."

Ginger nodded. So did Frank Bailey, who added, "But until then, I could do with a little food."

Eleven peas lined the ledge above Ginger's sink.

Four days had passed without food. The prisoners' stomachs were hollow. They did not exercise. Jeremy's voice was tired as he told the old tales, and Ginger and Frank Bailey had difficulty listening. They were just waiting for food, or for whatever else might happen next. And finally, when they had begun to think they never would, they heard the moan of the wall, the squeal of the cart, the clinking of dishes. And there was the baker, smiling, a white cloth blanketing the serving cart.

"*Hallå,*" he said. "Is it not a great day to be alive? Is everybody comfortable? Is everyone sleeping well?"

Ginger and Jeremy stared at him.

Frank Bailey stared at the cart.

Like a magician, the baker whisked away the white cloth

to reveal four platters covered with metal domes. He lifted one dome to reveal a savory cut of roasted beef. A rich aroma bloomed into the air.

The prisoners looked at the food with the dilated eyes of predators.

"Roasted beef," the baker said, "mashed potatoes and gravy, fresh roasted beets, just-baked rolls, and a pleasant little dessert. But first"—he set the domes back over the beef—"I need each of you to write a little note to your loved ones."

It took several moments for the baker's meaning to settle in.

"No," Ginger said in a stony voice. "The answer is no. If you're going to abduct and hide us and do who knows what, okay. But don't expect us to help."

The baker smiled at her, then turned to Jeremy. "And you?"

Jeremy shook his head. "Same."

The baker turned to the other enclosure, lifted the plate cover, and tilted the platter to display more clearly the delectable beef. "And what does Frankie say?"

Several long moments passed before Frank Bailey pried his gaze from the plate. In a small voice he said, "I'm with them."

"Ah, I see," the baker said, slowly setting the cover back over the plate. "Frankie is now with them."

He scanned the chamber and sighed. "I understand. But please don't say I didn't offer," he said, and with that he began to wheel the serving cart away.

Something changed in Jeremy's face—I had the presentiment that some idea had occurred to him. "Wait!" he called.

The baker stopped and peered back.

"I'll write the letter," he said. He looked from Ginger to Frank Bailey. "We all will."

Ginger and Frank Bailey both looked at him in wonderment.

"We'll write the notes . . . but only if tomorrow night you bring us spaghetti with lots of good spaghetti sauce. We all like Ragu spaghetti sauce"—and here he glanced meaningfully at Ginger and Frank Bailey—"but we want the real thing, made from scratch."

"Spaghetti with sauce? Of course, of course," the baker replied, a smile widening behind his white beard. "And truly, I would have hated to have this wonderful food go to waste. And now we must hurry so that it won't grow cold!"

He slipped pen and paper through the food slot of each cell and then stood in front of Frank Bailey. "Please tell your mother that you have taken a job as a cook on a private yacht that will have set sail by the time your letter is received. You will be gone six months, perhaps longer. You look forward to the travel. There is no need for worry."

He waited as Frank Bailey wrote. So, too, did Ginger. But Jeremy began writing on his own. When the baker saw this, he said, "Dear boy, if there is one word not to my liking, you will have to redo it completely."

Jeremy nodded. "I know. All I want to do is let my father know how much I . . ." His voice trailed off.

"Of course," the baker said in a sympathetic tone. "How much you miss him."

He turned then to Ginger. "You will advise your grandfather that you are sorry not to have written for some time and that it may be a while until the next letter because you and Jeremy are staying with some really nice"—a smile—"no, make that *fabulous* people who grow all their own food and live off the grid."

When Ginger pushed her letter through the slot, the baker

made a close study of it before nodding his approval. As with Frank Bailey, he gave Ginger an envelope to address, then folded the letter into it. Then he turned his eyes toward Jeremy.

"Almost done," Jeremy said, and added a last word or two before signing his name. He passed it through, and while the baker read it, I read it, too.

> Dear Dad,
>
> Still thinking of you while we
> travel across the country going
> everywhere almost. Miss you day &
> night wherever I go, but I am
> still having lots and lots of fun
> (but not when we hoe weeds
> at this far-off place where we're
> staying now). Ginger says we found
> Easy Street. I'm not so sure, but
> maybe we did find our way to
> Escape Street—from the place where
> nothing was going right. But I want to say
> Thank you, Dad, for everything. I love you.
>
> XXX, Jeremy
>
> P.S. I probably won't write again until we get to a place
> closer to a post office.

"Poignant," the baker said when he was finished. "Touching, even." In his Saint Nicholas–like smile, I thought I detected a knowingness that I did not understand. "If something does happen to you—God forbid, of course—this will provide some solace to your father."

He set the bundle of letters on the lower shelf of his rolling cart.

"And now your reward," he said, and slid his long carving knife from its case to begin slicing the beef, which fell smoothly in thin, neat slices.

As he worked, he talked. "All is well in the outside world," he reported. "There were several more legal notices posted on the door of your bookstore, Jeremy, but"—a brief flourish of the knife—"life goes on. Your father has arranged to rent a room in Mrs. Bathgate's boardinghouse"—the baker cast a wink toward Jeremy—"conveniently located just across the street from the home of Jenny Applegarth."

The captives said nothing, yet I could not help but notice how Jeremy eyed the fork and knife in the baker's hands as he began adding the sliced beef to the plates of potatoes, beets, and hot rolls. Then, as the baker set the meals onto the ledges outside each cell, Jeremy said in a low voice, "That food is poisoned."

The baker looked at him with surprise, and then began to laugh. "This food is untainted, my dear boy. You have my word."

"Why don't you have a bite, then?"

The baker paused only the barest moment. "Of course!" he said. "Why not?" With fork and carving knife in hand, he approached the platter on the ledge of Ginger's cell. "What would you like me to try, dear girl?"

Ginger chose the beets, and watched him cut away a piece and take it into his mouth without hesitation.

He crossed to Frank Bailey's chamber. "And you, Frankie?"

Frank Bailey shook his head. "Nothing, Mr. Blix. I know you wouldn't poison it."

He moved then to Jeremy's cell. "And you, my dear boy?"

Jeremy stood to look more closely at the food. "The beef, I guess."

The baker set his fork into the beef and began to cut away a small piece. At that very moment, Jeremy shot his arm through the bars and grabbed at the knife!

I was completely surprised by his action—but the baker was not.

He snatched the knife back, and Jeremy's hand closed . . . not around the handle but around the blade. His scream pierced the quiet, and when he released the knife and held his hand open before him, a long, clean incision brimmed with bright blood, which spread in red profusion.

"Jeremy!" Ginger said, and at once tried to tear a strip of gray cloth from her bedding, but the baker was already offering a cloth napkin. "There," he said in a strangely consoling voice, "tie it tight and the bleeding will stop."

It was true. For a time, the blood wicked into the napkin, but then it ceased, and the baker said, "Well, well, Jeremy. Quite gallant, really." His smile narrowed. "But, really, my dear boy, what would you have done with the knife if you had gotten it?"

Jeremy sat on the edge of his cot staring at the ground and holding his bloodied hand in his lap. "Whatever I could," he said in a low voice.

"Of course," the baker said. "Whatever you could. But, really, what would that have been? A few more days without food and water for you and your dear friends, and you would have had to push the knife meekly through the bars so you could all go on living."

His luminous blue eyes fell on Jeremy. "But I believe you knew that."

Jeremy said nothing.

"Oh, yes," the baker said evenly. "This was your little diversion."

Ginger issued a harsh, derisive laugh. "Diversion from what?"

The baker's cold blue eyes turned to her. Then, very slowly, he reached down to the cart and retrieved Jeremy's note to his father. "From this, my dear girl."

He unfolded the note and, with a pencil, drew a long loop that encircled the first letter of each line. He then held the note up for Ginger to see.

S	till thinking of you while we
t	ravel across the country going
e	verywhere almost. Miss you day &
n	ight wherever I go, but I am
s	till having lots and lots of fun
(b	ut not when we hoe weeds
a	t this far-off place where we're
s	taying now). Ginger says we found
E	asy Street. I'm not so sure, but
m	aybe we did find our way to
E	scape Street—from the place where
n	othing was going right. But I want to say
T	hank you, Dad, for everything. I love you.

Everything was quiet until Frank Bailey said, "You aren't going to take away the plates now, are you, Mr. Blix?"

The baker turned a cruel look on Frank Bailey. "I am afraid I must. Even yours, Frankie." His eyes locked on the poor, hapless boy. "You are part of the cabal, Frankie, with your plots and your jokes about Rangu spaghetti sauce."

Oh, how chilling the implications of these words were! The captives all grasped it, but Ginger was the first to speak.

"You *listen* to us?"

The baker's laugh was almost a sneer, and yet I sensed there was pride, too, in the comprehensive nature of his powers. "Yes. I listen." His lips formed a false smile. "Though most of what I hear is awfully tedious." He turned to Jeremy. "Those tales you tell, for example. I notice you leave out all the good ones."

Jeremy said nothing, but Frank Bailey asked what the baker meant.

Sten Blix did not even glance at Frank Bailey. He kept his eyes fixed on Jeremy. "He only tells you the ones with happy endings." His voice was cold—Ginger hugged her arms to her chest for warmth. "But there are other tales, too. Tales with dark endings even for heroes who"—he let his gaze move from prisoner to prisoner—"*resisted, adapted, never gave up.*"

He set the plates on the cart and pushed it forward a step or two, and then, as if remembering something, drew himself up. "Yes," he said, "it is true that there are people in the village who may miss you—the dwarfish deputy and Jeremy's father and Frankie's mother, and . . . well, I am sure there must be others. But then, when Frankie's and Ginger's new letters are received and passed around, their minds will be put at ease."

As the baker watched them absorb this news, it fell deeply quiet until, at last, Ginger whispered, "What did we do to deserve this?"

The baker smiled and looked away. "The pretty girl has to ask? The pretty girl who devised a plan to enter my house for the sole purpose of playing me for her fool?"

In a soft voice, Frank Bailey said, "What about me, Mr. Blix? What did I ever do?"

The baker did not look at him. "Oh, poor Frankie. Who has been wondering this from the first day of his visit, and now, at last, he will know. Does he remember that I presented him with two choices—one to stay in the bakery and work with me, and the other to go off to a fancy cooking school in San Francisco?" The baker's cold voice turned colder. "That was Frankie's trial. A test of his allegiance. I had hoped he would choose to stay to work with me in the bakery of his own accord, but . . ."

He touched his hand to his white beard. "Here is something I have learned. Some people crave Prince Cakes. Some people crave friendship. But neither one provides anything that lasts. Friendship, too, is just butter, flour, and sugar."

"No," Jeremy said, his voice low and vehement. "That isn't true."

The baker turned and seemed to be studying him as one might a specimen in a laboratory. "Now, why Jeremy is here is a question not so easily answered." His gaze drifted to the picture on the wall. "Even from the first days when your mother came into the bakery . . . I told you that you were a burrower, and that is true, but do you know that you burrowed down into your blankets only when you caught sight of me? Yes. Only then. It was

299

as if you could see in me what no one else would. Your mother would laugh at your burrowing, but I knew that you saw me, and I knew what it meant." The baker's blue eyes fell into a calmness that made my ancient spirit quiver. "It meant," he said quietly, "that you would come visit me here in the great chamber."

He exhaled, then walked over to the painting of the family sitting cozily before the glowing fire. He reached out as if to do something with it—take it down, perhaps—but he changed his mind and merely straightened it slightly. He returned to the serving cart and took up the plates, one after another, and scraped them so that the food fell on the stone floor just outside each cell. Then, without another glance at his prisoners, he pushed the cart away. The wall moaned closed behind him.

At once, two things happened: Frank Bailey knelt to the ground to pull scraps of food through the bars and Ginger placed her hands over her eyes and moved her lips without speaking. Jeremy watched her. When finally she took her hands from her eyes, he said, "What were you doing?"

She looked at him with wretched eyes. "Praying," she whispered.

Frank Bailey paused in his collection of food. "You know what they say, though—the Lord helps those who help themselves."

Well, what is true is what must be reported. Jeremy and Ginger exchanged shameful glances, and then they, too, were reaching through the bars, bringing rolls to their mouths, lemon cuts, pieces of beef, bits of potatoes, and beets. They licked the gravy from their fingers. They kept their eyes from one another so that they would not see the creatures they were, at the hand of the baker, becoming.

Soon thereafter, the dungeon fell into darkest darkness.

§

§

Schrecklich is my native word for miserable, and, oh, what a *schrecklich* time this was! The night of the rodents, which had seemed interminable, was child's play compared with what the prisoners endured that night. There was again the whisking of mice, but then, after a time, we heard something new and terrible: a subtler, softer sound, a kind of slithering that suggested vipers exploring the dungeon's nooks and crannies for prey.

And then—the sound seemed to shoot forward from the wall and grab at the throat—there was a small, sudden squeal, as if a mouse had just been slain.

"Oh, jeez," Frank Bailey said, his voice wavering.

"Sound effects," Jeremy said. "It's got to be sound effects."

Yes, I said, *it must be. I smell nothing, and vipers have a musky smell.*

"The thing is," Frank Bailey said, "they sound pretty real to me."

"He can hear you, Frank," Jeremy said, trying to keep his voice even. Closer by, Ginger whispered, "They do, though, don't they, Jeremy? They do sound real."

The slithering seemed to come from one direction, then another.

In the darkness, Jeremy could be heard taking a deep breath. "Okay," he said. "I'm going to lie down on the floor."

"With the snakes?" Ginger said. "Are you crazy?"

"I've got to. It's the only way to find out if they're real."

Jeremy could be heard easing himself slowly down.

"Okay," he announced. "Feet on the floor . . . Rear end on the floor . . . Lying down on my back . . . Totally flat." A few seconds passed. "And totally okay."

"Really?" Ginger said.

"Yep. Nothing going on down here."

But then he fell quiet just as the whisking and slithering suddenly increased, and Jeremy let out a sudden, bloodcurdling shriek, followed by, "*Oh . . . my . . . God!*"

"*What?*"

"Nothing, actually," he said in a matter-of-fact voice. "I was just kind of bored. Saw a chance there to break the ice."

"You're a droll boy," Ginger said, but she sounded reassured.

Jeremy could be heard standing up. He cleared his throat. "So is that it?" he shouted up at the ceiling in his loudest voice. "Is that the best you can do? Sound effects of phantom snakes and phantom mice?"

Almost at once, the whisking and slithering sounds abated.

The ensuing silence did not feel comforting.

The prisoners were waiting for whatever might happen next.

And then it came: a new sound, one so faint I could barely detect it.

"Did you hear that?" Jeremy whispered.

"Yeah, I did."

"Me too."

"It's like a horrible moaning or something."

"What is it?"

Everyone knew the answer, but no one wanted to say it. Finally, Ginger did. "It's human," she said.

It was true. The sound emanated from a human, one in great misery.

"Maybe it's just a recording."

"Yeah, but what of? It sounds like somebody dying."

Everyone was quiet.

"It could be an actor," Jeremy said. "Who's playing someone dying."

"Yeah," Ginger said. "A really good actor. One who you'd bet anything was actually dying."

The faint, terrible sounds of misery changed in tendency but did not cease. They moved from a sobbing wail to a hopeless whimper and back again. They went on minute after minute, hour after hour. And then, when the sounds seemed as if they had wrapped the room with agony and squeezed from it the last breath of hope and oxygen, they stopped.

Had the human died? Fallen asleep? Had the recording merely ended? Who could know? Who but the baker could know?

§

§

"Fifteen," Ginger said when the lights gradually brightened and she had set another pea in the line above her sink. The baker had not appeared since the eleventh day. The prisoners would spend this day as they had the day before: lying on their cots listening to the old tales Jeremy told them, talking about their hunger, and sipping foul water from their flower vases and hoping that it would not sicken them. When Ginger covered her eyes to say one of her silent prayers, Jeremy said, "Make it a good one."

She gave a pale smile and, hands still over her eyes, replied, "I'm *trying*, you idiot."

Time passed with agonizing slowness. I added more and more scenes to the tales, and fashioned happier endings. "That was a good one," Frank Bailey said after one such tale. Then, before Jeremy could summon the strength to begin another, Frank Bailey said, "I wish you guys were big like me."

Jeremy looked at him with dull eyes. "Why's that?"

"You'd have more for your bodies to feed on to keep you from . . . you know, starving."

Ginger managed a soft laugh. "You're a ray of sunshine, Frank," she said, and they all fell into benumbed silence until I said, *Jeremy! Jeremy! Another tale!* And he took a deep breath and began again.

The prior two nights had been mercifully quiet, but on this night, after the lights slowly dimmed to darkest darkness, the prisoners were met with a more vivid form of terror, for the moans that they heard were those of a young boy. The cries went on and on, growing weaker and more desperate. "Help me, please," he whimpered. "Please help me. Please, please, please." And then at last the voice was quiet.

None of the prisoners said anything.

The next day, the baker did not come, nor the day after. If the prisoners moved, their movements were slow. Their naps, if they came, were disrupted by ghastly dreams. Frank Bailey, as if it were the riddle that stood between them and freedom, said again and again that he could not believe that Mr. Blix was doing this to them. Ginger covered her eyes and said her silent prayers. And, though his voice was nearly too weak to be heard, Jeremy told the tales, on and on.

Once, when she could hear Frank Bailey snoring softly as he napped, Ginger faced Jeremy on her cot and waited until the story he was telling had come to its happy end: "And so the little tailor was and always would be king."

She smiled softly. "Remember my grandfather saying that the bad thing about going far, far away is that you always wind up finding that you brought yourself along? Well, I just want to say how glad I am that you brought your nerdy little fairy tale–telling self along." She gave him a tender look. "I think it's made all the difference."

For a moment, the weariness lifted from his eyes. "I'd say the exact same thing about you."

"Know one good thing?" she whispered. "The enchantment can't be undone."

Jeremy seemed not to understand.

"The enchantment of the first bite," she said. "It can only be undone by the touch of a salted tear on the parted lips of the spellbound." She tried to smile. "Meaning me—the spellboundee."

"So?"

"So that can't possibly happen to me in here. I'm beyond reach of your tear, salted or unsalted." She laughed a small, raspy laugh. "The thing is, I think you're stuck with me, Jeremy. And you might be stuck with me in the sweet hereafter."

"That's fine by me," Jeremy said. "Being stuck with you, I mean. But I'd like to put off the sweet-hereafter part."

He seemed to be considering something, then took a deep breath and began recounting "The Singing Soaring Lark," a solicitous choice, I thought, for the tale features a brave and resourceful heroine, much like our own.

That night in the darkness, instead of whimpering voices, they heard symphonic music, the same music the baker had listened to when he drove Jeremy and Ginger into the woods.

The next morning, when the chamber began to lighten, Ginger and Jeremy were again holding hands through the bars that separated their cells. They withdrew their arms slowly, as if reluctant to let go of the solace the other provided.

§

§

There were nineteen peas—all shriveled and faded—lining the shelf the day the prisoners again heard the moaning wall and the squealing cart.

"*Hallå, Hallå!*" the baker said as he entered. "Is it not a great day to be alive?"

None of the captives rose from their cots, and none of them spoke.

The baker pulled the white cloth from the cart to reveal a single plate piled with scraps of stale pastries and bread of the type that would normally be set out for stray dogs, and each of the prisoners looked upon the scraps as a starving dog might.

The baker talked as he divided the bits of food among three plates. "A little news," he said. "Frankie's mother and Ginger's grandfather have received their letters, and everyone feels reassured now, knowing that Frankie is making his way as a chef on a private yacht and that Jeremy and Ginger have found a hospitable home in some unknown remote location."

He began distributing the plates—the prisoners rose slowly to position themselves at the edges of their cots. "And now, my dear children," the baker said, "you will each begin to become a memory less and less frequently visited."

Jeremy, Ginger, and Frank Bailey all raised themselves with difficulty and moved closer to their small feeding doors.

"Yes, yes, it is not always flattering, but it is the human design. For a while, we miss the departed"—he gently shook his head—"and then we forget them."

With a push of a button, the small doors opened and the prisoners—they could not help themselves—reached through and grabbed the scraps. They ate greedily, which brought a laugh rumbling up from the baker's great belly.

Ginger swallowed, wiped her mouth with her sleeve, and said in a tight, rasping voice, "What is wrong with you?"

The baker produced a smirking smile. "That you, looking as you at this moment do, can ask such a question of me is rich with irony."

In a leisurely manner, he took out his tobacco, seated himself in his rocking chair, and tapped clean his pipe.

"I will tell you something interesting," he said. "Whenever I used to read one of those stories that Jeremy likes to tell, the ones where a genie or a talking fish grants somebody three wishes, I always thought I would ask for only two. And do you know what they were? One was to have a single friend who could take me as I am and upon whose loyalty I could always rely. And the other"—the baker pulled smoke from his pipe and released it slowly—"*was to do whatever I wanted.*"

The baker rocked and smoked. The prisoners—this was not an easy thing to watch—began actually to lick their plates. When they were done, he said, "I think the time has come for me to tell you a certain story. This is not one of Jeremy's feel-good fairy tales. It is even better, and do you know why?" His eyes grazed from prisoner to prisoner. "Because it is true and has a certain application to your present circumstances."

He drew from his pipe, then let white smoke flow through his lips. "This, dear children, is the story of the Nyköping Banquet. Do you know of it?"

The prisoners stared at him. They had not heard of this notorious occasion, but I had, and a fearful tremor passed through my spectral form.

"The Nyköping Banquet," the baker began, "was an unusual dinner party hosted in the early fourteenth century by Sweden's King Birger. Seven years before, at the Håtuna Games, the king's two brothers had staged a bloody coup to dethrone him, but they were rebuffed by the king's forces. With the passage of time, the king publicly forgave his two brothers and, shortly before Christmas of 1317, he announced his intention to reconcile with them. They were invited to a magnificent banquet at his castle in Nyköping. But after royally feeding his brothers and plying them with nectar, King Birger threw them into his dungeon." The baker stood and drew close to Jeremy's cell. "But before he did, do you know what he said to them?"

No one spoke, so the baker said, *"Kommer ni ihåg Håtuna spelen? Jag kommer klart ihåg dem."* He paused. "Do you want to guess what that means?"

I gave Jeremy a basic translation, and he repeated it. "Do you remember the Hatuna Games? For I remember them clearly."

The baker cocked his head in surprise. "What did you say?"

Jeremy repeated it.

"So you know Swedish?" the baker said.

I was unsure what to suggest Jeremy might say, but it did not matter, for a strange resolve had settled into his face. He sat straighter and said, "I don't speak Swedish. But there is a ghost who stays near me. He's the one who knows Swedish."

The baker stared at him for a moment and then began to laugh. "A boy in the middle of the United States with a Swedish-speaking ghost," he said even as he continued laughing. "That is perhaps too much to believe."

"He speaks a lot of languages, not just Swedish," Jeremy said. "He is the one who knows all about the fairy tales. He is the one who watched you go into Elbow's Café when we were bound up in your delivery van. He is the one who floated nearby while you ate beef pot pie and talked about me with my father." Jeremy fixed his eyes on the baker. "And he is the one who will haunt you until your last breath if you hurt any one of us here."

The baker's eyes had grown wider—for a moment, his face seemed made of stretched rubber—and it was so quiet that you could hear a mouse blink. But then his face regained its shape, and he issued another laugh, one that was smaller and harder. "You are very clever, dear boy, but what you saw was through comatose eyes and what you say your ghost heard is untrue."

It is completely true, I told Jeremy, and then I told him something else.

"And you tried to plant the idea with my father that I might run away with Ginger."

The baker shrugged. "Again, untrue. Perhaps your ghost does not hear well or"—he smiled slyly—"perhaps your ghost does not exist."

After a moment, Jeremy pointed to the baker's chair. "See that rocker?"

The baker regarded his rocking chair, which sat empty and still.

"Yes, my dear boy. I see it very clearly. Can your ghost make it vanish?"

"No," Jeremy said. "But he can sit in it."

"Yes? And is he sitting in it now?" He sniggered. "Why not make it three ghosts sitting in it, or"—another small laugh—"a whole baker's dozen?"

"Just one," Jeremy said. "And he will sit in it and make it rock."

It took me a moment to understand what Jeremy was asking me to do . . . but then I threw myself into the task, swirling past the chair, front then back, again and again, until the rocking began, and so furious was my swirling that it gained speed and the chair was soon rocking quite madly.

When finally I stopped and the rocker gradually grew still, Ginger, Frank Bailey, and the baker were all staring at Jeremy, who said, "My ghost seems to like your rocker."

A few moments passed in silence, and then, to the surprise of everyone, the baker began nodding and smiling as if in amusement. "So," he said. "So."

The prisoners, with their hollow eyes, stared as one.

"A mystery has been solved," the baker said. "So many boys our Jeremy has been. The boy who upon seeing me burrowed into his blankets. The boy who heard voices. The boy who knew fairy tales. And now he is the boy with his own ghost." His eyes settled on Jeremy. "I knew you were destined to visit me here in the great chamber, and I knew that it was important, but *I did not know why*. And now I do. I see why we had to meet here." His blue eyes twinkled. "For you and for me, Jeremy, it is our great opportunity." His face seemed to shine with luxurious anticipation. "Here, in front of our friends, we will match our . . . *talents* and see . . . how it all will end."

The baker took in and expelled a deep breath. "You are the cleverest of boys, Jeremy Johnson Johnson. But"—he was serene now, poised and assured—"even if you had a dozen personal ghosts, they would be no match for my demons."

Then, unhurriedly, he went to the painting on the wall and turned it over.

And there, on the reverse side, was a far different work of art, as ghoulish as the other was benign. In this woodprint, a haggard mother, who had been cooking a scant meal at her fire, looks on in anguish as a skeleton pulls her small child from their tumbledown hut. The terrified child reaches back through the smoke for its mother even as the skeletal form pulls it inexorably away.

"God," Ginger said in a faltering voice. "What *is* that?"

The baker's eyes gleamed with pride. "It is one of many prints collectively called *The Dance of Death*. Each is designed to remind us how Death is always with us, waiting to lead us away." The baker leaned toward the print. "The woodcutting is superb, and yet for a long time the identity of its creator was not known." He turned a smile to Jeremy. "Perhaps your ghost knows his name?"

I told Jeremy, and he said, "Hans Holbein."

The baker made a show of not being surprised. "The Elder or the Younger?"

I again supplied the answer. "The Younger," Jeremy said.

"Very good," the baker said in his most pleasant voice. "Your ghost is good at the esoteric question, and yet"—a rich laugh tumbled from his lips—"when it comes to the Disney version of *Snow White* . . ."

He did not finish the sentence. With stately calm, he pushed his cart from the dungeon, the wall moaning closed behind him.

§

§

For several moments, the chamber was deeply quiet.

Then Ginger said, "That was pretty freaking fabulous, Jeremy. I think you actually had him going there for a second or two."

"More than a second or two," Frank Bailey offered from across the room.

Jeremy waved a hand dismissively. "Didn't scare him enough, though, did it?" he said. "We're still here, aren't we?"

"Yeah," Ginger said, "but that rocking-chair poltergeist thing was amazing." Her eyes were fixed on him. "So how'd you do that? And where'd you come up with that personal-ghost stuff?"

Jeremy sat on the edge of his cot and said nothing.

"Jeremy?"

He breathed heavily in and out. "Promise you won't laugh or anything?"

"Promise."

"Okay," Jeremy said. "I didn't make it up. It's true."

From their stares it was clear that they did not believe him.

"Really," Jeremy said, looking earnestly at Ginger. "True."

Frank Bailey was searching all around. "And he's, like, in here with us?"

Jeremy nodded. "Unless he slipped out with the baker, which I doubt, because he promised me he would stay with us."

Ginger's eyes darted here and there in the chamber. "How do you find out?"

Jeremy touched his temple and whispered, "You here, Jacob?"

Yes.

"He's here," Jeremy said.

Ginger was having a difficult time grasping what she was hearing. "So he's here, and you can hear him, and you call him *Yaw-kub?*"

Jeremy nodded. "That's his name. He lived in Germany about two hundred years ago. His last name's Grimm. He and his brother are the ones who collected the household tales."

They were all silent for a moment or two, then Ginger said,

313

"So do you think we're in some kind of weird fairy tale, and that's why he's here?"

Jeremy shook his head. "I don't know. And I don't think my ghost does, either."

"But it *is* like we're in some kind of fairy tale," Frank Bailey said. "It's got enchantments and dungeons and potions and forbidden rooms"—his face fell; he seemed suddenly to remember something—"except this time it's all real."

Another silence stretched out. Then Ginger said, "And this ghost—he sees and hears everything we do and say?"

Jeremy nodded.

"That's kind of creepy," she said.

"Actually, he's pretty good about respecting people's privacy."

Something had occurred to Ginger. She put a finger to her lips, and then she leaned forward and whispered, "Are you just saying this so Sten will hear it and believe it?"

"No," Jeremy said in his usual voice. "I don't care whether Sten believes it or not. But I do know my ghost won't let him rest if he does anything bad to us."

She stared at Jeremy. "Yeah," she whispered, "but why didn't he do something to keep us from being abducted to begin with?"

Well, there it was: a sharp knife in the sheath of a short question.

It is true, Jeremy. I was not vigilant. Then I steeled myself and said something I had been needing to say. *And I think that the terrible mistake I made has led me to make another.*

He was waiting for me to go on, but Ginger spoke up first. "So what does your ghost think we should do now?"

I told him, and from his expression, I could see that it made him anxious. Still, he was cautious, lowering his voice to a whisper to say, "My ghost says that he needs to slip out with Sten." Then he added even more softly, "If Sten ever comes back."

"Maybe your ghost is the answer to our prayers," Ginger said, and managed a dry laugh. "You should tell him to bring back the cavalry—and some Oreos."

"That's the thing. He can't bring anything back. He can't even tell anybody anything. But at least he can find out what's going on out there. Right, Jacob?"

Yes. I can do at least that much. I had other ideas, too, but I did not mention them.

"It's okay," Jeremy said in a low voice. "We'll be okay."

For the first time, I detected something fatalistic in his tone, and what he meant by being okay, I did not want to guess.

All right, then, I said. *I will slip out the next time I can.*

§

§

Twenty-five peas, and the baker had not visited, then twenty-six and twenty-seven.

"That's all," Jeremy said in a soft voice.

His face had grown haggard and seemed composed of uncolored candle wax. All of their faces did. I must say it: the prisoners looked like the drawings one sometimes sees of ghosts.

"Twenty-seven days," Ginger said.

"Which means fifty-even for me," Frank Bailey said. "It seems like fifty years." His eyes were unlighted lanterns. "I still can't believe Mr. Blix is doing this."

"I think it's time to believe it," Jeremy said, but Frank Bailey, instead of nodding in agreement, merely lowered his eyes.

Ginger brought out all the peas from the ledge above her sink and laid them on her cot. "Twenty-seven's divisible by three," she said. "Nine each."

She began lobbing peas across the dungeon to Frank Bailey. Seven rolled into his cell; two fell short. She tossed two more. Frank Bailey collected them from the floor, eating them as he did. She then gave nine to Jeremy, who returned one so that the two of them would have eight each. They looked down at the peas, gathered in their cupped hands.

"Down the hatch?" she asked.

He shrugged. They opened their mouths, threw in the peas, then sucked them as one might candy, until at last they were gone.

"Nothing quite like a shriveled pea," Jeremy said.

She gave a weak laugh. "Fabulous appetizer. Now, where's the entrée?"

At night, the dreadful sounds of suffering still came through the walls, but now the prisoners stuffed their ears with small bits of cloth torn from their bedding.

One night, however, the whimpering and pleading ceased, and a short while later a new series of sounds came from another source—Jeremy himself.

"Please," he murmured. "Please." His pleading grew more fretful. "Please! Please!"

Jeremy! I said, and then I shouted, *Jeremy! Wake up! Wake up!*

He did not wake up, but his cries awakened Ginger, who pulled the wadding from her ears. "Jeremy!" she shouted, grabbing his arm through the bars.

He came slowly back from wherever he had been.

"What?" he said in a thick voice.

"You," Ginger said. "You were yelling in your sleep. You said, 'Please! Please!' again and again." She paused. "Please what?"

"I was asking . . ." He hesitated, as if trying to piece it together. "It was like I was hearing several voices, but it was different . . . I was seeing people, too."

Ginger gave a small laugh. "Most of us call that a dream."

"No. I mean, it was *like* a dream except . . . it was more real than a dream."

"So why were you saying *Please*? Please what?"

"It was a party for a little boy, a long, long time ago, and I was there, except somehow *I* was the ghost and nobody could see or hear me. Everyone was speaking German and laughing and singing except a man standing in the doorway half in and half out, with longish gray hair and wearing, like, an old smoking jacket or something, and kind of half smiling in a way that made me know he wasn't happy." Jeremy lowered his voice apologetically. "That's how I knew it was Jacob."

I listened, perfectly still. How had he done it? I did not remember telling Jeremy of this episode, but even if I had, how could he know where I was standing, what I was wearing, the length and color of my hair? How had he slipped into the rooms of my own memory?

317

"Then the little boy—Jacob's nephew, I think—asked him to sing, and he didn't want to, but I knew he should, that it might make him happy, so I tried to ask him, too." He waited. "That's probably why I was saying *Please* again and again. He wasn't hearing me."

I said nothing. This memory, as ever, did nothing but sadden me. Perhaps Jeremy sensed this, for he said, "It wasn't Jacob's fault he couldn't sing."

"You mean he couldn't carry a tune or couldn't bring himself to try?"

Both, I said. *And for the former I could not be blamed. Still, for the latter I must.*

"I don't know," Jeremy said, as if to Ginger, though I knew he meant it for me, too. "You can try to be different, but in the end we always are who we are."

They were quiet for a few moments. Then Ginger whispered, "No tape recordings tonight. I wonder what that means."

Jeremy did not answer, but I could tell from his breathing that he still lay awake. After a time, Ginger said softly, "Remember the story you told about Faithful John—the part about leaves and tongues when the prince sees the painting of the princess? Could you repeat that part?"

Jeremy needed only the slightest prompt from me. "When the king's son sees the portrait of the princess, his love for her is so great that if all the leaves on all the trees were tongues, they could not declare it." He paused. "That part?"

It was pitch-black in the dungeon and the circumstances could not have been more wretched, and yet her voice was tender. "Yeah," she said. "That part."

§

§

When at last the wall again moaned open, followed by the squealing wheels of the baker's serving cart, the prisoners did not move on their cots. They merely raised their eyes.

"*Hallå! Hallå!*" the baker said, but he did not ask if it was not a great day to be alive. He seemed, in fact, a bit weary himself—though weary of what, I had no idea. Still, he regarded the prisoners and pretended concern.

"Oh, my. You don't look at all well, my dear children. There is now hot water—or were you too lazy to notice?"

The prisoners did not speak. They did not even move on their cots.

The baker pushed bundles of clothes and flowers onto each of their shelves, and opened the serving doors to provide access, but the prisoners lay still.

"I've brought spaghetti, as promised," he said. "And with my own special spaghetti sauce. None of the *Rangu* stuff you were talking about." He gave a tired smile. " '*Resist, annoy, never give up.*' Wasn't that the rallying cry?"

None of the prisoners spoke. Their eyes were now on the plates that he was filling with small portions of pasta.

"I'm afraid these are leftovers," he said.

The food smelled rancid, and the tiny bits of meat were coated with a furry gray mold. He pushed the flowers and clothes through the small doors and onto the floor of the cells, and left the plates of moldy food on the shelves.

The prisoners stood with difficulty and pulled the plates through the door. There were no utensils. The baker stood watching as his prisoners ate with their hands and wiped their faces with their forearms.

Finally, when there was nothing left on their plates to lick, the prisoners picked up their parcels of clothes. Ginger unrolled hers first. They were all black. So, too, were Jeremy's. They looked from the clothes to the baker.

"Just like the night of your famous stealth mission," he said.

"And his?" Ginger said in a low, raspy voice, pointing to Frank Bailey's clothes. "Why are they black?"

The baker shrugged. "Who knows? It just seemed to suit the occasion."

He turned then and, rolling the serving tray before him, headed for the door.

And I with him.

"You're going, right?" Jeremy said.

The baker turned. "Who are you talking to?"

"You," Jeremy said.

"But why, my dear boy? You can see that I am going."

"I don't know," Jeremy said. He dropped his head. "I'm just really tired."

Yes, I am going, Jeremy, I said. *I must try to change our fortunes.*

Jeremy nodded very slightly, but otherwise held himself completely still. He looked like he was fighting back tears.

The wheels squeaked as the cart rolled on.

I moved quickly past Jeremy so that he would feel the slight current of warmth.

Lebewohl, Jeremy, I said. *Good-bye. Do not give in and do not give up. Perseverance is all.*

But just as the baker was turning out of view, Jeremy called to me: "You'll come back, right?"

Again the baker stopped his cart. His expression seemed almost consoling. "Yes, my dear boy. I will be back. But I cannot say with certainty when."

I again swept close to Jeremy. *Yes,* I said. *I will return. It is a promise. I will.*

The baker's cart was moving again, and this time, when he pushed the numbered buttons and passed through the wall, I followed. After mounting the stairs and tidying his kitchen, he stepped into the garden to cut flowers. I hastened past him, close enough to stir the air, for he said in a low voice as if to himself, "Ah, is that you, ancient ghost, or a gentle breeze?"

I darted close again, this time from the other side.

"So it is you," he whispered. "But it is too late, old ghost, and you are too weak. Yes, try, by all means try. But don't waste time playing parlor tricks with me. Be off to do what you cannot do! And who knows, dear ghost? Perhaps you will protect the next children better than you have protected these."

So I fled the Finder of Occasions, fled him as he bent close to examine his bed of irises, separating the long, upshooting stalks, searching for the showiest flowers for cutting.

§

§

Main Street was quiet. The light was harsh, and though I could not feel the heat, I could see its vapors rise from the black asphalt. I hastened at once to the Twinkle Tub Laundry. During the time in the dungeon, I had nurtured an idea. Now I would test it.

Mrs. Truax was there, and the door was open. I slipped close to her at her ironing board, within an inch of the hood of her musty cloak.

Mrs. Truax! I shouted. *Mrs. Truax! Listen, if you will!*

The washing and drying machines that lined the walls hummed and thumped.

I shouted louder. *Mrs. Truax, I need your help! I believe I know what happened to your son. Mrs. Truax! Your son, Possy! He may be alive!*

I believed what I said. But Mrs. Truax heard nothing. I darted by her, back and forth, and swirled about her in hopes that she would pull back her hood to hear me better, but this hood had been her hiding place for years, and it protected her now from the stirring air. She detected nothing. She turned a shirt on the padded board before her, and pressed the iron along its sleeve.

Mrs. Truax! Mrs. Truax, please!

Nothing. She continued to iron, a woman who had worked for years in the same laundry and lived in the same tiny trailer so that her son would know where to find her if he ever came back, a woman who could not hear the hopeful news I had come now to deliver.

I hastened down Main Street to Elbow's Café, where citizens were dining heartily and Jenny Applegarth bustled from table to table. The everyday busyness of it all was alarming. Three children were missing, locked in a dungeon a stone's throw from this very café, and here were the villagers eating and talking and laughing as if nothing at all was wrong!

I drew close to Jenny Applegarth and said into her ear, *Listen, if you will.*

But she was taking someone's order for chicken and potatoes. When she was finished writing on her pad, I tried again, this time even louder: *Listen, if you will!*

She did not hear me. I followed as she bumped through the swinging door into the kitchen, where Mr. Johnson looked up from his dishwashing and offered a blank smile, which she returned. I have seen such blank smiles before. They belong to intimates sharing a common grief. The blankness comes from waiting—waiting for something to be revealed, or written, or understood.

She pinned up her order. "Lemmy Wittle says kudos on the pepper steak," she said in a dull tone to Elbow Adkins, who, spatula in hand, nodded and mopped his brow before leaning again over the hot black fry-top.

In this town, Jenny Applegarth was my last faint hope for communication, so I waited as patiently as I could until the crowd had finally abated and she had stepped into the back alley with Mr. Johnson to sit and sip a glass of lemonade.

"Busy," she said.

Mr. Johnson stared off toward the smoke rising from the encrusted hot springs.

Jenny Applegarth said, "Now that Pittswort's calling the kids runaways, everybody is. Cassie Willis called them runaways today, and so did Bill Kibbs."

Mr. Johnson turned toward her. "What did you say to them?"

"What you always say. That Jeremy's no runaway."

She sipped her lemonade.

It became perfectly quiet. This was my moment. *Listen, if you will!*

Jenny Applegarth looked wonderingly toward Mr. Johnson.

I shouted this time. *Listen, if you will!*

She shook her head, and peered in my direction.

Listen, if you will! I shouted. *Listen, if you will! Listen, if you will!*

"Did you hear that?" she said to Mr. Johnson.

"What?"

"The wind through the trees," she said in a soft voice. "It was almost like faraway words. Pretty words. Like they were coming from heaven."

"Don't say that!" Mr. Johnson said with sudden vehemence. Then, more gently: "Don't say that. He's not dead." His eyes drifted again toward the hot springs. "He's not a runaway," he murmured, almost to himself, "and he's not dead."

I know where he is! I shouted. *I know where he is!*

But Jenny Applegarth only gazed out at the trees, where, she believed, the wind made the leaves whisper.

The screen door behind us swung open and young Conk Crinklaw stepped through. "Hey," he said, and Mr. Johnson and Mrs. Applegarth nodded.

"Elbow said you were back here." Conk took off his hat and held it in his hands. "Guess you haven't heard anything."

Jenny Applegarth shook her head.

Conk sat down and turned his hat in his hands. He wanted to say something, and finally he did. "Just seems so strange that

Ginger'd do this. And then to write to her *grandfather*, who couldn't care less about her, and not write . . ." His voice trailed away.

Jenny Applegarth turned to him. "Not write to you?"

"Well, yeah. Or Maddy or Marjory—somebody who actually cares about her."

He turned and tightened his face so that nothing—a tear, for example—might escape, but this did not fool Jenny Applegarth. She laid an arm over the boy's shoulder and then they were staring off, all three of them, waiting and waiting and waiting, with only eroding hope to soothe their fears.

Listen, if you will! I shouted one more time, then again, and again, exasperation and even anger hardening my voice.

Nothing. She heard nothing. This time she did not even look toward the trees.

§

§

I left those grieving people. I left that town and searched out others, moving from person to person, from ear to ear, whispering, cajoling, and shouting ever more desperately, trying to find just one mortal who might understand my words and repeat them to a sheriff. I traveled farther and farther from the town by the red buttes. Several days passed, and several more. I found a few other dead souls.

Three children in a dungeon, I told them, *and yet I can find no one to help.*

The ghosts were indifferent.

We should not interfere, one dead man told me.

Perhaps it is for the best, another said. *Between death sooner and death later, there is little to choose.*

This was a fatalism I could not accept. Perseverance is all: this had always been my belief. And so farther and farther I went, speaking into the ears of mortals of every description—*Listen, if you will! Listen, if you will!*—but no one heard my words.

I found no one able to hear me. No one, and I was far from home.

That was what I thought to myself. *Far from home.* A phrase that carried within its ribs a meaningful surprise.

Home, as I now thought of it, was where Jeremy Johnson Johnson was.

"My ghost." That was how he had described me to Ginger.

Suddenly, my fear for his safety and my need to see him one more time came upon me with such force that I gave up my search and hastened back to the little town by the red buttes. I had no trouble finding my way. It was as the wanderer had told me years before: *It is difficult to find, but, once found, you will never lose it.*

§

§

It was nearly dusk by the time I reached Main Street, which, except for a few trucks parked in front of the Intrepid Bar & Grill, was almost deserted. Elbow's Café was closed and so was the bakery, but, far down the block, the Green Oven Bakery truck stood parked in front of Crinklaw's Superette. Inside the market, I found the baker himself, carrying a basket of groceries toward the cash register.

"*Hallå*," he said to the clerk, "is it not a great day to be alive?"

He asked his question dully, without his usual exuberance.

The clerk seemed to notice this, for she said, "You okay, Sten?"

"Yes, yes." He hesitated. "The truth is that I am sorry to see summer ending. I had such fond expectations for it, and now—" He made a vague wave with his hand.

The clerk tried to jolly him by saying, "Well, don't forget autumn. We usually get two or three full hours of autumn before blowing full-tilt into winter."

The baker chuckled politely, and the clerk weighed a cluster of bananas, then ran a few more items through and said, "So, Sten. What about it? When're we going to get some more Prince Cakes? It's been a while, or did I miss something?"

An odd expression crossed the baker's face. He glanced around—there were no other customers nearby. "Well," he said, "I will tell you a little secret. I have been thinking of giving up the Prince Cakes." He sighed. "They take a certain toll. So I think I will give them up"—he smiled—"after one last batch."

"What? Tell me it ain't so!" the clerk joked. "But okay, then. If it's the last batch, put me down for a double portion. I'll freeze me some for a rainy day. When will you be doing them?"

The baker raised his shoulders in a shrug. "Soon, I think. The idea has taken hold, and that is always the first step."

All the while, the clerk was pushing buttons on the cash register as she slid goods past—a carton of oatmeal, a half pound of bacon, a bag of walnuts, a red box of raisins, and then a small carton of rodent poison.

I had been in Sten Blix's bakery, I had been in his storerooms, and I had been in his dungeon. I had never seen the smallest sign of rodents.

§

§

My foreboding grew as the baker drove home with his groceries, as he wearily stored his kitchen goods, as he set water for boiling, as he steeped and stirred his peppermint tea. Finally, he carried his cup and saucer to a dim, windowless room that was clearly his sleeping quarters. Hanging on the walls were several more of the woodcuts from *The Dance of Death*. A television sat perched on a metal shelf mounted near an upper conjunction of the walls.

The baker switched on this television, and, oh, it must be said: Not even my darkest fears could prepare me for what I saw. Instead of a normal show, the lighted screen displayed three panels, each showing different views of his dungeon—one of Frank Bailey's side of the chamber, one of Jeremy's and Ginger's cells, and one of the massive metal wall that separated the dungeon from the world.

So! The baker did not just listen to the prisoners. He observed them from the comfort of his bedroom.

The images were alarming. Ginger and Jeremy lay on their cots, turned toward the bars between them. Their hands lay close but did not touch. They both wore baggy black pants and shirts. They were both still. In his cell, Frank Bailey lay on his cot, tucked into a sickle-like curve. He, too, was still.

A fear of the most terrible kind took hold of me.

It seemed the baker felt it, too, for he drew close to study the screen.

A full minute passed, and none of the prisoners moved.

The baker set down his tea and approached one of the macabre woodcuts hanging in the room—one of a woman glancing lovingly at her husband as Death approached unbeknownst. At the baker's hand, its hinged frame swung open to reveal a panel of buttons, one of which he pressed.

A sudden piercing human shriek could be heard from the television screen, and the heads of the prisoners jerked up almost as one. They stared starkly about, and then, when the shrieking stopped, their heads dropped back down.

Ginger could be heard to say, "What was that?" Even though her voice was weak and low, it could be heard clearly.

"Just one more memento from the past, my dear girl," the baker whispered, then went to his closet and turned a valve on a water pipe.

On the television screen, the prisoners could again be seen raising their heads. Jeremy rose with difficulty and moved slowly

329

toward his small bathroom. On the screen, these movements looked like a series of detached images played in staccato, one stuttering into the next, an effect that made Jeremy look other than human.

When he came out of the bathroom, he said, "Water."

The baker watched as Frank and Ginger pushed themselves up from their cots and moved toward their bathrooms, then he turned the television off.

He knelt at his chest of drawers and pulled out the lowest drawer. Neatly folded within it was an array of shirts of various styles and sizes. He began to sort through them, regarding each one, then setting it aside. His manner was almost tender. Then, a shock: he picked up the pink shirt that had been Ginger's, the one with *As Is* written on it in glittery letters. And below that was Jeremy's faded blue T-shirt and Frank's formal white shirt, clean now and carefully folded. The baker set aside all these shirts, and a frightening number of others, too—each one, I feared, representing a lost life—until finally he came to a small shirt in dingy green. This was the shirt he wanted, for he placed all the others back into the drawer and carried the green shirt with him to the kitchen and laid it on the counter.

He sighed, looked around, and set to work. While a large pot of oatmeal boiled, he fried three thick strips of bacon. He slowly sliced apples and walnuts. He stirred the porridge and set down his wooden spoon. Then he took out a mortar and pestle, poured a liberal measure of blue pellets from the carton of rodent poison into the bowl, and began to grind the blue pellets into powder.

When they had been ground fine, he opened a small jar and tapped some of its granular contents into the bowl, and then he added three drops from a dark vial.

To himself, in a strangely dull voice, he said, "A pinch of this, a dash of that."

When all these ingredients had been combined, he stirred them into the porridge.

Three bowlfuls were portioned out, each topped with apples, nuts, and brown sugar. The baker arranged the bowls along with strips of bacon and fresh pastries onto platters that he covered with polished silver domes. His movements were slow, almost laborious. He set the green shirt among the platters and carried the tray down the stairs to his serving cart, which he pushed to the third storeroom.

When he stepped forward and depressed the series of buttons that opened the moaning door, I rushed past him and was struck at once by the fetid stench of the dungeon. I flew to Jeremy and hovered at his ear. *Jeremy!* I cried. *Listen, if you will!*

His eyes fluttered open. "You're back," he murmured, and the faintest smile appeared on his scabbed and swollen lips.

Yes. Yes, I am back.

He allowed his eyes again to fall closed. "Does anybody know about us?"

The baker's footsteps approached.

No. Not yet. What could I say? I said, *But I have not given up.*

"I'm happy you're here. I missed you. We're so hungry." His smile stretched ever so slightly and blood welled in one of the fissures of his cracked lips. "I've been having that dream-that's-not-a-dream thing," he whispered.

Yes? I said. *The one in which I do not sing?*

"Mmm. But I like being there. I like being the ghost trying to talk to you."

Jeremy again in the role of the ghost? It was too terrible to consider, but I could not speak—already the baker's cart was rolling into the great chamber.

"*Hallå!*" he said. When he asked if it was not a great day to be alive, he did not wait for an answer. He laid the small green shirt over his blue armchair, then raised the domed metal lids to display the food and release the savory aroma of bacon. "Porridge, bacon, and pastries." He made a wry, tired smile. "Of course, it may be poisoned."

It is poisoned! I said. *It is poisoned! Do not eat it!*

Jeremy stared intently at the food. So did Ginger and Frank Bailey. They looked as unalive as the living can look. Their eyes were swollen and their skin was stretched thin over their bones.

The porridge is poisoned! I said again.

"My ghost says it's poisoned," Jeremy said in a cracked, dry voice.

Sten Blix's laugh was hollow. "Your ghost. Well, I'm sure your ghost is right. And I'm sure he'll bring you another meal you'll like better, won't he?"

He slid the poisoned food into the enclosures.

The bacon and pastries are fine, I said. *But do not eat the porridge!*

But there was only one rasher of bacon for each prisoner, and the baker had withheld the pastries.

Their hunger was too great.

They could not be stopped.

They ate the porridge—ate it greedily—until at last their wooden spoons clacked on their empty wooden bowls. The baker distributed the pastries, and they ate them, too. Only then did the baker settle himself in his rocking chair. He regarded the small green shirt that he spread across his hands, then ran his gaze thoughtfully from prisoner to prisoner.

Jeremy stared back as fiercely as a weak and failing creature could stare. "My ghost," he said in a stiff whisper, "will never forget and never give up."

Ginger covered her eyes with her open hands and began moving her lips.

Frank Bailey, in a small, earnest voice, said, "You could just let us go, Mr. Blix. You could just let us go."

The baker looked at them almost sorrowfully. It was as if this had been a hunt, but the predator had lost his appetite for hunting.

"One last story," he said, and lighted his pipe.

§

§

"It is about a little boy in a town like our own, a mute boy who could hear but wouldn't speak."

"Possy," Frank Bailey whispered. He sat slumped on his cot. His voice faded into almost nothing. "Possy vanished."

"Yes," the baker said. "Let's call him Possy—because when someone talked to him, it was as if he were playing dead." The baker drew in and then exhaled a great stream of smoke. "Possy was a strange little creature. He would wear only green. Most of the people in the town were amused by the way he wandered about the streets in his green shirt and green corduroy pants, staring at people, shedding his clothes as the day grew warm, forgetting where he'd left them. The town's baker, however, went to the sheriff to say there must be some law against four-year-old boys wandering the streets unattended, leaving their clothes here and there. The sheriff only laughed. 'You mean Possy?' he said. 'Why, everybody knows Possy. Nobody'd cause Possy any harm.' Everyone made a mascot of the wandering boy, even the sheriff. He could be seen driving about with Possy riding up front, grinning his idiot grin. One such day, the sheriff pulled alongside the town's baker and said, 'Possy and me are *on patrol!*' and then he turned to the pathetic child and said, 'Ain't we, Possy?'

"So what could the town's baker do? He tried to reason with the child, tried to get him to speak, and to put his shirt and pants back on, but Possy paid him no mind. In fact, he found the baker's attempts to help him comical. 'Put your pants on, Possy,' the baker would say, and the boy would laugh with delight—or perhaps derision."

Ginger's eyes were nearly closed.

Jeremy's were clouded.

Frank Bailey stared blankly ahead.

The baker seemed so immune to this inattention that I wondered for whom he was telling the tale. Yet he pulled at his pipe and continued.

"The town's baker was the only one on earth who heard the boy speak. That is right. The boy *could* speak. It surprised the baker, and it might have surprised the boy, too. One day, in exasperation, the baker said, 'There's something wrong inside you.' And the boy laughed and laughed, and then he looked right back at the baker and said out loud, 'There's something wrong inside you.' Oh, it wasn't perfectly clear. The words were thick and muddy, but it was clear to the baker what he said, and then the boy said it again, 'There's something wrong inside you.' He laughed and began to repeat it, again and again, until the town's baker had no choice but to offer the boy frosted cookies to get him off the street."

Ginger's eyelids drooped. Jeremy's eyes fell closed. So did Frank Bailey's.

"The boy was not seen again. But that was not the surprise. The surprise was that the baker felt no remorse. No, instead, he felt set free. The hidden door to the secret place that was his true home had swung open before him."

The silence in the dungeon seemed to deepen.

"The baker went out in his delivery truck. When he came back, he told the sheriff that he had seen Possy out by the highway. He wondered if the boy had gotten home safely." The baker again stared at the green shirt he held in his hands. "He had not, of course."

He brought the shirt close to his face, sniffed it, laid it back down. "Even though the baker washed the shirt many times, it still bore faint traces of the boy's scent."

Ginger's eyes fluttered open. "What did the baker do with the body?" she whispered. "Did you bury him here?"

The baker gave a small laugh. "Oh, my dear girl, if I had to dispose of a body, and I am not saying I did, why in the world would I do it here when right next door I have a walk-in oven?"

These words hung in the air.

Jeremy's whisper could barely be heard. "Why are you telling us this?"

The baker did not answer.

"Aren't you afraid we'll tell somebody?"

Sten Blix actually laughed. "No, I am not afraid of that."

Possy is alive, I said. *Tell him that. Tell him Possy is alive.*

In his faint voice, Jeremy said, "Possy is alive."

The baker, betraying nothing, let his blue eyes fall on Jeremy. "So you are the Fairy Tale Boy to the last, still in search of a happy ending."

He lives in the forest. Tell him that. Possy lives in the forest.

Jeremy parted his lips but did not speak.

"What?" the baker said, leaning forward. "Do you have some profound last words?"

"Lives in the forest," Jeremy whispered.

The baker's eyes registered nothing. He gave a tired laugh, in fact. "Did your ghost tell you that? Because if he did, your ghost is telling stories."

He waited then, as if for Jeremy to say something more, but there was nothing more for Jeremy to say.

The baker laid the green shirt on his chair and turned to leave. To the prisoners, he said something he had never said before: "*Farväl.*"

Good-bye, in Swedish.

The baker was leaving, and I did not know what to do.

I yearned to stay with Jeremy and the others, as I had stayed to the end with my dear nephew, but if I stayed, it meant giving up all hope.

I must go, I said.

Jeremy nodded so subtly it could almost not be seen. I could sense that he felt his nearness to death. Still, he raised his head slightly.

"Bye," he whispered.

He seemed to want to say more but could not.

The baker moved forward, and I with him. I looked back to see Ginger slip her arm through the bars so that her hand and Jeremy's could meet.

When the baker pushed the buttons that opened the wall and then, on the other side, secured it, I recorded the sequence in my mind.

One three one seven.

1317.

The year the Swedish king hosted the Nyköping Banquet and had his guests escorted to the dungeon, where they were left to die.

§

§

It had grown late. Slowly, methodically, the baker straightened his house and tidied his kitchen, just as he had done at his hut in the woods on the fateful day that he gathered Ginger and Jeremy into his net. He hid the rodent poison in an empty carton of baking soda, which he placed in the refrigerator. And then, after a last look about, he sighed a great sigh and whispered, *"Sa börjar det igen."*

So another moment has come.

He unlocked the door and stepped out into the night.

I hovered in the darkness and watched him. He locked the gate behind him, turned the corner, and headed toward the bakery under the light of a full moon.

I did not know what to do.

In the tales, as I have noted, malevolence is not just subdued but punished, and through some intercession of goodness, virtue is restored.

But in this tale, Jeremy and the other innocents lay dying, and I, the agent of intercession, did not know what to do.

I will tell you the ineffectual things that I tried. I will number the parties into whose ears I vainly shouted:

• Mayor Crinklaw, as he stood in his backyard grilling meat over a charcoal fire.

• Maddy and Marjory, as they played a game of cards in Maddy's kitchen.

• Conk Crinklaw, as he and his friends watched car races at the county fairgrounds.

• Jeremy's father and Jenny Applegarth, as they sat in her living room blankly watching TV.

• Elbow Adkins, as he sat on his back porch reading a magazine called *Field & Stream*.

• Frank Bailey's mother, as she drank weak tea by her radio.

By this time, gray smoke had begun to rise from the bakery chimney.

I felt as impotent as I had felt long ago, as my dear young nephew gasped for air before finally expelling his last breath.

The sound of shifting leaves played in my ears, and I let the warm night breeze carry me north. I felt myself borne along without plan or intention. I drifted past rustling brown cornfields, past fences and pastures, past listless arid lands, until, not quite to my own surprise, I was on the fringe of the bleached-white escarpments and gaunt ravines of the Badlands. The moon threw long shadows. I moved through the tall, bony spires and ascended to the peak of the tallest one, where I was hidden from nothing.

And here, where I waited only for some merciful end to it all, I began to feel the world spreading out. Time slowed to the threshold of stillness. I felt a kind of accepting presence. I fell into the caress of the dead, not the wretched influence of the specters of the *Zwischenraum* but something benign and accommodating. I breathed deeply. I revisited the rooms of my youth, and then of my middle age. It was as if I could feel the books I picked up, and the feather of a falcon, and the smooth stone shaped like a heart, and then—oh, soft and reassuring sound— I heard the words of a small child.

Da sind Sie, lieber Onkel.

There you are, dear uncle.

Singen Sie, Onkel.

Sing, Uncle.

Had my ancient eyes closed? Had I, who could not sleep, been sleeping? It did not matter—I had heard this voice, and it came again.

Singen Sie, Onkel, bitte.

Sing, Uncle, please.

And then another voice, Jeremy's voice: *Please. Please, Jacob, please.*

I cannot explain it. There are marvelous aspects of both your world and mine, and on rarest occasions one can slip into another. Such slippages cannot be explained, nor can they be ignored.

I turned at once toward town.

Never had I hastened as I hastened then, across canyon and pasture and field. The round moon threw uncertain shadows, but at last, for me, I had a course.

I knew where I was going.

I knew what I must do.

It was not yet midnight, and the smoke pouring from the bakery chimney was still gray.

Jenny Applegarth had raised a window to let in the night air, and now she lay asleep under a white cotton sheet with her head on a white pillow.

I drew close but was for a moment unnerved. I could not sing, never could I sing, but now, on this night, a melody visited my memory, and I sang.

I sang: *The keeper did a-hunting go.*

Jenny Applegarth turned in her sleep but did not waken.

I sang: *And under his coat he carried a bow.*

Mein Gott! Her eyelids lifted! She raised her head and peered into the darkness.

It was the song that she and Mr. Johnson had sung, with its dark hints buried within its cheerful melody: *All for to shoot the merry little doe—*

"Harold?" she said.

Among the leaves so green, O.

She sat upright, alert, frightened, perhaps, but listening. "Harold?"

> *The first doe he shot at he missed;*
> *The second doe he trimmed he kissed;*
> *The third doe went where nobody whist,*
> *Among the leaves so green, O.*

I eased from her room, singing still, and she rose and followed. She seemed to expect to find someone in the living room, but no one was there. When she peered out the front door, I slipped through, singing more. My song seemed full of meaning to me, but she seemed only confused. Still, I led, and she followed, searching for the source of the voice.

> *The fourth doe she did cross the plain;*
> *The keeper fetched her back again;*
> *Where she is now, she may remain,*
> *Among the leaves so green, O.*

"Harold?" she called, peering into the night. "Is this some kind of joke?"

I moved toward the baker's house, along the silent, moonlit streets. I sang the menacing story, and she followed, confused and apprehensive, yet unwilling to turn back.

> *The fifth doe she did cross the brook;*
> *The keeper fetched her back with his crook;*

> *Where she is now you may go and look,*
> *Among the leaves so green, O.*

We had reached the house itself, looming and ghastly to my eyes. There I stopped and sang the last verse.

> *The sixth doe she ran over the plain;*
> *But he with his hounds did turn her again;*
> *And it's there he did hunt in a merry, merry vein,*
> *Among the leaves so green, O.*

It seemed to me this strange house covered in leaves must scream my meaning, but Jenny Applegarth stared at the darkened windows without understanding and, again, said only, "Harold?"

They are here! I shouted at her. *Here!*

But these words did not penetrate her ears. She was looking in the wrong direction, back down the lane, as if wondering how she had come to this spot.

And, then—*Nein! Nein! Nein!*—Jenny Applegarth turned back toward home.

Again I sang, but this time with the slightest alteration:

> *Where they are now you may go and look,*
> *Among the leaves so green, O.*

She stopped short. "What?"

> *Where they are now you may go and look,*
> *Among the leaves so green, O.*

"Where *they are* now?" she said. "That's not how it goes."

She stared at the baker's vine-covered house and said the words to herself: "Where they are now you may go and look, among the leaves so green, O." She did not understand, but then—and here I felt a silvery rush of hope—she said, "You mean *they*? Jeremy and Ginger?"

And then to the same tune I deviated further:

> *In the baker's dungeon you must go and look,*
> *Among the leaves so green, O.*

"*What?*" she whispered. "What baker's dungeon?"

I sang the verse again, and added another:

> *The poison is blue, and sullies their food,*
> *Among the leaves so green, O.*

Jenny Applegarth stared in disbelief. Now it was she who did not know what to think or do.

And then she did.

She stared at the baker's house, and a look of resolution formed on her face.

She began to run.

§

§

When Mr. Johnson awakened to Jenny Applegarth tapping frantically on his window glass, he rose at once and hurried to the front door.

She took several deep breaths and composed herself. "You're not going to believe this," she said, "but I might have an idea where Jeremy and Ginger are."

"What?" he said. "Where?"

"The baker's house."

For one long, still moment, Jenny Applegarth and Mr. Johnson stared at one another. Then he said, "Let's go get the sheriff."

He fetched her an old robe and turned toward the sheriff's house, but Jenny Applegarth grabbed his arm.

"It's Friday night," she said. "He'll be playing cards at the bar."

As they hurried down the deserted street, they saw something and stopped short. Across the street, the lights of the Green Oven bakery burned bright, and there, in the back kitchen, one could see the dark shadow of the baker moving about.

"Look," Jenny said, pointing. Above the bakery, rising in front of the round white moon, was a steady plume of green smoke.

§

§

There were four or five trucks parked in front of the Intrepid Bar & Grill. Inside, men sat or stood at various stations drinking and playing at cards. Several friends of Conk were also there, intently playing a table game that involved a ball kicked by hand-operated players. They had been whooping loudly, but upon seeing Jenny Applegarth and Mr. Johnson come through the door, they fell quiet. So did all the other men, and no wonder.

Mr. Johnson was dressed in pants, boots, and a nightshirt—unusual attire for public appearance—and Jenny Applegarth—barefooted, dressed in a nightgown and old robe—was even more informal.

Sheriff Pittswort, looking up from his game of cards, regarded their dress and said, "Well, howdy-do, folks. Did you lose your way from the *bou-doir?*"

A remark that seemed more cruel than comical, but no matter—it received appreciative chuckles from the cardplayers at his table, and even from Conk's school friends, though not from Conk himself, whom I now saw seated at a corner table, along with Maddy and Marjory. He'd been sitting sideways on a bench with his legs extended, but he straightened himself and gave Mr. Johnson and Jenny Applegarth a little nod.

Jenny Applegarth turned to the sheriff and said, "I think I know where the missing kids are."

"They're in the remote regions, Jenny. *Living off the grid.* That's what they wrote us themselves."

"No. They're not. They're here. They're here and can't get out."

Sheriff Pittswort's attention became keener. "Can't get out of where?"

Jenny Applegarth glanced around the room. She did not want the whole room to hear what she had to say, so she moved close to Sheriff Pittswort and whispered what I had told her in song.

The sheriff leaned back, stared at her a long moment, then broke into a harsh laugh. "They're in the baker's house?" he said loudly, and wagged his eyebrows at the other men. "You suppose Sten's fattening 'em up to cook 'em?"

Oh, how impenetrable this man was! And how indulgent his companions, who murmured and chuckled at his witless remark.

"I didn't say that," Jenny Applegarth protested. "I just said I think they're there."

Sheriff Pittswort's eyes narrowed on her. "Why do you think that?"

"I heard it."

"Who from?"

Jenny Applegarth cast her eyes down. "A voice told me," she whispered.

"What?"

A little louder, Jenny said, "A voice told me. A singing voice. It woke me up and told me."

The cardplayers and cowmen joined in low laughter, and Sheriff Pittswort's tight focus loosened to amusement. "Well, *who exactly* did this singing voice belong to?" he asked.

Jenny was flustered, and even Mr. Johnson was now looking at her anxiously. "I don't know," she said. "I just know I heard it. And the voice said the kids are in the baker's house."

Snickers and murmurs spread through the room. The only ones who did not seem amused were the ones off in the corner: Conk and Maddy and Marjory. And there was someone else, too: Deputy McRaven, sitting by himself on a high stool at the dimmest end of the bar.

Jenny Applegarth straightened her back. "The voice said they're being poisoned in the baker's house."

This was a new revelation to Mr. Johnson, who turned to her in shock and began to speak, but Sheriff Pittswort intervened. "Now, my question is," he said, grinning, "where exactly would the baker be hiding and poisoning grown kids?"

"In the dungeon," Jenny said.

"In the *dungeon*, you say . . . So the baker's got himself a *dungeon*?" Sheriff Pittswort was nodding and smiling. "Now, I just got to ask. Did you and Harold have a tipple or two tonight, Jenny?"

All at once Jenny Applegarth's face stiffened and reddened. She moved toward the door, but before she left, she turned back. "You're supposed to help find these kids, Victor Pittswort, not make fun of people who bring you leads."

The sheriff grinned and lazily scratched his neck. "Well, first of all, Jenny, those kids are runaways who'll come back when they're good and ready. And second of all, it's a little bit hard to take real seriously a *lead* that comes from a man who's spent most of his adult life laying up in bed and from a mysterious singing voice that your town waitress hears while trying to sleep on a hot September night."

This did not seem funny, but several of the men in the room found it so, and their laughter followed us out. Well, that is how people can be.

On the street, Jenny Applegarth turned to Mr. Johnson. "Now what?"

Mr. Johnson glanced toward the bakery. The lights still blazed and green smoke still rose from the chimney. I sensed the quiet approach of footsteps from behind, but Mr. Johnson did not. "Looks like the baker's in his shop," he said. "So I guess we better go over to his house alone."

A low, steady voice from behind said, "We'll come, too."

347

It was Conk Crinklaw. Behind him stood Maddy and Marjory. Jenny Applegarth looked at the three of them. "You know," she said, "if I'm wrong—"

But another voice from the shadows cut her off. "We're burning time here," the voice said.

They all turned around and had to adjust their gazes downward. It was Deputy McRaven.

"Not in uniform," he said. "Acting only as a concerned citizen." The look on his oversized face was deadly serious. "So what are we waiting for?"

The group moved as one down the street, but something caused me to look back. There, in the door of the Green Oven Bakery, Sten Blix was observing the movement in the street. He stepped onto the sidewalk and watched until the group turned the corner, out of view. He stood there another moment or two, as if in contemplation, then went back inside his shop.

§

§

In the alley behind the baker's house, Conk and the others helped Jenny Applegarth and Mr. Johnson climb onto the trash cans and over the fence. Everyone hurried. No one worried about noise. No one worried about the mud. They all slogged straight through it to the front door, which was locked.

Conk and the girlfriends quickly circled the house in search of open windows, but they were all secured. The party gathered again near the very window through which Jeremy and Ginger had peered that fateful night long ago. Maddy and Marjory cupped their hands around their eyes and stared into the darkened house. Mr. Johnson and Jenny looked at each other, wondering what to do next. Deputy McRaven did not look at anyone. He took off his outer shirt, wrapped it around his fisted hand, and turned to Conk.

"Boost me up," he said.

The deputy was built like a boulder, but Conk, straining mightily, raised him up, and McRaven, without hesitation, drove his covered hand through the window.

A clamorous crash of glass.

Immediately, a light went on in a yard across the street.

McRaven punched free a few more shards of glass and hoisted himself through. Moments later, he was opening the front door from within, and the party streamed through, branching off in every direction, searching every room. Jenny and Mr. Johnson were the first to find the stairs and follow them down to the storage rooms, but when they did not know where to look next, I began again to sing.

The fifth doe she did cross the brook.

She stopped and looked sharply at Mr. Johnson. "There. Quiet! It's the voice again!—the singing voice! Did you hear it?"

Mr. Johnson had not, of course, and shook his head.

What he has done you must go and look, I sang, moving toward the third storeroom, and Jenny followed my voice as if in a trance.

> *Hidden on the wall a numbered square,*
> *Among the leaves so green, O.*

"What?" she asked, her eyes darting around. And then, with others spilling down the stairs, she yelled, "Quiet! For God's sake! Everybody quiet!"

I sang the line again and she repeated it: "Hidden on the wall a numbered square?"

At once Conk and McRaven were searching the walls. It was Conk who swung the plate cover away to reveal the numbers. When he touched one of them, it lighted dimly from within. He turned to Jenny. "Now what?"

I spoke the code first, and though it was quiet, no one heard, so then I sang:

> *Jacky Boy?*
> *Master.*
> *Sing thee well?*
> *Very well.*
> *Thirteen,*
> *Seventeen.*
> *Derry, derry down.*
> *Among the leaves so green, O.*

"What?" Jenny Applegarth said. "Again?"

And so I sang it again, and she said, "Thirteen seventeen?" Then, to Conk, "Try it—thirteen seventeen."

At his touch, the wall moaned open and they pushed through.

The dungeon was in low light, so we could all see our way, but when I rushed ahead and spied the enclosures, my ancient heart fell.

Frank Bailey lay very still.

Jeremy and Ginger lay with their arms extended through the bars and entwined. They also were motionless. I swept in and searched frantically for the subtlest movement of faint breathing but found none.

Jeremy! I cried. Jeremy! Listen, if you will!

Conk remembered the numbers—1317—and by pushing them on the keypad near the enclosures, the gate latches dropped.

Conk slipped his arms under Ginger's head, and Mr. Johnson took his son's limp body and pulled it to his chest. Empty, dreadful seconds passed. And then Mr. Johnson's face contorted into a strange expression of flooding, grateful relief.

"Alive," he said in a low, strangled voice, his eyes squeezed shut, as if the only wish that ever mattered had just been granted. "He's alive."

"Ginger, too," Conk said, holding his face close to hers. "I can feel her breath."

Just outside the cell, Deputy McRaven had been standing rigid and brittle, but upon hearing that Ginger was alive, his big face gathered around his mouth and then—he could not help it—the strange, dwarfish deputy began quietly to cry.

Jenny Applegarth had slipped into Frank Bailey's cell and lifted his unconscious head. After a moment, she, too, nodded and said, "Alive."

She turned to Maddy and Marjory and said, "Go get the sheriff."

Whatever Sheriff Pittswort's speculations may have been before reaching the baker's house, they changed upon seeing Ginger, Jeremy, and Frank Bailey being carried from the home. He assumed quick control. He commandeered three patrol cars, put one patient along with an adult in the backseat of each, and sent them off, lights flashing, to the nearest hospital, some twelve miles away. Deputy McRaven drove the car with Ginger lying in the backseat, eyes closed, her head in Conk's lap.

The sheriff used his radio to advise the hospital that three youths were en route, near death, suffering from starvation and possible poisoning. Then he turned to Maddy and Marjory and asked them to show him the way to the dungeon.

As they proceeded down the stairwell and toward the third room, Maddy explained how Jenny Applegarth had led the way and how, when they got to the third room, she told them to look for the keypad and then figured out the combination of numbers that opened the wall.

The sheriff stopped short. "Figured out *how?*"

"I think the voice told her," Maddy said.

"Right," the sheriff said. "The voice."

Once they reached the dungeon itself, the sheriff drew himself up as if to absorb what he was seeing. He stared at the cells, the beds, the windowless walls. Then he approached the rocking chair and picked up the small green shirt.

He held it for a time, taking in what its presence in this dungeon must mean. Then something hardened in his face. "Okay," he said. "I've seen enough."

Outside, he thanked Marjory and Maddy and sent them home. He stood alone then for a moment, leaning against his patrol car, holding the green shirt. The last time he'd seen it, there had been a little boy wearing it, and he was sitting in a patrol car like this one, not saying a word and smiling out the window as if at a world he'd never before seen. A strange but good little boy, and then one day the town baker had gotten hold of him. Perhaps these were the kinds of things Sheriff Pittswort was thinking, and now he lifted his gaze from the shirt to the sky. The smoke still rose from the chimney of the bakery, visibly green as it drifted into the moonlight. The sheriff expelled a deep draft of air. Then, still holding the shirt, he slid into his patrol car.

I believed I knew where he was going next—it was where I, too, was going.

§

§

The sheriff had not yet reached the bakery when I arrived.

To my surprise, the door was ajar. The front area of the shop was dark, but lights shone from the kitchen. I found the baker there, wearing his white apron, applying frosted rosettes to the top of one Prince Cake after another. He was intent on his work, yet there was something different in his composure. From time to time he glanced through the kitchen door to the front of the shop, as if he was expecting someone.

And what of the fire that leapt and danced behind the open door to the giant oven? This was not how one baked—was it?—with unbridled fire.

On the counter to the side of the tray was a small note that said:

> To the citizens of Never Better:
> Thank you for seeing me as you wished to see me and allowing me to do all that I wished to do. That my wishes were unusual was neither your fault nor mine.
> Yours sincerely,
> Sten Blix, The Town Baker

There was something more self-pitying than apologetic in this note. Really, if not his fault, then whose? If he could not control his desires, could he not control his mastery over them?

But there he stood, setting rosettes on his pastries, the smallest smile forming when he had set one just so. The heat must have been intense. Repeatedly, he raised his apron to wipe his pink glistening brow.

He worked without haste, shaping perfect frosted roses for one domed cake after another. Where was the sheriff? I wondered. Why had he not arrived?

The baker went to the furnace to feed in more crystals and several lengths of wood—so furious was the fire that the logs instantly burst into orange ignition. He leaned back from the intensity of the heat, but he did not close the oven door. It was at this moment that the bells jangled above the shop's front door.

The baker stayed where he was, staring into the furnace.

The sheriff said nothing as he entered the kitchen. Behind him stood two of the men who, only an hour before, had been playing cards with him and laughing at Jenny Applegarth. Now they were tense and somber. Each wore a metal badge. Each carried a gun. The sheriff held only the small green shirt, draped in one hand, but he carried it as if it was the only weapon he needed. Yes, in the tales, justice is often merciless and horrific, but nothing had prepared me for this sheriff at this moment. His face was stone. He held the small green shirt in his hands and he was beyond pity or mercy.

But the baker was immune. His gaze moved from the green shirt to the sheriff's hard eyes. "Your little Possy"—he gave a broad, taunting wink—"who disappeared right from under your nose."

Something dreadful was going to happen, I could feel it.

I was right—and not right.

The baker unfastened the apron he was wearing and let it slip to the ground.

In a soft voice he said, *"Sa börjar det igen."*

So another moment has come.

Then, in the half instant before the sheriff could lay his hands on him, Sten Blix, the town baker, the Finder of Occasions, with a look of utter calmness on his face, stepped into the raging flames.

Sheriff Pittswort and his two men stared into the orange fiery space and watched the baker's brightening, writhing silhouette.

I hastened to the roof. At the chimney's edge, I let the smoke flow through me. I felt no heat, but I smelled burned flesh, and leaned away in revulsion.

But here—and this was what I had come for—the spectral Sten Blix rose to me and regarded me without surprise.

Yes, he said, *I thought the boy might really have such a companion. In Sweden I had heard of it many times. And were you in time? Were any of them still alive?*

All of them. I spoke with a kind of vindication. *All of them are alive.*

He smiled and shook his head. *No,* he said. *Not all of them. Only these three. You have saved those you could save. I have taken those I could take. So do not think that you have prevailed.* He cast his dead eyes over the dark village. *You think that you have won, but I did not lose. I grew indifferent to winning.* He gave a weary shrug and then, less to me than to himself, he said, *There was too much of them.*

I did not understand. *Too much of whom?*

He gazed back into the smoke that rose from the bakery built above a dungeon. *Them,* he said, and contempt crept into his

356

voice. *The girl with her prayers. The boy with his ghosts. And poor wretched Frankie, with his belief in my goodness.*

I was afraid he would leave. I asked what I had come to ask: *What happened to you that you could do such things as you have done?*

He did not answer. He leaned far over the chimney and, breathing deeply of the smoke, rose with it and slowly disappeared.

I tried to follow and called after him—*What was it you wanted? How were such desires formed?*—but the baker had gone wherever such souls go.

§

§

In the pale green hospital room, Jeremy Johnson Johnson was sleeping. So, in their chairs nearby, were his father and Jenny Applegarth. Nourishment dripped through a transparent tube leading from a machine to a bandaged area of Jeremy's wrist. The prisoner had become a patient, and though he looked waxy and frail, the physicians had pronounced that he would slowly recover to full strength, that all the prisoners would.

A few minutes before, when a doctor quietly visited, she opened a folder to read notes and add some of her own. I observed a strange array of words and phrases—"chronic poisoning," "warfarin," "vitamin K," "enhanced excretion," "whole bowel irrigation"—which, together, presumably indicated what had been done to Jeremy by the baker and what the doctors had done to reverse the effects.

I hovered there, watching Jeremy breathe in and breathe out, for I felt his breathing almost as if it were my own. Something had occurred to me. I felt disencumbered. For the first time since that day in September when the elm tree in the garden extinguished, I felt release. From what, I was not sure, yet I felt no urgency to know. I was enjoying too much the image of Jeremy, alive and breathing.

At last, I moved close. *Listen, if you will*, I whispered. *Listen, if you will.*

He eyes fluttered open. He made a faint but actual smile. "Oh, hi," he said.

At once, Mr. Johnson and Jenny Applegarth jerked awake.

"Hey, buddy," his father said. He reached out to touch Jeremy's hand.

Jenny Applegarth gave Jeremy's other hand a squeeze, then stepped away. "Think I'll give you two a minute alone," she said.

I, too, respected their privacy and followed Jenny Applegarth to a room near the end of the shiny corridor. Inside, Mrs. Bailey sat on the edge of her son's bed, gently massaging his arm. The boy slept. He, too, had a tube running to his wrist. Mrs. Bailey and Jenny Applegarth exchanged nods.

"Doing okay?" Jenny Applegarth said.

"He is," Mrs. Bailey said. "They say he is, anyhow. Though he doesna' look so good."

"How about you?"

"Well, you know. . . ." She gazed at her son. "At least now I can see him and hold his hand and fuss over him." Her eyes moved to Jenny Applegarth's. "He's a good boy," she said. "He couldna' be better, if people just knew."

"I know," Jenny Applegarth said.

"The Crinklaw boy told me what you did. How you went right in and held my boy and rode with him when they brought him here."

Jenny Applegarth looked down. "It wasn't hard."

They were both quiet, then Mrs. Bailey said, "Conk said you heard a voice, a voice that sang." She paused. "It made me think of an angel."

"That's right. I did hear a voice." Jenny Applegarth smiled. "But I'd hate to think an angel couldn't sing a little better than that."

The women both laughed at this, which I found irritating.

"Do you still hear it, then? The singing voice?" Mrs. Bailey asked.

"I don't, no."

This was true. I *could* sing, in my tuneless way, but there was no longer the need.

"You know, I can never repay you," Mrs. Bailey said as Jenny began to take her leave, and Jenny replied, "I don't know why you'd try."

A kind woman, even if she did not appreciate my singing.

From Frank Bailey's room, she walked to Ginger's. In the passing instant that the door was swinging open, Conk could be seen leaping from the edge of the bed into a chair. His fearful expression turned to relief, however, when he saw that it was Jenny.

"Hoo-boy," he said. "I thought it was McRaven or her grandfather. I was just sitting on the bed, holding her hand. But her grandfather . . . I don't know. He's like Attila the Hun or something. And McRaven keeps coming in and just staring at her like she's a goddess or something, which is kind of creepy since she looks half-dead."

Jenny Applegarth gave a murmuring laugh and looked at Ginger, who slept peacefully in spite of—or perhaps because of—the liquid dripping into her arm. "So how's our patient?"

"Okay, I think. She woke up a while ago. First thing she asked was how's Jeremy. Then she asked about Frank. I told her they were okay, and she fell right back to sleep."

Jenny Applegarth said, "What they've been through . . ."

Conk nodded his head and said, "Yeah."

Ginger stirred ever so slightly but continued to sleep. While Conk kept his eyes on Ginger, Jenny Applegarth regarded Conk. She seemed to be looking at him in a new way. I did not blame her. He had shown considerable valor in this episode.

From the corridor, the squeak of a cart gave me a strange start, but it merely preceded the appearance of Mr. Johnson in the doorway, with Jeremy just behind, holding himself stiffly upright, with one arm on the rolling medical stand to which the nourishment tubes were still attached.

"Hello?" Mr. Johnson called softly. "Anybody home?"

Conk looked at them, then leaned close to Ginger's ear. "Ginger. Can you wake up? Jeremy's here."

Her eyelids fluttered open, closed momentarily, and opened again. Her gaze fell on Jeremy and a weak smile came to her lips. "Hey," she said.

With help from his father, Jeremy rolled his medical stand forward. "How're you doing?" he asked.

"Better. How about you?" She closed her eyes. "How're things in Johnson-Johnsonville?"

"Better," he said.

She looked at him then and extended her hand, and as he stepped forward to take it, his face twisted and he seemed about to cry, but he tightened against the tears and held them back.

Everyone but Jeremy slipped away from the room. Ginger again closed her eyes. In a weak, whispery voice, she said, "My grandfather. He said nobody believes that a ghost . . ." She laughed softly. She seemed almost asleep. And then she was talking again. "I do, though. And you do." She raised her eyelids and looked at him. "That's all that matters, right?"

This time the tears Jeremy had been suppressing could be suppressed no more. "Yeah, that's all that matters."

When he had wiped his eyes and regained himself, it was quiet. In a soft voice she said, "You want to kiss me?"

What followed was a long, suspended moment, in which she closed her eyes, and as Jeremy leaned forward, one last residual tear welled at the very edge of his eye directly above her slightly parted lips. And then, before I could shout in alarm, the tear spilled free—and there was nothing for me to do but rush past and, with the smallest draft, ever so slightly alter its flight.

The tear landed, safely, on her cheek.

Her eyes snapped open in surprise. "That was close," she said. But she did not explain further. She merely closed her eyes again so that she might still collect her kiss.

§
§

And so to this tale, there is little more to add. I will tell you that my suspicions—and perhaps yours—regarding Possy Truax were happily confirmed. He was indeed alive. For the past twenty years, he had been living, if it may be called that, under the influence and authority of Sten Blix. He lived in a rude hut not far from the baker's cabin, and for all those years he did as the baker bade him. The search party, including the sheriff and Mrs. Truax, came upon him in the forest, raking the grounds around the baker's cabin, and when his mother, looking upon this large blank-faced man, pulled back her hood so that he might see her face, he let the rake fall from his hands and walked toward her and held on to her for a long time. He would not release her hand even while they walked to the patrol car, nor all the way back home. And yet, when a doctor who specialized in such matters came to see him, and asked whether he feared Mr. Blix, or hated him, or liked him, or depended on him, Possy nodded only at the latter.

"It will take time," the doctor said to Mrs. Truax, and Mrs. Truax said, "I've got time."

During Jeremy's convalescence, Mr. Milo Castle called to ask about his well-being. When he inquired about the financial difficulties of the bookstore, Jeremy explained that the lender was in the process of taking possession of the bookstore. He tried to sound positive. He said he was "still hoping something would turn up."

"Maybe it will," Milo Castle said. "Maybe it will."

And a few nights later, at the end of the last round of *Uncommon Knowledge*, Milo Castle reminded the audience of Jeremy (a small portion of his appearance was shown on the screen, during which he answered the question regarding Rapunzel), and then he explained that after that show had been taped, Jeremy—"like some innocent in one of the Grimm Brothers' own tales"—had been abducted and poisoned (here photos of news coverage appeared on the screen, including the newspaper headline THREE YOUTHS HELD CAPTIVE IN MODERN-DAY DUNGEON). Milo Castle mentioned the Two-Book Bookstore and the debt that had been incurred. Then he cleared his voice and said he was proud to announce that *Uncommon Knowledge* was sending a check in the amount of twenty-two thousand dollars to cover this debt. "And, if anyone else would like to help, here is how you can contact Jeremy at the Two-Book Bookstore."

Since this announcement, the store has had a good deal more traffic. Supportive letters have come in from all corners, some with monies enclosed. Visitors, too, have journeyed to this little town, many of them morbid sightseers coming to stare at the baker's vine-covered house and the Green Oven Bakery, now locked and shuttered. But many of the travelers come to meet Jeremy and visit the bookstore and, sometimes, buy a book. They also stop at Elbow's Café and shop at Crinklaw's Superette and stay at the Red Buttes Motel, helping everyone prosper, so the citizens have adjusted their view of Jeremy Johnson Johnson.

*   *   *

Jeremy and Ginger stick to themselves, often just sitting easily together in the park or the bookstore attic without speaking at all. Saturdays, Ginger helps Jeremy with Jenny Applegarth's yard work, and always, at ten o'clock, Jenny brings out cucumber sandwiches and lemonade. Occasionally, Ginger and Jeremy invite Frank Bailey for a lakeside picnic or they join the girlfriends and Conk to play horseshoes or watch TV at Mayor Crinklaw's house. More and more often, Maddy can be found in Conk's company, and sometimes Jeremy and Ginger ride with them to a nearby town to see a movie.

The mayor himself has been magnanimous about Jeremy's change of fortunes. He accepted repayment of the principle but refused all interest, and one evening before the fall *Konzert,* while standing in the park band shell with Lemmy Wittle and the other music makers, the mayor made a few announcements.

"Now, before I turn things over to the conductor," the mayor said, "I want to give a little update on Possy, because I know you all have been asking. The answer is, he's just plain been through it, and for a lot of years, and so we all just have to take it slow and easy. What I'm told is he's not capable of a lot. In fact, what they tell me is all he can do is listen good and follow orders." The mayor paused a moment to survey the crowd. "Now, I know just exactly what all you married gals are thinking: All he can do is listen good and follow orders—I married the wrong man!"

Raucous laughter worked its way to the back of the crowd, where Conk, Maddy, Marjory, Jeremy, Ginger, and Frank Bailey stood loosely together. Conk, shaking his head, turned to the others and said, "That's why he's the mayor."

"But I got some good news," the mayor continued from the bandstand. "Mrs. Truax doesn't want to move Possy from her trailer, but she said it's okay if a couple of us old boys build her a room addition so her and Possy don't bump into each other quite so much. And, on another front, last night the Council and me approved a position for Possy, raking up leaves in this very park, and from what I heard this morning, he's taking right to it."

The heads in the crowd nodded as one, and the applause was loud and long.

"Okay, then," the mayor said, "I've got one more item of business."

He held out the promissory note from Jeremy for the crowd to see. Then he said, "Okay, Lemmy," and with Lemmy Wittle providing a prolonged drumroll, the mayor set the promissory note on fire, to general applause.

"How about it, Jeremy Johnson Johnson?" the mayor called out to the back of the aggregation when the note was in ashes. "You happy?"

As the smiling crowd turned around to look at him, Jeremy's cheeks began to redden. "Yeah," he said. "Yeah, I am."

And then these townspeople, to Jeremy's surprise, and to mine, and perhaps to the surprise of the townspeople themselves, gave him such hearty and sustained applause that Jeremy could only cast down his eyes and wait for the acclaim to cease, but it did not. It seemed, if anything, to swell louder.

Finally, when it began to trail off, the mayor called out, "How about you, Ginger? You happy? And, Frank Bailey, how about you?"

They both nodded and grinned. Ginger even provided an

actress's graceful bow, which drew appreciative whistles and cheers.

"What about you, Conk?" the mayor shouted. "You happy for once?"

"I would be," Conk called back, "if you'd stop your yammering!"—which gave rise to more hoots and laughter.

The mayor, nodding, raised his hands for quiet. "Oh, I'll quit yammering, but I got to say something first." He surveyed the crowd, which grew quiet. "This is the truth. It don't matter how young you are or how old you get or how brittle your bones are or how leaky your gray cells, you are still going to flat like a happy ending. And that's what this is, folks. A happy ending"—he stretched a grin across his broad jaw—"or as close as any of us in this part of the country is likely to find."

It was true for me as well. A great relaxation had come over me. I had felt it for days, and had only to wait for a gentle wind to close my eyes and give myself up to the vast beyond. I was hopeful I would find Wilhelm, and Dortchen, and little Jacob, who had somehow reached through and saved not just Jeremy and the others, but me as well.

Yours is a good story, Jeremy, I told him one day. *You should put it to paper.*

"I wouldn't even know how to start," Jeremy said.

I do, I said quietly because I had spent hours and days with it, thinking it through, and that night, when we sat down at the library table and I began to speak, it came with remarkable ease, as if I were merely reading my own tale.

This, I began, *is the strange and fateful tale of a boy, a girl, and a ghost.*

Several days later, it was all on paper, all but the final few pages.

§

§

Jeremy and Ginger will soon return to school. They have arranged to take the same classes, study the same texts. They are teaching each other French, and less and less often they ask for my assistance. They have one another. And yet Jeremy does not entirely neglect his old friend.

One evening, when we are alone, he unwraps for me a book he has purchased by mail. It is a handsome old edition of the *Household Tales*—bound in brown leather, with a fine illustration of Rapunzel on the cover—and when he opens the volume, there is an even more pleasant surprise. The text of the tales runs in two separate columns, one in English and one in the original German, exactly as Wilhelm and I transcribed them. When I see this, I am quite powerfully affected.

"Do you like it?" he asks.

Yes. I do. Very much.

He does not need to speak. He is brimming with pleasure. He is happy. Through the open window I feel a gentle wind.

May I ask a favor?

"Sure."

Could we sit here and read our way through this volume together?

"Sure," he says again.

And that is what we do over the next several days, reading slowly, at the speed of mortals. And then, upon turning the final page of the final tale, we both are quiet. The *hoo-hooing* of a mourning dove carries on the breeze.

Jeremy, I say, but there must be something in my tone or inflection, for in a low, deflated voice he says, "I know."

Again we fall silent.

"Will you come back?"

I do not know.

I see the contortion of his face, the swell and slide of the first tear. He rushes a hand to his face.

It is all right, Jeremy. There is no one here to see but me.

"Yeah," he says in a small, snuffling voice, and suddenly he seems the boy I found years before, "and when you're gone, there'll be no one here to see at all."

You have Ginger. Your father. And then there will be more people at university.

He wipes at his eyes with the sleeve of his shirt. "I'll remember to study."

Yes. It is important to study. But also to enjoy.

Again he snuffles, but he has composed himself. He takes a deep breath and clears his throat. "Okay," he says. "I've been thinking about this. I didn't get to say it to my mother or to my grandfather before they left, but I'm going to say it to you."

But, oh, I cannot bear it. *I know. You do not need to speak the words. I know.*

He looks toward me with watery eyes. "Okay."

And you know. You know, too.

He nods, and tears again swell in his eyes.

I must go, Jeremy. I must go now.

"Okay."

Your grandfather was right, Jeremy. You are a dear, good boy. This is all I have set out to say, but something draws me further. *And I love you more than the sun and the moon.*

He tries to smile. In spite of his wretched state, he tries to smile.

"I love you, too," he says, and it is upon these whispered words, as upon a magical carpet from some ancient tale, that I have traveled on.

Acknowledgments

The author would like to express his gratitude to the National Endowment for the Arts for its support during the writing of this book; to Jack Zipes and, especially, Maria Tatar for their extensive and illuminating research in the field of fairy tales; to Mimi Sidwell, Christine Stotz, and Françoise Bui for their expert assistance with the Swedish, German, and French translation; to Jacki Rhoton for her demonstration of at least one female's invincibility in the art of Indian leg wrestling; to Sam and Hank McNeal for odd notions that found their way into the book; to Dana Reinhardt, Allison Wortche, and Jeremy Medina for their critical assistance; to George Nicholson, Joan Slattery, and Nancy Hinkel for their belief in the book and their assistance in bringing it to print; and, as always, to Laura McNeal, for everything, first page to last.

About the Author

Tom McNeal has written several young adult novels with his wife, National Book Award finalist Laura McNeal: *Crooked*, *Zipped*, *Crushed*, and *The Decoding of Lana Morris*. He has also written two critically acclaimed adult novels, *To Be Sung Underwater*, named one of the five best novels of the year by *USA Today*, and *Goodnight, Nebraska*, winner of the California Book Award. He lives near San Diego with his wife and two sons. To learn more about Tom, as well as his books with Laura, please visit mcnealbooks.com.